"You are obviously suffering under some delusion, Cousin Belinda, if you believe that you are entitled to an elite position in society. Whatever your past connections, you are an orphan now, a penniless orphan. It is only my generosity that has saved you from poverty, and possibly starvation. In return for the comfort and protection of my household, I expect you to earn your keep," Cady informed Belinda coldly.

She glanced up, wondering what he would say next.

"My servant, Hannah, will be leaving and it will be your obligation to take her place."

Belinda gasped. "You cannot be serious? I . . . I am to become your woman-servant?"

Without a word, Cady reached for a heavy birch switch, turned to Belinda, and before she had time to move, Cady brought it whistling down about her shoulders.

"I warned you against interrupting . . ."

Books by Jill Gregory

PROMISE ME THE DAWN
TO DISTANT SHORES
THE WAYWARD HEART

PROMISE ME THE DAWN

JILL GREGORY

BERKLEY BOOKS, NEW YORK

PROMISE ME THE DAWN

A Berkley Book/published by arrangement with
the author

PRINTING HISTORY
Berkley trade paperback edition/April 1984

ISBN: 0-425-06814-5

Berkley Books are published by The Berkley Publishing Group,
200 Madison Avenue, New York, N.Y. 10016.
The name "BERKLEY" and the stylized "B" with design are
trademarks belonging to Berkley Publishing Corporation.

PRINTED IN THE UNITED STATES OF AMERICA

To Larry and Rachel, with all my love

ACKNOWLEDGMENT

I wish to thank my wonderful editor, Meg Blackstone, for all of her guidance and support during the writing of PROMISE ME THE DAWN. Her wisdom, insights, and loving attention to the manuscript all contributed much to my endeavor. I am also grateful for her friendship and her counsel. I would also like to thank Susanne Jaffe for providing the inspiration and concept for PROMISE ME THE DAWN, and for her encouragement and confidence in my work. Last but not least, I must express my gratitude and affection for my agent, Ellen Levine, who works tirelessly on my behalf, and who has been a source of encouragement throughout our association. I feel fortunate to have the opportunity to associate with such fine professionals and such lovely people. They have my deepest respect, my warmest thanks, and my enduring friendship.

PROMISE
ME THE
DAWN

CHAPTER ONE

A MANTLE OF DARKNESS shrouded the great merchant ship *Esmeralda* as she plunged through the icy March sea. Belinda Cady gathered her woolen skirts in one hand and determinedly mounted the companionway, her heavy blue velvet cloak billowing about her as the winter wind roared in her ears. It was a bitter, starbright night, a night for blazing fires and thick, downy coverlets. There were no hearths on the *Esmeralda*, however, and the only blanket Belinda had use of was a shabby gray woolen one, worn thin in many places. But it was a pleasure for her merely to be up on deck, away from that stinking, noisy hole below. Her green-gold eyes sparkled rebelliously as she gained the top of the companionway. She didn't care that she was disobeying the captain's orders by coming above after dark, she didn't care that Sarah Cooke had scolded and frowned in displeasure when she had fled the crowded cabin jammed with immigrant women and children! Purposefully, she crossed the creaking, slippery deck and placed both hands upon the wet wooden railing. She lifted her face to the wind and breathed deeply of its fresh saltiness, shaking her head so her hair flowed free. Ah, the last night. The last night of this wretched journey. She couldn't wait to be rid of the foul, rat-

1

infested ship. Whatever lay ahead in the unknown Massachusetts Bay Colony had to be an improvement over this repulsive state of affairs.

Great milky clouds swirled across the charcoal sky, obscuring the stars. Thunder boomed in the distance. There would be rain come morning. Belinda wiped the salt spray from her delicate oval face and peered across the churning, inky sea. Her past life in the village of Sussex seemed as distant as old England. The colonies lay ahead, and therein her future. What would it hold?

Her heart beat faster as she tried to imagine the life awaiting her in the home of her father's cousin, Magistrate Jonathan Cady of Salem. She couldn't help wondering, with a gleam of mischief in her eyes, if he was as sober as his title. If so, she must indeed try to remember to behave. It would not do to anger her benefactor, for she was an orphan now, and penniless. If he chose to cast her out, there was nowhere else to go. So Sarah Cooke, housekeeper at the Cady Manor house since long before Belinda's birth, had been continually reminding her. As if, Belinda thought with a small sigh, she could ever forget.

Her parents had been killed in a fire in London when she was fourteen, and for the next three years there had been only she and Grandmama in the comfortable manor home nestled in the English countryside. Now even that indomitable old woman was gone, dead and buried these six months since. Her loss had been a severe blow to the usually resilient Belinda. Then immediately following the burial there had been yet another. She learned, to her shock and dismay that Bryant, the estate agent charged with looking after Squire Cady's property after his demise, had been grossly careless and inefficient in his duties. The comfortable circumstances in which the Squire had left his daughter upon his death had been wasted away by poor management. The orphaned Belinda found herself without sixpence to her name. The period following these disclosures had been a dark time indeed, a time Belinda did not care to remember. The long, anxious days wondering wildly what was to be done, the nights alone in the parlor when her grief for Grandmama welled up so painfully inside her that she thought she would burst with the agony of her loneliness. No, it had not been a pleasant time, not by any means. If Cousin Jonathan, her only remaining living relative, hadn't offered to bring her to the New World and take her under his protection, she didn't know what she would have done.

I am indebted to him for his generosity, Belinda reminded herself, trying to stifle the resentment she felt at being in such a position. *I must not repay him with troublesomeness. I must learn to be a quiet, biddable girl, the kind Grandmama always preached of. The kind of girl I most detest.* Knowing her own temperament, Belinda knew that such prim and proper behavior would not be easy. She was a termagant, from the top of her flaming head to the tips of her dainty toes. At least, that is what everyone had been telling her all her life, and she saw no reason to doubt her elders.

A troublemaker, a rebel, a girl too high-spirited and headstrong for her own good. That's what they branded her, the good people of Sussex. They blamed it on her hair, that bright, flame-colored mass which flowed in rippling waves down her back and shoulders to her waist. *With hair like that, no wonder she has a temper*, Sarah Cooke had always muttered when she didn't know that Belinda was eavesdropping. *The devil's hair, that's what it is. You mark my words.* But she was excused for her mischief-making and outspoken manner because she was the Squire's daughter. *Oh, the Squire's daughter is up to her tricks again, plucking the roses in Farmer Greer's garden. The Squire's daughter is astray again, hiding in the woods instead of taking her lessons. Miss Belinda? Aye, the Squire's daughter is the one—threw apples at the village boys and ran laughing all the way home.* Belinda's lips curved upward at such memories, but she immediately schooled her face into a frown, and sighed. Such pranks must be relegated to her childhood, she decided regretfully. She was a young woman now, almost eighteen, and she must make a good impression upon Cousin Jonathan, or else she would find herself truly alone in the world. This harsh prospect daunted even her. The seventeenth century offered little future for a girl with neither money, nor family, nor husband. Poverty and servitude were all such a young woman might expect, and Belinda had no wish for either. Therefore, she must try to please her unknown kinsman and put her wild ways behind her. It was her only alternative, disheartening as it was.

Her thoughts shifted to the New World ahead, and curiosity and excitement began to flow through her. Her brilliant green eyes shone as she stared out at the blackened horizon, trying to pierce its tantalizing mystery. *Tomorrow I shall see you for myself,* she thought triumphantly. *I shall see the land which I shall make my own.*

She was so immersed in these reflections that she failed to notice another figure creeping up on the deck behind her. He lurked in the shadows near the mainmast, watching her intently. He was dressed in a black woolen cape and patched knee breeches, and wore soiled black boots. A stubby, pale beard clung to his jutting chin, and there was a half-drunk spirit flask in his large farmer's hand. His eyes shone drunkenly in the darkness as he stared at the unsuspecting girl. He could see only the back of her velvet cloak and hooded head, but he recognized her at once. He'd been watching her secretly during the entire length of the voyage. Now a grin spread slowly across his broad, not unhandsome face. He took another swig from his flask and smacked his lips. It had come. The hour he had lusted for all these months at sea was now at hand. . . .

Belinda felt a rustle of movement along the hem of her skirt and she jumped aside, startled. She gasped, and the goose bumps rose on her flesh as a pair of rats scuttled by, their eyes shining redly in the pale starlight. Horrid, detestable creatures! Shuddering, she turned away from the rail, resigning herself to return to the crowded cabin below. *One more night*, she told herself as she began to cross the deck. *Then I'll be on dry land once more, free of these rats, free of this ship. . . .*

"Ohhh!" Belinda cried as a man suddenly loomed out of the shadows to block her path. She stared at him with widened eyes as the wind rose about her and sent the long, flame-colored tresses flying.

"You—you startled me, sir!" she gasped.

"Did I, now? I did not mean to, Mistress Cady," he replied softly, but from the grin on his face, Belinda knew that he lied. She recognized him now that she had had a moment to study him; he was a young, brutish fellow in his twenties with sandy hair and great, bulging shoulders, not unlike the village youths whom she had thrown apples at as a child. She had seen him about the ship with his young wife, a plain, sallow-faced creature heavy with child. Phelps. Lettie Phelps. That was his wife's name, for Belinda had spoken to her once, briefly. An odd pair, she had thought at the time, for he had not seemed the type of man to marry so young, and to such a timid, wilted-looking girl. No, he had reminded her strongly of the village louts who worked the fields by day and drank in the tavern by night, pinching and poking and bedding the tavern wenches. Belinda had suspected that the child Lettie carried was the cause and not the product of the marriage. It had seemed likely at the time, and Belinda's heart had gone out to the girl, doubting that she would find happiness with her brutish lout of a husband. She had only been thankful that *she* was not tied to such a beast. Now, alone with Tom Phelps on the dark, creaking deck, she eyed him warily and with dislike, pulling her dark blue velvet cloak more snugly about her.

"Excuse me, sir, I wish to return to my quarters," she informed him coolly, attempting to pass him, but he stepped quickly into her path once more, his wolfish grin widening, an odd light in his eyes. He took a final swig from his spirit flask, then tossed it over the rail into the swirling black sea. He laughed, a grating, unpleasant sound which made Belinda stiffen.

"Not yet, Mistress Cady," he replied, moving a step closer. "There is something I'm wanting to say to you."

"I've no interest in hearing it. Step aside, if you please."

He ignored her. "Don't you know, miss, that the captain ordered all passengers to stay below tonight? You're going against him, being here on deck like this."

"As are you, Yeoman Phelps," she retorted coldly, angered by the leer in his face and manner. She lifted her hand imperiously and repeated, "I wish to return to my quarters. You have detained me quite long enough. Step aside!"

"Ah, you'll not be rid of me so easily," he warned, slowly advancing toward her, his huge arms spread apart. "I've been watching you all these months...waiting for my chance." A gleeful chuckle sprang from his lips, and his eyes shone like rubies. "I never saw such a comely wench, never in all my life! You're a true bewitching beauty, Mistress Cady, that's what you are, and I—"

"Save your flattery for your wife!" Belinda broke in furiously, backing away from him toward the ship's railing. "Spare me such pathetic utterances, for I assure you

I have no interest in them!" With these words, she tried to break past him, but his long, thick-muscled arm shot out and grabbed her wrist, clamping her in a ruthless grip.

"Gentry!" he hissed, resentment and hatred throbbing in his voice. "You're all alike! You think you're above me, don't you?" His fingers tightened cruelly on her delicate flesh. "You'd send me back to that mealy-mouthed, good-for-nothing wife of mine, wouldn't you? Ah, but I won't go, wench, I won't go! I've made up my mind, and it's you I'll be abedding tonight—like it or not!" He gloated down into the horrified face of the slender girl struggling in his grasp and stroked her flaming hair with one large, callused hand. "Oh, you're a beauty, all right, and there's fire in you. *Fire...*" He wet his thick lips, but before he could say or do anything else, Belinda wrenched away with sudden, fierce strength, throwing herself back against the wet railing of the ship. Her heart hammered wildly in her breast.

"Don't—don't you touch me!" she gasped, fury shining wildly in her brilliant green-gold eyes. "I'm warning you—let me go!"

Yeoman Phelps threw back his shaggy head and chortled. In his black woolen cape and baggy knee breeches he was a formidable sight, standing with his booted feet planted apart and his hands stretching toward her greedily. "I've no mind to let you go, my pretty wench, not until I'm finished with you!"

Suddenly, as he took a stride forward, Belinda's hand deftly moved inside her cloak, emerging instantly with a knife. It was a kitchen knife, sharpened to deadly degree. It glittered in the misty night, and she brandished it threateningly, her eyes gleaming as brightly as the metal. "One more step and I'll kill you," she warned, holding the weapon aloft. To her great satisfaction, Phelps checked his advance and stared in amazement at the slender, flame-haired creature with the blazing eyes who crouched so threateningly before him.

"Where—where did the likes of you be getting *that?*" he demanded, breathing heavily.

A contemptuous smile curved Belinda's lips. "You men think so little of women, do you not?" she almost whispered. "Did you really think I would undertake a long, dangerous sea voyage like this, totally alone, without some manner of protection for my person? Do you really think me such a fool? Hah! Think again, Yeoman Phelps! Now I suggest you move aside quite slowly and allow me to pass. If you dare to step closer, I will drive this into your heart!"

His eyes narrowed. He shook his great, shaggy head. "Nay, nay, you won't have the stomach for it. A wench like you... well bred, gentry! It's a bluff!"

"'Tis not!"

"I'll be taking my chances!" he sneered suddenly and lunged toward her. Screaming, Belinda slashed out at him with the knife. The blade cut his right forearm, and he drew back howling, dripping blood upon the slippery deck. She would not allow herself to look at it. Instead, pale and trembling, she stared into his furious, contorted face.

"Leave me *be!*" she hissed. "I'm warning you!"

"Murderous bitch! You'll pay dear for this!" he bellowed and sprang forward again like a crazed bull. Belinda struck at him once more, but this time he dodged the knife and seized her arm, twisting it viciously behind her back until the weapon slipped from her grasp and clattered onto the deck. She screamed again in agony, but the rising wind drowned out the high, wailing sound. Phelps jerked her head beneath his burly left arm, holding her helplessly, her face pressed into his rough cloak. The man reeked of sweat and liquor and fresh blood;

Belinda forced back vomit in her throat as she fought frenziedly to free herself. Like a wildcat she clawed and writhed and bit, but he was far too strong for her.

"Fiery wench!" Phelps muttered hoarsely as she savagely tried to jerk her head free of his heavy arm. "You'll not escape me, gentry bitch. I mean to have you, and so I will. I'll teach you to swipe at me with a knife, too! You won't soon forget this night, Mistress Cady! That you won't!" With a thick laugh he dragged her down onto the cold, wet boards of the deck and straddled her, his breath hot on her neck. His hands pawed at her breasts and he pressed his thighs against hers, more animal than man.

"No! No, you damned, foul brute!" she shrieked, engulfed by a rage so overpowering she thought her body would burst with it. Wildly, she twisted and turned, spat and kicked, attempting to free herself, but she could not move the tremendous man atop her. Revulsion swept through her anew as he squashed his wet lips against her tender mouth, forcing her lips apart with his tongue. *I'd rather die than endure this*, she thought frantically as hatred and rage shook her slender frame. *He shall have to kill me or I him before I submit!*

Suddenly, she managed to free one slim leg and she brought it up savagely toward his groin. It was a trick she'd learned by accident while play-wrestling with the head groom's son years ago, but it served her well. Phelps cringed and yelled in pain, shifting away from her. At that moment, the *Esmeralda* lurched, and both Belinda and her captor rolled sideways. They fell into a row of barrels, and as they went sprawling, his grasp upon her loosened. Belinda scrambled to her feet. The knife! Where was the knife? Even as she turned her head wildly to look for it, Phelps moved heavily, sitting up with a grunt. Her fists clenched; there was no time to retrieve the knife; she must run instead. With the agility of a doe she darted away from him, her heart thundering. The memory of his brutal fondling, his nauseating kisses, spurred her on even faster. Once, she glanced back. "Oh no!" she breathed in fresh dismay, for Phelps was pursuing her more rapidly than she had hoped, lumbering along like a great, wounded bear, his arm dripping a trail of blood.

Suddenly, she reached the companionway, almost tumbling down the steps in her haste. On she fled, her breath coming in ragged gasps. Then, in horror, she realized she had made a terrible mistake. Somehow she had taken a false turn, and instead of finding herself in the corridor which led to the cabin she shared with the other women, she was in a strange, deserted corridor, lit only by the pathetic flame of one small candle which flickered eerily in the drafty hall. In the dimness she made out a row of doors, and she knew instinctively what she must do. She had reached the third door when she heard Phelps's boots stamping down the companionway. Panic surged through her; then, mercifully, even as she heard the heavy clamp of boots drawing closer, the knob twisted in her hand. She pushed the door open and slipped inside, her heart pounding.

She found herself in a tiny room crammed with canvas and barrels of tar. It was very dark, and would grow darker when she closed the door. She hesitated, her fingers fumbling for a lock, but there was none. With a sharp intake of breath, Belinda shut the door. It was pitch black and the darkness was thick and suffocating, almost as frightening as the man hunting her outside. She picked her way as carefully as she could into the room, tripping over an unseen coil of rope. When she reached a row of barrels, she edged around them and crouched down behind the tallest one. Rats squealed and ran all around her, and Belinda shuddered violently, clenching her clammy hands together and summoning all her restraint to keep from shrieking aloud.

She could hear nothing at all from the corridor, though she waited what seemed an interminable time. The sound of her thumping heart gradually subsided. Maybe he had gone away. Maybe he had given up and returned to his cabin, and the danger was over. She took a long breath and was just about to rise when she heard the click of the doorlatch. A pale beam of light trickled into the room as the heavy door swung slowly open. She caught her breath, her nails digging into the palms of her hands. Silhouetted against the doorway she saw the hulking figure of her pursuer. In the shadows cast by the candle in the corridor, his huge form seemed to fill the room.

"Mistress Cady...Mistress Cady..." It was a grotesque whisper, hoarse and eerie in the darkness. The flesh on the back of her neck crawled at the sound of it. "I'll find you, Mistress Cady. I'll have my revenge on you. Aye, I will! You'll regret this night, Mistress Cady! Mistress Cady..."

He peered into the room, searching into the darkened corners. Belinda could smell his male scent, the blood lust and fury of the man, and she huddled in her hiding place, praying he would not discern her in the inky darkness. Suddenly, he took a step into the room, and she froze, preparing to battle him with all her strength should he find her, but he immediately retreated and, to her intense relief, stepped back into the corridor and shut the door. Belinda could not move. Her muscles ached from the discomfort of her position, but she could not rise, not yet. At last, slowly, she got to her feet. Her body was damp with perspiration, despite the icy winter chill of the room, but elation flowed through her. She had escaped!

She edged cautiously toward the door and put her ear to it, listening. There was no sound. She inched the door open a crack and peered out. The corridor was deserted. Silent as a ghost, she slipped outside and up the corridor, glancing nervously about her. At any moment, she half-expected Phelps to bear down upon her out of the gloom, but he did not. She reached her own cabin and darted inside, pushing the door shut firmly behind her. She leaned against it and took a deep, shuddering breath. She was safe! Then she turned. All eyes in the cabin were fixed on her. The other women, already in their nightdresses and caps, stared up at her from their cots. They were frowning at her in disapproval, their incredulous faces taking in her disheveled appearance and wild, tangled mane of hair. Brushing her thick, bright locks from her eyes, Belinda's gaze traveled to where Sarah Cooke's cot was placed. She made her way there, her head held high and her shoulders erect, determined not to be intimidated by the scowling women. Inwardly, she was still trembling in fear, but outwardly she was a model of rigid composure as she ignored the severe stares of the women she passed. When she reached Sarah's cot, she found the housekeeper sitting bolt upright, her plump, round face bright red with indignation.

"Miss Belinda!" she whispered furiously, her blue eyes snapping, "where in the world have you been, you naughty, wayward child! Do you have any idea—" She broke off, her eyes widening in dismay as she suddenly grabbed the girl's hand convulsively. "Merciful heavens, child, there is blood on your cloak! *What has happened to you?*"

There was a short silence.

"If I tell you, Sarah, you will only say that I have received my just desserts for disobeying the captain's orders, so I think I shall keep my story to myself," Belinda said grimly, her lips clenched together. "I am in no mood for a lecture!"

"Miss Belinda, I will have an answer! What catastrophe has befallen you?" Sarah demanded, true horror in her eyes.

Belinda gazed defiantly down at the woman who had been her housekeeper for so many years. How she had resented Sarah as a child, hating her rantings and ravings whenever Belinda misbehaved. This was the woman who had scolded and stormed at her when she stole scones from the kitchens and pears from the orchard. But she was also the woman who had held her and rocked her like a child on the day Grandmama had died. Sarah, for all her scoldings and complaints, was devoted to her. She had even embarked on this journey so that she might look after her. Oh, it was true that Sarah's widowed brother, a blacksmith in Boston, had asked her to come into his household for many years now, but she had only accepted after the death of Belinda's grandmother so that she might care for Belinda on her long journey to the colonies. But Belinda knew that if it were not for the fact that *she* was traveling all the way to the colonies, Sarah would have chosen to retire to a quiet, comfortable cottage in old England instead of uprooting herself to join her brother in the New World.

Thinking of all this as she stared into Sarah's pale, worried face, Belinda forgot all her resentments. Her defensiveness ebbed away, replaced by a surge of affection. Poor, dear, fat, scolding Sarah! So stern and yet so softhearted! Impulsively, she leaned down and kissed the housekeeper's wrinkled cheek.

"It is all right, Sarah," she said soothingly. "I am not injured."

"Child, I've been beside myself! What were you thinking of, running up on deck like that—alone! I didn't know what to do! And now look at you! Oh, my poor lamb, what has happened? You have been hurt? I can see for myself that you have been hurt!"

"No, no, don't alarm yourself." Wearily, Belinda knelt down beside the narrow cot and for just a moment rested her head against the housekeeper's pillowy shoulder. "I . . . I am all right. But it was so dreadful. . . . There was a man . . ." Suddenly, Belinda felt an intent gaze fastened upon her and she glanced up, her eyes traveling to the cot beside Sarah's. Lettie Phelps's wan, pale face peered anxiously back at her. The girl was listening, her body rigid with fear, her trembling hands fluttering upon her swollen belly. Belinda bit her lip. She dropped her eyes. When she continued speaking, her voice was quiet, calm. "Oh, it doesn't matter, Sarah. Let's not think of it anymore."

Sarah gripped her shoulders in agitation. "But Miss Belinda, are you certain you're not hurt? Pray, child, I don't understand—"

"Hush." Belinda rose quickly to her feet and shook her head. "I assure you, I am well." When she saw that Sarah intended to question her further, she met the woman's eyes, a glint of steel in her own. "Sarah, go to sleep. I'll see you in the morning." She patted the housekeeper's shaking hand and turned firmly away, leaving Sarah no choice but to watch helplessly as her charge departed.

Belinda threaded her way through the teeming cabin, past the dreary rows of creaking cots and shivering women until she reached her own narrow bed. She removed her wet, bloodied cloak and threw it beside her. Exhaustion seeped through her as she sat down. Oh, how in that one moment she had longed to tell her tale to Sarah, to report that despicable man and see him punished! But looking into the eyes of his wife, she had been unable to bring herself to speak his name. She had suddenly realized all the grief and shame she would cause that pathetic girl and had changed her mind. What did it matter, after all? Tomorrow she would leave the ship and never lay eyes upon Tom Phelps again. Why should she destroy him in the eyes of his wife, the woman bearing his child? Lettie's pain would not be worth the pleasure of seeing him flogged. And besides, Belinda reasoned, she had escaped, hadn't she? Much as he might have liked, he had not succeeded in doing her any real harm.

Wearily, she climbed into her cotton nightdress and pulled the woolen coverlet about her, but sleep remained far away. Her entire body quivered, not only from the cold, but from her memories. She kept hearing Yeoman Phelps's voice in that hoarse, eerie whisper, echoing her name, vowing revenge. A chill finger of fear traced its way down her spine and she shivered uncontrollably in her cot. When at last sleep overtook her, it was an uneasy rest, punctuated by vague, disturbing dreams which tormented her, making her toss and turn upon the narrow confines of her bed. In the morning when she awoke there was only one dream that remained with her. It carried with it a strange, unceasing horror. She had dreamed of a rope knotted about her neck and of a man's soft, gloating laughter. And she had looked down the length of the rope to see the broad, grinning face of Yeoman Phelps, his eyes bright and leering and his huge hands grasping the rope which ensnared her. His fingers tautened, and the rope bit into her flesh. She was choking, strangling, the breath squeezed agonizingly from her body. When she awoke, her pillow damp with perspiration, she could still hear the horrible echo of his laughter. Over and over his voice reverberated in her head.

I warned you, Mistress Cady! I warned you!

CHAPTER TWO

THE *ESMERALDA* DOCKED in Salem Harbor amid joyous cheers from her passengers and crew. Belinda strained to see the harbor and the town, caught up in the crowd milling on deck as everyone prepared to depart the ship. It was difficult to see clearly, but she caught glimpses of a series of wharves lined with crates and sacks and oxen, of narrow streets, shops and houses with gabled roofs. The rain had ceased by midmorning, but a mistiness hung over the day, and it was now late afternoon, so dusk was stealing in, spreading its shadows across the land. Everything was gray and very bleak. She scanned the faces on the dock, wondering which of the men in their high-crowned hats and long, sober coats with rapiers at their sides was Cousin Jonathan. Well, she would find out soon enough, she told herself. With Sarah plodding along behind her as they shuffled with the throng, she tightened her grip on her trunk and fixed her eyes forward. She crossed the gangplank carefully, aided as she stepped down onto the wood-planked dock by the hands of a rough-faced sailor. Suddenly, her heart stopped. She had spotted Yeoman Phelps and Lettie up ahead, disappearing into a group of people near some wagons, and an

16

alarming thought had suddenly crossed her mind.

"Sarah," she said, turning with sudden urgency to the woman behind her. "Do you know the destination of Lettie Phelps and her husband? They're not...not settling in Salem perchance...are they?"

Sarah's brow puckered. "Lettie Phelps? That poor mite who's saddled with that brute of a husband? Nay, they'll not be settling in Salem. Andover County, the girl told me once. Her man's been given a small grant of farmland there. Why do you ask, child?"

"I only wondered," Belinda murmured, relief flooding through her. So all was well. She really would never see Yeoman Phelps again. She resolutely put all thoughts of him and her nightmare out of her mind as she and Sarah made their way through the milling throng on the dock. Her journey was over, and so was last night's ordeal. She was in the New World now, and her future beckoned. Belinda's knowledge of the Puritan settlement known as Salem was limited, but what she did know intrigued her. It had originally been called Naumkeag when settled by Roger Conant in 1626, and both Conant and John Endecott, leader of the New England Company, had worked diligently to build the area into a Puritan refuge, a place where Charles I could not readily harass those whose religious beliefs contrasted with his own. Though not a Puritan herself by either birth or upbringing, Belinda could empathize with their desire for freedom and admired the spirit and determination of the masses of people who had left the familiarity of their mother country to brave the dangers of the unknown, unsettled Bay Colony. At first, the hardships of the bitter winters and wilderness terrain had proven nearly insurmountable, but with the formation of the Massachusetts Bay Company things had greatly improved.

In 1630 the turning point had come. John Winthrop

set sail aboard the *Arbella* accompanied by a fleet of ten ships consisting of seven hundred passengers and a staggering amount of livestock and supplies. Their arrival in Salem in June of 1630 marked the beginning of real settlement, and the Massachusetts Bay Colony flourished. The small, ragged settlement at the harbor town of Salem grew slowly but steadily as the Puritans strove to achieve a holy community. Now more than sixty years had passed since that shaky beginning, and Salem had become a thriving port, humming with activity. These facts Belinda knew, but little else. The colonies of the New World remained somewhat of a mystery to the English, and consequently she scarcely knew what to expect now that she was leaving the *Esmeralda* and entering the new life awaiting her. She realized that there would be a certain amount of hardship, for certainly the colonies could not match the luxuries of the mother country, but other than that, she was ignorant. She did not fear the future, though, but welcomed it. She was determined to make a place for herself in this New World, to find her home and her happiness.

Her pulses quickened as she glanced about, hoping to discover her cousin. Suddenly, she felt a sharp tap on her shoulder and she turned in surprise. A hawk-faced, angular woman in a black bonnet and brown woolen cloak peered down at her through narrowed eyes.

"Be you Belinda Cady?" the woman demanded.

Belinda nodded. "Yes, and who might you be?"

"Hannah Emory. I work for Magistrate Cady, and he sent me to fetch you home. I've been waiting a long hour for you, and I've got chores yet to do, so let's be getting on."

Belinda stared at the brusque little woman with slightly raised brows. Hannah Emory appeared to be in her forties, a homely, sharp-faced creature with slitted brown eyes and steel-gray hair beneath her dark bonnet. Nowhere in her demeanor was there the slightest hint of friendliness or welcome. Instead, Belinda noticed that the woman had addressed her with every appearance of disdain, her small eyes flicking up and down. Even as Belinda studied her, Hannah Emory did the same, and from the scowling expression on the woman's face, she plainly did not approve of what she saw. She pursed her lips together, a gesture filled with judgment, and made a clicking noise with her tongue.

"Is something wrong?" Belinda inquired coolly, faintly amused by this examination. For answer, Hannah gave a short, contemptuous bark of laughter.

"Master Cady told me you'd be traveling with an older woman," she said in her harsh, clipped voice, "and all the other girls who left the ship had men with them, so I guessed who you might be, but still"—she shook her head slightly—"you're not what I expected. Not at all."

"Indeed?" Belinda stared at her, uncertain whether to be amused or indignant at the woman's rudeness, for she had never encountered such contempt before, particularly from a servant. In amazement she wondered what Hannah saw that disturbed her so. Belinda knew she looked presentable, even quite attractive. She had managed to remove the bloodstains from her cloak this morning, and it looked tolerable. Her coppery-red hair was tied back from her face with a green velvet ribbon, and beneath her cloak she wore a gown of olive green silk with three-quarter-length sleeves, and a green and gold lace-embroidered underskirt. What was there about her appearance to inspire such derision?

"I am sorry to have disappointed you," she remarked, meeting the other woman's gaze with a hint of hauteur in her own. "Pray tell me, what exactly did you expect?"

Hannah Emory opened her mouth to reply, then shut it quickly. "Never mind that now. You'll find out soon enough what's afoot, my fine lady. It isn't my place to be talking of what's to come."

"I quite agree," Belinda said smoothly, but inwardly she was worried. Something was amiss; she could sense it, not only from the woman's words and manner, but from her own feelings, her instincts, ever since they had encountered Hannah Emory on this dreary little dock. She tried to shake off her feelings, for she had no time to fret over them now. Instead, she tilted her head to one side and addressed the servant again.

"Where *is* my cousin?" she inquired. "I had hoped he would meet me himself."

"He had better things to do," Hannah returned sneeringly, tying her bonnet more snugly beneath her jutting chin. "There were important goings-on in the village today, and Master Cady was needed to officiate." Impatiently, Hannah gripped Belinda's arm. "Now come along, girl. Your cousin will be wanting his supper when he does reach home, and he'll want to see you, too. It's best not to keep Master Cady waiting, as you'll soon learn for yourself!"

This was too much. Indignantly, Belinda jerked her arm away, but before she could utter a word, Sarah Cooke charged in. "Just a minute, just a minute. Don't you go speaking to Miss Belinda in that tone!" The housekeeper's plump face was almost purple with rage. "Who do you think you're speaking to, you stupid woman? Imagine, addressing the Squire's daughter in such a manner! I never in all my life—"

"Squire's daughter, eh?" Hannah's eyes lit up unpleasantly. "From what I hear, the Squire is dead."

"Well, so he is, but—"

"But nothing!" Hannah snapped, her piercing gaze leaving Sarah's face to fasten upon Belinda, who was listening with growing fury. "You're no more a wealthy woman than I am!" she exclaimed, shaking a gnarled finger in the girl's face. "You're a pauper, for all your fancy clothes and fine airs. Well, you'll soon have the wind taken out of your sails, my fine lady. Master Cady will know how to deal with the likes of you!"

"How dare you!" Belinda's green-gold eyes sparkled dangerously. Her hands were tightly clenched, and she felt the heat of her wrath seeping over her entire body. "You are an insolent, mean-spirited shrew, and I shall report your conduct to my cousin the moment we arrive at his home. Perhaps you think it fitting to bandy words with your employer's kinswoman, but I doubt very much that he will agree with you. If you think to insult me with impunity, Hannah Emory, think again, for I shall not easily be appeased. Moreover, I understand that every colonial village has its stocks and whipping posts for disobedient servants, shrews, and criminals, and I should not be at all surprised if you find yourself spending a day of punishment for your conduct this afternoon!" she finished, regarding the unpleasant woman with cold triumph, but to her further amazement, Hannah threw back her head and laughed.

"What do you know of life here?" she said with a smirk, her eyes narrowed to slits. "You're mighty sure of yourself now, Belinda Cady, but you're in for a few surprises before the day is out, and that's the truth! We'll just wait and see!"

"What do you mean?" Belinda demanded, suddenly uneasy, but Hannah merely pressed her thin lips together and would say no more.

Trying to disguise how troubled she was by the servant's words and manner, Belinda turned back to Sarah, who had listened in shock to the exchange. The two women stared into each other's eyes.

"I don't like this," Sarah said in a lowered tone,

biting her lips nervously. "The woman must be mad, possessed by demons. I don't understand...."

"I don't either," Belinda admitted, "but I'm certain everything will be fine when I meet Cousin Jonathan. Don't worry, Sarah, you know that I am well able to care for myself. Everything will work out, and I'm convinced there will be a harmless explanation for this odious woman's behavior. Do not fear!" Despite her cheerful words, however, Belinda was disturbed. She couldn't understand why Hannah dared treat her so disrespectfully, and she wondered grimly exactly what Cousin Jonathan had told the woman about her. With every second that passed she grew increasingly anxious to make her cousin's acquaintance and find out what kind of a man he was to have such a woman in his employ.

"What about you, Sarah? Let me help you find your brother before we move on our way."

"Oh no, child, he's going to meet me at the inn tonight. 'Twill be dark before he rides in from Boston, and then it will require the entire day to travel back there." Sarah turned with a sniff to Hannah Emory. "If you'll be so kind as to tell me where the Wickham Tavern is located, I'll be off to settle in and wait."

Hannah pointed a bony finger toward a two-story, slope-roofed clapboard building along the main street of the town. It faced the waterfront, and there was a sign posted in the yard with neat lettering: *Wickham Tavern.* "Look for yourself," she answered sullenly. "You have eyes, don't you?"

Sarah bristled and began to reply, but Belinda touched her arm quickly. "No, Sarah, don't bother yourself over her. It will do you no good, and she is probably past learning to behave civilly to *anyone.* Leave us now, and do not worry. I can handle Hannah, you know— and Cousin Jonathan Cady, too!"

Tears entered Sarah's enormous blue eyes as she gazed for the last time at her former mistress. "Yes, *you* can take on anything, you naughty child, but I hope—" She bit her lip, and began again. "Do take care, miss, and try to remember to be a good, dutiful girl. Don't cause any trou—"

"Yes, yes, Sarah, I know." Belinda couldn't bear to hear any more advice. She leaned forward and kissed Sarah's cheek, then suddenly threw her arms around the housekeeper's neck. To her surprise, a hard, painful lump rose in her throat and she felt tears prick her eyes. "Fare well, Sarah," she gulped, smothered in a soft, yet fierce embrace. "I will miss you terribly!"

"Oh, Miss Belinda..." Sarah Cooke wiped at her own eyes, which were flooded with tears, and gazed miserably at the girl before her. "I worry so about you. I wish I could stay with you...watch after you...."

"We both know that is impossible." Belinda smiled through her tears and pressed Sarah's hands warmly. "Do not fret over me. Go in peace, with the knowledge that you have served me well all these years and that I shall remember you always. Our paths must be divided now, but I am certain we will meet again. Do not fear, my dearest Sarah. All will be well."

Sarah nodded, then slowly turned and, lifting her stout trunk, shuffled away toward the Wickham Tavern. As Belinda watched her go, she had to fight back the impulse to run after the woman, to gaze for just a moment longer upon her fat and kindly face. Sarah Cooke represented her last link with her former life, with the days of her girlhood in Sussex. From this day on, no person she met would be familiar, no one would share a single memory of her past. She would be alone as she had never been alone. An ache came into her throat, and a powerful loneliness engulfed her in great, drowning waves. She

suddenly wished fervently that she and Sarah could rush
back onto the ship and sail home to England. When they
returned she would find that this, the present, was all a
horrible nightmare, that Grandmama was still alive, that
the manor still belonged to them, that Bryant had not
really bumbled everything so that she was penniless and
forced to...

No. Such thoughts were useless. That part of her
life was over and the present could not be changed. The
future was what counted, and it must be faced. Belinda
straightened her shoulders, grimly remembering the
presence of Hannah Emory. She turned slowly to the
woman, a cold, composed expression fixed upon her delicate face to mask the overwhelming sadness and uncertainty inside. "I am ready," she said quietly. "Let us go
to the home of my cousin."

With head held high, she followed the woman along
the dock, squaring her shoulders like a soldier prepared
for battle. Hannah, her lips set in a tight line, led Belinda
to an unpainted wagon hitched to a single gray horse.

"Get yourself inside—and quick," she ordered. "It's
starting to rain, and we've five miles to the village."

With an effort, Belinda managed to heave her trunk
into the wagon, and then she climbed upon the seat
alongside the hard-faced woman. As Hannah drove she
had an opportunity to gaze about her at the surrounding
countryside. Through the mist and drizzle and shifting
shadows of the late afternoon, she stared in awe at the
dark, brooding forests all about her. What a wilderness
this Massachusetts Bay Colony is, she thought. The trees
seemed to huddle together, whispering secrets while she
passed beneath. The road was little more than a muddy
path, and the landscape was one of thick, gnarled trees,
boulders, and hills, a scene so dark and bleak-looking
that Belinda yearned for a big, glowing fire where she

could warm her hands and brighten her spirits.

The forest seemed to engulf everything, a force so wild and primitive it swallowed up all who might attempt to tame it. Staring about her at the encroaching hills, the looming trees, Belinda wondered about the people who inhabited this fierce wilderness. Were the Puritans as dark and grim as the land itself? She shuddered. Yet who could live amid these ancient hills and primeval forests without feeling their influence? Who could resist the dark powers of nature, powers so heathen and strong they seemed to dominate every inch of this desolate countryside? She tried to shake off the uneasiness which prickled her flesh like skeletal fingers, but as she left the open sea behind, drawn inexorably into the waiting darkness, her foreboding deepened.

Belinda's mood grew even more depressed as the drizzle heightened to a downpour, and she clutched her soaked hood about her head, shivering violently. Once she thought she made out a farmhouse, set back amid cleared fields, but it was only a blur in the gloomy mist of trees, so she could not be certain.

"How far is it to my cousin's house?" she shouted over the drum of the rain as Hannah turned the horse into an even darker section of woods. The bare branches of the trees, like ugly black claws, tore at the greenish-gray patches of sky, which could barely be seen above.

Hannah ignored her. Belinda gritted her teeth. "How far is it to my cousin's house?" she repeated more loudly, tapping the woman's arm insistently until Hannah threw her a dark glance.

"About three miles," she replied sullenly. "Salem Village lies yonder, five miles outside of Salem Town by the harbor."

"Is it a part of the same community?" Belinda was determined to learn something about her new environment. At first she had thought that Cousin Jonathan lived in the little town she had glimpsed at the dock, but it had become clear to her that he lived instead somewhere amid this wilderness, in a place called Salem Village. The farther they drove from the town, the more desolated the region seemed and the more downcast her spirits became. She felt cut off from civilization, from the bustle of people and activity which made up a community. Cold and weary, anxious about the meeting with her cousin, she felt a strange fear descend upon her. She didn't understand it, for she was not a person to indulge in silly fancies, but there was something about this place which sent a shiver of apprehension over her. She tried to shake it off as she questioned Hannah Emory about Salem Town and Salem Village, but the more deeply they drove through the dark, streaming woods and the more she dealt with this unpleasant servant woman, the more uneasy she grew. She managed to elicit a few answers from the reluctant Hannah and learned that Salem Village was indeed a part of Salem Town, though it was a farming community located on the farthest outskirts of the town settlement. The farm people, according to Hannah, had as little as possible to do with their town neighbors. "We have our own ways," she told Belinda, almost warningly. "Remember that, girl, if you're going to live among us. The people of Salem Village know the path to righteousness, and we know how to deal with those who stray from it."

"What do you mean?" Belinda asked from between chattering teeth, and Hannah threw her a sidelong glance.

"You'll see. I'll show you," she replied, flicking the whip over the horse's wet and glistening back and sending it into a gallop. Belinda clutched tightly to the sides of the wagon as the vehicle jolted across the marshy trail. A few strands of red-gold hair escaped from the velvet ribbon which had secured them and clung damply to her

face as she peered through the mist, wondering what
Hannah had meant.

A moment later they emerged from the woods upon
a wide, open clearing, which she instantly realized must
be the village square, for there were several buildings
clustered together around an open court, and nearby she
noticed the raised platform where the stocks and whipping post were located. On the far side of the square
squatted the ugly prison building, recognizable because
of the heavy iron bars across the tiny, high windows set
into its frame. They drove straight across the square at a
gallop, scarcely giving Belinda a chance to observe anything, though she did wonder in amazement where all
the people were. The village seemed deserted, a ghostly
remnant of a civilization that had mysteriously vanished.
Then she heard the chanting. Faintly at first it filtered
through the trees beyond the village square, beyond the
jail and the stocks.

"What is that? Where are we going?" she asked suddenly, as she realized Hannah was headed directly toward the sound. Hannah didn't answer. The wagon
careened onward into the woods until all at once, about
a hundred yards ahead, Belinda caught sight of a line of
people marching single-file, their heads bent against the
rain. They were chanting, and some carried torches which
had been extinguished by the rain. Hannah slowed the
gray horse and steered it alongside the marching throng.

"You there, Rebecca Sampson! Is it done?" she called,
and a stout woman in a scarlet cloak lifted her head and
nodded with a satisfied smile.

"Aye, the righteous have prevailed," she called, and
about a dozen villagers chorused "Amen."

"Master Cady will be home by now," Hannah muttered. "But I must see for myself the deed of this day.
We will make haste."

She nodded quickly to several people who lifted their

hands in greeting and shot curious glances at Belinda, and then she prodded the horse into motion once more. As they drove alongside the stream of people moving in the opposite direction, Belinda couldn't help being aware of the piercing stares directed at her. One man in a dark green cloak even stepped out of line and called to Hannah.

"Who be that with you, Hannah Emory?"

"This is the girl come to live with Master Cady. Belinda be her name."

It seemed to Belinda that his stare was suspicious and unfriendly as he approached the wagon to examine her more closely, but she told herself it was only her imagination. Nevertheless, she wished more than ever that she were already at Cousin Jonathan's house, out of the rain and away from this dismal throng.

"Where are we going, Hannah?" she demanded as they reached the end of the line of villagers and began to climb a low hill. "Didn't you say that my cousin would be home by now and that he doesn't like to be kept waiting? I recommend you to hurry homeward as quickly as possible. We're both soaked and nearly frozen—"

"Hush!" Hannah was staring straight ahead with glittering eyes. She raised one arm and pointed. "There she is, yonder. Look you now, Belinda Cady, and look you hard. Now you see what happens to those who stray from the path of righteousness!"

Belinda followed her gesture. What she saw made her gasp and recoil in horror. Upon the crest of the hill stood a gallows, from which dangled a woman's corpse. She swung limply in the gusting wind, her black cloak billowing about her lifeless form. Her dark hair whipped about her grotesquely drooping head as though trying to shield her poor face from any onlookers. Belinda stared at her, sickened. Her hands instinctively slid to her own throat. "Ohhh...how...awful!" She felt nausea rising in her and looked quickly away. "Who...is she? What had she done?"

Hannah was regarding the swinging corpse with satisfaction. "That was Elizabeth Foster. She was a witch. And she's received her just reward for consorting with the Devil!" Her voice had a smug, hard edge to it that sent a chill over Belinda. "I only wish I had been here myself to witness it, but the master sent me to fetch *you*."

"Cousin Jonathan...was he here today?" Belinda asked faintly, glancing with a horrified shudder at the grisly figure on the gallows.

"Of course," Hannah returned, her small brown eyes fastened intently upon Belinda. "He was the judge that sentenced her to hang!"

CHAPTER THREE

BELINDA STARED at Hannah Emory in shock. "Cousin ...Jonathan...is responsible...for this woman's death sentence?" she repeated incredulously, and Hannah nodded.

"Magistrate Cady is an important man here. What would we have done without him this past year while the village has been cursed? I shudder to think."

"The village has been cursed? What do you mean?"

Hannah's eyes narrowed. "We have been engaged in a battle against the Devil! He has unleashed a host of witches upon us, a black plague of evil. Do you think Elizabeth Foster is the only witch to have died upon Gallows Hill? Nay, there have been many! And the prison is full of Devil's servants, awaiting the fate to be dealt out to them by righteous souls such as Magistrate Cady!"

Belinda listened to her in stunned silence. She had heard of witch-hunts before, for the trials of women accused of practicing witchcraft sprang up occasionally in England and throughout all of Europe, but she had never before witnessed such a spectacle nor heard of a town or village being accosted by a host of witches. Usually the cases were random, isolated incidents which occurred from time to time across the continent. Never before had she heard of a concentration of witches in one place or a long series of trials. This, she concluded from Hannah's statements, was the case in Salem. She turned back, as if mesmerized, to the grim sight upon the gallows. Only a few hours ago that woman had been alive. And now...

"What did she do?" Belinda asked abruptly, her eyes fixed on Elizabeth Foster's grotesquely swinging feet. She couldn't bear to look toward the woman's face. "Why was she condemned as a witch?"

Hannah drew her dark bonnet more closely about her face. The rain had tapered to a drizzle, but droplets of water still ran from the brim, soaking into the brown woolen cloak. "She cast a spell on Goody Dunbar, for one thing," she replied savagely, her lips a thin line in her sharp face. "Gave her the stomach cramps—nearly killed her! And Goody Dunbar's cow stopped giving milk that same week, and half her chickens were killed by a wolf pack." She gathered up the horse's reins and began to guide the animal back down the hill, away from Elizabeth Foster's dangling corpse. "The Devil's work, that's what it was! 'Twas a blessing the witch was discovered and put to death before she could do even worse!"

Belinda's head flew up in amazement. "What?" she gasped. "Are you telling me that that girl was hanged because someone contracted stomach cramps? It can't be possible!"

Hannah rounded on her venomously, her slitted brown eyes crackling beneath her thin brows. "The evidence was clear, you ignorant wench! Witch Foster had quarreled with Goody Dunbar less than two weeks before these things took place. And Frances Miles had a dream where it was revealed to her that Elizabeth Foster was a witch! What further proof would be needed? There was no doubt of her guilt. Master Cady sat in judgment at a legal trial and reached the verdict justly."

"It's horrible," Belinda cried. "How can you know

that Mistress Foster caused Goody Dunbar to become ill
or her chickens to be killed—or her cow to go dry? It
could have been coincidence that these misfortunes befell
her. And as for that dream—"

"Blasphemy!" Hannah screamed, and slapped Belinda hard across the face. The girl recoiled in shock,
raising one trembling hand to her stinging cheek as Hannah raged at her. "Speak no more of this Devil's blasphemy, Belinda Cady, or I will report you to the master!
He will know how to deal with you!"

Hannah turned her attention back to the horse and
wagon as they proceeded once more into the woods.
Belinda stared at her in barely controlled fury. She spoke
in a low, warning tone, her voice throbbing.

"Don't you ever touch me again. Never! If you do,
I will make you sorry you were ever born!"

Hannah threw her a twisted smile, her own malice
and dislike bright in her eyes, but she said nothing.

Belinda fell into a shocked silence. *What kind of a
place have I come to?* she wondered, a knot of fear twisting
in her heart. The fear of witches in Salem Village was
widespread, almost hysterical in its nature from all that
she had gathered. It seemed that only the flimsiest evidence was needed to condemn someone to death. She
shivered, huddling deeper into her cloak. Her thoughts
shifted to Cousin Jonathan. What sort of man was she
going to find when she finally reached her cousin's house?

When at last the wagon emerged from the woods
into a large clearing, she saw a long, rectangular wooden
house with a sharply sloping, wood-shingled roof set
amid neat fields and flanked by a row of sheds and a
barn. It was difficult to see clearly, for the darkness of
the late afternoon had deepened and the mist had grown
more dense, but the building appeared large and dark,
a long, sturdy fortress overlooking the cleared farmland
surrounding it and facing the woods and hills with solid

endurance. Light glowed from within, seeming to beckon welcomingly. Here was her new home, for better or worse.

Belinda felt a surge of nervousness, but also a yearning for the shelter and comfort the house would provide. She was thoroughly soaked, chilled, and exhausted, and when the horse drew up before the two-story house, she climbed quickly down from the wagon. A silent manservant hurried out to lead the horse and wagon toward the barn, and he handed down her trunk. Hannah led the way to the massive double oak doors and swiftly opened them. Belinda stepped inside. She set down her heavy trunk and glanced about her. The large entrance hall was dusky, lit only by a single taper in a wall sconce. Ahead stood a steep staircase, narrow and uncarpeted. Before she had opportunity to note anything further, a man's voice rang out of the dimness to her left.

"Hannah! I am in the parlor. Bring my cousin here at once."

Hannah seized Belinda's arm and began to propel her forward, but Belinda shook her off wrathfully. "I am quite capable of moving forward without your assistance," she flashed, her eyes glittering in the candlelight. "I have told you once before, keep your hands off of me, Hannah Emory. Is that clear?"

Without waiting for an answer, she swept past the open-mouthed Hannah and into the parlor adjoining the hall. Her heart was pounding rapidly, despite her assured appearance. She found herself in a large, austere room with a low-beamed ceiling and leaded glass windows. Candles flickered in pewter candlesticks atop a handsome oak court cupboard on the far wall, and a roaring fire in the broad brick chimney sent shadows dancing about the room. Belinda scarcely had time to note the simple yet elegant furnishings: the gate-legged trestle table with the pewter cistern of wine atop it, the long pine table and low bench, the Turkey carpet on the oaken floor. She was gazing at the man opposite her, the man staring so piercingly into her face, searching his eyes as he searched hers. Jonathan Cady sat majestically in a tall carved chair at a writing desk near the fire, his large, bony hands resting upon the arms of his chair. As he stared at her without speaking, Belinda saw his thin lips tighten. It seemed to her that his eyes never blinked.

"Will there be anything else, Master Cady?" Hannah's voice, coming so suddenly from directly behind Belinda, startled the girl, and she jumped, then immediately felt like a fool. Nervously, she returned her attention to Cousin Jonathan, who replied to Hannah without his gaze ever wavering from Belinda's face.

"No, Hannah, that will be all. Leave us now."

Alone with her cousin, Belinda tried to smile. "Cousin Jonathan," she began formally, taking a tentative step forward. "It is good to meet you at last. I must thank you for inviting me here, into your home. It was...a most kind and generous act, sir."

Slowly, Jonathan Cady nodded. He was a tall, gaunt man, almost cadaverous in appearance. His bony face was long and narrow, with a sharp, pointed chin on which rested a distinctive black mole. His forehead was high, his nose long and aquiline and of a patrician line. His mouth was stern, his lips so thin they seemed not to exist at all. In his solemn black waistcoat and fine damask breeches he was a sober, humorless figure. But it was his eyes that most fascinated and repelled Belinda as she stood uncomfortably before him. They were small and set close together and of a pale, sickly greenish hue, opaque, even cloudy in nature. She had never seen eyes like that before, so odd a color, so lacking in human warmth. She shivered inwardly as he ran those strange, pale eyes over her straight-backed figure, still in her wet garments, her hair a damp, tangled mess. She wished he would invite her closer to the fire or at least to sit down and remove her wet cloak, but he had said nothing to her since she had entered the parlor, and her uneasiness grew almost unbearable. What was wrong? Would he never speak to her in greeting, never welcome her to his home?

"May I . . . may I come near the fire?" she asked finally. "I am rather chilled, Cousin Jonathan, after a long drive through the rain. I'm sure you won't object if I remove my wet cloak?"

She began to do so, but he surged to his feet and commanded her to halt.

She froze, her eyes widened, for he looked as though he were quite mad. Cady stepped closer, his pale eyes burning. He cupped her lovely, fine-boned face in his hand and tilted her head upward. "So, *you* are the daughter of my cousin Arthur and that French wife of his! I might have known. An unfortunate liaison if ever I saw one!"

Belinda stiffened. Slowly, she reached up and removed his hand from her face. A slow, boiling fury began to grow inside of her as she stared into her guardian's frowning face. Yes, it was true. Her mother, Lizette, had been a French noblewoman who had left her home and her family to wed. Owing to the long enmity between the English and the French, many had disapproved of the marriage, as Cousin Jonathan obviously did. But Belinda well remembered the strong and tender love between her parents, and she resented her cousin's sneering tone. "Yes, my mother was French," she responded coldly, her gaze locking with his. "She was a great beauty and a most accomplished woman. It is a pity you were never privileged to meet her, cousin."

He snorted. "Your father was a fool! The French are devils, every one of them. When you have lived here a short time, you will see how they threaten us. Between the French and the Indians we are in constant danger of being overrun. Therefore, it is a rule that you shall never mention your mother in this house again! Do you understand?"

"No!" Belinda cried, her cheeks flushed in anger. "I do not understand! My mother never harmed you or any Englishman! She was a gentle woman, a great lady!"

"She was French, and I will not have her name mentioned in my home." Cady sneered disdainfully at her from his towering height and then turned on his heel to return to his chair. "You may now remove your cloak and sit on that bench, cousin. I wish to have a better look at you."

Her breast heaved with indignation, but she followed his instructions. She was only too glad to shed the wet cloak and hang it upon a peg near the fire. Then she seated herself upon the hard wooden stool he had indicated. It was customary that children never sat upon chairs, only upon stools or benches. She was hardly a child any longer, however, and he might have offered her the small cushioned chair near the fire. Instead, she sat uncomfortably opposite him, her bones chilled and her flesh craving the warmth of the flames. She gazed defiantly back at him, her eyes blazing as brightly as the fire, as he scrutinized her once more. First the woman-servant and now Cousin Jonathan! She could not tolerate being treated so rudely, and her temper flared like a torch.

Jonathan Cady watched her every mannerism, her every expression. He noted the long, thick coppery-red hair pulled back from her face in its green velvet ribbon. Some strands had escaped to wisp delicately about her face, and they glimmered like golden threads in the light of the fire. He saw the loveliness of her dainty features, her brilliant eyes and satiny, peach-colored complexion, and he also observed, with a jolt of violent emotion, her soft, full breasts and narrow waist beneath the rich folds of her green velvet gown. She was an exquisite creature, this Belinda Cady, this kinswoman of his. A temptress. A woman-child who would know how to tantalize a man, to drive him mad. His bony hands clenched on his desk. A woman like this caused trouble, led men from the path of righteousness and decency. He had expected a quiet mouse of a girl who would do his bidding in fearful haste and never open her lips to dispute him. One who would not draw unseemly attention to herself merely by her appearance. But this is what he had received instead. A beauty. An obstinate, willful beauty, that's what she was; he could read it in her eyes. A thin smile touched his lips as she glared rebelliously back at him. He would deal with her. Yes, indeed. It was his duty, his obligation to protect the community from her lures. He would subdue her, teach her to fear and respect him and the laws of decency he upheld. She would not have the opportunity to torment any man as he had once been so cruelly tormented.

"You are not what I expected, Cousin Belinda," he remarked slowly, intertwining his fingers on the desk before him. "Your appearance displeases me."

Belinda's eyes widened incredulously at this insult. "There is little I can do about *that*, Cousin Jonathan," she retorted, clenching her hands in her lap. "My features were bestowed on me at birth. If you are dissatisfied with them, I suggest you address your complaints to our Maker, for He is the responsible party!"

"Do not bandy words with me, you insolent wench!" Jonathan leaned forward, his long, pale face ablaze with fury. "I will not tolerate impudence—nor blasphemy! Now you will sit there and listen to me and you will hold your tongue. You will not speak again until I require you to do so. Is that clear?"

Belinda stared at him in mounting indignation. Her experience of the world was limited, sheltered as she had been by her quiet village life, but she was an intelligent girl, and she knew a tyrant when she saw one. Jonathan Cady, with his small, cold eyes and high-bridged nose, was a tyrant, indeed. He was an important member of the community; Hannah Emory had shown her that. As a magistrate, a man of power and authority, he clearly enjoyed exercising his will. And unless Belinda was much mistaken, he intended to exercise it over her. Every muscle of her slender body quivered with rage. She who had run free in the woods and meadows, barefoot and with flowing hair, rebelled instinctively at his tone and manner. To be dictated to by this sour-faced, sneering man! Was this the future in store for her? Her new guardian was worse than any of her imaginings, and she fought against a wild, furious impulse to sweep from the room and out of his house. But that would be sheer idiocy. Where would she go? To whom? And how? He was her guardian now, and her fate was in his hands. Her heart sank at this prospect, but her spirit never flagged. She met his stern gaze unflinchingly and answered his question with rigid calm.

"Yes, Cousin Jonathan, you have made yourself quite clear. I am listening, as you see, but only because I have no choice in the matter."

His stare seemed to grow even colder. "Very well. I will continue, and I recommend you to pay close attention." He began to pace slowly about the parlor, his hands clasped behind his back. "When I invited you into my home, Cousin Belinda, I expected a different sort of a girl. An ordinary girl. I can see immediately that you are not ordinary. Your looks are . . . striking, and it is that to which I object. Young women of uncommon prettiness such as yourself, are, I believe, inclined to be vain and lazy. Such conduct will not be permitted in this house. As you know, I am a man of considerable importance in Salem Village, and my household must serve as an example for the rest of the community. Your appearance, the way you speak and behave, will be noticed by all and will reflect upon me. Therefore, I will exercise strict supervision over all of these elements." He paused before the fire and frowned at her, his face harsh. "You will wear a cap at all times. That is the first rule you must obey." He stepped closer and his hand stretched forward. He lifted a long curl of her magnificent hair and fingered it slowly. "This hair," he said softly, "the color of flame, is a sign of the Devil. You must hide it beneath the cap. It is an affront to decency, a symbol of hellfire. I will not gaze upon it, nor will anyone else in Salem. Do not let me find you without a cap upon your head from this day forward! Do you understand?"

Belinda wanted to scream, to stamp her foot and rage about the room, but a small voice inside her warned her that this would do no good and would in fact be foolhardy. With great effort she mastered her emotions and replied between clenched teeth, "I understand."

"Excellent. Regarding the rest of your garments, I must inform you that sobriety and practicality are of the utmost importance. We of the Massachusetts Bay Colony have passed a law prohibiting the lower classes from wearing garments above their station. No excessive frills, lace, silks, and so forth—"

"Pardon me, Cousin Jonathan," Belinda broke in angrily, unable to control herself any longer. "I am hardly a member of the lower classes. My father was a squire, my mother a gentlewoman of the nobility—and you, my only living relative, have just informed me that you are an important member in this community—"

"Silence!" Cady thundered at her, his eyes shining with fury. "You will not interrupt me again or I will take a switch to you, wench!" He rose above her, towering over her, trembling with rage, and Belinda feared he would indeed strike her. She paled and gazed at him with ill-disguised hatred. His next words rang even more harshly in her ears, each sound striking her like a blow.

"You are obviously suffering under some delusion, Cousin Belinda, if you believe that you are entitled to an elite position in society. Whatever your past connections, you are an orphan now, a penniless orphan. It is only my generosity that has saved you from poverty and possibly starvation. I trust you will remember that in the future. I have given you a home, a fine roof over your head, and the sustenance of food. There are certain things I require from you in return."

She glanced up, preparing herself for whatever he might say next.

"In return for the comfort and protection of my household, I expect you to earn your keep," Cady informed her coldly. "My servant, Hannah Emory, will be leaving in a week's time. Her sister's health is failing, and she will remove to Andover to nurse her. It will be your obligation to replace her in this household."

Belinda gasped. "You cannot be serious? I...I am to become your womanservant?"

Without a word, Cady strode to the corner of the parlor and lifted a heavy birch switch from a shelf on the wall. He returned to Belinda and raised it above her head. Before she had time to move, he brought it whistling down about her shoulders with a heavy blow. She screamed and fell from her stool. He stood over her, fingering the switch, as she lay sobbing upon the floor.

"I warned you against interrupting. Now get up and sit upon this stool without another word."

Tears streamed down her cheeks. She had never been so ill-treated in her life, and she longed to fly at Jonathan Cady with her nails, to claw his face and bite and kick and strike him. At the same time she wished to run to someone, anyone, for help and comfort. Instead, she rose, whimpering as her shoulders burned with a fiery pain. She sat once more upon the hard wooden stool, her head bent and her shoulders shaking. In her mind's eye she pictured her past life, the lovely manor house in Sussex, her own room with the yellow and white satin canopy over the bed, Sarah Cooke patting her head as she served her a tray of tea and buttered scones. She saw once more her grandmother smiling at her in the parlor as she gazed dreamily into the fire, and a hard lump rose in her throat, nearly choking her. Such a lovely, simple life, gone, gone forever! Oh, why had everything changed? How had it happened that now she was here in this cold, austere house in the Massachusetts wilderness, servant to this odious man? Her tears flowed bitterly as she hunched on her stool, contemplating Jonathan Cady's words. She was to be his servant, to cater to his whims and scrub his floors, to obey every command or . . . or be beaten into submission. The humiliation and injustice of it tore her apart, but there was nothing she could do. Through her sobbing, she heard his harsh voice relentlessly pounding at her.

"You must learn to obey, little cousin. That is of the utmost importance. Do not speak again unless I bid you, or your punishment will not be so light!"

He tapped the switch against the palm of his hand as he resumed his pacing, his heavy black shoes scraping against the oaken floor. "As I explained, you will take over the duties of Hannah Emory within a week's time, and until then I expect you to work closely with her, learning what will be expected of you. Defer to her in all situations, as she shall teach you the proper way to serve in this household. You will begin in the morning; I have decided that tonight, since it is your first night here after a lengthy journey, you may rest." He replaced the switch on the shelf and turned back to her with a thin, cruel smile. His was the most heartless visage she had ever seen. "Hannah will show you your quarters now. Then, after you have altered your appearance with a suitable cap and gown, you may come down to the kitchen for your supper. I daresay there shall be some hasty pudding and brown bread remaining from the noonday meal. I shall dine presently here in the parlor, and I do not wish to be disturbed for the rest of the evening. Have you any questions?"

Belinda stared up at him, her face tear-streaked and her green-gold eyes shining with hatred. "How long is this arrangement to last, cousin?" Her voice was low and taut. She clenched her hands tightly in her lap. "Even indentured servants are released from their indenture after a period of years. For how long is my servitude to last?"

He regarded her fixedly with those strange, pale eyes, and then a corner of his mouth lifted in a twisted smile. "When I deem it fitting and proper, I shall begin to look about for a suitable husband for you, little cousin. Someone stable and firm, who will know how to control your vanity and laziness. He will see that you are looked after as you deserve. Do not fear. When the time is right, I shall end your service in this household. But," he concluded with a little shrug, "you have only just arrived. You shall not be leaving for several years yet." He sniffed and waved his arm at her. "That will be all. You are dismissed." He called to Hannah, who appeared seconds later in a long white apron and cap, her sharp face alight with malicious satisfaction, revealing to Belinda that she had overheard the entire scene. Belinda bit her lip so hard it bled, but she rose and walked with quiet dignity toward the woman.

"Show my cousin her room," Jonathan Cady ordered, "and then bring my supper." He turned to Belinda, a haughty expression on his bony features. "I regret, cousin, that our first meeting was marred by such unpleasantness. It was necessary, however, to impress upon you the realities of your circumstances. I trust such action will not be necessary again. It is my sincere hope that we shall get on well together, and that you will find contentment in your new home."

Her eyes glittered as she faced him, standing straight and proud in the doorway of the parlor. "You have given me a unique welcome, cousin—one which I assure you I shall never forget," she replied with lifted chin. "I do not know how to begin to thank you for this greeting. Perhaps one day I shall find a way." Without waiting for a reply, she whirled quickly and swept from the parlor, Hannah trailing behind her. Together they mounted the narrow flight of wooden stairs in the hallway. At the landing, Belinda caught a glimpse of a single chamber, containing an iron bedstead with a green tapestried coverlet and matching hangings, a large, carved oak chest, an escritoire, and two chairs with green embroidered cushions.

"This is the master's room," Hannah informed her with a motion of her wrist. "Beyond it is a small sitting room the master uses on occasion. Mind you keep it scrubbed and dusted just like all the others."

Belinda turned to her. "Where is your bedchamber—and mine?"

"Stupid wench—I don't sleep in this house. 'Twouldn't be fitting, there being no mistress. I live in a cottage at the end of the road with the Carters, Will and Patience. Will Carter works the farm here for the master, and his boy, Seth, is the groom. He's the one who took the horse and wagon when we drove up."

"I see. But where am I to sleep?" Belinda inquired wearily. "I don't see any other rooms on this floor."

Hannah grinned spitefully. "This way, my fine lady. Follow me." She led Belinda to a rickety wooden ladder in the corner opposite the sitting room and pointed upward. "The loft is where you'll be sleeping. It's a bit cold up there—dark and stuffy, too, but that won't trouble the likes of you, will it?" Her laugh echoed harshly in the dim corridor. "Up with you, then. And here's your trunk. You'll find your way to the kitchen when you're ready to eat. If not, you'll go hungry. It's all the same to me."

Still snickering, she disappeared down the narrow stairs into the gloom below. Slowly, Belinda managed to climb the steps to the loft, dragging her suitcase along with her. When she reached the top, she pulled herself into the dreary little room. A tallow candle in a tarnished pewter holder rested on a small square chest of drawers beside the door. She lit it with trembling fingers and shut the door. Then she stared about her at the ugly little cell where she found herself. It was a cold, pitiful place. There were dark clapboard walls and a dusty wooden floor. A small, square window was set on the far wall, and there was a thin pallet on the floor near the chest, a faded blue wool blanket folded upon it. The sheets beneath looked coarse and yellowed. On the chest of drawers, beside the candlestick, was an iron pitcher and basin, almost as badly tarnished as the candlestick. Belinda gazed about her in dismay, feeling the tears well up in her eyes. The room was musty, and dust clogged her nostrils. She covered her face with her hands. *What am I going to do?* she wondered in anguish. *How am I going to endure this?*

Wearily, she sank down upon the straw-filled pallet that was now her bed. Sobs shook her as all of her pain and fear and loneliness flooded through her. Never had she felt so desolate, so lost. Her head ached and her body shuddered as she finally allowed all of her pent-up tears to flow. When at last she raised her head, she felt spent, exhausted. She realized that it had begun to rain again, that the night outside her window was filled with thunder and the rush of the wind. The cold, damp air crept in through the walls and sloping ceiling, chilling everything. Belinda drew a painful breath, shivering.

One thing was certain. She could not tolerate living

here with that tyrant, serving him, bowing and scraping. It was intolerable. But, she thought with a helpless frustration which pierced deeply into her heart, what could she do? Cousin Jonathan had brought her to the colonies to be his servant, and there was now no escape. *At least*, thought Belinda, suddenly glancing up with alacrity, *not yet. Perhaps I will find a way*, she whispered, her brilliant eyes glowing with a sudden purpose. *Yes, yes I must! I will pretend to acquiesce, I will deceive him into thinking me a poor, spiritless puppet, and then I will escape!* Sitting up on the floor of the loft, she prayed that she would find the means to free herself of her enslavement, to seek a new life elsewhere, anywhere but here! She crept to the window and peered out at the wet, driving blackness, knowing that the New England wilderness crouched out there, the dark, looming trees and mysterious hills. *I will conquer them all*, she vowed vengefully, shaking her small fist as she knelt upon the floor. *I will win my freedom and my happiness, and may heaven help anyone who stands in my way. I will be free!* And she leaned her head against the icy glass and closed her eyes, summoning all of her strength for whatever lay ahead.

CHAPTER FOUR

BELINDA STIRRED on her straw-filled pallet and rubbed her eyes as dawn broke hesitantly through the gray winter sky. Her body ached and her mind felt foggy, as though her head were stuffed with cotton. She longed to sleep until noon, but dared not tarry another minute. Within the half-hour Cousin Jonathan would expect his breakfast served, and before that time she had much to accomplish.

She sat up with a groan, shivering in the morning chill. She had been in Salem more than a week now, and she was becoming accustomed to the day's routine. Hannah Emory had departed two days ago, much to Belinda's relief, but before that she had instructed the new servant scrupulously as to every detail of her duties. It was a rigorous schedule, with no opportunity for rest or diversion. Even mealtimes were brief and consisted of only the simplest fare. Belinda's passionate hatred for her new home grew stronger each day. She thought constantly of escape.

Gasping from the cold, she bathed her face and hands in the basin of icy water she had brought in from the well the night before. She dressed quickly in the gloom, fastening the plain buttons of her black wool gown with frozen fingers and brushing her long, flaming hair with quick, even strokes. Carefully, she pulled it into a knot and tied it with a black ribbon, then pinned a white lace cap upon her head. *I must look like an ugly old crone*, she thought bitterly. Since she had no looking glass, she was unaware that even the dark, severe clothes and prim cap could not spoil her vibrant beauty. She climbed hurriedly down the ladder leading from the loft and slipped past Cousin Jonathan's room, running nimbly down the stairs. Her first task was to rake out the ashes from the previous night's fire and then build the morning's fire, using hardwood logs and pine kindling until she had a cozy blaze in both the kitchen and parlor. Then she threw on her cloak and rushed outside to fetch water from the well. Her breath came in white puffs in the morning frost, and with great difficulty she carried the heavy wooden bucket brimming with water back toward the house. Cousin Jonathan was just descending the staircase as she entered, his stern, unsmiling expression the same as it was every other morning. Belinda felt a knot tighten in her stomach as she glanced at his hated figure.

"Good morning, cousin," he said coldly, strolling past her into the parlor. "Make haste with my breakfast, if you please. I have important business awaiting me at the meetinghouse today."

Belinda grimaced behind his back and brought the water to the kitchen, proceeding to prepare the hasty pudding in the big iron pot used for that purpose. Then, while the water for the coffee boiled, she warmed the remains of yesterday's corn bread in the brick oven. She knew what the business in the meetinghouse involved and wished there was some way to prevent her cousin's attendance there. Another witch trial was in progress, and today was the day Cady, as chief magistrate of the village, would issue a sentence.

The woman now on trial was a middle-aged widow with five grown children. The only evidence against her, as far as Belinda had heard, was that Frances Miles, an eighteen-year-old girl from one of Salem's finest families, had accused the woman of "tormenting" her with witchcraft. A group of Frances's friends had all attested the same. It was absurd! On the basis of testimony from a group of superstitious, impressionable girls, a woman might die! Belinda had never met the accused woman, Widow Smith, or Frances Miles, but Goodwife Fletcher, who lived only a mile from the Cady house, had told her on the road only yesterday that she believed the Miles girl was lying.

"She enjoys all the attention it causes when she flies into her fits and swoons," Goodwife Fletcher had whispered, glancing worriedly about to be certain no one was approaching to overhear. "I think she . . . imagines most of these attacks," she had continued, shaking her gray head. "But what is to be done?"

"Someone ought to speak out against her!" Belinda had cried, staring in chagrin at the stout, kindly neighbor who had been one of the few people to welcome her to Salem Village. "She cannot be allowed to go on accusing innocent people, causing them to be tried for witchcraft and hanged! It's horrible!"

Goodwife Fletcher nodded wearily, her blue eyes growing sad. "Some have tried to speak against her and the other girls. They were accused in turn—and hanged like the rest. A body doesn't know what to do. To disagree with those girls, and the rest of the village, casts great suspicion upon a person. I—I do not dare to even appear as though I disapprove of what is happening . . . but I do. I do, child." To Belinda's distress, the old woman had begun to cry. "There are others who feel the same as I. But our numbers are few, and we dare not

raise our voices against those who see witches at every
turn. We dare not show our doubt, even our pity for
those accused."

Belinda had been shocked by these disclosures. This
morning, as she served Jonathan his breakfast in the parlor, she thought of Widow Smith, manacled in that ugly
prison, awaiting the announcement of her fate. *I must
speak*, she thought uneasily, despite the warning voice
inside her head which bade her to be careful. *I cannot
allow that woman to die without attempting to sway my cousin's
judgment. I cannot.*

She took a deep breath. "Cousin Jonathan," she began with forced calm, as she poured coffee into his gleaming pewter cup. "May I have a word with you about
the . . . the trial of Widow Smith?"

Cady regarded her disdainfully. "What would you
have to say about it, wench? You have not attended at
the meetinghouse."

"N-no, but I have heard about the trial from . . . from
various people," she murmured, not wishing to identify
Goodwife Fletcher in any way. "I must tell you, cousin,
that I don't understand how the mere word of Frances
Miles and her friends could bring a woman like Widow
Smith to trial. From all I have heard, she is a decent,
righteous woman who never did an injury to another in
her life."

"Cousin Belinda! Are you accusing those poor tormented girls of falsehood?" he demanded, a cold light
emanating from his small, close-set eyes.

"No . . . no, that is . . . I don't know. They might be
lying, or perhaps they merely *think* someone is tormenting them with witchcraft."

"Speak no more of this. You have not seen them
weeping in the courtroom, screaming in agony. You have
not heard their tormented wailings. The Devil acts in

mysterious ways and chooses strange creatures for his servants. It is clear that Widow Smith has succumbed to his lures and is acting on his behalf, and it is my duty to stop her. I must protect the people of this village!"

"Can you not even conceive that she might be innocent, that there is an error somewhere, a terrible misunderstanding?" Belinda cried, her eyes imploring him, but he threw her a glance of icy contempt.

"Silence! Who are you, to advise me on matters of law and justice? Get on with your chores, wench, and do not try my patience any longer!" He brushed roughly past her and removed his long scarlet cloak from its peg near the door.

"Cousin Jonathan, you cannot do this! You will be sending an innocent woman to her death!"

His gaunt frame turned slowly to face her, and she read the cold, cruel implacability in his eyes. "One more word from you, Cousin Belinda, and I shall send you to the stocks for a day. Perhaps that will teach you to hold your tongue." Opening the door, he paused and glanced back at her once more. "Here comes Lucy Brewer, servant to the Miles family. She is come to bring some garments for you to embroider for Miss Frances. Do not dawdle with the girl; send her on her way quickly and return to your chores. I shall return at midday for my dinner, and I expect it to be served promptly."

The door closed firmly behind him. As she cleared the table, Belinda controlled an impulse to send one of the pewter plates flying across the room. She chewed her lips, wondering bleakly if she hadn't hurt Widow Smith's cause more than helped it by her defense of the woman. She could scarcely believe what was going on in this seemingly quiet little village. How many people would have to die before this oppressive witch-hunt ended? Who would be the next victim of Frances Miles's imagination?

Suddenly, she remembered the girl approaching on

PROMISE ME THE DAWN   51

the road, Frances Miles's servant girl. She set down her
armload of plates and hurried to the door, opening it to
the slowly warming day. Now that the sun was fully
risen, much of the chill had left the brisk March air, and
she shivered only slightly as she watched the approach
of the figure on the road.

Lucy Brewer was a thin girl of no more than sev-
enteen summers. Clad in a long gray cloak, she moved
quickly up the path to the house, a basket over one arm.
In the pale sunlight, her features appeared washed out
and bleak, but as she drew nearer, into the shadow of
the timbered house, Belinda saw that she was a pretty
girl—fair and pale, with velvet-brown eyes and ash-blond
hair, a small nose and chin, and hands that were unusu-
ally graceful. She seemed nervous and smiled timidly at
Belinda.

"Good morning to you, Mistress Cady. I bring some
garments for my mistress, which she wishes you to embroider. News of your skill with the needle has reached
her ears even in the short time you have been in Salem."

Belinda smiled rather wryly. Once he had learned
that she was a talented needlewoman, Cousin Jonathan
had wasted no time in hiring out her skills to the neigh-
borhood. In addition to her daytime chores, she spent
several hours every evening placing fine, dainty stitches
upon rich garments of lace and silk for the elite ladies of
the area. Though the poor and lower classes were pro-
hibited from wearing finery, the wealthy and powerful
displayed their worldly goods as they wished. She found
it hypocritical and distasteful, yet she was still grateful
for the work. Cousin Jonathan allowed her to keep half
of the profits from her needlework, and in this way she
hoped secretly to save money toward her journey to freedom. She beckoned gracefully to Lucy Brewer to enter
the house and bade her welcome.

"Please call me Belinda," she told the girl with a

smile. "I am a servant here, the same as you. It would not do to put a distance between us."

A pleased smile lit the other girl's face. "You are kind. I thank you—Belinda." Lucy opened the basket and removed a fan-shaped neck ruff and a wine-colored damask gown with a pink and white satin underskirt. The richly colored finery billowed around her small, gray-cloaked figure like rainbowed clouds. She handled it reverently. Watching her, Belinda realized that Lucy Brewer had probably never owned or worn anything half so fine in her entire life. No, the silks and damasks were reserved for the likes of Frances Miles, not her servant girl. Yet, Belinda observed, noting the wistful expression in Lucy's velvet-brown eyes as she placed the exquisite garments in Belinda's arms, Lucy would look beautiful adorned in finery such as this. There was a quiet grace and elegance about her which could not be hidden even by her plain, homespun clothes. Dressed in this gown of rich, wine damask with a lace-edged neck ruff, her pale hair tied with ribbons of satin, she would outshine any well-born lady. Unfortunately, Belinda reflected, she would probably never have the opportunity to do so. She was a servant, and to wear finery such as this, even if she could afford to purchase it, would draw harsh censure down upon her.

Lucy's soft voice broke into Belinda's thoughts. "Mistress Miles wishes you to embroider the underskirt with ruffles and lace, and also the sleeves of the gown's bodice to match. She requested lace edging to the neck ruff as well."

Belinda nodded, fingering the soft fabric of the gown. "Very well. How soon need the work be finished? I have several orders placed already which must be completed first, naturally."

An uneasy look darted into Lucy's eyes. "Oh, y-yes,

I understand but... but Mistress Frances would like them completed by the end of the week. She... she is not a patient lady."

Belinda tossed her head, thinking of the girl who had accused so many of witchcraft in this village. Perhaps others in Salem were intimidated by Frances Miles, but she was not. "Then she must learn to be patient. At least in this case," she informed Lucy coolly.

Lucy's eyes widened. "Oh, please... Belinda, is there not some way you can accomplish the work more quickly? I fear Mistress Frances shall be very angry!"

"Indeed?" Belinda's small, delicate features were determined. "Then so it must be. I work according to my schedule, not Frances Miles's wishes."

Lucy's alarm increased. She wrung her hands together nervously. "But she... she specifically told me that she wished the damask gown be embroidered at once. It... it was an order!"

"She will be disappointed then. It is impossible."

To Belinda's amazement, Lucy's face suddenly crumpled. She burst into tears, her sobs echoing loudly in the quietness of the sunlit parlor. Belinda stared at her in chagrin, then moved quickly to her side.

"Please, try to calm yourself. Tell me what is wrong. I don't understand!"

Lucy had by now covered her face with her hands and was weeping bitterly, but she allowed herself to be led to the pine bench flanking the table, where she sank down beside Belinda. Belinda put an arm across the girl's shoulders and spoke to her gently.

"It is your mistress, is it not? You are afraid of her." She bit her lip as Lucy nodded. "Do you mean that *you* will face her wrath if these garments are not completed within the week?"

"Y-yes," Lucy gasped, "and so will you! You are

new here, you do not know my mistress!"

A glitter came into Belinda's brilliant green eyes. "For myself, I do not fear her! I have heard a great deal about Frances Miles. She is the one who has accused Widow Smith of witchcraft, and she testified against Elizabeth Foster also. I gather she is hardly the kindest of persons!"

"She is horrible!" Lucy began to cry again, trembling violently. "And if she ever learned the truth about *me*—"

"You? What about you?"

The pale-haired girl stopped crying abruptly and stood up, her face registering horror. She stared at Belinda with wide, dilated eyes. "Nothing! N-nothing! Please, Mistress...Belinda! Do not pay any heed to me! I am distraught, I am being foolish. I will leave now and allow you to return to your chores."

She flew to the door, but Belinda ran after her and laid a gentle hand on her arm. "Wait, Lucy, don't be afraid. I wouldn't do anything to hurt you. You can trust me."

Lucy peered at her uneasily. Apparently what she read in Belinda's face reassured her that this was true, for she relaxed and drew a deep breath. A wan, watery smile washed across her features.

"Yes...yes, I can see that you are kind," she replied in a low tone. "But you must not ask me to explain myself. I cannot! I must not! It isn't that I do not trust you, but...but I am so very frightened."

"Shhh. Never mind." Belinda smiled. Whatever Lucy's secret involved, it obviously terrified the poor girl, and in some way her fear of Frances Miles contributed to the problem. Puzzled and concerned, Belinda realized it was useless to question Lucy further at the moment, for she was determined to hide her secret. But Belinda suspected that she needed a friend, and so she beckoned the girl back into the parlor.

"Why don't we have a cup of tea? It will only take a moment to put the kettle on," she invited warmly.

"Oh, but I couldn't! I must be getting back." Lucy reached for her basket. "The...the master and his lady expect me to hurry...."

"Ten minutes," Belinda promised, "and then you may return to your mistress and tell her that the embroidery will be completed within the week."

Lucy lifted her head. Her warm brown eyes held tears of gratitude. "You are very kind," she said simply.

Belinda smiled. "I won't allow you to suffer at your mistress's hands because of me. I am pleased to help you, and pleased to have your company." Suddenly she laughed, mischief brimming in her vivid eyes. "Since this is a special occasion, I will even bring out a dish of honey to spread upon our corn bread, though you mustn't ever, ever let on to Cousin Jonathan or he would undoubtedly send me to the whipping post. My dear cousin does not allow anyone but himself to use sweeteners such as molasses or honey or sugar. But I defy him as frequently as I dare!"

"You are very brave. Magistrate Cady is a stern man."

"He is a tyrant, and I abhor him," Belinda stated frankly. "From the sound of it, your Mistress Miles is not much better!"

Lucy looked down at her hands.

Belinda changed the subject then, moving efficiently between the kitchen and the parlor as Lucy helped her prepare their little feast. In only a few moments they were sitting cozily at the pine table before the blazing fire, chatting amiably, warm and comfortable with their tea and corn bread and honey. Belinda watched Lucy's timidity slowly ebb, and she herself felt the knot of tension inside her begin to loosen. Some of the loneliness of the past weeks lifted, leaving her spirit refreshed. It was so good to find a friend. She had become so accustomed to Cousin

Jonathan's cold orders and disdainful frowns that she had begun to wonder if she would ever find kindliness again. Yet here she was now, feeling almost as content as she had in Sussex, surrounded by all those she held dear. Despite the quiet kindness of Goodwife Fletcher, Belinda had not felt nearly as comfortable as she did with this girl of her own age. Though they spent only a brief time together over their tea, both Lucy and Belinda bid farewell with the feeling that a bond of allegiance existed between them. Each felt more hopeful about the future and more able to endure the present. They went on about their respective chores inwardly warmed by the glow of newfound friendship.

Belinda had learned a great deal about Lucy during their brief chat. The girl, like herself, was an orphan who had been taken on as a servant in the Miles home at the age of ten. She had grown up with Frances Miles, for they were the same age, though always the difference in their status was brought heavily to bear upon her. Last year, Lucy had become engaged to Henry March, a young man of twenty and the son of a farmer, whom, Belinda could see, Lucy loved deeply. When she spoke of him a smile came into her eyes and her fluttering, nervous hands stilled. Unfortunately, Henry had left for Philadelphia the previous autumn. He had an uncle there who had offered to bring him into his leather tanning business. Henry, for whom farming held no appeal, had eagerly accepted the opportunity. One day, Lucy had informed Belinda proudly, Henry would inherit his uncle's business and be a man of importance in the growing city of Philadelphia. The only drawback to this bright future was that he and Lucy would have to remain separated until he had established himself and earned enough money to support a new bride. Lucy hadn't heard news of him in almost three months now. Belinda wondered, with a stab of pity, if this might account for some of the nervousness and traces of unhappiness she had first noticed in the girl. She still pondered what secret Lucy harbored which terrified her so. She had refrained from questioning her, however, deciding that if and when Lucy chose to share her problem, she would have opportunity enough to help her. After Lucy had departed, Belinda felt able to face her tasks more optimistically. Her daily life might be dreary and arduous, but at least she had found companionship.

The weeks crept by in an endless repetition of tasks. The cold, gray days of March gave way to April and a hint of spring. Warm, tangy breezes drifted down from the mountains and swept in from the bay. The days grew less bracing, and the sky brightened in hue from whitish gray to a magnificent blazing blue. Belinda had little time to observe the changes of nature, however, for her life was imprisoned in a tedious routine. In the morning she built the fires, fetched water, cooked breakfast, and scrubbed the house from floorboards to rafters. At noon she served Jonathan Cady his dinner meal, usually beef or mutton stew or fresh-cooked fish, succotash, parsnips, and onions, followed by a dessert of "Injun pudding," a concoction of corn meal sweetened with molasses and accompanied by cider. After the meal, she spent the remainder of the afternoon tending the herb garden, creaming butter, and spinning yarn at the big wooden spinning wheel near the hearth in the kitchen. She also tended to the laundering, which involved paddling the clothing in a big wooden "bucking tub" in the shed beside the house, an exhausting chore and the one she most despised. Supper was served at sundown, and then, when she had scrubbed the last pot and banked the fires for the night, she retired to her loft. There, by flickering candlelight, she worked meticulously at her embroidery, her body sagging with exhaustion, her fingers moving wearily as she automatically placed the delicate stitches in appropriate patterns. Once or twice a week she drove the wagon into the village to make household purchases. Even these trips, despite the welcome change in routine, were not entirely pleasant, for the villagers gazed at her severely, whispering and nodding to each other as she passed. Lucy told her once that they distrusted Belinda's beauty, that her magnificent flame-colored hair, even hidden as it always was by a plain cap, stirred unease.

"They say that the child of the Devil possesses such hair," Lucy informed her quietly, her gentle brown eyes worried. They had met upon the road, Lucy on foot, Belinda in her wagon. She had immediately taken her friend up beside her. "You must take care, Belinda, with everything you do. The slightest offense could spark all types of rumors."

"You mean rumors suggesting that I am a witch?" Belinda inquired, half amused and half scornful. "Surely the villagers are not so superstitious as *that!*"

Lucy shook her head. "Do not be so sure. There is a . . . a madness afflicting them. They need only the slightest excuse to cast the blame for their troubles upon someone who draws their suspicion—and it might be anyone! I beg of you, be careful in everything you do, everything you say!"

At this, Belinda's green-gold eyes smoldered. "I will not be intimidated!" she cried. "How I would love to toss this wretched cap into the mud and dance through the village with my hair loose and flowing. I fancy that would shock them!"

"Oh no, don't even think such a thing," Lucy begged, her eyes round with horror. "They would probably clap you in the stocks at the very least—and who knows what else they might do!"

"Wretched, fanatical fools," Belinda muttered bitterly. "One day we will escape them, Lucy, both you and I. You will settle in Philadelphia with Henry, and I...I shall run off and begin a new life, too—although I have not yet decided where. I must save up enough money, however, because once I flee this place I shall never, ever return no matter how desperate my circumstances!"

"Perhaps you shall marry, too, Belinda. You are so beautiful that I am certain there are many young men in Salem Village who would be eager to—"

"No." Belinda set her lips firmly together. "No, I shall never marry. I have never yet met a man whom I did not find to be a fool." She smiled a little ruefully, her lovely, delicate face shadowed with a fleeting sadness. "I refuse to marry a man I cannot respect, a man less clever than I, and I...I have given up hope of ever finding one. They are all either brutes or idiots. These boys in the village—I have seen them stumbling around their business. They are a dull, lifeless bunch. Not one of them has the wit to question the life he leads, to doubt the values of these superstitious Puritans who order every facet of their lives so rigidly."

"That is here. Perhaps elsewhere you shall meet a man who—"

"No." Belinda shook her head. "It was the same in Sussex. Men are fools, Lucy. They drink themselves to oblivion, chase strumpets in the taverns, and preach endlessly of a woman's duty to obey her man. They expect total subservience, and *that* I could never give. Being tied to a husband like that would be even worse than this servitude to Jonathan Cady! At least he doesn't feel it is his right to...to *touch* me." A sharp memory of Yeoman Phelps's wet, brutal kisses and pawing hands made her shudder in revulsion. No, no, if that was what it was like to be with a man, she wanted nothing whatsoever to do with the lot of them. She would rather die than submit to such handling.

"You will meet a man," Lucy was whispering softly, her voice so low it was barely audible. "You will fall in love...hopelessly in love...and soon."

"Is that so?" Belinda asked laughingly, glancing at her friend's face and then breaking off in astonishment. Lucy was sitting perfectly still, like a statue. Her pretty brown eyes were glazed, and she was staring fixedly at the road ahead. She appeared to be seeing nothing. She neither blinked nor moved her eyes nor gave any sign that she was alive. Only her lips moved, as she very softly spoke.

"You will have a man...a love...both beautiful and dangerous....You will know pain, and joy, and..." Suddenly, Lucy's eyes closed. Her entire body sagged, as if with exhaustion, swaying so dangerously upon the seat of the wagon that Belinda quickly grabbed her arm to prevent her from toppling into the road. The girl shuddered quickly, then her eyes opened and she stared about her as if she did not know where she was.

"Lucy, are you all right?" Belinda pulled the wagon to a halt and stared at the girl fearfully. "You were acting so strangely, and you said the oddest things."

Lucy grew pale, and panic seemed to seize her. "No, oh, no," she whispered, trembling. She grabbed Belinda's arm. "Please, forget everything I said. Forget what you saw. Please!"

"Lucy, I don't understand."

"One day...perhaps I will explain....Not now, not yet." Lucy suddenly leaped down from the wagon. "I must go....I must go!" She had run off toward the Miles house without another word, leaving Belinda to stare after her in concern and bewilderment. The next time they had met, neither girl mentioned the incident, but

Belinda puzzled over it for many a night. She couldn't forget the strange expression in Lucy's eyes or her words, preposterous as they might seem. She did not believe her friend for a moment and knew with a bitter certainty that she would probably spend the remainder of her days alone, but still . . . sometimes at night as she lay upon her pallet and strove to sleep, a yearning came over her, a hunger to be held and loved and touched. Not by a man like Yeoman Phelps, but by someone gentle and tender, and . . . oh, it was hopeless. She would force her thoughts to other things, but occasionally in the middle of the night she would awaken for no reason at all and begin to cry. Loneliness ate away at her, feeding like a greedy parasite upon the emptiness in her heart.

One morning in mid-April Jonathan Cady departed to Salem Town. He had official business to attend to with the general court regarding the evidence to be permitted at future witchcraft trials and would be away the entire day. He informed Belinda not to expect him to return before sundown.

"At that time I expect to find my supper prepared as usual and everything else in order." He glared at her, his narrow face stern and cold, the black mole on his pointed chin more noticeable than ever against the pastiness of his skin. "Do not think to escape your chores because I will not be here to supervise. I will inspect the house thoroughly at sundown to be certain you haven't shirked any of your duties. Idleness is a sin of the Devil, and I will not countenance it under my roof."

"You accuse me unjustly, cousin!" she cried, flushing with anger. "I have never given you cause to accuse me of idleness!"

"Only because I am usually present to assure that all runs smoothly. If it were not for your fear of me and your realization that I will not hesitate to administer the switch if need be, you would not work so diligently." His thin fingers gripped her arm, cruelly tightening around her tender flesh. "You are a wicked girl, Belinda. Lazy, impertinent, and wild. Oh yes, the wildness is there. I see it in your eyes, wench, you cannot deceive me. I knew another girl once who was wicked like you. For a while she deceived me, I thought she was good and pure and—" He broke off abruptly, staring down with renewed fury into Belinda's face. "Enough. I can see through you, little cousin. I know the secret sins of your soul, the malice and deceit and ugliness. I will conquer them all. Do you hear me? I will conquer them! One day you will thank me for saving you from the evil seething within you!" Contemptuously, he shoved her away from him and then stalked out the door, leaving Belinda to rub her bruised arm and to angrily ponder his words.

I cannot bear it another day! she thought frantically, tears of helpless rage trickling down her cheeks. *I cannot live like a chattel, enduring his insults and commands! I shall go mad!* She strode to the window, watching through blurred eyes as her cousin mounted his gray gelding and set off toward the road to Salem Town. She watched until he had disappeared, and then slowly the mist before her eyes cleared and she became gradually aware that in contrast to her spirits, the day was lovely and mild. She stared in wonder at the blooming wilderness, and a sudden idea came to her. She ran to the door and threw it open, exulting in the fresh, warm April breeze which swept through the stolid, airless house. It was a clear, glorious morning. Tiny green leaves fluttered delicately on the branches of the tall oak and elm trees, and a carpet of grass had sprung up over the earth. The New England landscape looked green and dewy, as if it were awakening from a heavy winter's slumber to the breathless beauty of spring. Belinda's eyes began to glow. Why not?

Why shouldn't she? She would work quickly and finish all of her chores in shorter time than usual this morning. Then she would pack herself a picnic lunch and go off into the countryside. It would be lovely to strip off her heavy buckled shoes and knitted stockings and run barefoot across the new earth. Perhaps she might even discover a pond or a stream where she might bathe. *Yes, I shall do it,* she decided excitedly, tossing her head in rebellion. *Cousin Jonathan need never know, for I shan't be away more than an hour and I shall be certain to complete all my tasks before sundown—yes, yes, I will have an hour to myself, to bathe and doze and bask in the sunshine.* It sounded irresistible, and she threw herself into her work with feverish energy.

Several hours later, when the sun was a glowing golden orb in the sapphire sky, she almost skipped from the house with a basket of food over one slim arm. She was wearing a pale blue muslin gown with elbow-length sleeves and an embroidered underskirt edged with white lace. It was a gown she had brought from England, one she associated with festive occasions since she had worn it to a fair only last May. For the first time in weeks she felt soft and pretty, and she felt all her dreary discouragement evaporating. As she moved gracefully across the cornfields, she glanced about for any sign of the yeomen working Cousin Jonathan's farm. She had had little contact with the men, but she knew that at noon they would return to their families for dinner; thus she had planned her departure time carefully. She didn't know if they would report her excursion to their master if they discovered her, but she wasn't taking any unnecessary chances. When she returned, she would skirt the fields and take the longer route to travel the road, hoping not to meet anyone. The nearest house was a mile away, so she felt little cause for worry. The day was too beautiful to allow unhappiness to darken her thoughts, and her heart was too full to let anything dampen her enthusiasm.

Once she entered the still thickness of the forest, she breathed deeply of the earth-scented air, noting with delight the marigolds and white and blue violets already blossoming among the rocks and patches of grass. A rabbit skittered from behind a hemlock and disappeared through a grove of maple trees to her left. She followed it leisurely, listening to the chatter of the squirrels and chickadees. A pink flush tinted Belinda's cheeks as she strolled deeper into the hilly woods. She climbed slowly upward, rejoicing in the smells and sounds of the awakening forest, so alive with nature's creatures and the magic of spring. She felt herself relaxing, smiling delightedly as the forest enclosed her protectively.

At length she glimpsed a small clearing beyond some birches and headed toward it, only to halt with a sharp intake of breath as she reached the edge of the trees. Her eyes sparkled with pleasure, for beside the grassy clearing dotted with dogwood and azalea, there was a pond, its clear blue water shimmering in the sunlight. She gave a cry of joy and darted forward, dropping her basket upon the grass as she began to peel off her clothes. The exertion of her walk had brought perspiration to her brow and dampened the wisps of hair about her forehead and ears. She could think of nothing more delightful at that moment than to bathe in that cool, inviting water. Free, finally, from all her garments, she plunged into the rippling pond, laughing aloud as the icy liquid enveloped her silken skin. She had tossed her cap to the ground and unpinned her hair, which now swirled freely about her, a thick, fiery mane clinging to her shoulders and breasts as she splashed gaily about. It felt wonderful to be unhindered by clothes or pins or caps, and she reveled in her newfound freedom. Like a child she played and frolicked, caught up in the sheer joy of being alive. A bird, perched on a tree limb, sang to her; a deer peeked timidly through the trees. Belinda's heart felt as though it were bursting with happiness. This charming spot seemed like a magical hideaway destined especially for her, especially for this day. She wished she could remain here forever, hidden from Cousin Jonathan, hidden from the grim confines of Salem Village. The tiny, glimmering pond, and grass-carpeted clearing set amid the spring-time forest presented her with a splendid haven. As she bathed, all of her unhappiness seemed to wash away, leaving her heart and soul as clear and clean as the lovely droplets of crystal water surrounding her.

When at last she emerged from the pond, the spring air felt much cooler than before, and she shivered as she slipped hurriedly into her petticoat. She was about to don the muslin gown once more, but as the shock of leaving the water subsided, she felt the warm rays of the sun upon her bare arms and legs and shook her head. No, she would sit here and bask in the sunshine, wearing only her petticoat and with her hair spilling to her waist like a glistening veil. It seemed almost wicked to feel so happy and free and close to nakedness, and she laughed to herself, knowing Cousin Jonathan would faint from shock if he knew of her behavior. She prettily arranged the white cotton blanket she had packed upon the grass and then set out her lunch. The turkey pie and cheese and the apple tart she had brought tasted more delicious than anything she had eaten since her arrival in Salem, and afterward she repacked the basket and lay back with her face toward the sun, drawing a deep, satisfied breath. Warmth and peacefulness enwrapped her. The forest was fragrant with the scent of new earth and wildflowers, and the small rustling and chirping noises all about her were like music, lulling her into blissful peace. The clearing, indeed, seemed enchanted. A pleasant drowsiness began to overtake her. It had been a lovely repast, but soon it would be time to return to the drudgery of her chores, to Cousin Jonathan's censure and domination. She sighed, wishing she could prolong this interlude, wishing she need never go back. Lying upon the blanket, she stared at the sky. Its piercing blueness made her shut her eyes, smiling gently. Just a few more moments of this beautiful calm, she promised herself. She would hurry back to the house then, with ample time to complete her work. . . . Just a few more moments of freedom . . .

Somehow, she drifted off to sleep. She didn't know when it happened or for how long she slept. Suddenly, though, she sensed something which made her stir in her slumber. Her eyes opened slowly to gaze dreamily into the hard, handsome face of the man looming above her. She felt sure she must still be dreaming.

Her first impression was that he was the most powerful-looking man she had ever seen. His face was strong-boned, like a granite statue, with a firm, arrogant nose and a determined chin. His hair was black, raven black, and it fell recklessly over his brow. His shoulders beneath his white lawn shirt and rich-looking blue damask coat were wide and muscular. But it was his eyes which caught and held her attention in that first instant she gazed at him. They were gray, a clear, light gray, as keen as a sword blade and equally cold. He was very close to her, leaning over her and smiling faintly, a smile which somehow never reached his eyes.

"Ah, the beauty awakens," he spoke in a deep masculine voice which held a sardonic note. His smile deepened. "I thought to wake you with a kiss, but you did not quite give me the opportunity. Nevertheless, my beauty, a kiss you shall have."

Amusement touched his cool gray eyes as he leaned

closer. Belinda suddenly came fully awake. She realized with a rush of panic that this was no dream. This man was real, he was going to kiss her, he was going to—

She gasped and pushed him away, struggling to sit up. To her horror, he merely laughed and pushed her down again upon the ground, easily grasping her flailing wrists and pinning them above her. He was overwhelmingly strong, she realized as she fought in futility against him. A black-haired, wide-shouldered giant imprisoning her beneath him. Her breast heaved in terror as she cried out.

"No, no! What are you doing? How dare you—"

He paid her no heed. He merely chuckled softly and bent over her again. Then, quite ruthlessly, he pressed his mouth to hers.

CHAPTER FIVE

HE KISSED HER long and hard, savoring each second. To her further fury, he seemed to be thoroughly enjoying himself. Helpless in his hard-muscled arms, she braced herself for the expected rush of revulsion, the nausea which had surged through her when Yeoman Phelps had attacked her. To her astonishment, it never came. As the stranger's mouth captured hers, his lips firm and cool, she felt rage, yes, and murderous fury, but not revulsion. In fact, she realized in shock, shutting her eyes for just a moment as her soft lips parted in surprise, she felt something else entirely.

Suddenly, her lips closed once again. Even as she relaxed for one insane instant, the shock of her response and its impropriety made her freeze in renewed outrage. She began to struggle again, but to her dismay he continued to ignore her struggles, holding her in an iron grip and kissing her with the masterful determination of a man accustomed to getting his own way. His mouth teased and explored the softness of hers, sending strangely delicious shudders throughout her body which she fought against. When at last the black-haired stranger lifted his head and gazed down at her again, smiling mockingly, her eyes were shut and she was lying quite still, only her breasts rising and falling rapidly beneath the thin silk of her petticoat. Dazed and breathless, she opened her eyes, staring into his lean, darkly handsome face.

"Let...me...go," she uttered through clenched teeth, searching for some sign of mercy in his impassive features. She found none. In fact, his smile merely deepened to one of insolent mockery. Icy fear ran through her. This man was unlike any she had ever met. He was different from that drunken brute, Tom Phelps; different, too, from her gaunt, cadaverous, nasty cousin. There was strength and self-assurance in his face and bearing, and a gleam of keen intelligence in his cold gray eyes. Toughness and arrogance and iron-clad determination were reflected in the face that stared so boldly into hers. Every instinct warned her that he was a man to be reckoned with, and Belinda, little used to fearing others, felt the danger of her position. This man would do whatever he wished with her. What if he....She gave a cry, half terror, half frustration. Angry tears suddenly pricked her eyes.

"I told you to let me go!"

Her captor regarded her coolly. "Don't be frightened, little beauty," he commented, loosening his grip on her wrists as he noted the red marks forming there. "I have no intention of harming you. On the contrary, I have something most pleasant and intimate in mind. I've been studying you as you slept, and you are an extraordinarily beautiful wench." His eyes traveled leisurely along the slender length of her body. A glint of appreciation shone in them. Yes, she was indeed a treasure. A rare treasure. He had never seen hair like that before, bright and glorious as fire, yet silky soft as it cascaded about her small, fine-boned face. Her eyes were a molten green-gold, a tigress's eyes, dangerous and fascinating. He drew in his breath as he observed the proud swell of her breasts, two creamy mounds almost totally revealed by the décolletage of her petticoat. Then he let his gaze wander downward across the soft curves of her hips and thighs. Stunning. She had the delicate, radiant beauty of a princess, yet there was something fiery and passionate about her, something intangible which suggested that here was a woman of burning spirit who, once ignited, would enflame any man with almost unbearable desire. Studying her as she lay helpless beneath him, he had been struck by the realization that she was probably the most breathtaking wench he had ever encountered. More beautiful, even, than Gwendolyn.

His lips formed a hard, ruthless smile. "I am considered something of an expert on the subject, my sweet, and I assure you that seldom have I been so impressed by a young woman." His eyes narrowed. "Your services for a brief hour, that is all I require. Naturally, you will be well paid—and handsomely rewarded if you please me. Which," he added nonchalantly, "I am quite certain you shall."

Belinda stared up at him in shock. This couldn't be happening. Not to her. It was outrageous, impossible. She felt the color draining from her cheeks, and then, just as he released her wrists and instead cupped her breasts in his warm, strong hands, the truth hit her in a shocking realization. He thought her a common harlot, a wench from one of the local taverns! He didn't mean to rape her—merely to buy her! She gasped and twisted in fury under the onslaught of his exploring hands. "You . . . you conceited, ignorant beast!" she spat, clenching her teeth in rage. "Let me go! You've made a grievous error, one you shall live to regret! I am no strumpet! I am a pure maid! Did you hear me? Damn your impudence, let me go!"

He paused, regarding her with a sudden frown. "What did you say?"

Once more she struggled to push him away, and this time he allowed her to do so. She sat up, breathing hard, and straightened her petticoat across her breasts. Venom and fury sparkled in her eyes as she glared at him. "You heard me correctly! I am no strumpet, to be bought for a pine tree shilling! How dare you assume... how could you insult me like this? Oh, you monster, I could kill you!" And with these words she dived at him in a frenzy of rage, her nails clawing at his face. The stranger reacted with lightning swiftness, gripping her wrists and pulling her close against his chest.

"You may not be a strumpet, but you are a firebrand," he remarked coolly, giving her a hard shake. "Calm yourself, wench, and explain your words. Chaste Puritan women do not lie about half-naked in the woods— they have homes and families and duties to keep them occupied. If you're not a harlot, then who the hell are you?"

"That is none of your business!" Belinda cried indignantly, flashing him a glance filled with hatred. She suddenly observed, just behind him on the grass, his rapier and scabbard, which he had obviously removed before kneeling down beside her while she slept. Her fingers itched for the sword. There was something so cool and arrogant about this man that she longed to strike him. It wasn't only his recent offenses, which were considerable; it was his arrogance, his damned attractiveness combined with his careless self-assurance which seemed to proclaim a vast superiority over all others. She yearned to revenge herself upon him. Suddenly, an idea formed in her brain. She ceased struggling and glanced up at him with wide, imploring green eyes.

"Please," she whispered, in a demure, subdued tone, "please let go my wrists. You're hurting me."

He looked down at her helplessly pinioned hands

and then released her. A scowl had come over his features. "I apologize."

Belinda put an unsteady hand to her head. "I...I feel suddenly faint," she uttered in weak accents. "I...I'm not accustomed to such...I...I..."

"Steady, girl. There's a wineskin of ale in my pack. It will soon help to revive you," her opponent said quickly, his voice not ungentle. She watched from beneath her lashes as he strode to his horse, a tall, chestnut stallion tied to a spruce tree near the northern edge of the clearing. Her heart pounding, she waited until he had reached the animal. Then, with the agility of a doe, she sprang to her feet and darted toward the rapier. The stranger whirled in surprise at the sudden movement, but Belinda already had the weapon in hand. A triumphant smile curved her lips as she brandished it, but to her chagrin, instead of showing fear when he gazed at her, her insufferable enemy threw back his dark head and roared with laughter. She gripped the rapier more tightly, her knuckles whitening, and a dangerous sparkle entered her eyes.

"So you laugh, do you, rogue?" she cried with rage. "Perhaps you think I will hesitate to run you through. You err! Only recently I stabbed a man and received great pleasure from the deed! It will be my delight to kill you here and now to save other innocent women from your insults and unsought advances!"

He chuckled. "A firebrand, indeed! Well, you are free to make the attempt, little wench, but I doubt that you will succeed."

"I think otherwise!" Belinda retorted, lifting her chin.

He replaced the wineskin in his saddle pack and began walking slowly toward her. Warily, Belinda studied him. He was tall and powerful-looking, with broad shoulders and a muscular chest beneath the elegant fit of his blue damask coat. His physique tapered to a taut, flat belly and lean hips encased by black silk knee breeches, which did much to illustrate the muscular shape of his thighs. His long, muscled legs wore heavy jack boots which appeared mud-spattered from his travels. Belinda couldn't help feeling a flutter in her chest as he approached her. He was a commanding figure of a man, one who would always draw the notice of women. His raven-black hair and handsome features were intriguing, and had they met under different circumstances, Belinda might have allowed herself to admire him, but as he approached her, she found the gleam in his eyes infuriating, and she suddenly sliced the rapier through the air, causing him to halt on the spot and stare at her sardonically.

"You do not frighten me, firebrand."

"Then you are a fool!"

"You are the fool." All of a sudden, his voice held a warning. His gray eyes raked her slim, defiant form. "Take care. I could disarm you in an instant, you know. You cannot hope to emerge the victor from this encounter. Be a good, wise girl and put down the rapier."

Belinda only laughed grimly at him. "Yes, you would like that, would you not?" she mocked. "A surrender before the battle is joined. But I shall not make things so easy for you. I am no fainting miss, to shudder at the thought of blood. In fact, I would dearly love to shed some of yours in payment for the insult you have given me! It is what you deserve!"

"A flogging is what *you* deserve," he commented coolly, a hard light entering his eyes. "Your resourcefulness and courage are commendable," he continued, "but your skill with a rapier and your strength to wield it against me are, I fear, lacking. I am running out of patience with you, wench! Put down the weapon immediately, or I will not answer for the consequences!"

Red rage flashed before her eyes. He scorned her, ordering her to desist. And she was the one who was armed, who held him at a disadvantage! Well, perhaps Cousin Jonathan had the power to order her about, to scold and criticize, but this arrogant, insolent stranger did not! "I will kill you before I lay down this weapon!" she cried, lifting her chin rebelliously. "Do what you dare!"

For answer, he suddenly raised his hand and with a sharp, flicking movement uncoiled a wicked-looking whip. Belinda gasped. Too late she realized that he must have removed it from his saddle when she'd grabbed the rapier. He had held it hidden as he approached, and she had failed to notice it. Now she could not help staring for it was an ugly weapon, and she could imagine how it would feel upon her flesh. She swallowed, feeling the rapier slipping in her hands from the sudden perspiration on her palms. "You . . . you despicable . . ."

"Precisely." He smiled coldly. The cruel look upon his face frightened her even more than the whip. When he cracked the weapon through the air with artful expertise, she jumped. His smile deepened. "For the last time, firebrand, put down the rapier."

Belinda's voice throbbed. "Never!" she cried, overcome with fury. She lunged at him with the rapier, throwing all her strength into the thrust. Her opponent leaped aside, his lean face nonchalant. Then, very deliberately, he raised the whip. Belinda screamed and swung her weapon toward him again, but he sidestepped deftly and uncoiled the whip with a sharp thrust of his arm. It made a hissing noise in the quietude of the clearing and caught the long blade of the rapier. An instant later the sword was jerked roughly from her grasp as the stranger gave a sharp pull upon the whip. Instantly he threw it down beside the fallen rapier and advanced toward Belinda, a dangerous glint in his eyes. She gasped, retreating.

"No. Oh no, you—"

She suddenly came up against the trunk of a maple tree, and her enemy closed in upon her, placing his hard-muscled arms on either side of her so that she could not escape. He stared down into her white, upturned face.

"I warned you, didn't I?" he demanded, noting against his will how enticingly her flame-colored hair spilled over her bare shoulders. "Only a fool begins a fight he cannot win."

"Let me go." Belinda gritted her teeth. "I don't know what you want from me! I am no strumpet—I've already told you that! You have no right to keep me here by force!"

"I want some answers, wench! What is your name?"

Her eyes blazed with defiance, though her body trembled. "I shall never tell you—you're an abominable, unscrupulous scoundrel, with no morals whatsoever, who abuses helpless women—"

"May I remind you that you were the one who raised the sword against me?" he put in cuttingly. "I was merely defending my life."

"After you attacked me for no reason!"

He grinned suddenly, his darkly handsome face lighting with amusement. "Attacked you? I think not. I kissed you, as I recall."

"Against my will!" Belinda tried to break past his arm, but was unable to move him an inch. A cry of despair rose in her throat, but even as she uttered it, she straight-ened her back, refusing to allow him to cow her. "What do you want with me?" she cried furiously.

His gray eyes captured hers with a blaze of intensity which almost took her breath away. Belinda's heart gave a strange, crazy leap and a wave of searing heat suddenly rushed through her veins. She wondered madly if she had the fever. Nothing, nothing like this had ever happened to her before. *Who is this man?* she wondered weakly, frightened by the enormity of his impact upon her senses. *What is happening to me?*

"Little firebrand, don't be afraid," the black-haired stranger murmured softly, and before she could move he had tangled his hands in her hair. Belinda stood like a statue. Slowly, he leaned forward and kissed her again. This time Belinda made no move to resist. She realized with a pounding heart that she *wanted* him to kiss her. A small shudder went through her as his arms enclosed her. When his mouth covered hers and she felt herself pressed hard against his muscular frame a thrill of excitement such as she had never known shot through her. The male scent and power of him overwhelmed her; her arms slid to his massive chest, then slowly upward to his powerful shoulders, and finally around his neck, drawing him even nearer as their mouths met and clung. Her whole being shook with emotions she didn't understand and couldn't begin to control. His hands explored the slender length of her body, searing the curves and hollows of her flesh beneath the indecent thinness of her petticoat. She felt as if she were drowning, drowning in ecstasy, and at the same moment she felt tinglingly alive, as though she had never truly been alive before. Long, heart-pounding moments later, the stranger drew back and reluctantly released her. Belinda stared at him through burning eyes, her delicate face flushed pink. What would happen next? She wanted more, more, and was surprised by his sudden hesitancy. In fact, she noticed, startled out of her feverish bliss, his face was dark with anger now, and he was breathing as heavily as she.

"That's enough," he muttered in a voice hoarse with emotion. "You did say you were a virgin, did you not? Well, unless you're prepared to forfeit that state here and now, firebrand, I recommend you put on your clothes as quickly as possible and stand away from me!"

He turned on his heel and walked swiftly toward the edge of the clearing, leaving her stunned and puzzled. His harsh words stung her. Unless she was prepared... to forfeit her virginity? No! No! Crimson color flooded her cheeks as shame swept through her. What had she done? Was she insane? She had behaved like a... like a common strumpet, kissing this stranger, allowing him to touch her, to stroke her. She ran to her blue muslin gown where it lay upon the grass and donned it with shaking fingers. A shadow had fallen over the afternoon. The sun had disappeared behind some clouds, and the breeze now blowing down from the hills was cool. She shivered as the stranger turned to face her once again in the little clearing. He was buckling on his sword belt with the rapier securely inside, but his eyes were fastened intently on her face. He moved toward her with a long, easy stride and lifted her chin with one strong hand.

"You're a beautiful creature, firebrand," he said in a gentler tone than he had used before. "And most unusual."

"You... you must think me..." she began, biting her lip in mortification, but he only laughed.

"I think you enchanting."

"I've never done this before! I'm not a loose creature! I don't understand what happened."

His eyes softened, and his thumb gently massaged her cheek. "One day you will understand. It's a pity I won't be able to—"

"*What is going on here?*"

The shrill words reverberated through the clearing, sending a dawdling squirrel fleeing deep into the protection of the forest. Belinda froze in horror, recognizing that voice with dread certainty. She turned, her face ashen, to see her cousin standing at the edge of the clearing, his gaunt frame trembling with wrath.

"No!" It was a hoarse whisper that emerged from her tightened throat. She felt as if she were about to faint. Cousin Jonathan's cold, pale eyes fairly jumped from their sockets.

"Yes!" he screeched. "I have caught you, you wicked, unholy slut! You will pay dear for this Devil's work, wench, indeed you will! You will pay with both your body and soul!"

Belinda screamed as he picked up a fallen twig and advanced murderously toward her.

CHAPTER SIX

"JUST ONE MOMENT." The tall, raven-haired stranger stepped purposefully between Belinda and Jonathan. "Perhaps I can help you, sir," he commented in a cool, relaxed tone which made Cady's pasty skin darken to purple.

"I don't know who you are, rogue, but you'd best stand aside! I will deal with this slut first, and then we shall see what is to be done with you!"

"I think not." The stranger smiled coldly. Shaken as she was at being caught in this position by Cousin Jonathan, Belinda couldn't help admiring her defender's imperturbability. Then she realized that he probably didn't understand the true seriousness of the situation. If he had known to whom he was speaking and the position of authority Jonathan Cady held in Salem, he would probably have shown more concern. Yet, gazing up at him as he stood so firmly between her and her cousin, she thought he did not seem the type of man to cower before anyone. No, indeed, he seemed more likely the one responsible for making other people cower with fear.

Still, she couldn't allow him to bear the brunt of Jonathan's anger. "Cousin, if you will allow me to explain—" she began, but Cady cut her off with a derisive snarl.

"Silence! I have no interest in your lies! My only wish, indeed, my only duty, is to see that your evil ways are punished!" He brandished the tree branch threateningly, but the stranger spoke before he could make a move toward Belinda.

"If you think to harm this lady, you are sadly mistaken! I don't know who the hell you are or why you believe you have the right to call her foul names, but I recommend you to put down that damned switch before I break your arm!"

Cady froze, staring in disbelief at the man before him. Both gentlemen were tall, but while Jonathan's frame was thin and bony, the stranger was so powerfully built that there could be no question as to the outcome of any physical altercation between them. Frustration blazed across Cady's narrow face, and his knuckles whitened on the stick he held.

"Put it down," came the stranger's order again, and after only another moment's hesitation, Jonathan complied, throwing the weapon to the ground in chagrin. His small, chilly eyes fixed themselves like clamps upon his adversary. His voice shook with rage.

"Sir, you are making a grave mistake in preventing my disciplining of this wench! She is my cousin and my ward, and is a servant in my home. It is my right and my duty to punish her. She was supposed to attend to certain duties in my home. Instead, when I return early from my business in Salem Town, I hear voices in the woods—and whom do I discover there? My ward! My servant! In the company of a stranger! A man!" Jonathan seemed nearly beside himself with fury. His face worked convulsively as he spoke. "From the first day that she came to me, little better than a beggar needing a home and sustenance, I recognized her for the lazy, wicked sinner that she is, but only now have I seen how totally doomed she is to hellfire! I demand, sir, now that you are informed of the circumstances, that you step aside and allow me to deal with this Devil's wench as she deserves!"

Slowly, the tall, lean stranger turned to Belinda. It was impossible to read his thoughts behind the cool mask of his eyes. "Is this true, what he says?"

"It is true that I am his cousin and servant," she replied, tossing her head. "But I am not lazy or wicked! I intended to return to the house and complete all my chores before his return! But as you well know, I was detained against my will."

A half-smile curled the tall man's mouth. "Yes, I know what occurred to detain you," he remarked. His gaze returned to Jonathan Cady, hardening.

"If anyone is to be held accountable for this incident, sir, it is I," he commanded. "I accosted your cousin and detained her with conversation. I am a newcomer to this region and sought directions to the Four Bells Tavern in Salem Village. I was most interested in learning something about the good people of Salem, and we became so immersed in our conversation that we failed to notice how much time had elapsed." Carelessly, the stranger rested his hand on the hilt of his rapier as he went on. "If there is a price to be paid for such a harmless incident as this, then I must be the one to pay it. But I warn you, sir, I am no defenseless girl who will helplessly submit to a beating. It will be no easy thing for you to exact your conception of justice from *me!*"

Cady's mouth drooped. Then he shut it with a snap and drew himself up to his full height. Once again he was the Jonathan Cady Belinda recognized: cold, cruel, controlled. Her hands clenched unconsciously into fists as she watched him, wondering what his response would be to the stranger's thinly veiled threat.

"You tread on dangerous ground, rogue!" Cady replied in his most condescending tone. "Do you know to whom you are speaking? I am Magistrate Jonathan Cady, an esteemed official of the village you intend to visit. I exercise considerable authority here, and it would be an easy thing for me to have you clapped in the stocks for your interference in this matter. However," he went on hastily, eyeing the stranger's muscular frame with unease, "I would be willing to forget your intrusion, and indeed to welcome you to our village, if you will go on about your own business and leave me to deal with this wench in my own way. Her deceit and laziness are my concerns, not yours. I will handle them as necessity dictates."

"You intend to beat her," the stranger retorted, his keen eyes glinting like steel daggers. "I cannot allow it."

"You—you cannot—" Jonathan sputtered, and the stranger smiled contemptuously. One eyebrow lifted.

"You heard me correctly."

Before Jonathan could speak, the dark-haired man held up a hand, decreeing silence. "You have told me your identity, Magistrate Cady," he went on smoothly, one hand still resting on his rapier. "Now allow me to present myself to you—and to your lovely ward. My name is Harding. Justin Harding. Does it bear any familiarity to you?"

Justin Harding! Cady's gaunt frame stiffened instantly. He stared at the stranger in astonishment and then quickly scrutinized his elegant dress and arrogant bearing, making mental notes and judgments. At last his gaze rested briefly on the tall, mysterious man's hard, chiseled face. Yes, Jonathan conceded uneasily, as he lowered his gaze beneath that cold, glinting stare, it was entirely possible. This scoundrel could well be the man widely known in the colonies as the Gray Knight, the aristocrat friend of King William of Orange who had amassed a fortune as a pirate for hire and who in recent years had built a spectacular plantation in the Old Dominion of Virginia. He certainly had the look of a pirate and a rogue, and yet there was an unmistakable air about him which proclaimed to any observer that he was well bred, an aristocrat with solid family connections at the king's court. Silently, Jonathan Cady cursed. Few people in the colonies would dare oppose the Gray Knight. He was too close to the king, too powerful a figure by merit of his own dashing reputation. Salem Village certainly would not welcome the scrutiny of the royal eye, for the Puritans' greatest dread, besides the Devil, was persecution by the Crown. Cady wet his lips, thinking hard. This must be handled carefully, for it would not do to antagonize Justin Harding further. A stiff smile stretched across Jonathan's lips, though his eyes remained cold and watchful. He bowed ever so slightly.

"Sir, you are correct. Indeed, I am familiar with your name. May I, as a magistrate of Salem Village, welcome you to our colony and offer you my assistance in whatever your business might involve here?"

Harding's eyes gleamed mockingly. "You may go on about your damned way and allow me to do the same," he returned. "I've tarried long enough in this wood; I wish to reach the Four Bells and refresh myself with a tankard of ale and a hearty supper. So let us all be upon our way."

"Certainly." Jonathan glanced at Belinda, still standing in the shadow of Harding's powerful frame. "Come here, wench," he ordered in a gratingly civil tone. "I have much to say to you, but we will not detain Mr. Harding any longer. What we have to discuss can wait until we reach my home."

Belinda took a deep breath. Her startled mind was still taking in the oddness of Cousin Jonathan's behavior in showing respect to this stranger. Obviously, Justin Harding was an important man, but she did not know for what reason. She had never heard of him before this day, but apparently her cousin was in considerable awe— or was it dread?—of him. She glanced swiftly at her protector, but he was now gazing at her with only a cool, expectant eye. Well, she could not stand here forever, hiding behind this unpredictable man. She moved with slow dignity toward her cousin, wariness coursing through her body. When Jonathan's hand shot out and gripped her arm, she winced but did not resist. He stared down at her. "Come along, Belinda. You have many chores awaiting. Suppertime is already upon us."

"One moment, sir." Harding's commanding voice made both Belinda and Jonathan freeze. "A word of advice."

"Yes?" Cady's teeth clenched on the word.

Harding surveyed him through narrowed eyes. "If it ever reaches my ears that this wench has suffered due to today's incident, I shall feel it my personal responsibility to take action. In the past, such action on my part has been deemed most violent and terrible. I should dislike being forced to repeat such behavior, but make no doubt of it—if you cross me, I shall certainly do so."

"Do you threaten me, sir?" Jonathan demanded.

"I do." Harding smiled unpleasantly. "How clever of you to deduce it."

Jonathan shook with anger. "How dare you— you—"

"Enough bandying words, Cady! Let this girl be. Or I'll teach you a lesson in beatings you won't soon forget." He turned to Belinda. "Farewell. My apologies for all the trouble I have caused you today."

His tone was cool and casual, as though he were thanking a serving girl for having fetched him a tankard of ale. Something inside of her wrenched painfully at these indifferent words, but pride forced her to present a calm facade, hiding the painful turmoil within. "Yes, you have been much at fault today," she returned coolly. "I tried to explain that I could not tarry long, engaging in idle conversation with a man who found it difficult comprehending even the simplest directions, but you detained me nevertheless. I hope in the future," she added with a sparkle of fire in her brilliant eyes, "you will sharpen your wits sufficiently to heed what is told you."

"Belinda!" Jonathan Cady glared at her. "Show more respect to Mr. Harding, you impudent wench! He is a gentleman of considerable esteem in the eyes of our king, and of all good men. Curtsy and thank him for all his trouble."

At this she flushed and glanced angrily at her would-be protector. His eyes were gleaming with amusement. "Thank you, kind sir, for all your trouble," she spat, and made him a curtsy as mocking as it was graceful. "Farewell!"

With that she gathered up her white lace cap and hairpins and stuffed them into the basket with the remains of her picnic. Then, without another glance at Justin Harding, she followed Cousin Jonathan through the wood. His horse was tied to a sapling at the side of the road. He mounted it and stared down at her, his face white and taut with fury.

"You will walk beside me, and you will not speak," he ordered. "Not a word."

For once, Belinda was only too glad to obey. Her mind was seething with emotions she sought to tame. Dread of her cousin's wrath when they reached the Cady house competed with a strange, heady excitement still possessing her as a result of her meeting with Justin Harding. *Justin Harding!* Who was he? What was he doing here? Most important, why had he had this unsettling effect upon her, a girl who thought she was immune to the powers of men? She was both disturbed and wary, but much as she tried to banish his image from her mind, it remained firmly fixed there, filling her with a breathless exhilaration she was powerless to subdue. This irked her all the more because she had the bitter belief that Justin Harding, whoever he was, had already forgotten her existence. She would have been much surprised to discover that for some while as he rode his tall, chestnut stallion through the dusky woods, this was not the case.

Harding had watched them go through narrowed eyes. He was not a man to feel the stirrings of pity often, for he had led a hard life and had done his good share of cold-hearted deeds, but now, gazing after that exquisite, flame-haired beauty with eyes like green fire, he couldn't help feeling a twinge of regret for the life she no doubt led at the hands of her cousin. He knew many men like Jonathan Cady, tyrannical, self-righteous bastards who delighted in the subjugation of those about them, particularly women. He had long hated them and knew how to deal ruthlessly with them. It was a pity that a lovely, spirited girl should be tied to such an existence in this Puritan colony, restricted to a drab life of chores and strictures, when by the looks and spirit of her, she ought to have been a gypsy. He grinned suddenly, remembering the triumphant glow in her eyes when she had brandished his own sword in her hands. She reminded him in an odd way of himself ten years ago, when he had been a wild youth of twenty, defiant and filled with pride, battling everyone because of his own painful wound. *Damn the memories*, he thought with sudden ferocity. *It will all be over soon, and the error rectified. Gwen-*

dolyn will be mine at last. She will belong to me. His mouth tightened with determination. He spurred his stallion to a gallop and ruthlessly banished all thoughts of Belinda Cady from his mind.

The hills had grown silent. Like dark, jutting fortresses they watched and waited as the man and girl moved homeward. The sun still shone as brightly in the sky, but now it lacked the dazzle which had beckoned Belinda from her home. Instead, it glared pitilessly down upon the landscape, spreading its white, harsh light across the wild land. Even the wind had died down, as if lurking in wait amid the trees. All was quiet and strangely still, but it was an uneasy stillness, a stillness lacking both peace and serenity.

Jonathan Cady stared straight ahead as his horse drew near the long wooden house. His face was stony and set, except for his eyes, which glowed as though lit by the depths of hell. His rage had simmered slowly at first, but soon it boiled with greater intensity. His mind recounted the wrongs Belinda had committed in disobeying him, and he concluded that he was indeed harboring a vile sinner. He deemed her a wicked temptress who would grasp any opportunity to defy him and the laws of decency to cast out her evil lures to whatever unsuspecting man came within her range. He had known another like that, a long, long time ago. Alice, that alluring beauty with the honey-colored hair and clear blue eyes! How he had worshiped her once. His mind traveled swiftly back, vividly recalling those days when he had been a gaunt, pale boy, gawky in his love for the blacksmith's innocent daughter. Oh what a sordid deception it had been. Alice, beautiful Alice, had whispered to him, teased him, sometimes even taunted him. She had encouraged him to hope...but then the day of discovery

came. He had found her, not far from the very spot where
he had discovered Belinda today, lying in the woods,
naked as a heathen, coupling with the strapping, swag-
gering candlemaker's son. His heart had stopped in
disbelief and horror. And then she had seen him peering
through the bushes. *Come out, Jonny,* she had giggled,
her voice all sugared malice. *Come and see. Don't be so shy,
like a frightened toad.* He could still hear her high-pitched
laughter. *Why, Jonny, whatever is the matter? Poor Jonny,
you didn't think I would want an ugly, bumbling toad like you,
did you? It was all a game—the most amusing game! Come
and see, you foolish boy, what you will never, ever have. Never,
never, never.*

Cady's thin face grew livid with that agonizing memory. Somehow he had managed to flee through the woods,
sobbing and sick. He had never mentioned the incident
to a soul. But he had never forgotten. Even though Alice
had died of malaria less than three years later, Jonathan
Cady had kept her memory vividly alive, though buried
deep within his mind. He loved her and hated her still.
She tormented and sustained him throughout all the cold
New England winters, and she haunted him when he
sweated in his bed during searing summer nights. Wicked
Alice. Beautiful Alice. Taunting Alice. Temptress Alice.

Never had her memory been so vibrant as it was
this late afternoon, as he stalked stiffly through the doors
of his home. Belinda was like her in every way. Lovely
and evil, a menace to all decent, respectable men. But he
was no longer a frail, humiliated boy. He was a man now,
a leader of his community. And the wicked were in his
power, to punish as he saw fit.

"Ah, yes, sinner, you have good cause to be anxious," he muttered in a dazed tone as he almost absent-
mindedly glanced at Belinda's face. Silently, she had followed him into the parlor. "You are wicked . . . you are a

temptress. Just like *her*. Another Alice!" Slowly, he walked to the shelf where the birch switch rested. He lifted it and fingered it lovingly. "You shall pay, Belinda, you shall pay. Indeed, I will see to it that you pay."

"No!" Belinda whitened, and backed away from him. Panic filled her as she noted the insane expression on his face. "Cousin Jonathan, listen to me!" she cried, trying to keep her voice strong and calm. "Let me explain what happened. Let me—"

She darted aside just in time as he swung the switch viciously at her head. "You're mad!" she screamed and fled toward the entrance hall and the stairs. "Don't do this! You're insane!" she gasped. "Please!"

Jonathan watched her through rage-blurred eyes. He no longer saw Belinda Cady with her flame-colored hair and brilliant green eyes. He saw Alice, golden-haired and cruel, the temptress who had tortured him, and he gave a cry of twisted fury. Then he rushed up the stairway after her, his long legs overtaking her as she reached the upstairs hallway. He grabbed her arm and raised the switch, bringing it down upon her with a stunning blow. The girl screamed and crumpled at his feet, sobbing. She began to rise, to crawl away, but he raised the switch again, his eyes swimming with tears.

"You shall pay, sinner, you shall pay!" he screamed, and raised the switch again...and again...and again....

CHAPTER SEVEN

BELINDA SAT DULLY before the kitchen fire, staring into the flames. Aside from the hissing and crackling of the logs, there was silence in the Cady house this morning. It was past dawn, yet Jonathan Cady had not stirred from his bed. Belinda had crept downstairs at the usual time and prepared everything for his breakfast, but still he slept.

Slowly, she shut her eyes. Her entire body throbbed with pain. The long, puffed-sleeved black wool gown hid the welts and bruises on her arms and back, but she knew all too well that they were there. Every time she moved, she had to fight to keep from moaning aloud. Only her face, pale and drawn, was unmarred by the switch. No, Cousin Jonathan, even in his madness, had retained enough sanity to beat her where the bruises would not be readily apparent. Even though it was perfectly acceptable for a master to discipline his servants in his own home, too much attention would be generated if Belinda Cady showed a bloodied face to the world. Jonathan would not welcome such attention. So he had carefully avoided her face and neck, even at the height of his rage, and had satisfied himself with flailing the rest of her body. Fortunately, she had lost consciousness before long, only to awaken at dawn to find herself lying in a bloody heap at the top of the stairs. With the onrush of pain, the memory of the beating had come flooding back, and she had begun to sob quietly, her head in her arms. Almost immediately though, she had ceased her crying, fearing her cousin might hear her. Half-crawling down the stairs, she had hobbled to the well to wash her wounds. Then somehow she had managed to get herself up to the loft to change her dress, but that had sapped her energy completely. Now she sat in the kitchen, aching and sick, too weak to eat or drink, shutting her eyes against the cruelties of the world.

I cannot stay here any longer, she thought. *Jonathan Cady is a madman, and he will kill me if I remain in his house. I cannot live according to his rules or according to the restrictions of this village. I must go!* She opened her eyes, and there was desperation in their shimmering green-gold depths. She knew what she had to do. She would collect her moneys for the embroidery work of this week, and then she would leave. Whatever sum she had accumulated thus far would have to be enough. She would make her way to Boston and the home of Sarah Cooke. Sarah would help her. At least she would provide shelter and food until Belinda could decide what to do next. Her heartbeat quickened with excitement, and some color returned to her chalklike cheeks as she realized that soon she would be far from this grim, stifling little village, far from Jonathan Cady's fanatical eye. She must try to be patient and careful until the week was out.

A knock sounded quietly at the front door, startling her. She hurried to answer it, wincing as she moved. Lucy Brewer stood upon the porch, looking pale and worried.

"Belinda—are you all right?" she asked quickly, and Belinda raised a finger to her lips.

"Shhh. Cousin Jonathan is still abed. Come into the kitchen, Lucy, so that we may talk."

When they were seated together on the pine bench, Lucy looked anxiously at her friend with her soft brown eyes. "Something horrible has happened. I know it!" she cried. "Tell me at once! Are you badly hurt? Did that monster harm you greatly?"

Belinda stared at her incredulously. "How... how did you know?" she gasped, her hands moving immediately to the hidden bruises on her arms.

"Then it's true!" Lucy exclaimed in distress, putting her hands over her face. "Master Cady beat you senseless! I saw it all so clearly—I knew I couldn't be mistaken, yet I hoped... I *prayed* that I was!"

Belinda trembled, suddenly overcome by the relief of having someone to confide in. "Yes, Lucy, it's true! It was a nightmare. I can't even bear to think of it!" Suddenly, she began to weep, all of her tension and pain swelling uncontrollably within her.

"You must leave here—you must go away!" Lucy declared with surprising vehemence for someone usually so mild. She gripped Belinda's shoulders firmly. "I know you have been planning to run away. Let me help you. I have some money saved from my wages. I intended to use it to set up my new home when Henry and I are married, but *you* must have it. You must use it to run as far from Salem Village as you can!"

Belinda dried her eyes on the corner of her apron. She shook her head with a tremulous smile. "Lucy, you're too kind. I cannot accept such a gift."

"Yes!" Lucy whispered furiously.

"No." Belinda took her hand and squeezed it gratefully. "Listen to me. It isn't necessary. I have enough money to go away on my own—or I will, when this week is up. I've been planning this very carefully ever since I arrived in Salem. I know exactly what I'm doing." She paused, staring at Lucy piercingly for a moment. "But there is one thing I would like from you."

"Anything," her friend responded eagerly.

"An explanation." Belinda watched her thoughtfully. "I'm very confused. How did you know what happened to me yesterday? For you did know—before you even saw me, before I spoke a word!"

"Yes." Lucy bit her lip, and stared down at her hands, which were twisted tensely in her lap. "I'm going to tell you my secret, Belinda. I know I can trust you. It's just that...it feels so strange to think of confiding it to anyone. I've lived with it for so long, you see, knowing that if I told anyone, I...I would be hanged!"

"Hanged! What are you talking about?"

Lucy met her gaze, speaking quietly. "I...I *see* things. Faraway things, future things. It's called the Sight. They say that witches have it." Now Lucy's eyes filled with tears. "I don't understand it. I don't want it! It's just there. All my life I've known beforehand about certain events. It terrified me, and it still does. It is as if I'm dreaming while I'm awake. Oh, Belinda, you can't imagine what it's like, knowing I'm different from everyone else, always fearful that someone will discover it! I live in dread that Mistress Frances will learn of it and point her finger at me for being a witch! I fear it is only a matter of time!"

Belinda could scarcely believe her ears. She stared at her friend in fascination and with a kind of apprehensive awe. "Can you...can you always predict the future, Lucy? Can't you then foresee your own fate as well as that of others?"

The small, pale-haired girl shook her head. "I can't control it. Sometimes I have flashes, glimpses. But always of other people or events. I've seen nothing of my own future. That remains black. Only events involving others

are illuminated occasionally, like a candle flickering somewhere in the night. That is what it seemed like when I
witnessed what Master Cady did to you yesterday." She
shuddered. "Oh, Belinda, I wept for you last night!"

"Thank you." Belinda took a deep breath. "And don't
worry. I shall keep your secret at all costs. I'd hang on
Gallows Hill myself before I breathed a word to anyone."

"I knew I could trust you!" Lucy whispered.

Belinda grew thoughtful, staring absently at the copper andirons of the fireplace without really seeing them.
She marveled at the wonder of her friend's strange gift,
and at the same time she feared for her, and her terror
was well founded. For if anyone in Salem Village discovered her secret, she would certainly be branded a
witch. Belinda only hoped that one day soon Henry March
would come for Lucy and carry her off to Philadelphia
as his bride. Perhaps among the gentle Quakers, Lucy's
secret would not so greatly endanger her life. Her thoughts
shifted to the odd things Lucy had said and done on
previous occasions, now so easily explicable. With a sudden shock she remembered Lucy's dazed prediction that
Belinda would soon find a man—and a love. For some
reason she now thought instantly of Justin Harding, and
a flush rose to her cheeks. She turned to her friend, trying
to appear calm, though a disturbing excitement flowed
through her at the memory of that overwhelming man.

"Lucy, did you ever hear of a man called Justin Harding?" she demanded. "I met him in the woods yesterday,
and Cousin Jonathan appeared to know who he was."

"Justin Harding!" Lucy stared at her with wide eyes.
"Everyone in the colonies knows of Justin Harding! They
call him the Gray Knight! He's a . . . a sort of pirate!"

Pirate! Yes, Belinda decided grimly. The description
aptly fit him. Despite his elegant clothes and aristocratic
demeanor, she could well imagine him the captain of

some daring pirate vessel plundering the high seas. For a moment when he had held her helplessly beneath him on the grass, there had been an expression in his eyes which had warned her that he was capable of anything— anything at all. She shivered, yet her own green eyes were alight as she bombarded Lucy with questions.

"Why do they call him that? Is he really a pirate? He looked like a gentleman—a rogue and a rake, but an aristocrat for all that!"

"Oh yes, he is, of course," Lucy continued, with a slight laugh. "He is very well born, the younger son of a family well connected at the royal court. He is an intimate friend of King William and indeed is rumored to have saved his life. He left England, oh, more than ten years ago, I've heard, and set himself up as the captain of a ship for hire. He offered protection to merchant ships against pirates, guarding them for huge sums of money and fighting horrible sea battles against the real pirates. He is whispered about almost as though he were the Devil himself. He is very powerful, partly because of his influence with the king, partly because of his own wealth and reputation—" She broke off suddenly and stared at Belinda in amazement. "Did you say you met him? He is in Salem? But why?"

Belinda tried to appear nonchalant in this discussion of the Gray Knight. "I have no idea. Cousin Jonathan seemed curious, too. He asked if he might help him with whatever business had brought Mr. Harding to Salem Village, but Justin Harding had no patience with him and forbore to answer."

Lucy shook her head. "The whole town will be talking of it. The Gray Knight here in Salem Village! Perhaps we'll learn more about it at the meetinghouse lecture today."

"Yes, perhaps." Belinda's heart skipped a beat as

she wondered suddenly if Justin Harding might even attend today's Thursday lecture, might even walk about the village square and mingle with the citizens after the minister's sermon in the meetinghouse had adjourned. Would they meet and speak again? Would he even notice her? She had no time to ponder, however, for both girls jumped in alarm at the sudden creak of the staircase. They stared uneasily at each other as they heard the deliberate clunk of Jonathan Cady's heavy buckled shoes on the wooden steps.

"I must go," Lucy whispered and hurried into the hallway, followed by an inwardly trembling Belinda.

"Good...good day to you, Master Cady," Lucy exclaimed rather shrilly as the tall magistrate reached the foot of the stairs and fixed her with a chilly frown. She curtsied nervously. "I...I stopped by to tell you and Belinda that there is to be a...a barn raising next week for the Oakes family over in the North Meadow. I...I hope you will grace the gathering with your presence, sir—and Belinda, too."

Jonathan's mouth was a thin, tight line. "Get on about your business, girl. I don't require an invitation from Eben Miles's servant. I'm well aware of the barn raising and will attend if I so choose. Go on with you, and don't tarry on the road. I'm certain Mistress Frances has more important things for you to do than gossiping with your fellow servant girls. Now be off!"

With a fleeting glance in Belinda's direction, Lucy scurried out the door. Slowly, Belinda closed it behind her, then turned to face her cousin. She stood with her shoulders straight and her head held high, meeting his flinty stare with every appearance of calm, though inwardly all of her terror from the previous day had come rushing back and was now pulsating through her battered body. She wondered if he planned to beat her again today and resolved that this time she would fight against him with any weapon she could lay her hands upon. Her throat dry as burning sand, she began to speak.

"Your breakfast awaits you, cousin," she said, her voice carefully empty of emotion. "I will bring it into the parlor."

"Wait! Come here, wench," he ordered softly, and panic leaped into her eyes.

"I said *come here!*" he snapped when she hesitated. Slowly, warily, she edged forward.

He seized her arm, and she gasped in pain, for his fingers were pinching the bruises he had only yesterday inflicted. "Did you tell that girl anything of your punishment? Did you?"

"No!" Belinda lied brazenly, knowing it was for Lucy's protection as well as her own. "She knows nothing! Of course I didn't tell her. I was...too ashamed."

He nodded and released her arm, a satisfied expression in his pale greenish eyes. "And well you might be. Sinner! You deserved what happened, and well you know it. Still, I warn you not to speak of it."

"Yes, I understand. Mr. Justin Harding would not be pleased to learn that you crossed his wishes, would he, Cousin Jonathan?" she retorted, unable to contain the contempt in her voice.

"Impudent girl!" Cady shook his finger in her face. "Mr. Justin Harding does not tell me how to conduct my household! I, too, am a man of importance, at least in this colony!" He regarded her piercingly. "You spoke with him yesterday, didn't you, girl? Tell me, did he mention anything of his reason for visiting Salem?"

"No."

"Don't lie to me! Are you certain? He said nothing?"

She met his suspicious gaze steadily. "He merely asked directions to the Four Bells. He scarcely confided his private business matters to me, and I would have been much surprised if he had. Now I will fetch your breakfast into the parlor before the bread grows stale and the soup turns cool." She was aware of his eyes following her as she walked quickly into the kitchen. Out of his sight, she drew a breath of relief. She began ladling soup into a pewter porringer, while her mind spun furiously. *Even if Justin Harding had confided the reason for his journey to Salem to me, I would not have repeated it to you, dear cousin,* she thought venomously. *You're obviously displeased by his presence. Good! I hope he remains a fortnight and causes a great deal of trouble for you. I will be long gone from this place by then, and your worries will be no concern of mine!* With this consoling thought, she returned to the parlor to silently serve breakfast.

That afternoon Belinda perched herself carefully in the wagon beside Jonathan Cady. Her magnificent hair was demurely pinned beneath a plain white cap. Her hands were folded decorously in the lap of her black woolen skirt, and a white linen neckerchief was draped in the common style about her shoulders. It was a cool, cloudy afternoon, and the wind that gusted down from the hills threatened rain. Even if a downpour began immediately, however, the meetinghouse hall would be crowded with villagers. Few would let inclement weather keep them from attendance at the Thursday lecture, almost the only social diversion in the village aside from an occasional barn raising or stoning bee. Everyone in the region looked forward to the lectures, and it was a cruel disappointment when one was denied the opportunity to attend the sermon and afterward to stroll briefly around the village square, greeting neighbors and exchanging news. Even Belinda, who knew few people and was apt to draw more censorious stares than pleasant greetings, looked forward to the lecture day with antic-

ipation. This was a respite from her work, providing her
with an opportunity to speak to Lucy and Goodwife
Fletcher and to mingle with other human beings. Her life
was so isolated and tedious that every diversion was eagerly sought. Today, in particular, she wished to be present. If Mr. Justin Harding were indeed to attend, he would
create quite a stir among the stolid Puritans. She told
herself that this was the only reason she anticipated the
lecture with such excitement today—merely to observe
the reactions caused by the Gray Knight—and that her
excitement had nothing to do with the desire to see him.
After all, he was only a man—a man who had caused
her a great deal of trouble and anguish. If they happened
to meet, he would be well served if she refused even to
speak with him. Nevertheless, she couldn't control the
impulse to swiftly scan the meetinghouse when she entered. The benches lining the long, narrow hall were filled
with people, and others stood against the raftered walls,
but in all the throng she did not perceive the darkly handsome face she unwillingly sought. With great impatience
Belinda sat through the seemingly interminable sermon
by Reverend Wilkes, who, upon his unpainted wooden
pulpit, spoke out passionately against the wearing of wigs
by men, proclaiming that they were the "Devil's device."
The congregation seemed deeply stirred by his words,
but Belinda paid scant heed. She was wondering if Justin
Harding had been merely passing through Salem on his
journey to a different destination and if he was already
far from the New England wilderness. Disappointment
stabbed sharply at her with this thought, but she angrily
tried to assuage it. Why should it matter if that man, who
was so arrogant and high-handed, should disappear forever? she asked herself sharply. *You're behaving like a fool.
This is madness.* Yet she kept remembering the fierce, demanding way he had kissed her, the iron strength of his

arms around her waist, and she quivered with the desire to see him again. Disturbed by her feelings, she tried to thrust them aside, to concentrate on the sermon, but as Reverend Wilkes preached endlessly on, her mind seethed with the image of the tall, powerful stranger with his raven-black hair and glinting eyes, and she was powerless to think of anything else.

At last the sermon ended and the villagers filed outside upon the green. Cousin Jonathan was holding court with a group of village officials and prominent men of the community, so Belinda escaped alone to amble about the square, scanning the faces of those around her. As if drawn by an overpowering force, her gaze traveled to the Four Bells Tavern opposite the meetinghouse, with its swinging signpost and bright green shutters. No one could be observed through the windows, and not a soul appeared at the door. She bit her lip and turned abruptly away.

"Ohhh!" A girl's high-pitched shriek rang out as Belinda inadvertently collided with her. Belinda spoke a quick apology.

"Haste leads always to accidents," the girl snapped, her bright blue eyes fixed disapprovingly upon her. "Who might you be, and where are you going in such haste that you do not even take care whom you knock aside?"

Belinda paused and leveled a piercing stare at her accuser. She had never met Frances Miles before, but she had seen her in the village on other occasions. She was a stout, robust girl with thick yet mousy-brown hair, a round and heavy face, and very red cheeks. Her most striking feature was her eyes; they were astonishingly blue and veiled by short, dark lashes. She was not at all a pretty girl. Her full, frowning lips and angry glare served only to accentuate her unattractive appearance. She was wearing a gown Belinda had embroidered for her. It was of russet cloth, with a full skirt which was turned under and looped back to reveal a somber gray underskirt. Both the skirt and the sleeves of the gown were daintily embroidered in gray and white lace. The bodice was tight and pointed, emphasizing Frances's buxomness, just as the full, rounded overskirt called attention to the stout hips beneath. As she stood with her feet apart and her hands on her hips, glaring at Belinda, she raised her chin, a trace of hauteur entering her expression.

"My name is Belinda Cady. And I fancy I know who *you* are, Frances Miles."

"Mistress Miles to you!" the girl exclaimed, her bright eyes flashing. "So you are Magistrate Cady's servant, the one who does my embroidery work. Well, you have a delicate hand, Belinda Cady, but you've provêd your clumsiness today by charging into me in this manner. You ought to look about you more carefully!"

"I have already apologized." Belinda spoke with cool firmness, disliking Frances's high-handed tone more with each word she spoke. From everything Lucy had told her about her mistress, combined with Belinda's knowledge that the girl was the chief accuser of witches in the village, Belinda had been prepared to dislike her, but this accidental meeting brought home with vivid clarity the true pompousness of the supposedly pious Puritan. She had no patience with such airs of superiority, and did not hesitate to show it.

Frances recognized this and was infuriated. She took in Belinda's slender, graceful form, her small, exquisite features and huge, glimmering green-gold eyes, and noted the glory of her red-gold hair coiled tightly beneath the prim cap. The servant girl's arresting beauty was not lost on her, and the ruddy flush deepened in her own fat cheeks. She was accustomed to being the center of attention in the little village, being the acknowledged leader of all the young maids in the region, especially since coming to fame as a victim of witchery. She enjoyed the power she wielded, the attention created by her swoons and screams. Over the past months people had come to treat her with great respect, even with fear. But this arrogant girl appeared not the least fearful or respectful. She looked as haughty as a princess and completely indifferent to the reprimand which had been delivered to her. Frances narrowed her eyes and spoke sharply.

"And where were you going with such haste? Answer me, if you please."

"My comings and goings are my own concern," Belinda retorted. "Ah, Lucy. Good day. How pleasant to see *you* here."

Lucy had walked quickly up behind her mistress. She appeared to have summed up the antagonistic situation at a glance. "Good day, Belinda," she put in hastily. "I...I trust you enjoyed the sermon, and...and you, also, Mistress Miles."

"Oh yes!" Belinda gave a short laugh, her face suddenly sparkling with mischief. "Reverend Wilkes's address was most...inspirational. Did you not think so, *Mistress* Miles?"

"Reverend Wilkes's lectures are always worthy of praise," Frances replied with prim superiority. "You would do well to listen to them carefully, Belinda Cady, especially those regarding piety and humility. For a servant, your manners are fast and rude, and you do not show the proper respect for those above you in rank. Unlike my dear Lucy here, who understands her place. Lucy," she said with sudden command, "I wish you to run home at once. The herb garden needs tending, and you have neglected it these past three days. Go."

Lucy stared at her a moment, then bent her head to hide the anger in her eyes. "Yes, mistress." She glanced expressionlessly at Belinda, then turned away.

"Run!" Frances Miles ordered and smirked in grim satisfaction as her servant obeyed. She faced Belinda with a malicious twinkle in her eyes. "Lucy understands that a servant must obey, must show deference. It is something you have yet to learn. From all I have observed, you know little about exhibiting the proper respect."

"On the contrary," Belinda replied, taut with anger at the treatment meted out to Lucy. "I know well how to show respect. But only to those who are deserving of it."

"*What*?" Frances gaped at her. Never before had anyone spoken thus to her. She wanted to slap the face of this brazen servant. Instead, she held herself in rigid control and opened her mouth to issue a scathing retort. She was interrupted though, before she could speak, her attention being claimed abruptly as the door of the Four Bells Tavern opened suddenly, and a man emerged onto the porch. He was the most handsome, virile-looking man she had ever seen. Frances stared at him open-mouthed, forgetting all about Belinda Cady. Tall and powerfully built, the stranger strode across the porch. He made a dashing figure in his white ruffled shirt and black silk coat, with black satin knee-breeches encasing his muscular thighs, and dark leather boots glistening atop his feet. He wore an intricately arranged white linen cravat, and a long, gleaming rapier at his side. Frances could not tear her eyes from him, and Belinda, bemused, turned her head to see what was commanding the other girl's attention.

She, too, nearly gasped when she saw him. Color rushed to her cheeks, and she turned her head away swiftly, fastening her eyes upon a knot of Puritan matrons in dark gowns and sugarloaf hats who stood whispering several yards away. Suddenly, she felt a strong hand upon her arm.

"Belinda Cady, we meet again." Justin Harding smiled mockingly at her discomfiture.

"Good—good day to you," Belinda managed to utter, despite the butterflies somersaulting in her stomach. "I—I did not expect to see you again."

"Did you not?" he inquired, amusement touching his hard gray eyes. "Then you were mistaken, Belinda. Very much mistaken."

Gazing into his eyes, Belinda felt the mesmerizing pull of the attraction between them, but she fought it with all of her powers of self-control. "I don't believe...you have met Mistress Frances Miles," she continued, attempting to keep her voice calm and her composure intact. "May I introduce Mr. Justin Harding of..."

"Virginia. A pleasure, Mistress Miles." Harding smiled politely and sketched a bow. He instantly returned his gaze to Belinda.

"Oh, Mr. Harding—it *is* you—the Gray Knight!" Frances opened her blue eyes very wide. "It is an honor to have a gentleman of your fame and breeding visit our village! What brings you to Salem?"

"Personal business, Mistress Miles." The air of finality with which he spoke these words left no room for further inquiry, and Harding continued smoothly before Frances could respond. "Mistress Miles, I beg your pardon, but there is a matter I wish to discuss with Mistress Cady. You will excuse us? Thank you." Despite the polite formality of his words, Justin Harding gave her no opportunity to protest. To Frances's great chagrin, he placed his hand firmly upon Belinda's elbow and led her masterfully across the dusty square.

Frances glared after them in outrage. So the Gray Knight preferred a servant girl to herself? It was outrageous! Belinda Cady must have cast a spell over him! Her cold, bright blue eyes shone like icicles. *We shall see about this Belinda Cady*, she thought to herself as she marched toward the group of village maids who were her devoted followers. *We shall see.*

Justin Harding smiled sardonically down at the delicate girl beside him. Yes, she was as beautiful today as he remembered. A little paler, perhaps, and she moved with a certain weariness, but equally lovely as the memory which had disturbed him at odd hours throughout the past night. "Thank you for joining me on a stroll about this enchanting little village," he remarked. "I have not seen such a bright, cheery place since the prison hold of my ship."

She laughed up at him, her eyes glowing. "Do not let the villagers hear your disparagement," she warned. "They will clap you up in stocks—Gray Knight or no! This is a close-knit, protective community. They do not take kindly to criticism from outsiders."

"I shiver in apprehension." Harding stopped walking abruptly and turned her to face him, a frown in his eyes. "You do not belong here, Belinda. You are out of place. Like a jewel amid pebbles. Why don't you leave?"

"Perhaps I shall—someday." Belinda fought an overwhelming temptation to confide her plans to this fascinating man, but managed to hold the impulse in check. The fewer people who knew of her intentions to escape Salem, the better. She met his searching gaze with an equally puzzled one of her own. "And what of you? A man like you journeying here—it is most odd. What brings you to Salem?"

Something in his eyes changed with her question. They darkened to charcoal and pierced her face with keen watchfulness. "Did your esteemed cousin tell you to ask me that?" he inquired softly. "Are you now doing his spying for him, little firebrand?"

"No, of course not. What are you talking about?"

"Look at him—look at all of them!" Justin Harding jerked his head toward the small group of somberly dressed men near the meetinghouse door. "They've been watching us ever since I approached you. I can see the cunning glint in your cousin's eyes from here." He turned back to Belinda with an unpleasant smile. "Surely a man as stiff-necked as he would not permit you to stroll about the village green with a complete stranger unless it served his own purpose. The fact that he has allowed us private speech together suggests to me that he *wishes* us to speak privately—that he seeks to gain information through you. Am I correct?"

Belinda could not deny the logic of his words, for indeed, it *had* struck her as odd that Cousin Jonathan had not already interfered in their discussion. She remembered the way he had questioned her about Justin Harding's purpose for visiting Salem Village and realized that he probably did wish her to chat with Justin Harding today, to discover why he was in Salem, and then later to question her about it. That would be typical of Jonathan Cady, who was as devious as he was hungry for power. Yet, for Justin Harding to believe her a part of the plan, a willing conspirator! It was an insufferable insult. Her small, lovely face blazed with anger, and she clenched her hands into trembling fists. Burning green-gold eyes clashed with steely gray ones.

"Yesterday, Mr. Harding, you called me a harlot—today a spy! What else is left for you to insult me with? What else? I'm certain you will think of something, for you are most inventive, but fortunately, I will not be present to hear of it. Good day, Mr. Harding! I hope I never have the *dis*pleasure of seeing you again!"

She whirled quickly to flounce away from him, but his arm shot out and seized her, drawing her helplessly back. He held her tightly, his iron arm encircling her waist as she squirmed in vain, uncomfortably aware of the growing stares directed at them by the Puritans. "What are you doing? Let me go!" Belinda hissed. "How dare you—"

"I'm not quite finished with you, my beauty," Justin Harding replied coolly. "Come along."

He drew her irresistibly along with him across the square and past the stocks and whipping post where Zebariah Dunston was being lashed by the constable for idleness. Flushed and furious, Belinda resisted with all of her strength, but Harding dragged her relentlessly until they had left the prison building at the corner of the square behind and were quite alone in a grove of hemlock trees, with the sounds of a running brook somewhere deeper within the forest reaching their ears. Overhead, gray, murky rainclouds swirled in a hazy sky. The air throbbed with tension as Belinda met the hard stare of her captor.

"What do you want with me?" she cried, yanking her arm free of his grasp. He had further bruised the injuries from yesterday, and she rubbed her arm abstractedly. "I hate you—I want nothing more to do with you."

"I want you to answer some questions for me. I made inquiries at the Four Bells last night, but as you mentioned earlier, this is a close-knit community. They did not appreciate questions from an outsider, and I did not receive the answers I sought." His eyes narrowed ruthlessly. "You shall provide them for me, firebrand. Now. Quickly."

"I will do no such thing!"

But when she tried to flee, he dragged her to the ground and pinned her there, staring harshly down into her face. "You will leave when I dismiss you. As for the questions I wish answered, you will comply. Don't try to defy me in this, my beauty, for I have neither the time nor the patience to indulge you."

Belinda writhed desperately beneath him, her rage fueled by helplessness. "If you think I'm going to answer one question, or...oblige you in any way...you are greatly mistaken!" she gasped. "I'd rather die than aid you, Justin Harding!"

"That can be arranged." One hand slid to her throat. "It would be a pity for such a young and lovely creature to die so needlessly, but I could certainly accomplish it." Belinda's eyes widened as his strong fingers tightened. "Yes, it can well be arranged. Unless you cooperate."

Both hands now encircled her neck. Their pressure made her gasp futilely for air. Stars of light pierced her eyes as her thoughts swam. Then, as abruptly as it had begun, the pressure ceased. Justin Harding leaned back, his features hard and implacable.

"Well, firebrand?"

"D...damn you," Belinda croaked, rubbing her throat with shaking fingers. "You...you don't frighten me, you...you...pirate!"

He drew in his breath sharply at this response. Angry frustration pounded through his powerful frame. This slip of a girl with her silken, flaming hair and brilliant eyes was exhibiting more spirit than many strong men he had battled in his lifetime. She had courage, he granted her that, and a fierce determination to rebel which he couldn't help admiring, even though it thwarted his plans. "Damn it all to hell," he muttered at last savagely. "I wish I knew if I could trust you!"

Her green-gold eyes blazed up at him. "I'm not a spy, if that's what you mean!" she cried, and sat up on the grass, trembling with fury. "I...I hate my cousin. I would never do his filthy questioning for him. But I hate you, too! I won't lift a finger to help either one of you!"

"Oh? And what about Elizabeth Foster?" Harding

spoke softly, his eyes riveted on her face. "Would you be willing to help her?"

At mention of the name, Belinda stared at him in surprise. The grove was absolutely still in the silence that followed, except for the distant murmur of the brook.

"Elizabeth Foster? What does she have to do with any of this?"

"She is the reason I am in Salem. I'm investigating the circumstances of her death."

"For what purpose?"

He made an impatient gesture. "I'm doing the questioning, Belinda. Now, will you help me?"

Slowly, Belinda nodded. Her whole body ached from his assault, and she felt exhausted. He was too strong, too determined. She simply could not fight him anymore. Besides, a growing curiosity possessed her as she wondered why Justin Harding was so concerned about Elizabeth Foster. Had she been a relative? Or...a lover? She suddenly needed to know.

"What do you wish to know?" she asked, carefully studying his face.

"Everything regarding the circumstances of her death. And hurry, we don't have much time. I'm certain your cousin will search for us soon."

"Very well. She died last month. She was hanged—as a witch." Though she expected a strong reaction to this announcement, he accepted it without a trace of emotion.

"Yes, that is what I understand. Do you know why she was accused of such a thing?"

Belinda tossed her head contemptuously. "It was absurd! They say she cast a spell on Goodwife Dunbar, causing her to contract stomach cramps and her livestock to grow ill. Frances Miles, that abominable girl I was speaking with when you accosted me, had a dream that

Elizabeth Foster was indeed a witch. How do you like that for proof?" she demanded scornfully. "Did you ever hear of a woman being put to death for such reasons?"

"From what I hear, there is a great deal of witch hanging in Salem these days—for just such reasons," he replied, his face grim. "You say Frances Miles played a part in this? And what about you, firebrand? What was your role? Did you or anyone else speak out against this senseless hanging?"

His tone of condemnation made her leap to her feet in rage, fists clenched. "For your information, Mr. Harding, Elizabeth Foster died on the very day I arrived in Salem from England. There was nothing I could do to prevent her death."

He, too, rose to his feet and loomed over her, looking more dangerous than ever with his black hair and glinting gray eyes. He stepped closer to her and gripped her shoulders roughly. "There have been hangings since then! What did you do to stop them?"

Tension quivered through her as her rage mounted. "How easy it is for you to stand there in judgment!" she cried. "You are a man of power and authority and far-reaching influence, by all accounts I have heard. What do you expect *me* to do? I tried to reason with Cousin Jonathan about the verdicts he hands down; I tried to change his mind. You are a stranger here; you don't understand what it is like, living among these people! Everyone spies upon everyone else, everyone is required to dress according to code, to speak and sleep and eat and live according to their Puritan ethic!" Her voice and body shook with pent-up frustration. "I am powerless to change things, powerless even to fight! If I do—"

She broke off, thinking of the switch Cousin Jonathan kept handy at all times in the house, of the stocks and whipping post on the village green with which he threatened her. Her shoulders, beneath Justin Harding's strong hands, still smarted from last night's beating. How could she explain? This man looked as if he had never been fearful of anything or anyone in his life. How could she hope to make him understand how frightening and vulnerable her position was—how much she hated every moment of her life in this wretched, oppressive place?

His hands gripped her shoulders more tightly, and she winced. Something in his eyes changed, softened. She read what might have been compassion in their depths. For one wild moment, she thought he was going to kiss her. Then, abruptly, he checked himself. Whatever gentler emotions might have touched him momentarily were banished, and he turned a harsh, ruthless countenance toward the wide-eyed girl in his grasp.

"Poor Belinda," he mocked, giving her a hard shake. "Is it pity you want from me? You'll get none, I'm afraid. I'll save my pity for the poor souls who have fallen victim to this insanity. You and the rest of these pathetic sheep who blindly follow the dictates of men like Jonathan Cady merit only contempt. Some are too foolish and ignorant even to recognize the injustice being committed; the rest, like yourself, are too cowardly to speak out against it!" His eyes held a deadly coldness as they bored into hers. His fingers never slackened their cruel grip upon her shoulders. "If there is one thing I cannot abide, it is a coward!"

Belinda glared at him, white and trembling with fury. Her eyes more than ever resembled those of a tigress, a tigress who was cornered but still fighting. "How dare you judge me! How dare you compare me to...*them!* What do *you* intend to do about the witch-hunts, my self-righteous Justin Harding? How bravely do *you* intend to speak out against them?"

"That remains to be seen, for you and for your

cousin," he replied coldly. Despite his hard, impassive features, she sensed from the tension in his mouth and body that he was very angry. Suddenly, he thrust her away from him, and she stumbled backward, nearly falling.

"Get away, wench," he ordered. "You've served your purpose. Now go!"

"It will give me great pleasure to leave! And to inform my cousin of the exact nature of your business in Salem Village! I'm certain he'll be most interested to learn of it!"

"By all means," Harding nodded, his arms folded across his powerful chest. "Run off and file your report. Don't forget to tell him that if he has any questions, he must feel at liberty to call upon me at the Four Bells. I'd be delighted to have a few words with him." He laughed unpleasantly, and Belinda dug her nails deep into her palms. Without another word, she whirled and ran back toward the village, holding her skirts in one hand.

What a fool I have been, she thought, tears sliding down her cheeks, *to have thought him capable of compassion, of kindness. He is the most arrogant, cruel, heartless man I've ever met, and I'll be thankful when he leaves Salem for good!* Still, the tears flowed ceaselessly down her pale cheeks, and her chest was tight. She stumbled several times in her flight, but never slackened her headlong pace.

Justin Harding scowled, watching the slender, beautiful young woman dart away from him as though she couldn't flee fast enough. His features were dark with anger. Damn her. First she had haunted his thoughts last night, when he ought to have been thinking of Gwendolyn. Now, she had almost touched him with her sad story, almost made him feel sorry for her. Sly little vixen. He didn't want these emotions she stirred in him. He'd been immune to women for the past ten years, bedding and baiting them, enjoying their charms with a detached cynicism which he'd carefully nourished. Now, suddenly, this fragile, exquisite-looking hellion with the red-gold hair and glowing eyes had come dangerously close to piercing the armor he'd so deftly employed in self-defense. Impatiently, he ran a rough hand through his dark hair. He couldn't deny that he wanted her, that he longed to explore the soft curves of her delectable body, to kiss her fine-boned face and long, white neck, to tangle his hands in her cascading hair. But she was a virgin— forbidden territory, according to his own personal code of honor. Besides that, she was dangerous. She affected him in ways he didn't trust. He hadn't felt these emotions for a long time, not since Gwendolyn had first kissed him in the moonlight of the English countryside, amid the rose gardens and statuary. That had been ten long years ago. Now, on the verge of finally possessing what ought to have been his all along, fate had led him into the vicinity of this bewitching, spirited firebrand whose allure cast a strange spell upon him.

There was only one thing to do. Finish this business as swiftly as possible and leave Salem for Boston, where Gwendolyn's ship would be docking within days. Forget this damned Belinda Cady. He would have to erase her from his mind as ruthlessly as though she were dead. It shouldn't prove difficult, after all. Once he was in Boston, gathering Gwendolyn into his arms, this disturbing little minx would no longer matter. How could she?

The scowl still on his face, he strode purposefully back toward the village.

CHAPTER EIGHT

"SO HE DARES to inquire into our witch trials, does he?"

Jonathan spoke in a cold, dangerous voice. He stood in the parlor doorway, watching as Belinda polished the pewter candlesticks atop the oak court cupboard. His pale eyes noted her every movement.

"That Devil's scoundrel! Who is he to come to our village questioning and judging? It is the height of arrogance, and the Devil's own work! He deserves to be lashed at the whipping post for his insolence!"

"Do as you wish," Belinda shrugged. "I do not care what becomes of him."

Jonathan's eyes narrowed. Had she told him everything? What more did the lying wench know that she had kept secret? "Did he say anything else—anything about his connection with Elizabeth Foster?" he demanded. "Why is he so concerned about the hanging of that particular witch?"

Belinda set down the candlestick in her hand with a thud. "He didn't say. Cousin Jonathan, we've been over this again and again. I've told you everything I know!"

"You didn't tell me what he plans to do next!" Cady

114

snapped, his sharply pointed chin quivering. "What are his exact plans? Tell me!"

"I don't know!" Belinda gritted her teeth. "Why don't you ask him yourself, since you're so interested. He said he would welcome the chance to exchange a few words with you. Why not pose these questions to Justin Harding?"

Surprisingly, Jonathan Cady nodded. He was attired in his richest brocade coat, breeches, and silk stockings, and silver buckles gleamed on his black leather shoes. A sheer linen cravat was tied elegantly about his bony neck, and atop his head he wore an expensive beaver hat whose added height made his tall, gaunt frame appear even more gangly than usual. A thin smile stretched across his lips. "I intend to do precisely that, dear cousin. Reverend Wilkes, Constable Vining, and I shall confront the Gray Knight this very evening. It will allow us a perfect opportunity to question him."

His sly, satisfied tone made Belinda bite her lip uneasily. When Cousin Jonathan had first questioned her after the Thursday lecture about her conversation with Justin Harding, it had given her great pleasure to relate everything Harding had said. She had enjoyed Jonathan's rage and chagrin and his threats against the Gray Knight's impudence. Let him cause all the trouble he could for Harding! It would serve that despicable scoundrel right! She grew livid whenever she recalled the harshness with which he had treated her. He deserved whatever befell him! So she had felt at the time. Now, seeing the evil sheen in her cousin's strange, greenish eyes, she felt a shiver of apprehension. What did he intend to do about Justin Harding? He was capable of anything. The mention of Constable Vining made her particularly nervous. Was Jonathan planning to have Harding arrested tonight? Would he indeed be whipped at the post on the morrow or locked in the stocks for public scrutiny until he agreed to answer all the magistrate's questions? A knot of tension twisted inside of her at the thought of all these possibilities.

"Are you...are you going to arrest him?" she inquired, trying to keep her voice steady. "Is that why Constable Vining accompanies you?"

"My intentions need not concern you. You've already informed me that you do not care what becomes of the Gray Knight."

"I don't! I'm merely curious."

"You shall learn all you wish to know when the time is right. As for me, I must depart. The hour is near when I shall meet that blasphemous scoundrel face to face and teach him that a stranger cannot question the laws of our colony with impunity!"

He turned on his heel and swept from the room, slamming the heavy oak doors of the house behind him. Belinda threw down her polishing cloth in agitation and paced about the room, twisting her hands together. What was going to happen? What were they going to do to Justin Harding?

For a wild moment she wondered if she ought to try to warn him, but she quickly realized this would be impossible. She would be recognized in the village, detained at the Four Bells. A young woman alone would never be permitted to see a gentleman staying at the tavern. Word of her intentions would spread through the scandalized village like wildfire. Besides, how could she hope to reach the tavern before Cousin Jonathan? It was hopeless.

Uneasiness built inside her as a heavy silence settled over the gabled house. She moved through the large, gloomy rooms completing her chores, though her mind was not on her work. At last she decided that a bath might soothe her nerves, and she dragged the wooden tub, stored in the shed, into the kitchen. Laboriously, she poured buckets of water that had been heated over the kitchen hearth into the tub, filling it less than half full, lest it be too heavy to empty into the yard later, before returning it to the shed. She undressed quickly and stepped into the tub, sinking down as far as she could in the clean, hot water. Its warmth felt marvelous upon her sore body, still stiff and bruised from the beating. Sighing, she scooped up a cake of hard soap made from bayberry tallow and began to scrub her skin and hair. Outside the kitchen window, the dusk deepened to darkness and a cold night wind swept howling down from the hills. She was grateful for the crackling fire, which protected her naked body from the drafts which seeped through the edges of the doors and windows. She washed herself quickly, then rinsed with a fresh bucketful of water and shivered as she stepped from the tub. She wrapped a thick length of toweling about her dripping form and another, turban-style, about her hair. Then she hurried upstairs and deposited her clothes in the laundry bin in the corner of her loft and slipped into a thin white cotton nightrail.

Sitting on the pallet with her legs curled under her, she began to brush her flaming hair with vigorous strokes, the shining silver hairbrush which she had brought with her from England the only object of ornamentation in the small, dingy room. Wearily, she realized that the bath had done nothing to relieve the disorder of her nerves. Her heart was as heavy as ever, her anxiety even more severe. What if Justin Harding was in prison at this very moment? Manacled and chained like an animal in that dark, dreadful structure on the village green? It would be all her fault! Even though he had tauntingly invited her to inform Jonathan Cady why he was visiting Salem Village, she never should have done so. It had been pure spite that had led her to report her discovery. But if Justin should be harmed because of her actions...She gave a cry of anguish and threw the hairbrush aside. Unable to tolerate the grim confines of the loft another moment, she climbed down the ladder and ran downstairs.

Only the flickering firelight emanating from both the parlor and the kitchen illuminated the house, which had darkened with nightfall. Eerie shadows danced about the parlor as Belinda moved to the window and peered out. There was no sign of Cousin Jonathan's return. Only the black, forbidding wilderness crouched outside, lit by neither stars nor moon. The wind shrieked through the trees and tore across the meadows, echoing away into the hidden depths of the forest. Belinda shivered. The night chill pierced straight through her nightrail, as though the wind had somehow crept indoors. She edged closer to the fire, hugging her arms to herself. If only things had been different, she thought yearningly, aware of a painful ache in her chest. If only Justin Harding were capable of feeling a tiny bit of what she felt when she was near him.

Suddenly, she heard a noise. There was a tapping sound coming from the kitchen. Belinda stood up, wide-eyed, her heart racing. Wondering nervously what had caused the sound, she made her way to the kitchen and peered around. The tapping sounded again, but this time she noted with relief that it was caused by a branch from the elm tree outside the window, beating against the leaded glass. The wind drove the branch, bending and shaking it. She ruefully shook her head at her own jumpiness, but then saw the wooden tub still in the center of the kitchen. She realized she must empty and return it to the shed before Cousin Jonathan returned. Like most people of the day, he abhorred bathing. Immersing oneself in water was almost never done, although a monthly bath in which the body was washed with soap and water from a basin was considered acceptable. The dread of full immersion was one of the reasons why the ducking stool, usually reserved for nags and scolds, was such a hated punishment—and such an effective one. Most colonists shuddered in revulsion at the thought of being immersed in water. Jonathan Cady was no exception, and he had not the faintest idea that Belinda actually enjoyed bathing and did so whenever possible. He would no doubt be outraged if he learned of this practice, so she was careful always to bathe when he was away from home and to empty the tub and return it to the shed when she was finished. Tonight she had almost forgotten, but fortunately, the branch at the window had drawn her in here in time to correct her oversight.

Hastily, she dragged the heavy tub to the kitchen door. A blast of cold air greeted her as she opened it, and she gasped, tipping the tub to empty it into the yard as quickly as possible. Then she pushed it hurriedly toward the shed, stumbling in the darkness. When she had maneuvered it into a corner of the shed, she turned away, her teeth chattering and her thin white nightrail blowing about her slender form. Suddenly, out of the blackness, a hand clamped brutally over her mouth. She tried to scream as her heart skittered wildly, but the sound was muffled by the strong hand crushing her lips against her teeth. Belinda fought with every ounce of her strength as she tried in terror to break away, but a steely arm pinioned her closely against a man's unseen, granite-hard body. Suddenly, a deep voice chuckled in her ear.

"So I frightened you, firebrand, did I? Well, I may indeed murder you, but not just yet."

She recognized that voice! As Justin Harding dragged her struggling figure toward the half-open kitchen door, she kicked at his booted foot, but he only cursed and tightened his cruel hold upon her. She sobbed in frustration as he forced her through the kitchen door, her thinly clad body pressed close against him. Once in the kitchen, the firelight blazing beyond them, he suddenly shoved her away. She caught herself against the pine table and whirled to face him, fury shining across her face.

"What do you think you're doing?" she cried, rage almost choking her. "You nearly frightened me to *death*, and you hurt me, and you have no *right*—"

He cut her short. "I'm paying a farewell visit to you, Belinda. After tonight, we shall not meet again." His cold eyes raked her body, seeing everything through the flimsy nightrail, then returned harshly to her face. Her lips had parted in sudden shock at his words, and she appeared heedless of the fact that she stood before him little more than naked.

"You're . . . you're leaving Salem?"

"Correct. Thanks to you, my pet, the hounds are already in pursuit. In fact, I was fortunate to escape with my flesh still intact."

She clasped her hands together. "Cousin Jonathan! He tried to have you arrested!"

Justin Harding laughed shortly. "Oh, he did better than that. It was his intention that on the morrow, after having spent a night in the delightful Salem Prison, that I be whipped at the tail of a cart."

"Oh no!" Belinda whispered. This cruel punishment demanded that the victim be forced to follow a cart to which his hands were tied, while the constable followed behind and whipped him with every step he took throughout the entire village. Tears stung her eyes at the very thought. "I—I'm sorry! Please forgive me. You must leave. You must get away before they—"

She stopped as she noticed the sudden change in his expression. A strange look entered his icy gray eyes as she spoke. Suddenly, he took a stride toward her, and she drew away in apprehension. He grasped her wrist and pulled her closer. His voice was taut with mockery. "Why, firebrand, is this a note of concern in your voice? Can it be that you do not wish to see me sustain such a punishment after all?"

He was very close to her. Belinda was intensely aware of his powerful physique as she lifted enormous, green-gold eyes to his face. "I . . . I . . . of course not . . ."

"You were the one who sent them after me, were you not?" he demanded, watching her intently. "You were the one who swore you hated me."

"I don't! I didn't! I mean, I didn't send them after you! I told Cousin Jonathan why you were here, but . . . you told me I could!" she cried, further agitated by her own uncharacteristic confusion. Being so near to him had a dizzying, most unsettling effect upon her. She struggled to think coherently. "I never wanted him to arrest you or . . . to hurt you! You must believe that!"

Her lovely face searched his hard, impassive features. For some strange reason tears suddenly burned her eyelids. She would have brushed them away, but he was holding her wrists, and they slipped slowly down her cheeks. "You insist on thinking the worst of me!" she said, trembling. "And I don't understand why!"

Harding fought to keep his emotions in check. He had escaped Cady and his associates by use of brute force and had stopped here only long enough to bid a scathing farewell to this damnable little troublemaker. So he told himself. Ever since the first afternoon they'd met, he'd been fighting to contain his feelings for her, feelings as sudden and strong as though that first heady kiss in the woods had sent a poisonous, exotic drug through his veins. He'd been denying his feelings, resisting them ever since. Now he felt himself weakening. She was so damned beautiful. He wanted her. That was the real reason he had come here tonight. Not to say good-bye, but to torture himself with the urgent, unrelenting desire that encompassed him every time he was within fifty yards of this captivating, glowing girl. "Belinda." His voice was husky. "Do you want to know what I really think of you?"

Her heart hammered so loudly she thought he must surely hear it. But the only sound in the big, homey kitchen was the crackling of the logs in the hearth. She nodded slowly, her eyes huge, wondering. Justin Harding pulled her closer, enfolding her slender, shivering form within his cloak. "I'll show you," he told her, his gray eyes keenly alive. "Damn it, I've been wanting to show you ever since that first afternoon!"

And slowly, with fierce yet tender domination, he captured her lips in his own. Belinda felt herself enclosed in a crushing embrace that made her gasp for breath, yet rapture swept through her as he bent her head backward with the force of his kiss and proceeded to devour her mouth. In one swift motion he tore the nightrail from her luminous body and cupped her full young breasts in his hands. Naked and burning with passion, Belinda flung her arms about his neck and held him close, her mouth parting eagerly to meet and return his kisses, her tongue searching frantically for his. Justin paused only long enough to throw his cloak upon the floor and then they sank down together, engulfed by a raging fire which had simmered too long before exploding. His lips caressed her tautened nipples as their bodies lay entwined before the flickering hearth, and she gasped in ecstasy, tangling her fingers in his hair, sliding them across his broad, hard-muscled shoulders, thrilling to the ripples of the powerful muscles in his back. Justin left a searing trail of kisses across her breasts and shoulders and down the length of her arm, but suddenly he paused and lifted his head. He was staring at her arm.

"What the devil?" In the flickering firelight her body shone golden, but its satiny perfection was marred by the bruises still evident on her arms and back. He sucked in his breath as black fury coursed through him. *"Who did this?"*

Belinda turned her face away in sudden mortification. "Cousin Jonathan," she whispered.

He pulled her to a sitting position, facing him on the floor. His eyes were like flint. "He did this to you—after we met in the woods?"

She nodded. "He... he paid no heed to what you told him. I sometimes think he is a madman. He... confuses me with another girl he once knew."

"I'm going to kill him." Justin's voice was cold, deliberate. It sent chills like a thousand icicle slivers pricking up and down her spine. "He'll pay dear for this, Belinda. You can believe that."

"No!" Belinda clasped his arm, suddenly frightened. "Don't bother with him! It doesn't matter. I'm going away—I'm going to run away. And you must do the same!" She caught her breath and continued urgently. *"Now.* Quickly. If they find you here—oh, Justin, what have we been thinking of?"

"Don't you know?" He grinned at her and gathered her close. "Come here, my love."

He stared down into the beautiful, high-boned face and gently touched one long, red-gold curl which dangled over her shoulder. "No one is ever going to hurt you again," he told her and kissed the top of her hair. "I promise you that, Belinda. Upon my honor."

"Your honor? I wasn't aware that you had any!" she laughed saucily up at him. "You are a pirate, are you not?"

"Impudent wench. Shut up and let me make love to you. I did vow that one day you would understand the nature of passion. I am going to be your personal instructor, my fortunate little firebrand. And your lessons shall begin right now."

"No, Justin." She squirmed in his arms, alarmed by his recklessness. "You can't stay here. Cousin Jonathan might return."

"To hell with Cousin Jonathan!" His eyes narrowed as he raked the luminous beauty of her naked form. He felt the raw desire pumping through his blood as he sat so near to her, and the heaviness of his aching loins demanded action. He seized her firmly and stared into her upturned face. "To hell with everything but us, Belinda! You and I."

This time there was no stopping him. Fearful they would be caught, Belinda tried to resist, but he paid her no heed, his lips conquering hers, his hands driving her body wild with their masterful stroking. She moaned, trying to fight the wild urges building within her, but finally she could fight no more. She gave a low, tormented cry as his fingers probed the silken, red-gold triangle between her thighs. "Justin, Justin." It was a ragged whisper, repeated breathlessly over and over as she clutched him ever more tightly, drawing him to her, wanting him, needing him as she had never wanted or needed anyone before. There upon the floor before the blazing hearth they came together, a man and a woman driven by desire, beckoned by love. When he spread her legs with his powerful thighs and poised himself above her, she drew in one half-frightened breath, but he kissed her tenderly, his mouth clinging to hers. Slowly and carefully, he entered her, muffling her whimpers with his mouth and promising her that soon the pain would be gone forever. As his hands continued to caress her and his lips to enflame her mouth and the flesh of her throat and breasts, the pain indeed ebbed and a sweet, strange sensation replaced it. Gradually, but with growing intensity, a fierce, wild craving built inside her, spreading through her so that every part of her ached and tingled and screamed for release. She moaned, not in pain, but in a kind of tormented ecstasy, as he moved powerfully within her, thrusting and driving her until she thought she would die of pleasure. She clutched him closer, her nails digging into his back, her mouth sucking eagerly at his as together their passion soared. Belinda sobbed at the beauty and fierce exhilaration of it, her heart lifting as joyously as a captured bird suddenly set free. The dark world outside was forgotten. Only the beauty of the moment was real.

Afterward, it was quiet in the kitchen, except for their heavy breathing and the persistent tapping of the branch at the window. Justin held her tight within his arms.

"Belinda, my sweet, sweet love," he murmured, kissing her breasts very gently. "You are truly a jewel. A rare and precious and most beautiful jewel."

"That is how you make me feel." She smiled glowingly up at him, hardly daring to believe that this wonderful thing between them had truly happened. Silent moments passed between them while they gazed at something fleeting and yet eternal within each other's eyes. Slowly, Justin's fingers traced the bruises on her shoulder. He kissed them with great tenderness. Belinda murmured against his lips.

"Oh, Justin. I'm so glad you came to Salem Village."

"As am I, my firebrand."

"Only think what might have happened if you had not come to the colony," she breathed, gripping his mighty shoulders with her small hands. Her eyes were enormous pools of green-gold fire as she stared up at him. "We might never have met, never have seen or touched or known one another."

Justin's gray eyes burned into hers. "Impossible, my love. This is our destiny. I can feel it. I know."

His mouth pressed against her soft lips. He kissed her long and deeply, savoring every moment. Belinda responded eagerly, opening her heart and soul to him once again. Dreamy pleasure seeped through her as she swayed against him and felt herself clasped against his iron frame. Her lips and tongue sought his. Long, languid moments passed. They drew apart and smiled at one another. She lay her head against his chest and gave a small, trembling sigh. Happiness enclosed her as they lay quietly together before the fire.

Eventually, Belinda spoke again. "Justin, I . . . I must ask you a question."

"Yes?"

"Who was Elizabeth Foster?" She sat up, her eyes searching his face. "Why did you . . . care so greatly about what happened to her that you came to Salem to investigate?"

"Is this jealousy, my pet?" His voice was gentle, amused. "You have no cause to feel jealousy—not of Elizabeth Foster," he amended quickly, guilt suddenly stabbing him. He pushed Gwendolyn's golden image from his mind and returned to Belinda's question. "My investigation has been done on behalf of another man. His name is Simon Foster. Simon was my first mate for many years at sea and is probably the best friend I have. Elizabeth Foster was his sister."

"I see." Belinda traced a delicate pattern on his bare, bronzed chest with the tips of her fingers. "It must have been terrible for him when he heard what happened to her."

"Yes." Justin spoke grimly. "Simon wanted to come himself, to exact a pirate's vengeance upon those responsible, but I persuaded him to let me handle it my way." His mouth tightened. "Your cousin will not hold the reins of power much longer, my sweet. I will personally see to it that this witch-hanging madness is brought to an end. One way or another." He suddenly tilted her head up toward him. "But I don't wish to speak of such ugly matters now. I want only to look at you, for when I'm far from here, I want to remember every lovely thing about you—from head to toe." He grinned with wicked pleasure as he surveyed her glistening nakedness.

Belinda snuggled closer against him. "Justin, I wish you could hold me like this forever. I wish you could stay."

He chuckled at her. "You're not to be rid of me so easily, firebrand. I intend to stay with you many hours into this night."

"But Cousin Jonathan..."

Amusement gleamed in his gray eyes. "Do you really think I fear that damned cousin of yours? What a paltry fellow you must think me."

"Of course not!" She sat up beside him and lightly touched his hair. "But he set off to find you tonight with Reverend Wilkes and Constable Vining, and you said they already tried to arrest you!" A frown suddenly creased her forehead and she glanced at him questioningly. "By the way, how *did* you manage to escape them?"

"I'm afraid I was forced to resort to violence," he returned sardonically, enjoying her pleased expression. "The good reverend sustained nothing more than a bruised jaw, and your cousin is none the worse but for a bloodied nose. However, I fear the constable suffered a slight wound from my rapier." He shrugged unconcernedly. "Unavoidable, you see. He was not badly injured, though, and will certainly survive the loss of a bit of blood. My room at the Four Bells, however, will probably be uninhabitable for some time. To put it mildly, when I made my exit, it was a shambles."

She regarded him with open admiration. "So you

eluded all three of them!" Her eyes sparkled. "I think it was very clever of you. And here is your reward." She kissed him slowly and sensuously on the mouth, a kiss made all the more enticing because she pressed her breasts against his chest as she did so. Justin's eyes glinted at her, and he gave her bare bottom a light slap.

"Impudent tease," he growled. "One moment you're warning me to leave and the next you are seducing me all over again. There is only one thing to be done with you, Belinda Cady."

She gave him a look of complete innocence. "Oh, and what might that be?"

For answer, he scooped her up in his arms—cape, discarded clothing, and all—and carried her out into the hallway. "I suggest we find a more private spot, where I can show you," he chuckled.

He carried her up to the loft and firmly shut the door. Setting her down gently upon her straw-filled pallet, he glanced grimly about the dark, cell-like room. Deftly, he tindered the candle on the chest, then sank down beside her, anger pumping through him. "So this is where he keeps you. This place isn't fit for an animal!"

"I won't be here much longer. I'm leaving soon."

He glanced at her sharply. "Where will you go?"

"To Boston. My old housekeeper from Sussex lives there now. I'll find her and she'll help me." Belinda's eyes glimmered green-gold in the candlelight. "I don't care what I have to do. I'll become a seamstress or a servant—anything! Anything is better than living here with *him*. Any place is better than Salem Village."

"No." He seized her shoulders, and shook her gently. "You can't go alone, Belinda. It isn't safe. How would you ever find your way to Boston?"

"I have no choice." She lifted her chin. "I'm leaving. Just as soon as I've collected some moneys owed me for my needlework, I will run away."

"You little fool. How far do you think you'd get? If only I could take you with me—" He broke off in frustration, cursing inwardly. No. He had to see Gwen first— alone. It would be madness to bring Belinda with him now. She was in no immediate danger here. Better that he settle things first, instead of embroiling her in the whole damn mess. He studied her determined little face, weighing his options. Then he cupped her chin in his hand.

"Listen to me, firebrand. I don't want you to leave Salem alone."

"But I..."

"No!" His voice was commanding. "I'll kill you myself if you attempt anything so idiotic. Stay here. I'll return and take you away as soon as I can."

"What do you mean?" Her heart had begun to pound with excitement. He had not spoken a word to her of love or commitment. Despite the intensity of her own feelings, she had not dared to hope for a future with him. Now he was implying otherwise. She searched his eyes eagerly.

"I can't explain now. You must trust me. I can't take you with me tonight, but I will get you out of this place. I'll return for you—soon."

Suddenly she jerked away from him, her lips quivering. Disappointment and anger stabbed painfully at her heart. "So I am supposed to wait here for weeks, maybe months—holding my breath while you decide *when* you are going to come for me!" she exclaimed. She jumped up, her eyes flashing fire. "How dare you! I am no chattel, Justin Harding, no simpering, frightened fool who will plan my life around your whims and conveniences! I will leave when I choose! If you can't take me with you tonight, then I will make my own way! You cannot order me to stay in this horrid place! You have no right and no power to do so. I will go when I please, and not a moment later!"

Harding stood up, towering over her in the tiny room. His eyes glinted like steel. "You'll do as you're told," he informed her coldly. "If you set off on your own, you'll get yourself killed! You'll either fall into some river and drown, or get lost and starve, or be attacked by Indians or ruffians or wild beasts. America is not England, you know. The times are dark and dangerous. And the world, my innocent beauty, is cruel. It is unthinkable for you to travel alone outside of this village. If you had an ounce of sense in your lovely head, you'd see that."

"I see that you are no different from any other man— believing that you can order a woman about as though she was a slave, expecting that only *you* know what is best for her!" she spat. "Well, let me tell you something! I have no intention of obeying you in anything!"

Suddenly, he yanked her close and covered her mouth with his hand. Her ears picked up the sound of the double doors below slamming. She froze as the heavy tread of shoes across the lower floor confirmed her worst fears. Cousin Jonathan had returned. Her argument with Justin was forgotten as she gazed up at him in alarm. Terror flowed through her. What should they do? Where could he hide? Her eyes screamed questions at him, and he leaned down to whisper in her ear.

"Don't panic. My horse is hidden in the woods, so he has no suspicion that I'm here. Get into bed and pretend to be asleep. And don't look so frightened. I won't let him hurt you."

She nodded, too numb to tell him that all her fears were for *his* sake. She swiftly pulled on a fresh cotton nightrail and lay down upon the pallet, watching as Justin blew out the candle and quickly donned his breeches and sword belt. Coolly, he hid the rest of their clothing and then positioned himself behind the loft door. Belinda caught her breath as she heard Jonathan's footsteps approaching. When the loft ladder creaked beneath his feet, she smothered a cry of dismay and threw her head down on the pallet, feigning sleep, though she trembled beneath the thin blanket. Slowly, the loft door swung open. She heard it above the drumming of her heart and fought to keep from moving a muscle. Then Jonathan Cady's voice sliced through the dusky air.

"Wake up, you lazy wench!"

She jerked upright, pretending to be startled out of a deep slumber. She stared at his tall, thin form framing the doorway. Only two feet from him, on the other side of the door, Justin waited in the darkness, looking quite ruthless and deadly, a faint film of sweat gleaming on his naked chest and forearms. She dared not glance at him, however, and fastened her gaze upon Cousin Jonathan, feigning surprise.

"Cousin Jonathan—what is it?"

"I'll tell you what it is, you lazy wretch!" Cady's voice was edged with contempt. "Never in my days have I seen such an ungrateful, good-for-nothing! Get downstairs, girl, and finish your tasks! The fires have not been banked for the night!"

"I'm sorry—I...I will see to it now." He appeared about to enter the room and yank her out of bed himself, so she quickly added, "If you please, Cousin Jonathan, I must reach my dressing robe. Kindly step downstairs and I will bank the fires directly."

"See that you do," he snarled. It was then that in the faint, flickering light of the candle he held upright in his hand, Belinda noticed his red, bruised nose. She couldn't help the wave of satisfaction that washed over her and couldn't resist commenting, "Why, cousin, whatever happened? Your nose appears to have been bleeding. Are you hurt?"

"I had a confrontation with the Devil!" he snapped, his eyes bright with hatred. "Your friend the Gray Knight managed to elude the trap I set for him. We've been hunting him throughout the village all evening!" His fingers clenched on the candlestick until his knuckles showed white. "He may have escaped tonight, but he will receive his due in good time. Hellfire awaits him, and he will suffer the fate of all sinners on earth! One day he will pay. If Justin Harding shows his face in our village again, that day will come sooner, but if not, he is only delaying his fate. He cannot escape the wrath of the Righteous One forever. He will burn, he will suffer! He will know the horrors of hell when his time on earth is gone!" Jonathan's narrow face shone with the reflection of his rage and frustration at the evening's failure. He seemed ready to describe at length the agonies certain to befall the Gray Knight, so Belinda interrupted swiftly.

"Well, he is gone now, cousin. You and I need not concern ourselves with him. I will attend the hearthfires now, if you will kindly step down."

Cady grunted his assent and slowly descended the loft ladder. Belinda shot Justin a relieved glance, but he merely grinned nonchalantly, apparently undisturbed by her cousin's dire predictions. She slipped downstairs even as Jonathan slammed his bedchamber door, and set about banking the fires in the parlor and kitchen. By the time she returned to the loft she was cold and weary, and she stumbled up the ladder. Justin caught her in his arms as she entered the loft and kissed her gently. Then he gazed down into her tired face.

"Does that bastard always speak to you so?"

She nodded. "Do you see now why I must leave?

He is such a cruel man, Justin. I can't bear to live under his roof any longer."

"I understand." His face was grim. "I'm sorry I spoke so roughly before. It was only my concern for you that made me do so." He gathered her close and kissed her suddenly, fiercely. "I'll return for you, Belinda. I swear it."

"Justin, can't you take me with you tonight?" Hope surged through her, lighting her eyes. "I can be ready in an instant. I can travel anywhere you want to go. Oh, please..."

For an instant, staring down into her desperate face, a face so beautiful it almost hurt him to look at her, he wavered. Then another face swam into view, pale and patrician, with eyes of violet and hair of gold. Damn! In that moment, he almost told her about Gwendolyn. He almost decided to bring her with him, damning the consequences. But he steeled himself, adhering to his earlier decision.

"No, Belinda, I must go alone."

She choked back a sob, saying in a strangled tone, "I...see. You don't really want me, you don't care about me. What happened between us meant nothing to you—"

"Don't say that!" Angrily, he gripped her shoulders, shaking her. "I care about you, my little firebrand—more than I should! I cannot explain, dammit, so don't question me! Just promise me one thing."

Defiantly, she stuck out her chin. "What is it?"

"Wait a week. One week. If I don't return for you within that time—which, my darling, I swear I will—you may then do as you wish. Agreed?"

Belinda bit her lip. More than anything else in the world she wanted to go with him tonight. She had the terrifying feeling that if they parted, she might never see him again. He would forget about her; he would not bother to return. It wasn't that she doubted her ability to make her way to Boston alone, for it had been her plan all along, and she was fully prepared to follow it through. No, she didn't need Justin Harding to get away from Salem Village—but she wanted him! Desperately, wildly, she wanted him. Never in her life had she known such longing or behaved with such reckless abandon, but tonight, when he had held her in his arms and made fierce and powerful love to her, he had awakened intoxicating, passionate emotions inside her. Perhaps it was because she sensed they were kindred spirits, both strong-willed and independent, perhaps it was the raw strength of his personality and the physical chemistry between them, but she wanted Justin Harding with an overwhelming passion. She couldn't bear to lose him, not now, after they had only just discovered one another. She knew virtually nothing about him, and yet she knew everything. She prayed this was only the beginning of their relationship and not the end, yet she feared with all her heart that if he left her tonight, they would be parted forever. Her eyes searched his face, reading the implacability there. He would not change his mind. He was adamant. With a surge of pride, she knew she would not and could not beg him. She drew a deep breath.

"All right, Justin." Her voice was quiet. "I will wait. One week."

He smiled and caressed her cheek with his finger. "That's my girl."

Happiness swept through her at the gentleness of his tone, at the softened expression in his eyes. She clung to him suddenly, and tears sparkled on her eyelashes. "Must you...must you leave just yet?" It was shameless, it was wicked, but she couldn't control the desire pulsing through her. She placed her hands on his chest and stared up into his eyes. "Can you stay with me a little longer?"

He chuckled and began to remove her nightrail with deft, determined hands. She helped him strip off his sword belt and breeches, gasping in pleasure at the magnificence of his physique. As he lowered her beside him onto the pallet and kissed the tautened nipples of her full, creamy breasts, Belinda ran her fingers over his firm buttocks and thighs and then caressed his male hardness, savoring him, writhing sensuously in rhythm with his movements. She moaned as he kissed the pulse at her throat and whispered to her.

"I am in no hurry to leave, Belinda. No hurry at all."

Slowly, deliciously, they entwined themselves together, heedless of the howling wind which rattled the windows, heedless of the trees that sighed and shivered. They were snug and safe and warm in the dark, tiny loft. And morning seemed a long time away.

CHAPTER NINE

BELINDA AWOKE with a cold, empty feeling in the pit of her stomach. Before she even opened her eyes, she knew Justin was gone, knew he had slipped away sometime in the pink-gray hours of the morning while she slept. Her hand crept up and touched the pallet where his head had lain beside hers. *Justin, don't forget me,* she prayed, and clenched her fingers tightly as if she could somehow contain the essence of the man to whom she had given her love last night. Bleakness enveloped her, settling heavily in the gloom of the loft. Justin was gone.

It took tremendous effort to rise from the pallet. The day held nothing for her, nothing but toil, and scowling lectures from Cousin Jonathan. *Only one more week,* she reminded herself, taking a deep, determined breath. *Then I can begin a whole new life . . .*

Still, she was unprepared for the way the day dragged and the listlessness which encompassed her. By mid-afternoon, restlessness replaced her languor, and she desperately wanted to see Lucy, to share her feelings and draw reassurance from someone who would sympathize with her plight. Lucy, too, was in love and separated from her betrothed. She would understand.

Cousin Jonathan had business to attend to in the

village this afternoon, so Belinda set off after finishing most of her chores, confident that she could easily return home before he arrived for his supper. She left the soup pot simmering over the hearth and set off eagerly to find Lucy.

It was a warm, overcast day with little wind to stir the trees. The air was as thick as gravy. For once Belinda was grateful for the plain white cap which secured her thick hair off her neck. Her blue homespun dress clung damply to her body as she strode quickly across the grass-carpeted countryside. Her thoughts were distracted, turbulent, Justin's darkly handsome face swimming continuously in her mind, tormenting her.

How was it possible, she wondered, to love a man one had known for such a short time? A man one knew almost nothing about? Yet she did love him. She wanted to be with him so desperately she ached, and her heart was filled with a strange, hungry yearning which frightened her with its intensity. She reached the Miles house in a state of fevered frustration and was grateful that it was Lucy who opened the kitchen door when she knocked. Her friend stared at her in surprise.

"Belinda, what are you doing here?"

"I must talk to you. Is anyone about?"

"Mistress Frances will return from the village soon, but we can speak for a few minutes. Come in."

Belinda stepped inside. The Miles kitchen was as large and inviting as the one at the Cady house and, on this stifling day, equally warm. Over the fire, a great caldron of stew filled the air with a delicious aroma, compensating somewhat for the heat it generated. Iron pots and skillets hung on hooks beside the hearth, the andirons were made of brass, and a table board beneath the window casement held an array of pewter platters, porringers, and wooden bowls. There was a spinning wheel in the corner, and two cane chairs on either side of it.

Near the door was a low pine bench. Belinda sank down upon this, staring with haunted eyes at the slight, fair girl beside her. "Oh, Lucy, I don't even know how to begin to explain what's happened. It's...it's Justin Harding. We're...I mean, I—"

"Are you in love with him?" Her friend spoke softly.

"How did you know?" A horrible thought entered Belinda's mind and she stared at Lucy, aghast. "Lucy, you...you didn't have a vision of Justin and me...last night, did you?" she gasped.

"No, no, of course I didn't." Lucy shook her head, then suddenly burst out laughing. "It was merely a guess, Belinda. After the way you questioned me about him and the way he dragged you from the village after the Thursday meeting—the Mileses and everyone else were scandalized, you know—well, let me just say it was a guess. An instinct." She smiled. "It doesn't require the Sight to conclude that the two of you would make a splendid pair." She broke off suddenly and studied Belinda with her head tilted to one side. "What *did* happen between you and Justin Harding last night?" she inquired.

A tremulous smile touched Belinda's lips.

"We...we were together," she replied, and blazing warmth surged through her at the memory. "Throughout the night." She saw that Lucy had drawn back in amazement, and Belinda's chin lifted defiantly. "I'm not ashamed of it, Lucy," she continued, and her eyes held a determined glint. "I love him. I've never felt this way about anyone before. What we did last night was beautiful. Not wicked, not sinful, whatever Cousin Jonathan and the rest of the world might think. It was beautiful."

"What are you going to do?" Lucy asked quietly, and Belinda realized gratefully that there was no condemnation in her eyes, only concern. "Will you go away with him?"

Slowly, Belinda shook her head. "Justin has already gone. Cousin Jonathan tried to arrest him last night. He had to flee secretly." She bit her lip. "But he promised he would come back for me in one week's time! And I believe that he will!" she cried, realizing with an ache in her throat that she was trying to convince herself as much as Lucy. "I'm sure that he loves me. I know he will return!"

"I hope so." Lucy's pinched face reflected her own inner pain, and Belinda knew she must be thinking of Henry, from whom there had been no word in months. "Just as Henry March will return for you!" she added firmly. "We must both have faith."

"Yes." Lucy glanced down at her hands. "I do try. But...I miss him so!" She wiped away the tears that had gathered suddenly in her eyes.

Watching her, Belinda trembled. If her own misery was this intense after only a few hours' separation from Justin, she could imagine how lonely and abandoned Lucy must feel. She tried to think of words of comfort, but before she could speak, they were interrupted by a shrill voice from the entry hall of the house.

"Lucy! Lucy!" Frances Miles's strident tones pierced the silence. She burst in upon them before either Lucy or Belinda could move. "Lucy, come at once and fetch these parcels from...oh! You!" Her brows drew together as she noticed Belinda seated on the pine bench. "What are *you* doing here?" she demanded.

"I came about the satin gown you sent to me for embroidering last week," Belinda invented swiftly. She rose, squarely meeting Frances's chilly stare.

"What about it?" the girl rasped. "I sent Lucy with complete instructions. Is there some difficulty in carrying them out? They were simple enough!"

"Quite simple," Belinda agreed. "There is no difficulty at all. I merely wish to offer a suggestion."

"What might that be?" Frances's blue eyes gleamed unpleasantly. "Speak up, girl!"

"I believe that small gold buttons sewed on with gold thread would enhance the color of the gown more than the pewter ones presently in use. If you wish, I will purchase the gold ones in the village and substitute them for the others before returning the gown to you."

Frances considered this, apparently approving the idea. Her pudgy face broke into a grin. "Yes, gold will do most nicely. I wonder that I did not think of it myself. Very well, you may change the buttons. But I must have the gown returned before Thursday meeting next."

"Of course." Belinda and Lucy exchanged quick, hidden smiles. Belinda turned to leave. "Good day to you both," she said crisply.

Frances Miles did not bother to respond. She was already prattling on to Lucy in her most officious tone. "Do run outside at once and bring the parcels into the kitchen. Hurry, girl! And by the by, you haven't seen a sign of the Gersholm babe, have you? The silly brat has wandered off somehow, and half the village is out searching. Goodwife Fletcher noticed him missing more than two hours ago."

"Aaaaa!"

Frances broke off, and Belinda whirled from the doorway as Lucy gave a sudden, piercing scream. She was clutching her head, eyes closed.

"Lucy, what is it?" Belinda rushed to her side, watching her friend's ashen face in consternation. "Lucy, oh no, not *now*," she whispered, aware that Frances was staring at the blond girl incredulously. Lucy appeared not to have heard. She stood frozen, oblivious of everything around her. Belinda touched her arm almost pleadingly. "Lucy? Lucy, please..."

Suddenly, the girl's eyes flew open. The terror shining wildly in them made Belinda's skin prickle. Lucy swayed forward, clasping Belinda's arm.

"The child!" she gasped, pale as death itself. "The child—John Gersholm! I saw him in the pond!"

Belinda felt the color draining from her own cheeks. Her heart jumped. "Pond? What pond? Quickly, Lucy!"

Lucy's hands were trembling. She put one to her brow as though in terrible pain. "Whistledown Pond—in the Far Meadow," she managed to gasp before sinking down onto the bench, her knees giving out beneath her. Belinda was already darting toward the door.

"Care for her!" she commanded Frances over her shoulder, and an instant later she was outside, running headlong toward the Far Meadow.

She had seen the shock on Frances Miles's face at Lucy's odd behavior, and dreaded the consequences, but she couldn't pause to consider them now. Only the child mattered at this moment, the small toddler who was Goodwife Fletcher's grandson. She tore across the earth toward the Far Meadow, praying she wouldn't be too late. The north end of the meadow was thickly wooded, and branches clawed at her as she plunged through the thickets, but she didn't slow her pace. Desperately she ran, her arms pumping at her sides, her breath coming in sharp, painful rasps. A horrifying image of a child floating lifelessly in the crystal water drove her even faster, despite the agony in her lungs. Her gown ripped on a blackberry bush. Her feet tripped over unseen boulders and tangled undergrowth; still she ran. She felt as though she'd been running forever. Hot and exhausted, she pushed on, sheer desperation keeping her on her feet. Suddenly, she caught sight of Will Gersholm and his eldest son searching among the bushes just ahead. She summoned her strength to shout.

"The pond!"

No sound emerged, just an agonizing hiss. Gasping,

she stumbled toward them and tried again. "The pond!" she finally managed to croak, as the square-set, bewhiskered farmer and his lanky boy turned to stare at her blankly. "The...child...is in the...pond..." Belinda gasped out the words and, without waiting, staggered past them toward the water, which she knew to be only a short distance beyond a stand of birches. The crashing of boots upon hard earth behind her told her that Will Gersholm and his son were following. They overtook her and reached the pond first. Just as Belinda limped up alongside, the boy gave a shout.

"There, Pa!"

And as the three of them stared, a husky child of barely two summers crawled through the blackberry bushes on the far side of Whistledown Pond. His cheeks were smeared with blackberry juice. He was grinning delightedly. Before their widened eyes, he waved, laughed, and toddled straight into the water. Belinda screamed.

Will Gersholm plunged in, boots, work clothes, and all, and waded swiftly across the shallow water until he reached the child, who had only just begun to sputter in fear. He hauled the boy into his arms and carried him quickly to the shore, speaking gruff, angry words even as he hugged the child to his breast.

Belinda gave a sob of relief. It was over. The child was safe. She sank down upon the damp grass at the water's edge. Her breath was coming in short, wheezing gasps. Dimly, she was aware that Will and the elder boy were looking at her, speaking, but her head throbbed and her sides ached painfully. She shut her eyes and laid her cheek against the soft grass. Weakened, totally spent by her headlong race across the Far Meadow, she allowed herself to collapse. She had no idea how long she lay there, listening only to the labored sound of her own breathing, her eyes tightly closed, but suddenly, other sounds intruded into her numb oblivion, and slowly, dazedly, she pulled herself to a sitting position. She was stunned to find that she was no longer alone by the pond's edge with Will Gersholm and his two sons. A half-dozen people now stood among the reeds and cowslips, eyeing her with a mixture of fear and horror.

"The witch told her. That's how she knew!" Will Gersholm was exclaiming, his usually ruddy face pale beneath his whiskers. "Just in time I grabbed my boy from the water. Just in time!"

"Where's the witch now?" a man bellowed from the group.

Frances Miles stepped forward, her arms folded. "She's locked in our shed!" she declared. "My pa's keeping her there while Ned rides in to fetch the constable and Magistrate Cady from the village." She pointed dramatically at Belinda, her bright blue eyes glittering. "They ought to arrest this one, too! Both she and Lucy Brewer are servants of the Devil!" she announced.

"No!" It was Goodwife Fletcher, little John Gersholm's grandmother, who cried out as she cradled the whimpering child in her arms. "Belinda saved his life. She is no witch—she's a messenger of mercy!"

People glanced at each other uncertainly, muttering among themselves. They all grew silent as Belinda rose unsteadily to her feet. As one, they cast a wary gaze upon her, filled with suspicion. Belinda stepped forward to face Frances Miles.

"You sent for the constable—to arrest Lucy?" she asked disbelievingly. "How could you *do* such a thing?"

"How can you *ask* such a thing?" Frances mimicked her tone maliciously. "That girl is a witch! She has visions from the Devil, she consorts with him, serves him—"

"Will Gersholm!" Belinda strode toward the square-shouldered farmer, still soaking wet from the pond. He eyed her uneasily as she spoke. "Do you think Lucy

Brewer is a witch? She saved your son's life! The vision that came to her, the one that Frances Miles and I both witnessed, was a heavenly gift, one which spared the life of your own child! Can't you see that?"

Will's close-set brown eyes darted back and forth between Belinda and Frances. He shifted his weight uncertainly and rubbed his large, callused hands together. "I...I don't rightly know," he finally muttered. "I guess the magistrates will have to decide. I only know...'tis strange. 'Tis mighty strange."

"There is evil in the air today!" Frances declared suddenly, hugging her arms about herself. "I feel it! My bones are cold!"

Angrily, Belinda wheeled on her. "You're nothing but a vicious troublemaker, Frances Miles!" she cried. Her green-gold eyes sparkled with fury. "You speak of things you know nothing about. You're filled with ignorance and stupidity! But I won't allow you to harm Lucy when nothing but goodness lives within her. There is no more evil in that girl than in the flowers that grow in your garden. You see wickedness where there is none! Not this time, though. You won't hang Lucy upon Gallows Hill, not while I have a breath left in my body. I will refute you at every turn!"

"Refute me? Will you lie, then? Did she not go into a swoon and then cry out that the child was in Whistle-down Pond? Was this not the truth, as you yourself discovered? What more can you ask in the way of evidence? This is the Devil's work!"

"No. It was a miracle through which a child's life was saved." Belinda spoke very quietly, but with a firmness of voice and manner which drew rapt attention from the little circle of listeners. "You look only upon the dark side of things, Frances, never upon the bright. Therein lies your fault."

"And you defend a practitioner of dark magic."

Frances narrowed her eyes. "Let the magistrates decide! Justice will determine which of us speaks the truth!"

"Aye, the courts shall guide us!"

"Aye, Magistrate Cady will decide!"

"He is wise—and just!"

"Aye!" "Aye!" "Aye!"

Belinda heard the echo of their words with chill dismay. Lucy would be arrested, tried as a witch! Perhaps hanged! She could bear it no longer. Despairingly, she thrust past the group and started for the village at a run. Behind her, she heard Frances Miles's sharp voice.

"See how she defends the witch? She is her accomplice! I tell you, she is evil! Last night, I felt pins pricking into my flesh—and now I know why! Belinda Cady, the needlewoman, was practicing her black magic! She is dangerous, as dangerous as the other one."

Belinda didn't pause or look back in response. It was useless. Lucy's secret had been discovered, and now a harrowing ordeal lay ahead. Frances Miles was too narrow-minded and self-righteous to listen to reason, and the villagers, even Will Gersholm, whose child had been saved, were consumed by superstitious fear. She must try to reach Cousin Jonathan, in whose hands Lucy's fate now rested. Somehow, she must make him see that Lucy's power to see into the future was not a weapon of the Devil! She would speak out, argue, plead, and insist until Cousin Jonathan saw the logic of her words! For once the accused would be defended!

Even as she ran, the hopelessness of her mission loomed before her. Jonathan Cady believed in witchcraft every bit as much as Salem's most terrified villager— more, perhaps. Though Belinda might beg him to consider Lucy's innocence, deep within, she knew he would close his ears and his mind to her pleas. Her stern, towering cousin had no mercy in his heart. Failure taunted her, even as she staggered on. She would never convince

Cousin Jonathan of Lucy's goodness! Still, she told herself, half sobbing in frustration, she must try. What else could she do? She must at least try!

Belinda reached the village breathless and disheveled. She groaned as she saw the constable leading Lucy across the square in the direction of the prison. "No!" In seconds she was at Lucy's side, trembling. One look at Lucy's pinched, chalk-white face filled her with anguish. In horror, she noticed the thick rope binding the girl's hands at the wrists.

"Lucy! Don't be afraid," she began, as her friend stared with huge, terrified eyes. "I...won't let them harm you! I'll convince them of your innocence!"

"Belinda." Lucy's voice was so soft it was barely audible. "I am so frightened. I don't...want to...die."

"You won't! I will make them see—"

"Step aside, here!" Constable Vining jerked Lucy's arm roughly and shot Belinda a fulminating glance. "Be off with you, girl! I'm taking this witch to jail!"

"She's not a witch!"

"That's for the court to decide." His swarthy cheeks reminded Belinda of the great jowls of a vicious dog. It enraged her to think of Lucy in the custody of such a brute. With a prickling of satisfaction, she suddenly noticed the thick bandage bulging beneath his loose-fitting cloth coat. *Well done, Justin. Your rapier scored well.* Then, as she watched, the gray-headed constable dragged Lucy forward. "Go on with you, now! Or I'll arrest you for interfering with justice."

Lucy sent Belinda a helpless, beseeching glance as the lumbering constable marched her ruthlessly toward the prison. Belinda called sharply, "Where is my cousin?"

"He rode home after signing the warrant," Constable Vining returned over his shoulder. "And you'd best return there and see to your duties, Belinda Cady, instead of meddling in village affairs!"

"Lucy!" She once more caught up with the constable and the pale, shaking girl at his side. "I'll talk to Cousin Jonathan. I'll make him see reason. You must have faith and... and try not to be afraid. I won't desert you."

Lucy nodded bleakly. Her eyes were glassy and dull. Stunned by what had befallen her, she seemed to have no strength to answer. She stumbled as the constable pulled her roughly along the commons. Belinda watched, motionless, until the pair disappeared inside the dark prison building. Waves of anger washed over her as she thought of Lucy in that dreadful place, surrounded by all the other poor wretches awaiting trial. Wearily, she rubbed her temples. It had been an exhausting day, what with racing through the Far Meadow in search of the Gersholm child and then the trek to the village. Now she must hurry home and plead with Cousin Jonathan. Her back and shoulders ached, and her legs felt as though their muscles had turned to lead. She wanted to sit down and cry. Instead, she turned from the village square and began walking quickly in the direction of the Cady house.

She reached it just before suppertime. Hazy clouds swirled through the darkening sky. A mist was rolling in from the sea. She shivered slightly as she crossed the threshold. Despite the muggy heat of the spring day, the night would be chill. She wondered if Lucy would have a blanket in her prison cell.

Jonathan Cady glanced up from his desk as she appeared in the parlor doorway. His strange, unpleasant eyes gleamed at her in the twilight of the room. "So," he said very softly. "Your friend has been arrested. It speaks ill of you, my cousin, keeping the company of a witch."

"She is nothing of the sort, Cousin Jonathan. You must let me explain about Lucy."

"Explain? What is there to explain?" He rose slowly from his chair, his gaunt, bony frame towering above her. In the dim light of the low-beamed parlor, he looked as grim and eerie as death itself. "The creature had a vision from the Devil. She can foretell the future; she has powers beyond this earth. What more is there to say?"

"Her power stems not from the Devil. It is a gift; it can be used for good. Today it enabled her to save the life of a child! How can that be evil, Cousin Jonathan?" Belinda spread her hands imploringly. "Please, only consider. Lucy is a good, pious girl, she is everything you always demand of *me*. She is quiet and obedient and diligent in her work. There is no evil in her. Surely you can see that?" Impulsively, she put out a tentative, pleading hand to touch his scarecrow's arm. At her touch, Jonathan jumped as though she had bitten him. His small, icy-green eyes bored into her, sending a shudder up and down her spine.

"There is evil in us all, Belinda," he murmured. "You—me. We must constantly guard against it."

Something in his voice disturbed her. She wiped her palms on her apron nervously. "Not...not Lucy," she insisted.

He appeared to have forgotten Lucy. Slowly, stiffly, he reached up to touch the satin softness of her cheek. She flinched, drawing away with swift revulsion. "I...I must see to supper," she stammered, filled with cold dread and a new and ugly fear. She turned her mind from it, concentrating on the matter at hand. "P-Please think about...what I said. Lucy is...not a witch. She is kind and good."

He made no answer. She was uncomfortably aware of his strange gaze upon her as she hurried away. Glancing uneasily back from the doorway, she saw that Jonathan had not moved. His eyes burned with an unsettling light as they traveled over her graceful form, seeming to examine her every curve beneath the plain blue homespun gown. Flushing, Belinda escaped to the kitchen. She hoped that by the time she returned to the parlor to serve supper, her cousin's odd mood would have passed, for his strange, lingering way of watching her upset her even more than his cruelty. But to her dismay, the strangeness seemed to have settled upon him, for he studied her fiercely as she served the meal and kindled the fire, seeming to hold himself very still all the while. Once, his tongue flicked over his dry lips in the manner of a lizard anticipating its prey. Belinda gathered the pewter platters and dishes into her arms and sped back to the kitchen, trying to ignore her cousin's disturbing behavior. Presently, her thoughts shifted once more to Lucy, imprisoned like an animal in that dark, cramped cell. The thought made her cringe. She *had* to convince Cousin Jonathan to dismiss the charges against her!

Moments later, a dreadful sound made her pause in her work. Rooted to the floor, Belinda lifted her head and listened, icy chills creeping over her as she heard the horrible, anguished noises emanating from the parlor. Cautiously, she tiptoed to the hallway and then to the parlor door. What she saw made her start in astonishment.

Cousin Jonathan was seated at his desk, his head in his large, bony hands. Tears gushed down his thin face and dropped unheeded off his pointed chin. His bent shoulders shook with sobs. Horrible, choking noises of grief were torn from his throat.

"Alice! Alice!" The words were a weeping moan which echoed throughout the firelit chamber. He appeared lost in some awful nightmare, oblivious of his surroundings.

Shocked, Belinda hesitated, uncertain what to do. Suddenly, he glanced up and saw her. The sobs ceased. His grief-stricken face was transformed into one of fury. He rose, taut with wrath, swaying unsteadily in the shadowy room. One trembling hand lifted to point at her.

"You! Belinda Cady! Witch!" he shrieked. "Trying

to corrupt me, to seduce me! Just like *her!* Alice! You're
possessed of her spirit, and wickedness lives in your soul!"
He lunged around the desk, his face hideous, ravaged
by an indescribable grief. His arms were flailing wildly
in the air as he shouted, "But you won't succeed, witch!
You won't seduce me! I am a righteous man—I am
stronger than the lures of Satan! I will see you hanged
before I succumb to your bewitchment!"

"No! I never . . . Cousin Jonathan, be *reasonable!*" Belinda clung to the door frame for support, panic rushing
through her. "I am no witch! I know no one named Alice!
And I've done nothing to seduce you!"

"Lies. All lies." His raspy voice had dropped to a
whisper. He crept toward her, skeleton hands outstretched, and gripped her shoulders. "You have tormented your last, Alice. I will see you hanged. You and
your friend, Lucy Brewer. You will pay. Justice will be
done!" Suddenly, he yanked her closer and fastened his
wet lips to hers. Belinda struggled wildly to escape, twisting her head in revulsion, but he held her tightly, his lips
moving with brutal ferocity against hers. She kicked and
struck at him blindly, until finally he lifted his head. The
horror in her eyes was reflected equally in his.

"Devil!" This time the scream tore from his lips to
echo in the rafters of the house. He was shaking violently,
overcome by emotions of deadly power. "You will hang
for your sins!" he cried, in a high, shrill voice, and abruptly
he flung Belinda aside and hurtled from the parlor and
through the front doors like a man pursued by demons.

Belinda collapsed against the door frame, sick and
stunned. Dazedly she listened as his horse set off at a
wild gallop through the deepening twilight. Her face was
wet with tears as she wiped his kiss from her lips. Fear
bit into her. *What did he mean to do next?* The answer was
dreadfully apparent. Raw terror pulsed through her veins.

I must leave—tonight! she realized desperately. *He means to secure a warrant for my arrest, to toss me in prison with Lucy and the others! He will claim I torment him with witchcraft. And who will disbelieve him, the magistrate of the village? Frances Miles will surely add her own accusations, and the entire village already looks upon me with suspicion. I will have no prayer of acquittal.* She suddenly had a vivid recollection of that dark, chill day when she had first come to this fierce colony. She heard once again the chanting in the woods, the wind howling through the streaming trees. And she saw, with horrified eyes, Elizabeth Foster's lifeless form swinging grotesquely upon the gallows. She would never forget the sight of the girl dangling there, her dark hair blowing around a horribly ravaged face, her cloak billowing in the chill, black mist. Belinda shuddered in anguish as the image flooded back. Then the vision spurred her to action. Whirling, she flew up to the loft, lighting her single candle with trembling fingers. There was precious little time to pack clothes or provisions, but she snatched up her blue velvet cloak and stuffed the little pouch containing her embroidery money into a pocket. The tinderbox went into another pocket, and then she was dashing downstairs, her heart thumping wildly. At any moment she expected to hear snorting horses and shouting men as Cousin Jonathan and the other Puritans galloped up to arrest her, but so far the night remained silent. In the kitchen, she thrust a chunk of corn bread into the pocket with her money pouch, longingly eyeing her uneaten dinner. But there was no time to even consider eating. She slipped into her cloak, then made her way swiftly to the front door and threw it open. On the threshold, an idea occurred to her and she darted back to Cousin Jonathan's writing desk in the parlor. With shaking fingers she scrawled a message with his tall, quill pen.

Cousin Jonathan: I know you will never accept my innocence, so I am fleeing before you can falsely arrest me for witchcraft. Do not bother to search for me. By the time you read this, I will be in Salem Town Harbor, sailing forever from this village. I hope you will regain your senses about Lucy; she is as innocent as the angels in heaven. Farewell. Belinda.

Her lips curled in satisfaction as she dropped the quill pen and turned away. There. Let him think she was making for the harbor. It would give her more time to escape through the forests. But first, before she disappeared into the black woods, there was something she must do. Determination tightened her face as she bolted out the door, not even bothering to shut it behind her. With quick, light steps she began to run toward the village, her body quivering with fear and excitement. Her time for escape had come, far sooner than she had expected. But unless she was very cautious and very clever, there would be no escape at all. There would be only imprisonment—and death.

CHAPTER TEN

THE ROUGH DIRT ROAD to the village was strewn with boulders. In the darkness, Belinda tripped and stumbled along, unable to see where she was setting her foot, much less see twenty paces ahead into the blackness. Despite the difficulty, she was grateful that it was a moonless, cloudy night. The darkness swallowed every moving thing, and under the circumstances, that was reassuring. Even the wet mist which had rolled in off the bay, obscuring the stars, pleased her, despite its damp chill which made her hair curl in tiny, dew-frosted tendrils about her face and which made her shiver in her cloak. Shrouded as she was by the misty night, her hopes of success rose. She must remain hidden for as long as possible. Dawn would be her enemy, unless she was far enough away to be beyond those who would hunt for her. And hunt for her they would. They would be furious when they discovered that she had eluded them, and they would pursue her with a vengeance. She shuddered again, envisioning their wrath and seeing also the mad, glowing eyes of the man who would be their leader. Oh yes, the darkness was her friend. Her kindest friend.

She had not gone far when she heard the sounds.

Eerie in the swirling mist, the hoarse, angry voices and pounding of hooves 'seemed to swim out of nowhere, ghostly echoes in the wind. She had been waiting for them, expecting them, yet when they came, the hairs on the back of her neck rose, and clamminess coated her body. She dove off the track and scurried toward the forest, hiding herself within a web of darkly looming trees. Tension tautened her nerves like a whipcord, and the bark of the tree bit into the side of her face as she leaned rigidly against it. She waited, breathing hard.

It wasn't long. They appeared suddenly around a bend in the road, illuminated by the flaming torches they held aloft. They wore dark cloaks and tall hats, and passion gripped their faces. Some were on horseback, others ran alongside. Belinda caught a glimpse of Jonathan Cady's towering form at the head of the shouting mob, then she jerked back into the sheltering darkness of the trees. Though she could no longer see them, their words rang through the darkness like death bells.

"Arrest the witch!"

"That red hair has always been a sign of the Devil!"

"Hang the servant of Satan!"

The shrill, ugly words, so filled with hate, chilled her far more than the mist and the wind. Her fingernails bit into her palms. Then, almost as abruptly as they had appeared, the lights and the voices faded. She was once more alone in the night. She took a deep, shuddering breath as relief flooded over her. Then she pushed herself shakily away from the trees.

There was no time to lose. In moments they would discover her escape, and her diversion about the harbor would not delay them for long. She must hasten.

The distance to the village seemed interminable, yet at last she reached the edge of the square, noting the surrounding wooden buildings in apprehension. So far, no one was about. She pulled her hood more snugly around her head, hunching forward so that her face would not be visible, and then slipped across the commons toward the prison. She knew that Constable Vining went home to his supper at dusk, and there was no night guard to watch over the prisoners, since escape from their barred, heavily chained cells was virtually impossible. Quickly, she darted into the shadow of the building and clung to the wall beneath one of the high, barred windows.

"Lucy! Lucy!" Her voice was no more than a whisper in the night, and she feared it would not be discerned among the moaning and sobs of the wretched inmates within. She tried again, more loudly. Still there was no response, so she crept like a shadow to the farther window.

"Lucy! Can you hear me?" she repeated.

"Who...who is it? B-Belinda?" Lucy's soft voice sounded especially weak tonight, but Belinda gasped with relief at the sound of it.

"Yes, it's me," she called softly in return. "Are you all right?"

"Y-yes, but...Belinda, you must flee!" Lucy's words throbbed with urgency. "There was a great commotion in the village less than an hour ago! I...I heard it through the window, all the yelling and shouting. Magistrate Cady rode back toward your house with the constable and a crowd of villagers to arrest you!"

"I know. They passed me on the road." Belinda wished the window were not so high and so small. She would have liked to have seen Lucy's face to ascertain if she was really all right. Her voice sounded so distraught that Belinda feared for her all the more.

"Lucy, I'm going away where they won't find me, but I wanted to tell you first. I didn't want you to think I was deserting you."

She heard what sounded like a sob from within the prison. "I . . . I would never think that. There is nothing you can do for me, Belinda. You must save yourself!"

"I'm going to send word to Henry!" Belinda called. "I will do everything I can think of to help you. Don't fear that you're alone! I want you to know that, and have faith!"

For a moment there was no answer. Only a wail from some unseen wretch within the cell, and the stirring of the wind outside. Then Lucy's voice came, small and lost. "There is no hope for me, Belinda. I know that. But you . . . you will escape. You're so clever and bright. You will succeed."

"I will succeed in summoning Henry to your aid!" Belinda hissed back fiercely. "And don't you forget that, Lucy Brewer!"

"Go now, Belinda. There isn't much time."

"Yes, I know." Belinda felt tears sting her eyelids. She hated leaving Lucy to face this ordeal alone, but she had no choice. She gave one small, ragged sob and then forced herself to speak. "Farewell, Lucy! We shall meet again."

"Farewell, my friend. Go in safety." Lucy's voice was a thin whisper on the wind. "Farewell."

Steeling herself, Belinda turned from the wall.

Suddenly, light beamed into the square as the door to the Four Bells Tavern swung open, and two scarlet-coated figures stepped into the misty night. Belinda shrank back into the shadows, fear twisting inside her. She held her breath as the two men, deep in conversation, walked toward the commons, then exhaled softly as they turned into the road without even glancing in her direction. She had been biting her lip so hard she now tasted blood. Her hands were shaking. She tried to steady herself.

There was no time for this. She had to move. Now.

Quickly. She sprinted forward, toward the woods beyond the prison, the same spot where she and Justin had argued after the Thursday lecture. When she reached it, she kept on running until she melted into the hemlocks. Above the pounding of her heart, she heard the murmur of the brook and the rustle of the wind through the tall trees. Nothing else. No chanting or shouting or hoofbeats. They were not on her trail—yet.

Still, she knew it was only a matter of time before they abandoned the harbor and turned their pursuit to the woods. She pulled her heavy cloak closer about her shivering form and began, once more, to run.

On and on through the forest she plunged, desperately trying to keep to the south and west, where she knew, some sixteen miles ahead, lay the town of Boston. In the swirling, inky blackness, she often stumbled and fell or scratched her face upon low-hanging branches and shrubs, but she dared not pause to consider her hurts. Always in her mind was the dread that at any moment she would hear them crashing after her. It was this dread that kept her on her feet, dodging headlong through the wind-swept forest. Exhaustion dragged at her, but her fear kept her moving.

After the first few hours she could no longer run. Her breathing labored, she stumbled along. Weariness encompassed her. Surely now she could spare a few moments to rest? No, she told herself. They might be coming, they might be close. She pushed onward, her feet shuffling against the soft wet grass, her head hanging. She couldn't stop. Not yet.

At last she halted, unable to move another step. She leaned against an old oak tree, clinging to it as to a long-lost friend. A rabbit scurried by. Geese circled overhead, telling her, reassuringly, that the coast was not far away. At least she was headed in the right direction. She lis-

tened, hearing only the sounds of the forest. She began
to wonder if perhaps she was finally safe, finally far
enough away. Then, suddenly, a twig snapped, and she
froze, panic shooting through her in sharp, stabbing
needles. What was it? A horse? A man? The bile of fear
rose in her throat.

She screamed softly as something moved in the
bushes. Red eyes shone in the night. Then she saw the
red fur glinting, the long snout, and realized it was a fox
that watched her from the thicket. Then a new fear clawed
at her. She edged away, slowly at first, her eyes never
leaving the glaring animal. Suddenly, she began to run
again, faster and faster, deeper into the night. The forest
swam by, dark trees with wet, swatting branches, spongy
earth squishing beneath her feet, crickets filling the night
with their song. The woods seemed alive, vibrant, and
terrifying as she staggered through them. She felt herself
an intruder, a trespasser in this misty, midnight forest,
but she had no choice, and she glanced fearfully about
as she ran, cringing at the unseen perils about her. She
could not stop. Driven by dread and desperation, she
plowed onward, until at last, finally, she reached the limit
of her strength.

Boston was a full day's ride on horseback from Salem.
Her journey would require at least two days on foot, or
a night and a day if she traveled quickly. She would have
to rest and regain her strength at some point. Better to
do so under the cover of darkness than in daylight, when
she would need to be constantly on watch. So she told
herself as fatigue laid final claim to her and she sank to
the soft, reedy grass beneath an elm tree. She rested her
head against its trunk as the chill of the night penetrated
even more deeply into her bones. The mist had lifted in
the past hour, but the damp cold remained. Through the
web of tree branches high above, shredded clouds floated

slowly in the darkened sky. Belinda prayed it would not rain, and then, her eyes shut, the lids too heavy to stay open another minute. Sleep overtook her, sucking her into a world of shadows and fog. The hours slipped away.

She awakened with a start. Panic surged through her as she stared wildly about, expecting to see a ring of Puritans surrounding her with muskets and ropes. Instead, she saw only a chickadee hopping across the damp earth. Dawn pinked what she could see of the sky. Dew glimmered everywhere. Belinda sat upright, listening intently. All was rustling, murmuring peace in the forest. She reached into her cloak for her breakfast.

The corn bread was consumed all too quickly, and hunger still gnawed at her when the last crumbs had been devoured. *Well*, she thought with forced cheerfulness, *perhaps I will find some berries along the way. And a stream of fresh water where I may drink and bathe my face.* She pushed herself to her feet and slipped out of her muddied cloak, carrying it over one arm. It was going to be a warm, sunlit day. Already the dew was fading from the grass, and the sun poured down through the tree tops. She glanced about for her bearings and started off in what she hoped was a southwesterly direction. If she could only find the road. Then she could keep just to the left or right of it and hide if any travelers approached. As the sun rose higher in the sky, her dread of discovery increased. She would have to be very careful, very quiet. She prayed that her sense of direction would not fail her.

The day proved long and exhausting. After much anxious effort, she located the road, which was little better than a four-foot dirt track slicing through the swampy, wooded wilderness. She followed this most of the day, but was forced to hide in the forest whenever she detected the approach of other travelers, which fortunately was not often. She gobbled berries which she picked from nearby bushes as she walked, but they did little to appease her appetite. Weariness dragged at her, but she walked doggedly on, knowing that it was too late now to turn back. Only death awaited her in Salem Village. She tried not to think of Justin Harding, of the fact that he would return there for her and find her gone. She wondered once, with a surging hope, if he might come to Boston in search of her, but quickly dismissed this from her mind. He would probably be too angry with her for having left without him to bother. *If* he even bothered to return to Salem at all. She walked on, her shoulders sagging. If somewhere inside of her, something wilted and died like a flower plucked from the rich earth, she paid no heed. With almost mindless determination, she followed her course to Boston, placing one foot dully before the other. Justin Harding was a memory, a dream. This horror was all that was real. This endless, hilly wilderness where she must hide from man and beast. She walked on.

Her efforts at washing up went to waste when, while hiding from a wizened old farmer and his scolding wife, she fell into a swamp that sprang seemingly out of nowhere. Foul-smelling mud oozed over her, and it was all she could do to keep from crying aloud in dismay. Later, when twilight came and she was once more alone in the ancient forest, she did cry, tears of weariness and fear, tears of despair. She wrapped herself in her wet, filthy cloak and allowed her tears to flow freely, thinking all the while of Justin and wishing with a desperate loneliness that he were there to hold her. She would have given half her life away at that moment if only Justin could have been there to cradle her in his arms, to gently kiss away the tears. But he wasn't there. Instead, alone and forlorn, she cried until she sank at last into a heavy, exhausted sleep. This night she was not plagued by dreams.

She awoke in that eerie hour between night and dawn when the moon has not yet ebbed away and the baby sun still slumbers. The sky was charcoal, veiled by wispy clouds. Belinda lay still a moment, listening to her heartbeat, listening to the rhythms of the forest. Slowly, insidiously, a terrible new fear crept over her. She wondered if she would spend the rest of her life wandering alone through this forest. She began to doubt that she would ever reach Boston, that she would ever again stumble across a town or a cottage, that she would ever see another human face. A kind of madness seized her, a waking nightmare, shooting panic in gigantic rippling waves throughout her brain. She sat up, glancing wildly about, then staggered to her feet. Frantically, she began to run, flinging herself headlong through the trees, her throat throbbing with silent screams. She toppled over boulders, crashed into trees, yet she did not slacken.

Filled with frenzy, she ran and ran and ran....

It was a tattered, filthy creature who finally stumbled into the town of Boston shortly before noon that day. She looked more like an old hag than a young girl, her hair a tangled mass stinking of the swamp, her face caked with mud and dried blood from tree branch scratches and tumbles. Gown and cloak were torn and splattered. Belinda was dazed as she dragged herself forward to the edges of civilization, leaving the nightmare of the forest behind. With lifeless eyes she gazed about, barely remembering her purpose now that she had reached her destination. Sarah. She must find Sarah.

Head bent and knees trembling, she staggered through the twisting streets, vaguely aware of people staring at her, pointing. She reached a narrow lane and leaned weakly against the wall of a bake shop, inhaling the tantalizing aroma of fresh-baked bread. Tears sprang to her eyes at the thought of food. Her fingers moved shakily to the pocket with her money pouch. She began to inch her way toward the bake shop door.

Suddenly, she felt a heavy hand on her shoulder. Flinching, she glanced up, and her face whitened beneath its grime. A harsh-visaged man in a scarlet coat was frowning at her. Another stood at his elbow, nose wrinkled in disgust. Constables. Belinda gasped aloud in dismay.

"Who might you be, woman? And what are you doing here?" the first man demanded. His eyes reminded Belinda of a reptile, narrow and cold and watchful.

Before she could reply, the second one, pudgy and short, with a thick neck, spoke up contemptuously. "A beggar by the looks of her. An idler with no fit occupation."

"We don't like strangers here, woman," the reptile intoned. "Especially disreputable ones. We're a decent, hard-working community with no pity nor time to waste on those who don't honor the laws of cleanliness and honorable labour."

"I...I'm not..." Belinda began in a cracked, dry voice. She wet her lips with her tongue and tried again. "I...I'm looking for someone. Can you tell me—"

"I say we put her in the stocks for a day," the pudgy one interrupted impatiently. "That'll teach her to wander in here as though she'd just climbed from a pig sty!"

"No!" Belinda glanced desperately from one scowling face to the other. Horror filled her. They wouldn't listen, they wouldn't care. They would lock her in the stocks, imprison her, question her until they discovered that she was escaping from Salem, where witchcraft charges faced her. They would send her back!

"No!" she screeched again. Fear shone in her eyes. Desperately, she threw herself past the two men into the narrow lane. She began to run, dodging garbage and ruts, using the little that remained of her strength. Yelling, the constables pounded after her. Suddenly, Belinda tripped over a wooden plank and fell heavily to her knees. She felt herself grasped from behind and jerked to her feet, her arms twisted behind her. The constables, each one holding an arm, grunted in satisfaction as she sobbed and struggled. She even kicked at them, but they only tightened their cruel hold. "Let me go!" Belinda wept.

Suddenly, into the chaos of the altercation, an icy, calm voice rang out with the clarity and strength of a sword crashing against metal. "Halt!" it demanded. "Let the poor wretch go!"

The constables turned with Belinda to see who had interrupted them. She gazed upward with bleary eyes.

A magnificent caped figure was mounted before her on a tall chestnut stallion. Handsome and arrogant, he stared back at the three in the lane. Belinda blinked and looked again. Her heart began to hammer.

"J-Justin!"

The tall, commanding man focused his gaze sharply on her. He leaned forward in his saddle and caught his breath. Shock tautened his lean, bronzed features.

"Belinda?" His voice came quick and hard, filled with incredulity.

"Y-yes." It was a thin whisper, sounding as if it came from someone else's throat. She felt weakness seeping into her, and an icy coldness that spread through her as though icicles were melting in her veins, freezing her blood. She tried to speak again, tried to reach out to him, but then, through a darkening mist, she saw the white-hot fury clamp over his face and she shrunk away in sudden fear. Something was wrong. Justin was angry. He wasn't glad to see her; he was angry. She gave a sob. Then she could no longer see him. Misty blackness swirled before her eyes. She cried out, terrified, but there was no sound. Then, swiftly, the blackness rushed in one final time, swallowing her, and she knew nothing but the chill, dark emptiness of the dead.

CHAPTER ELEVEN

BELINDA AWOKE STILL IN darkness. Her body automatically tried to seek again the numbness of sleep. Yet her thoughts returned, like pinching fingers which touched and probed until she moaned aloud. It was the merest whimper, but it was easily heard by the trim little woman who sat in the corner with her mending, her agile fingers busily working the needle by the light of the fire. The woman dropped her mending and hastened to the bedside, peering down at the drawn face of the ragged girl in the bed. Yes, she was awakening. Good.

Belinda's eyes opened slowly. She stared unrecognizingly into the thin, kindly face. Before she could speak, a pleased smile curved the old woman's lips.

"Bless you, child. That's better. Now, don't say a word, and for heaven's sake, don't try to sit up. I'll run and fetch you some broth and a bit of bread to mop it up, and we'll see what we can do to muster your strength once again."

Belinda heard a door click quietly shut, and it seemed only a moment later that it creaked open again. The woman tiptoed forward, bearing a silver tray. A delicious aroma of hot soup filled Belinda's nostrils, and suddenly, her pain and weariness were replaced by ravenous hunger which made her want to grab the steaming bowl from the woman's hands and drink it down in one gulp. But she had no strength even to lift her head from the soft pillow it rested on. It was the woman who, setting down the tray on a maple bedside table, lifted her pillows gently so that she was half sitting up in the bed. Then, carefully and slowly, she began to feed Belinda the soup.

It was marvelous. Rich and meaty, it slid deliciously down her throat and warmed her empty belly. Silently, the woman handed her chunks of bread softened in the broth, and Belinda wolfed these down, tears stinging her eyes at the goodness of this simple fare. When every crumb and every drop had been devoured, she let out a long sigh, and then turned her head to smile weakly at her benefactress.

"Th-thank you."

"Oh, hush, child, don't thank me. I'm glad to do it, glad to help take care of a pretty mite like you, half starved and more than half dead by the time the master brought you home. Poor thing. I shudder to think what you've been through, little one."

"Who . . . are you?"

"My name is Mrs. Gavin. I'm the housekeeper. Now, don't be exhausting yourself thinking and worrying. You just try to rest a bit more and then—"

There was a bold knock on the heavy oak door, and the woman jumped.

"Who's there?" she called.

For answer, the door crashed open and Justin Harding stood on the threshold. His powerfully muscled arms were folded across his chest. His black hair fell in rumpled disarray across his frowning brow.

"Now, Master Harding, don't you go upsetting the poor child when she's only just come about. The fever could come back, you know. She needs her—"

"That will be all, Mrs. Gavin." Justin's icy tone left no room for argument. Mrs. Gavin took one look at his harsh face and pursed her little lips together, then scooted out of the room, bearing the tray. Justin didn't even bother to glance at her. His eyes were riveted upon Belinda. Slowly, he closed the door behind him and moved with the stalking grace of a panther toward the bed.

The sight of him brought Belinda's memory of what had occurred in the little lane rushing back. It was a miracle that he had found her, here in Boston. She didn't know how it had come to pass, but she knew that he had rescued her from those constables after she had fainted, and she knew that he had brought her here to this pleasant, quiet room with the crackling fire. But why was he glaring at her with such fury in his eyes? He looked as if he wanted to throttle her!

"Justin, what are you doing here? What am I doing here? I'm so confused. Why...why are you angry with me?"

His gray eyes narrowed to dangerous slits. "I thought we had an arrangement, Belinda. You made a promise to me."

Something in his voice frightened her. She fought to think clearly. A promise? What promise? And then she remembered. She raised her eyes to his face.

"Y-yes, I told you I would wait a week before I left Salem, to give you a chance to return for me. But Justin, you don't understand."

"Don't I?" His lip curled contemptuously. "You must have waited less than a day before running off on your own. You never intended to wait for my return, did you?" His hands were clenched into fists at his sides, the knuckles white. His voice flogged her. *"Did you, firebrand?"*

Belinda instinctively recoiled from the ferocity in his face and voice. She spoke weakly. "Of course I did. I wanted to see you again more than anything in the world."

He gave a short, mocking bark of laughter. "Is that why you ran off the very next day—not knowing where I was or how I would ever find you once you had left Salem Village? How did you expect us to meet again, my love? By magic?"

Exhausted as she was, Belinda nevertheless felt the first stirrings of anger. She pushed her tumbling red-gold curls from her eyes and sat up straighter in the bed, glaring at him. "If you would only give me an opportunity to explain, you would understand why I could not wait for you. I had to leave Salem immediately!"

"You chose to do so." His gray eyes glinted coldly. "It was pure coincidence and, for your sake, luck that led me to happen across you today when those constables apprehended you. Perhaps," he continued slowly, cruelly, "it would have served you properly if I had allowed them to carry you off."

Twin spots of scarlet color burned her cheeks and her eyes glittered with fury. "You're insufferable! How...how dare you speak to me so! I don't deserve your censure, Justin! I was forced to leave Salem—I had no alternative. And after everything I've been through..."

"Everything *you've* been through!" Justin gritted his teeth to keep the full force of his rage from exploding. His powerful frame quivered with tension as he exerted every effort to keep from laying hands upon her. How could he explain the past ten hours of waiting for Belinda to awaken, replaying over and over in his mind the tremendous danger she'd placed herself in, and from which she might not recover? Those hours of waiting helplessly while she fought the fever and exhaustion had been sheer hell, a torture more agonizing than any physical pain he'd ever undergone. It had left him shaken and spent, and more terrified than ever of losing her. When Mrs. Gavin had finally announced that Belinda had come around, relief had engulfed him in great, pounding waves, but it had been joined almost immediately by savage fury. Damn the girl for nearly killing herself! Damn her for tearing him to pieces this way! He didn't know whom he was more furious with: her or himself. Now, seeing her lying on this bed in this house, her face pale and luminous in the firelight, looking so fragile and so damned beautiful even though she was scratched and bruised and her hair a filthy mess, he was torn apart by warring desires. Part of him wanted to enfold her in his arms, to rain kisses down upon that enchanting little face and never, ever let her go, while another part of him wanted to strike her. Stupid, impatient wench, jeopardizing her life and his sanity with her recklessness! How could she be so foolhardy? The fury grew as he thought of how easily he might have lost her, how little she had cared for his advice or his promises. His eyes hardened as the anger pumped through him. All relief and rational thought were shoved aside by the unreasoning rage which took complete possession of his weary mind. It was this rage, borne of fear and pain and exhaustion, which spurred him to speak so brutally.

"Well, now that you've recovered from 'everything you've been through,' you can get the hell out! You don't want me or need me, that's obvious, since you made a decision that would have excluded me from your life. So feel free to leave, my love. No, feel *obliged* to leave. I don't want you in this house."

Belinda's eyes widened incredulously at this pronouncement. For a moment she could not speak or move. Her heart cried out in torment at this cruel turn of events, yet her mind could not quite believe it was really happening. She lifted her arms to Justin, wanting to beg him to hold her, to love her, but the words died on her lips. Her arms fell. His harsh expression forbade any appeal. She fought back the tears threatening to betray her anguish, struggling to retain some remnant of pride. Then anger came to her rescue. It flowed through her slender form in a burst of white-hot fire, lending her sudden, unexpected strength.

A cry of outrage tore from her throat. She threw back the bedsheets and jumped from the four-poster bed, trembling. Someone (Mrs. Gavin, she hoped) had removed her tattered gown and wrapped her in a soft, pale pink silken robe, and it flowed becomingly over her body as she faced Justin Harding. "Give me back my dress and I'll be more than happy to leave!" she retorted through clenched teeth. "I don't want your charity!"

He lifted what was left of the filthy homespun gown from the back of a chair and flung it at her. There was no emotion other than contempt on his rugged features.

"Thank you! Now kindly leave while I dress!" Belinda nearly shouted the words, choking back tears of rage. Her entire body was shaking, and her head felt strange. Hot, achy. She fought off a wave of dizziness, refusing to let Justin see her weakness.

For one long moment he stared at her. A muscle worked in his jaw. Then he turned on his heel and strode to the door. His hands grasped the brass knob, gripping it with fearsome strength.

There was a dull thud behind him.

Justin spun about and saw Belinda in a crumpled heap on the floor. The color drained from his face. In two quick strides he was at her side, kneeling and lifting her gently in his arms. Her eyes were shut and her breathing faint. Fear knifed through him, ten times worse than it had been before.

"Mrs. Gavin!" he shouted hoarsely. "Come quickly!"

Seconds later the little housekeeper rushed in. When she saw Belinda's limp form and ashen face, her hand flew to her mouth. "What have you done to the poor mite?" she demanded, momentarily forgetting to whom she spoke, but one glance at the fear and self-recrimination evident in Justin's face made her soften her words.

"There, now, she'll be all right, sir, never you worry. More rest and food, little by little. That's what she needs now. You run down to the kitchen and tell Cook to simmer some weak tea and prepare some of those little tartlets of hers. I'll see to the child myself."

And so Justin Harding the formidable pirate who had terrorized the worst blackguards of the sea, bolted from the bedchamber to obey his housekeeper's instructions. He vowed that when Belinda regained consciousness he would make up to her for everything. He would kiss away the pain in her eyes and warm her lips with his. He would beg her forgiveness and, damn it, he would listen to her explanation—whatever the hell it might be.

It was many hours before Belinda next fully regained consciousness. Throughout the night she would stir and moan and permit Mrs. Gavin to feed her some tea or broth, and then, choking and sputtering, she would sink once more into fitful slumber, her limbs seemingly weighted upon the feathery softness of the bed. By midmorning though, when sunlight brightened the cheerful room, she woke more naturally and, Mrs. Gavin noted in relief, her face had regained its color. She actually smiled as the housekeeper settled down beside her with a tray of thin gruel.

"Ugh, Mrs. . . . Gavin, isn't it? Must I eat that horrid stuff?"

The trim little gray-headed woman chuckled. "Yes, child, it will strengthen you. Although I must say, you look very much the better this fine morning."

"All thanks to you." Belinda touched the woman's hand. "I...I remember you being here with me all through the night, speaking quietly, feeding me. How can I ever repay you?"

"Hush, child. If you clean your bowl of this gruel, that will be payment enough." She slanted a look at the girl as Belinda reluctantly swallowed a mouthful of the gruel. Belinda hadn't mentioned a word about Justin's presence in the bedchamber. Did the girl remember, or had she even been aware, that he had paced the room until dawn, a dark, tense figure in the shadows, watching silently as she had swallowed a few drops of broth and sipped at the tea, stiffening in alarm every time she cried out tormentedly in her sleep? Mrs. Gavin wondered but thought it best not to speak. Let the two of them work it out. There was something quite powerful between them. Amazing, considering that in only a day or so, *she* would be arriving. What was the master up to now? Mrs. Gavin gave her head a little shake. She had long since stopped trying to predict the actions of the Gray Knight. He had never really gotten over his buccaneer ways. She only hoped he would do nothing to hurt this pretty little thing in the bed. Mrs. Gavin had taken an instant liking to the slender, flame-haired creature her master had brought home, half dead. And, she predicted, when the girl was cleaned up a bit and properly clothed, she would be quite ravishing. A fit companion to the master, who, in her admiring eyes, was the finest-looking man in the entire world.

Belinda finished the gruel with a relieved groan. "There, now please take it away! I hope that for luncheon I may have some *real* food."

Mrs. Gavin's almond-shaped brown eyes crinkled in her small, lined face. "Yes, by then, I fancy, you will be quite ready to handle something more substantial. Now"—and she cocked her head to one side appraisingly, looking somewhat like a sparrow—"do you think you feel strong enough for a bath, child? I don't like to speak of it, but your hair smells as though... well, never mind what it smells like. I bathed your face with a wet cloth when I changed those horrid clothes of yours, but you were so ill I dared not chill your flesh with water. But do you suppose—"

"Yes!" Belinda made a revolted face at her own unpleasant scent. "I must scrub the swamp out of my hair immediately or I'll go mad!" she declared. "Please, Mrs. Gavin, a bath will restore me faster than anything else."

A short time later she was relaxing in hot, soapy water, scrubbing her hair with bayberry soap. It felt wonderful to be clean and fresh once more. As she bathed she had an opportunity to study the pretty bedchamber she had been occupying. It was a warm, pleasant room, with a maple nightstand and clothes chest, a marble hearth which had been blazing all through the night, a Turkey rug of dark blue and plum and gray, and plum-painted shutters encasing the leaded glass windows. The four-poster bed was graced by a dark blue and white striped coverlet and plump pillows. It was a simple yet charming room, with none of the barren severity she had observed in her cousin's home. If this room represented the rest of the house as well, it was more akin to a gracious English manor house than a Puritan colonial home. To whom did it belong, she wondered? Justin had told her he owned an estate in Virginia. But here he was in Boston, the apparent master of this house, with a devoted housekeeper at his disposal, and free to bestow whatever guests he chose within its chambers. She knitted her brows. She had been trying all morning to push aside all thoughts of Justin. After that horrible scene between them last night, her stomach twisted into knots whenever she thought of him. Where was he now? What was he thinking, feeling? Did he even care that she had recovered? Or was he about to burst in at any moment and compel her to leave? Tears suddenly slipped down her cheeks, dropping into the bath water. Angrily, she swiped them away, and stepped out of the tub.

Wrapped in a thick white towel, she rested in the bed and sipped hot tea before dressing, trying to calm her turbulent emotions. What to wear was an additional problem. Her homespun gown was past salvaging, and she had of course brought no other clothing with her. Her problem was resolved when Mrs. Gavin reappeared bearing an armload of pale, shimmering gowns and undergarments.

"Here you are, my dear," she announced gaily, and began to hang the apparel in the wardrobe. "Now tell me, which of these lovely gowns would you care to wear this morning?"

Belinda sat up rigidly in the bed, teacup poised in midair. "Whose dresses are these?" she demanded, noting at once the delicate loveliness of the silks and muslins, the lace trimmings and satin ribbons adorning them. They looked more like the latest French fashions than anything one would find in the colonies. She hadn't seen gowns like these since she'd left England. "Where did you get them?" she cried, her throat tight.

Mrs. Gavin, usually so self-assured, hesitated. She did not meet Belinda's eyes. When she spoke at last, her words were careful and measured. "The master provided them, miss. They are indeed lovely, are they not? Now, why don't you tell me which one you fancy for this morning and I'll help you to dress."

Belinda couldn't tear her eyes from the elegant gowns which Mrs. Gavin was busily hanging away. The woman had never answered her first question. Whose gowns were these? Her mind jumped to the obvious conclusion. There must be a lady of this house, the house of which Justin was so clearly the master. His wife? Dear heavens, *his wife?*

"I don't want any of them!" She set the teacup in its saucer so violently that some of the hot liquid sloshed over onto the maple table. She jumped from the bed in agitation. Her eyes fell upon the pretty pink silk robe she had worn unquestioningly last night, and picking it up, she hurled it across the room. "Oh, how dare he?" she stormed.

"Child, child, don't upset yourself so!" Mrs. Gavin quickly laid the garments on the bed and hurried to Belinda's side. "This kind of strain really is not good for you. You'll collapse again!"

"No, I won't! I'm fully recovered! Tell me, do these clothes belong to Master Harding's wife?" She held her breath awaiting the answer, searching the housekeeper's shocked face with glittering green-gold eyes.

"No, miss! Oh, no. The master isn't married. Never has been!" Mrs. Gavin shook her head, and sighed. "Really, miss, I'm sure the master will explain everything. . . ."

Belinda did not even hear the rest of her words. She sank down on the bed, almost overcome with relief. Justin wasn't married. At least, she thought bitterly, he had not deceived her about *that.* But she still didn't know to whom these spectacular gowns belonged. She took a deep breath, trying to steady herself. So much had happened since she and Justin had spent the night in each other's arms, only two short days ago. All the happy intimacy and understanding they had shared had vanished. Last night, she recalled all too well, he had been furious with her, ordering her to leave. Maybe he didn't want her anymore. Maybe there was someone else, a mistress here in Boston.

Her throat ached. She rubbed it with trembling fingers and briefly shut her eyes. Mrs. Gavin's anxious voice broke in on her misery.

"No, no, Mrs. Gavin, I'm...fine." This time she spoke quietly, her words echoing hollowly in her own ears. "Where...where is Master Harding?"

"He had business to attend, miss." Again, that secretive, wary note in the housekeeper's voice. The same note she had used when Belinda had questioned her about the gowns. The girl nodded slowly to herself. So Justin was off, seeing to some mysterious business which was more important than learning whether she had recovered. No doubt he had not given her a thought since ordering her from his house, except perhaps to wonder how soon she would be capable of obeying. Well, she would not trouble him any longer.

She glanced dully at the delicate rainbow of gowns neatly arranged in the wardrobe. "I shall wear that one, I suppose," she said listlessly, indicating a sea-green muslin frothed with silver ribbons. Mrs. Gavin smiled as she reached for the gown.

"Tell me, Mrs. Gavin, do you know the direction of the blacksmith, Ambrose Cooke? His...his sister, Sarah, used to be my housekeeper in England, and I might like to pay her a visit."

Belinda kept her voice casual. Her temples were pounding, and tension vibrated through every nerve in her body, but she kept her eyes downcast so that the kindly little woman would not see the pain in her face. Mrs. Gavin spoke regretfully.

"I'm sorry, child, I have no idea. I'm a stranger to Boston, like you. Doubtless the master will know. You can ask him later, if you wish." She beamed at the silent girl. "Pray, may I help you dress your hair? It would look so fetching gathered back with a satin ribbon and falling down your back just so. It would show off even more of your lovely face, my dear."

"Do as you wish." Belinda blinked back her tears. She couldn't think of anything now except her bitter disappointment. All that was between her and Justin was finished. Somehow, in the past two days, her dreams had been shattered. He didn't love her, he didn't intend to share his life with her. She was ill and miserable under his roof, and what had he done? He had commanded her to leave, and then abandoned her for some business matter, proving that he cared nothing at all whether she recovered or not. Well, she would not burden him with her presence any longer. She would go to Sarah, and Sarah would take her in, hide her until the witch-hunt had died down. She stared up at Mrs. Gavin, pale as a lily. Her lips were dry as she spoke.

"I...I will dress now, Mrs. Gavin. Thank you...for all your help."

At the dismissive tone, the woman raised her eyebrows in surprise. "Don't you want me to help you, miss? I'd be glad to do it."

"No, thank you. I want a little time to myself."

The housekeeper gathered up the tea tray. "Very well, child. But I'll be back in a bit to dress your hair," she promised.

Belinda merely smiled, a strained and sickly smile. She knew that by the time Mrs. Gavin returned, she herself would be gone.

CHAPTER TWELVE

THIS TIME no one stopped her as she made her way through the twisting streets. She had tied a white silk shawl over her hair, and draped a linen kerchief about her shoulders, and she appeared a demure, quiet young woman as she wove her way northward from Oliver Street, where Justin's handsome brick house sat within a small orchard, toward the hub of the town, the marketplace. Surely there someone would be able to direct her. Many of the streets were only narrow cow paths, and she picked her way carefully. Boston was a crowded, bustling town reminiscent of many in England. It dwarfed Salem in size and appearance. Both sides of the streets were crammed with unpainted frame houses, with here and there a brick or stone building, like the one she had just left, set elegantly within spacious grounds. At Great Street, the main thoroughfare leading from the wharf, she discovered a crowded, raucous market, jammed with sailors and merchants and townspeople, all come to buy or sell their wares. She stared about in bewilderment, noting the boggy marshes to the east and the town center, meetinghouse, and commons to the south. Where might the blacksmith's residence lie? Someone jostled her arm, and she heard a man's voice apologizing formally. She turned and saw a soberly clad gentleman in a tall-crowned black felt hat, accompanied by a woman with kindly blue eyes. She smiled and spoke quickly.

"Pray, excuse me, sir and mistress, but can you tell me the direction of the blacksmith Cooke's residence? I have an errand to see to there, and do not know the way."

The man pointed gravely to the north of the market. "Milk Street," he replied. "Third house past the corner, clapboard roof."

"Thank you." Belinda saw that the woman's eyes were darting appreciatively over her delicate sea-green muslin gown, admiring the little satin ribbons and lace which added to its charm. She smiled again, rather grimly, being able to take little pleasure in this gown, which undoubtedly belonged to Justin's latest lady love. "You have been most helpful. Good day to you."

She hurried on, intent on her purpose. If Justin Harding didn't want her in his house, Sarah Cooke would. That was a certainty and, she told herself, a great comfort. Still, her heart twisted inside her as though great hands mashed and ravaged it. Something sweet and priceless had been snatched from her grasp, and she didn't quite know how or why. She only knew that it was over and that Justin would never hold her in his arms again, whispering those gentle, caressing words. The void inside her was almost unbearable. She gave a gasp of pure misery as she crossed the uneven cobbles of the street to reach Milk Street. The third house on the left, the man had said. Yes, there it was, a squat little frame cottage with a thatched roof and smoke billowing from the chimney. It didn't appear very large. She found herself hoping uneasily that it would accommodate an uninvited guest.

She tapped on the door. There was a long, unsettling

pause before the door creaked open and showed her a barrel-chested, full-bellied man of medium height and dark, grizzled hair. His large black eyes were red-rimmed as though he'd been drinking, and his ruddy cheeks were flushed. He glared at Belinda unseeingly for a moment, and then slowly, his eyes registered her presence. His fierce scowl almost made her step backward in alarm.

"What do you want?" The words were a guttural growl.

She summoned her composure with an effort, hardly reassured by his forbidding appearance. "I...I...are you the brother of Sarah Cooke?" A nod. "I wish to see her, if you please."

"Why?"

"Because I am a friend," Belinda responded, worried that he would turn her away without giving her an opportunity even to speak with Sarah. "She will know me," she put in quickly. "My name is Belinda Cady."

His face altered instantly. The scowl vanished and was replaced by open-mouthed wonder. "Belinda Cady? Heaven be praised! You are welcome, mistress. Quickly, quickly, come in!"

She found herself dragged forward into the cottage, where an unpleasant, sickly odor assailed her nostrils. The little house was modest and sparsely furnished with pine benches, plain wooden chairs, and a small, simple table set before the kitchen hearth, which was flanked by a court cupboard filled with wooden bowls and utensils. At first glance there appeared to be only two rooms, the kitchen just beyond the tiny hall, and the sitting parlor beyond. Belinda glanced about for Sarah.

"Where is your sister?" she inquired in bewilderment, for she had fully expected her former housekeeper to have bustled forward full of questions and exclamations. "Has she gone out?"

The blacksmith regarded her solemnly from beneath bushy brows. "My sister lies ill, mistress. Oh, very ill. It is good that you have come today. The physician claims she will not live to see the morrow."

His words, so stoically stated, made Belinda pale. "Sarah is... dying?" she whispered, and swayed unsteadily on her feet. One of the blacksmith's burly arms gripped her swiftly. "What... what happened to her? You must take me to her at once!"

Ambrose Cooke led the way toward two small chambers beyond the kitchen. Belinda had not even been able to see them from the entry hall. They were not much larger than the loft she had occupied in Cousin Jonathan's house. One obviously belonged to Ambrose, and the other...

"The fever came on her suddenly a week ago. She's grown weaker each day," Ambrose said, watching the shocked expression on Belinda's face as she beheld Sarah lying upon a bed in the corner of the smaller room. "She often speaks of you, mistress. It is a miracle that you have come. Maybe there is something you can do to ease her in her last hours."

Belinda darted across the planked floor of the chamber and dropped to her knees beside the bed. Dismay filled her as she gazed upon the shrunken, gray face of the once-stout housekeeper. "Sarah!" she whispered. "Oh, my poor Sarah."

Ambrose's heavy voice intruded on her pain. "I beg of you, mistress. I... I know little of sickbed nursing. She suffers so, and I... I can do nothing."

Belinda tore her gaze from Sarah's wasted countenance and stared up at his face. She realized suddenly that his red-rimmed eyes were the result of sleepless nights, and perhaps of weeping. This big bear of a man with his rough face and guttural voice was as tenderhearted as his sister. He was already grieving for her, grieving deeply. Her heart went out to him.

"Of course. If you will allow me, I will do what I can for her."

"Bless you, mistress." Ambrose wiped a tear from his ruddy cheek and turned away abruptly. "You are...very good. I cannot thank you properly."

"There is no need." Belinda turned back to Sarah, smoothing the dry, brittle straws of her hair from the shriveled brow. A lump rose in her throat. The air in this room stank of death and disease. Stale, yet sickly sweet, it merged with the smell of tallow candles and unwashed bed linens.

"Sarah," she whispered again. "It is I, Belinda. Do you hear me?"

The veined eyelids flickered. A slit of blue showed and then widened, staring for a moment until recognition dawned. Belinda thought that a gleam entered those round blue orbs as they fastened on her. Saliva dribbled from the old woman's blistered lips.

"B-Belinda. Child." Sarah gave a wheezing gasp. "Wh-what are you doing here?"

"I...came to visit you, Sarah. I have missed you so."

Belinda ignored the tears running in warm rivulets down her cheeks. She forced herself to speak cheerfully. "I'm going to make you more comfortable, dear Sarah. Ambrose will help me to lift you so that we may put on fresh bed linens, and then I will fix you some broth and some nice hot marigold tea, and bathe your face with rosemary water. Doesn't that sound pleasant?"

"Aye." Sarah moistened her cracked lips with her tongue, and her eyes closed momentarily. She spoke faintly. "And then don't forget to look in on your grandmama, child. She's been asking for you today."

Belinda gasped. Sarah's delirium unsettled her even more than her wasted appearance. "Poor Sarah," she murmured, stroking the fevered brow. "It will be all right, dearest, truly it will!"

But the words were spoken more to reassure herself than Sarah, and they failed in their ambition.

She was kept busy in the next few hours tending her patient. Forgetting that only this morning she herself had been recuperating from a state of collapse, Belinda threw herself into Sarah's nursing with vigor. After exhaustive effort, she and Ambrose succeeded in shifting Sarah to replace the damp, soiled bedclothes with fresh, crisp linens. She applied cool compresses fragrant with rosemary and gillyflowers to Sarah's burning face, spoon-fed her tea and broth, and spoke quietly and encouragingly throughout the afternoon. She was so absorbed in easing her patient's suffering that she did not even notice when Ambrose slipped away and disappeared to the entry hall of the house. She had not heard the authoritative knock on the front door which had sent the burly blacksmith lumbering from the sickroom.

It was only moments later that Justin Harding stood on the threshold of the tiny chamber. His muscular frame filled the doorway, and a frown darkened his features as he watched the wan, slender girl who knelt at the old woman's bedside. Belinda's head was close to her former housekeeper's; she was speaking in a low, soothing voice and clutching the woman's limp, blue-veined hand. She did not see him, so absorbed was she in her ministrations, but he watched her for some minutes, his expression unfathomable. Only when Belinda raised Sarah's hand to her lips and kissed it did the steely gleam in his eyes perceptibly soften. He took a breath, preparing to speak. Then, abruptly, he changed his mind. He turned in silence and left the room.

It was dusk when Sarah breathed her last. The physician had come and gone, shaking his gray head. Only Ambrose stood beside her, silent tears flowing down his cheeks as he muttered final, parting words of affection to his sister, while Belinda knelt at the bedside, head bent. They stayed that way for several minutes. At last, Belinda stroked Sarah's shriveled cheek for the last time. She rose unsteadily to her feet, gazing in anguish at the closed, cold face.

"Farewell, Sarah." Her voice broke on the words. "Go...in...peace."

Ambrose gently took her arm and led her from the room. "Come now, mistress. Nothing more can be done. You served her well today, and I'm thankful you were with her at the end." He cleared his throat and rubbed at his eyes with the coarse sleeve of his cotton shirt. "She spoke of you often, especially since she took sick, and I know it eased her heart, you being there with her. Aye, it eased her plenty, just knowing you were there."

"Thank you." Belinda sighed. "I...I am glad if what you say is true, and I only wish I might have come sooner."

A great weariness washed over her. Now that the ordeal was over, her own weakness and her sagging spirits took full possession of her. Before, she had been too busy to even think of her own health, but now she felt the desperate need to lie down and shut her eyes, to erase from her mind all the sorrow of this day. She realized that she must leave the house. Now that Sarah was gone, she could hardly remain here with Ambrose Cooke. She must find another place to stay. But where? Her foggy brain refused to think. Dizziness assailed her, and she put out a trembling hand to steady herself. "Ambrose...please. Before I leave, could I trouble you for...a bowl of soup?" she managed, hoping that nourishment would strengthen her enough to make some decisions. "If . . . if it wouldn't be too much trouble?"

A voice spoke from the sitting parlor. "My cook will be more than happy to prepare whatever you wish, Belinda. She is awaiting your pleasure at this very moment."

Belinda whirled to see Justin Harding leaning his broad shoulders against the window frame. His elegant buff-colored coat and holland shirt and his black satin knee breeches looked severely out of place in this modest setting, yet he appeared completely at ease. He moved forward with the determination that characterized him and grasped her arm, his gleaming boots thumping on the bare planked floor.

"Come along, Belinda. You look as if you need a brandy."

"What are you doing here? How did you find me?" she gasped.

His eyes locked with hers. "Mrs. Gavin told me of your inquiries about the blacksmith. It wasn't difficult to deduce the rest." Silence fell between them. Belinda wanted to wrench away from him, but weariness had turned her limbs to jelly. She merely stared at him, trying stupidly to think.

Ambrose had discreetly disappeared, and Belinda faced Justin quite alone in the low-beamed parlor. It was dusky, for the candles had not yet been kindled, and shadows played across his face, making it impossible to read his expression.

"You said you didn't want me," she said at last, her voice low and dull. "You ordered me to leave."

Justin drew her close, his strong arms encircling her in an unbreakable hold. "Don't be an imbecile, my love," he whispered in her ear. His warm lips found hers, brushing them lightly. *"Come home."*

The next thing she knew he was sweeping her toward the door. Ambrose reappeared with her shawl and kerchief. "Thank you, Mistress Cady." His deep, guttural voice held great respect. "You have done much good this day."

She took his hands. "Ambrose, is there anything you need? For Sarah, that is. For her burial or . . ." She began to dig into a pocket of her gown for the pouch which contained her meager funds, but Ambrose stopped her with a quick shake of his head. "Oh no, mistress, I can manage well enough. Besides"—he glanced toward Justin, and toward the kitchen—"Master Harding has seen to the arrangements—and more—this afternoon. Aye, he was busy while we sat by Sarah, indeed he was."

Dazed, Belinda saw the big basket of fruits and cheeses and bread and potatoes sitting atop the kitchen table. She turned to Justin in surprise, and he put his arm across her shoulders. "Everything is taken care of, Belinda. Your Sarah shall have a proper burial and resting place, never fear. And Ambrose will not go hungry tonight or for many days. Now I'm going to get you home before you faint on me again. You've exhausted yourself quite enough for one day, firebrand."

The two men nodded to each other, and Belinda next found herself out on Milk Street, where twilight shrouded the town. Justin lifted her onto the saddle of his stallion, tethered outside, then swung up behind her. She sat sidesaddle, his arms firmly on either side of her as they rode through the narrow, twisting streets of the North End. She leaned against him, closing her eyes, too tired to think. It felt so good being close to him, knowing that she was returning to the comfort and security of the house on Oliver Street. The rhythmic gait of the stallion, the everyday noises of townspeople in the street, and the familiar sounds of shops closing up and carts being dragged across cobblestones lulled her into a half-sleep. When they reached the house on Oliver Street, a man-servant hurried forward to lead the stallion. By the sil-vered light of a half moon, Justin carried her into the warmth and brightness of the house. He bore her directly to the dining parlor, a long, handsome room lit by a dozen candles in silver sconces, where even as Belinda sank into a cushioned wainscot chair, Mrs. Gavin was already bringing forth silver trays of ornately beautiful work-manship bountiful with food. A delicious aroma floated through the air, and Belinda's mouth fairly watered. The fare was sumptuous. There was fish chowder and turkey stew, kidney pie and mutton chops, hot corn bread drip-ping with honey, squash pies and blackberry tartlets. She ate ravenously, savoring every morsel, oblivious of Jus-tin, who watched her in silent amusement. When the feast was over, she leaned back in her chair and met his gaze. Smiling faintly, he drained the last of his ale tank-ard.

"Let's go into the parlor, Belinda. I must speak with you."

There was a roaring fire in the parlor, a splendid room with rich burgundy velvet draperies and oaken wainscoting, as well as comfortably upholstered sofas and chairs carved in the ornate, intricate style so well loved in the colonies. Justin pulled a chair before the fire and held it for Belinda. Then he handed her a crystal brandy goblet.

"Drink this."

Ordinarily, she would have balked at his peremp-tory tone, but shock and fatigue were making her shiver, and so she obeyed, sipping at the strong brew, which burned her throat and made her cough a little. She saw his eyebrows quirk in amusement.

"Now. You've had a decent meal and you're warm

and content, are you not? I think it is time for us to talk."

He leaned his massive shoulders against the mantelpiece, his keen gray eyes studying her. In her sea-green gown, with her burnished hair disheveled and falling loosely about her shoulders she looked irresistible. A flush of color, the result of the brandy, had entered her pale cheeks, emphasizing the high-boned planes of her delicate face. The firelight glowed in her green-gold eyes, making them appear even more brilliant than usual. Justin controlled the impulse to seize her in his arms and make love to her there and then before the fire as they had in Salem Village, to possess and savor the melting softness of her lithe body, the honey of her mouth. He wanted to inhale the sweet, womanly scent of her as he demonstrated the emotions which throbbed in his heart as well as in his loins. *But not yet,* he reminded himself, his jaw tensing with determination. *Not yet.*

"Are you indeed feeling better?" He was carefully polite.

In fact she was. Despite the dragging weariness which assaulted her and the sorrow over Sarah's loss, her head felt clearer than it had since she'd left Salem, and some of her spirit was beginning to return. Justin's very presence made her feel tingly and alive. She nodded, sending him a searching glance. "Yes, I am better. Thank you."

"Excellent." He regarded her piercingly as he spoke his next words. "Now suppose you tell me, firebrand, why *did* you leave Salem Village?"

Belinda studied his face, so cool and calm. Only yesterday he had raged at her about this very subject, without giving her an opportunity to explain. Now he was trying to be patient. Love and forgiveness welled up within her. *Oh, Justin, how I want you!* she yearned to cry, but she contained her emotions. She remembered the gown she was wearing, the multitude of elegant feminine garments conveniently at hand in this house, and wondered yet again to whom they belonged. There were too many questions that needed answering before she could again open her heart to Justin Harding. First she would answer his questions, and then he must and he would reciprocate.

She spoke quietly. "I fled Salem because I was about to be arrested. For witchcraft."

His knuckles tightened on the brandy goblet in his hand. He set it down with a thud on the mantel. "How the hell did that come about?" he demanded. A dangerous gleam entered his eyes.

She poured out the story then, of Lucy and the Gersholm child and, lastly, of Cousin Jonathan. When she finished, Justin strode to her chair, grasped her hands, and jerked her to her feet. "That damned old fool!" he rasped. "I ought to have killed him before I left Salem!"

"No, Justin, don't talk that way. It's over now. As long as no one discovers my whereabouts, I will be safe. But something must be done about Lucy. I intend to send word tomorrow to Henry March in Philadelphia and see what he can do to help her."

"Of course." Justin frowned. "I'll have one of my men set out at first light with a message." He cupped Belinda's chin in his hand. "I owe you an apology, firebrand. I should have let you explain why you broke your promise to me. But the idea that you braved the forest and the road and managed to reach Boston alone..." he shook his head in amazement. "I shudder to think what might have befallen you."

"No worse than if I had remained in Salem," she retorted. She tossed her head scornfully. "Why do men so consistently underrate women?" she demanded. "We suffer hardships every day—the hardships of servitude and obedience, and hard dreary labor as difficult as that performed by any man. There is strength in women, Justin, far greater than you can imagine."

He chuckled and tugged gently at a loose, fiery curl which dangled over her shoulder. "You have certainly proved *your* mettle, vixen," he acknowledged. "To my immense relief. If you had not made your way through the wilderness successfully, we might never have met again. And that is something I would have greatly regretted."

He bent forward and covered her mouth with his, but Belinda pushed him away. "No, Justin. Don't! I, too, have some questions that need be answered."

"Oh?" He raised an eyebrow at her maddeningly.

"Yes!" Anger gave her strength to resist the impulse to surrender to him. "To whom does this lovely gown I am wearing belong?" She brushed at the filmy skirt in agitation. "And all those others which Mrs. Gavin placed in my wardrobe this morning? *That* is something I must know before I spend one more moment in this house."

"They are yours, Belinda, naturally." He smiled, a slight lifting of the corners of his lips. "Gifts. As a token of my...affection."

"You didn't know I was coming here! These clothes were already in the house! To whom do they belong?" she cried.

His smile faded. A dark frown descended between Justin's brows. The impossible little minx questioned everything. She wanted all the answers before he was prepared to give them. *Well, we shall see about that,* he thought grimly. *I'll tell her the truth. But in my own time and way, when I'm ready to do so.*

"I think, Belinda, that we've had quite enough talk for one night. You are exhausted and tense, and you really ought to be in bed."

"Not before you tell me...Oh, what are you doing?"

Before she even realized what was happening, he had swept her into his arms as though she weighed no more than a feather and carried her toward the stairway. She struggled to escape him, but he held her easily. "Let me go!" she gasped and pounded on his chest, but to no avail. Fury consumed her, and she dreaded the possibility that Mrs. Gavin or one of the other servants would see her in this humiliating position. "Justin Harding, I'm warning you...!"

He ignored her, and bore her swiftly up the broad staircase to a bedchamber she had not seen before. It was a large, high-beamed room with a rich brass bedstead, an immense oak court cupboard on one wall, a pair of wainscot chairs with black and gold embroidered seat cushions arranged before a wide brick hearth, and a magnificent Turkey carpet on the floor. There was a silver tankard atop the court cupboard and a pewter flagon on the little trestle table in the corner, near windows draped in gold tapestries tied with black silk tassels. The room was handsome and elegant, and lit merely by the golden orange flames of the crackling fire. Belinda caught her breath as Justin deposited her rudely on the bed, and she scrambled to a crouching position, facing him. To her chagrin, he had already begun stripping off his boots, followed quickly by his buff-colored coat and holland shirt, and stood before her only in his black knee breeches. Muscles bulged on his gleaming bronzed chest and rippled in his forearms as he folded his arms and regarded her lazily. Hissing like a cat, Belinda sprang off the four-poster bed.

"No! Oh no, Justin Harding! I want nothing to do with you! Not until you've answered all my questions!"

"I'll answer your questions when it suits me!" he shot back and took a step forward. "Which will be later. Much later."

Furious, Belinda lunged toward the door, but he

blocked her path. He imprisoned her slim wrists in his hands. "Don't fight me, firebrand," he said with a laugh. "You cannot win. I wish merely to celebrate our reunion. Surely you don't object to that?"

"I most certainly do object!" She kicked at him, fighting wildly to free herself of his steely grip, but he only chuckled, his breath rustling her hair. "Let me go, Justin! I . . . I hate you!"

He dragged her backward and pushed her down upon the bed, pinning her there with his powerful body. "Liar." His voice was very soft, yet edged with steel. "I'm going to prove that you're a liar."

His mouth pressed against hers, his lips warm and hungry. She felt herself drawn into a spinning, magnetic vortex from which there was no escape. He kissed her eyelids, her brow, the tip of her nose, and returned to her mouth. As he urged her lips apart, his tongue explored the inner sweetness of her mouth, savoring and tasting her. Though his hands and body held her helpless beneath him, his kisses were gentle as summer rain. Belinda resisted with all her might, but it was futile, for she could not escape him, or the fire he was igniting within her. Slowly, alarmingly, her slender body began to tingle and to tremble. Delicious warmth spread through her, washing away all her will to resist, like sand swallowed up before the rushing tide. A soft moan escaped her lips. Justin lifted his head, grinning at her, his eyes gleaming like molten silver.

"No." Belinda whispered the word automatically, yet her own eyes, her own body betrayed her. He saw the desire shining on her flushed face, and he released her wrists, only to cup her breasts beneath the sea-green muslin. Through the thin material of the gown and the silky chemise beneath, his strong fingers caressed her nipples, and Belinda moaned again, stirring uncontrol-

lably. Deftly, he began to unfasten the delicate pearl buttons of the dress, but the small, gilt-threaded loops proved
clumsy. He swore under his breath. "Damn it anyway!"
In one swift motion, he ripped the bodice from her body.
He removed the gown, and his lips sank to the snowy
mounds of her breasts, tickling her hardened nipples with
his tongue. Belinda gasped in frenzied pleasure and began to tug at his breeches. Soon they were both naked,
lying together upon the four-poster bed as the fire cast
golden shadows across their bodies.

"Belinda." Justin's lips were warm on her throat.

Her fingers were circling the rippling muscles of his
back. She spread her legs to welcome him as he moved
his hips atop hers. Her fingers slid downward to caress
his maleness. "Yes, Justin?" she breathed, aching with
desire, her hands and arching body urging him to penetrate her. His next words made her cry out in torment.

"Shall I leave now, firebrand?" he whispered, licking
her ear. "I wouldn't want to force you..."

"Monster." She moaned, dragging his head down
to her lips almost savagely. "Don't...you...dare...."

"But are you sure this is what you want?" He rubbed
his powerful thighs against her legs in a sensuous, teasing
movement while he played with the taut nipples of her
breasts. "After all, you said you hated me, didn't you,
my darling?"

"Justin, please." He chuckled and began to enter
her, slowly, teasingly, pulling back as he sensed her in-
creasing fervor, then advancing purposefully to tantalize
her even more. His hands were warm and caressing on
her breasts, sending her senses reeling in ecstasy.

"Well, firebrand?"

She clutched him to her desperately, her fingers digging into the broad muscles of his back. "Yes, I want you!

I love you! Justin, please!" she cried, and her heart was pounding as wildly as her pulses.

Justin smiled, then kissed her very tenderly. Suddenly, he entered her completely, plunging in with surging ferocity, releasing all the coiled strength and energy he had so carefully controlled.

Belinda arched her back and opened herself to receive him. She wrapped her legs tightly about his long, lean frame as he thrust deep within her. Joy surged through her as he seemed to penetrate her very core. "Justin, Justin, I love you," she cried softly over and over as sensation and emotion blended in a splendid union which left her quivering and afire. Passion exploded in both of them. Belinda had never known such blazing, tumultuous rapture. She ran her hands over the length of his magnificent body, as her hips thrashed in frenzy, savoring the touch and smell and sight of him. "Oh, Justin," she gasped, breathless from the dazzling, delightful sensations which held her in their grip. "Don't ever leave me!"

"Never!" His voice was husky in her ear, his increasingly powerful thrusts driving her to shivering heights of ecstasy. "Never, my wild, beautiful love!"

It was a long time before their passion was spent. At last, Justin rolled aside and held her close against him, trying to still her trembling within the circle of his arms. He gently kissed her damp temple and the flaming ringlets which touched her shoulder.

"I missed you, Belinda," he growled. "Even the short time we were apart, I kept thinking of you—wanting you. And now you're here in the flesh, and ten times more beautiful, more desirable even than my memories."

"I missed you, too." She leaned over and kissed his flat, taut belly. Her mouth traveled slowly upward across his chest until it rested against his lips. "I longed for you so. Justin," she barely breathed the words, brushing her satiny cheek against his rugged one. "I do love you so."

He said nothing for a moment. Belinda lifted her head to stare into his eyes. Fear stabbed at her. Why didn't he say it? Why did he hesitate? Could she be mistaken about his feelings toward her? Pain and doubt shook her, and some of it must have shown in her face, for Justin quickly took her head between his hands and kissed her hard on the mouth.

"I love you, Belinda." He spoke with compelling purpose. "Heaven help me, I love you. More than you can know. Don't ever doubt that, my love. No matter what happens."

"I won't," she pledged. Her smile was radiant, and she felt like dancing with joy. Her eyes glowed brighter than the fire as she gazed up at him. "Just hearing you say it is enough for me." Her lips touched his shoulder, tasting the saltiness of his flesh. "Isn't it strange, Justin? I love you, and yet I know so little about you. I don't even know why you're here, in this house, when you said you live in Virginia." She tilted her head up at him, her red-gold hair cascading over her shoulders and half hiding her breasts. "Why *are* you in Boston?"

To her surprise, he frowned. A set, closed look descended on his features, and Belinda feared for a moment that he would refuse to answer this question, too. But a second later he did speak, in a cool, casual tone. "I'm meeting a ship. Someone is arriving from England any day now. I've rented this house for a brief time from an old friend. His name, my inquisitive firebrand, is Edward Brough." He grinned at her. "Edward knew me in my hired pirate days. He used to be my second mate. Then he came to Boston. Started shipbuilding and soon made himself a fortune, since Boston has become a port of such vital importance. We've kept in touch over the years, and when I sent word that I needed a comfortable place for myself and my guest during our stay in Boston, he offered me this house. He's in the Caribbean now, building himself a fine mansion on Barbados for a winter retreat. But he most kindly allowed me the use of his house so that I and my expected guest would be comfortable. For a small fee, of course." He laughed. "Edward was always a sly rogue. Never lets friendship interfere with monetary interests. That's why he made such an admirable pirate. Ruthlessness always triumphs, my love."

Belinda smiled at him. "Is that why you made a fine pirate, too, my Gray Knight? Are you ruthless as well?"

"Completely." He grasped her in his arms and kissed her roughly. Then he laughed again. "You ought to have realized that by now."

"Tell me of your visitor," she retorted, squirming out of his embrace and regarding him with thoughtful eyes. "You are certainly a generous host, going to all this trouble for the expected guest. It must be someone quite special."

Justin shot her an amused look. "Not as special as you," he replied and yanked her down once more on the bed. "Enough conversation for one night, Belinda. My guest will arrive all too soon and provide us with a great deal of conversation, I assure you." He began to caress her breasts with his warm, strong hands, driving all rational thoughts from her mind. "In the meantime, my darling, I have better ways to pass the hours."

Belinda was only too agreeable. Secure in his arms, enflamed by his kisses and the subtle teasings of his caress, she was only too glad to forget her doubts and questions, to forget the horrors of Salem, the forest terror, and her grief over Sarah's death. Tonight she was safe in Justin's bed, warmed by his love, sheltered from the world. Love and pleasure sizzled through her, blotting out all else. Tomorrow she would deal with the world. Tomorrow she would think, worry, wonder. But tonight... She sighed rapturously as she gazed into Justin's gleaming gray eyes. Tonight was for the two of them. Only the two of them.

The fire in the huge hearth gradually died down to flickering embers. But another kind of fire kept Belinda warm and glowing all through the chill New England night.

CHAPTER THIRTEEN

BELINDA CAME SLOWLY AWAKE, her lips still curved in a dreamy smile. Eyes closed, she stretched and reached out a hand to touch Justin, but he was not there. Her eyes flew open and she jerked upright in the bed.

Justin stood at the foot of the four-poster, a burgundy-colored dressing robe encasing his magnificent physique. He was lifting a china coffee cup to his lips, grinning at her.

"Sleep well, my love?" he inquired.

"Beautifully," she assured him, dimpling. "And you?"

"Oh yes. Rarely have I slept better. Though my bed partner was so insatiable, I slept rather less than usual."

She giggled. "Some wicked maiden, no doubt. You ought to beware of such breed of women. They are quite shameless."

"So I hear tell." Justin strolled to the oak court cupboard, which bore a square silver tray laden with two china cups, sugar bowl and creamer, and a gleaming silver coffeepot. "Would you care for some coffee, Belinda? Mrs. Gavin brought up a tray."

"Oh yes. Please." She yawned, delicately patting her

mouth. "Mrs. Gavin is certainly a treasure, isn't she? Has she been in your employ long?"

"Nearly six years. Her husband was one of my crew members and now keeps my books at the plantation. They're both indispensable to me."

"You seem to keep quite friendly with your former crew," she observed, pulling the sheets up to her chin, for it was cool in the bedchamber this early spring morning. "Do many of them still work for you in Virginia?"

"Most. We're an unusual bunch, I suppose. Once one has lived such an unorthodox life, it is difficult to readjust to the rest of society. We all work well as a team and understand one another, so it is convenient to have my former crew mates work for me. Also," he said, bringing her a cup of steaming black liquid, "they are all loyal to me. Loyalty is a most valuable commodity. It deserves to be rewarded."

He sat down on the bed as he placed the cup in her outstretched hand. Their eyes met, and they smiled at each other.

"Good morning, my love." Justin's voice was husky, filled with tenderness, and Belinda's heart skittered madly.

"Good morning." Her eyes held an unmistakable invitation. Justin flipped back the sheets and raked her naked form with glinting eyes. Then the coffee was left to grow cold as they slid together beneath the sheets. Belinda snaked herself across his chest, kissing him with insistent, languorous lips. Justin's hands were gentle as they explored and caressed every inch of her body. This morning their lovemaking was leisurely and tender. Belinda was dimly aware of the fresh sea breeze blowing into the room, of the gold tapestries at the window swaying with a soft, rustling sound. Even the bedsheets fluttered about them. She felt very peaceful, very safe, as Justin's handsome face, so strong and real in the light of day, bent over her. There was a lightness about the morning, a sense of relaxation and pleasure, which seeped through her body like warm, lapping waves. She ran her fingers over the rippling muscles of Justin's back, murmuring softly. He licked her breasts, arousing her nipples to taut peaks with his tongue. They savored each other, teasing, tasting, letting their feelings flow and swirl, until at length Belinda slid gracefully atop his powerful frame and smiled into his eyes. She felt the cool breeze on her naked back. His hands were warm on her breasts. The morning sun sent soft golden streams of light splashing into the room, illuminiating the couple twined in intimate harmony. Their bodies merged into one, arching, stretching, joining them together for one splendid moment of eternity.

It was a delightful way to awaken, Belinda decided. In fact, she wouldn't have minded their spending the entire day in bed, wrapped in each other's arms, except that presently there came a knock on the door, which interrupted their mood of pleasurable contentment.

"Damn!" Justin frowned and kissed her on the neck. "Who's there?"

"Simon," came the curt reply. "I've got tidings." Justin immediately sprang from the bed and slipped into his dressing robe, leaving Belinda to huddle beneath the sheets in embarrassment.

She listened intently when he opened the door a crack and spoke in a low voice to the man on the other side, but Belinda was unable to see or hear anything. When he finally shut the door and turned back to her, she could see that his gentle mood had been shattered. Apparently, the "tidings" had not been good.

"What is it?" she asked, brushing her tumbling locks from her eyes. "Is there some trouble?"

Justin seemed distracted as he answered her. "No, nothing that need concern you." He strode to the window and stared out into the street. His expression was cold, withdrawn. She felt left out of whatever problem occupied his mind. Her own lovely mood faded, and a chill pierced her flesh. She slid from the bed, wrapped only in a sheet, and stood there uncertainly. After a moment, Justin turned from the window.

"You'd best return to your room to dress," he said curtly. "Mrs. Gavin will draw you a bath. I'll meet you in the dining parlor shortly."

"Justin." She went to his side and touched his arm. He did not respond to her touch. "What is it? What's wrong? Please, can't you share this with me—whatever it is?"

He stared into her face. The frown still darkened his brow. He reached out a hand and stroked a tendril of her flaming hair, then leaned down and kissed her quickly on the mouth.

"Go, Belinda," he said quietly. "We'll talk later."

She saw that he was still disturbed and that he had no intention of discussing the problem with her. She turned and left, trying not to feel hurt. Last night she had thought only happiness lay ahead, but now doubt and uncertainty had returned. Justin was a stranger to her once again, and she felt bereft and lonely.

Mrs. Gavin was already in her bedchamber when she reached it. The housekeeper was laying out her clothes upon the bed, which had obviously not been slept in last night. The bath water had already been poured into the big tub, and steam rose from it invitingly. Belinda was assaulted by sudden embarrassment as the housekeeper turned and saw her clad only in a bedsheet. "Th-thank you, Mrs. Gavin. That will be all," she stammered, aware that she was blushing from head to toe. To her amazement, the pert little woman merely smiled at her in her usual warm manner.

"Certainly, miss. And may I say that I'm delighted

you've come back? I was quite worried about you yesterday, indeed I was. Imagine you running off that way, scarcely out of the sickbed. I never saw such a thing, never in all my days."

"I . . . I'm fine, now," Belinda managed to murmur. "There were no ill effects."

"Thank goodness. Now you take your time dressing, miss, because I'll keep breakfast good and warm for you. No need to worry."

"Thank you. You're most . . . kind." Belinda stared in wonder as the door closed behind the housekeeper. What an unusual household this was. A young woman spends the night in the master's bedroom and is treated as royalty. No sneers of disapproval, frowns, or sly, mocking stares. As if such occurrences were normal and expected and nothing at all out of the ordinary.

She discarded the bedsheet and stepped into the tub, her muscles suddenly tense. An unsettling thought rippled through her mind, like a pebble tossed into a placid stream. What if this was *not* out of the ordinary? What if "Master Harding" entertained women in his bed every night? That would explain the housekeeper's nonchalance. It would explain why the woman had not even raised her eyebrows when Belinda, dressed only in a sheet, had returned from the master's bedchamber in the middle of the morning, after having obviously spent a long and busy night. Her stomach lurched suddenly, and she felt ill. Was she merely Justin's newest toy? Was his ardor and the love she thought she saw in his eyes only the passing infatuation of a man who used and discarded women as a regular pastime? All of the happiness and trust she had felt only an hour ago vanished as uncertainty rushed back. The sense of mystery and danger which surrounded Justin had intrigued her from the first, but now it also tormented her. She knew she had to get some answers from him today, this morning. She had to penetrate his wall of secrecy, for if she didn't, she would go mad. Once and for all, she had to *know*.

She descended the staircase a short time later, filled with determination. She was attired in a pale violet gown of rustling organdy, with satin ribbons tied about her slender waist and intricately entwined through the full, flowing sleeves of the gown, which fell to her wrists in delicate, lacy ruffles. Her flame-colored hair was dressed in soft, loose curls which cascaded down her back. A violet ribbon to match her dress was threaded through her thick tresses. On her feet were white satin slippers. She looked the picture of delicate femininity, but her thoughts were not soft and pleasant, as might have been expected within the lovely head of such a creature. She was tense and nervous, yet filled with a sense of purpose which made her hold her head high as she entered the dining parlor. She immediately saw Justin seated at the head of the table. He rose when she entered and gave her a long, appraising look. His smile was one of great satisfaction.

"You are bewitching, Belinda." His eyes lingered on the soft curves of her figure, so alluringly revealed by the violet gown. They slowly returned to her lovely face, and he spoke again. "This is how you deserve to be dressed, my pet. Like a princess. Not as the scullery maid your cousin would have you be."

Belinda said nothing. She studied him as closely as he had surveyed her. She could read nothing but admiration in his cool gray eyes. Yet he was tense. She sensed it beneath the easy nonchalance of his stance. There was something different about him, a retreat from the intimacy they had shared this morning and all through the long, glorious night. He was holding himself aloof from her, despite his compliments. There was an invisible gulf between them which Justin did not want her to breach.

She slipped into a chair and stared at her plate. The
idea of food repulsed her. Justin, too, sat down again,
his eyes riveted upon her.

"What's the matter now, Belinda?" he asked, and
she heard the impatience in his voice.

She met his gaze, speaking in a low tone. "I'm very
confused."

"Oh?"

"What is there, really, between you and me?"

"Don't you know, my love? After last night? This
morning?"

"No, I do not."

"Come, Belinda." There was a sharp note in his voice
which stung her. "Don't be a coy, stupid woman. I'm in
no humor for games this morning."

"This is no game, Justin. I am in earnest."

His gray eyes narrowed, and a shiver ran suddenly
up her spine. She had a mental image of him then as
captain of his ship, barking battle commands, fighting
his enemies with the ruthlessness and single-minded determination to match the most fearsome pirate. He was
a dangerous man and would make a deadly foe. But was
he her foe? She felt now as though he were sizing her
up, estimating her mental and emotional strength to
withstand him. It was a lonely, terrifying feeling. She no
longer wanted to battle Justin Harding. She wanted to
stand beside him, to be loved by him, to share his life
and his trust and his dreams and to let him share hers.
But was that possible? Was this black-haired man with
the arrogant manner and hard, penetrating gray eyes
truly capable of love, or was it all merely an act, a charade
he employed with all women until he no longer desired
them and flung them aside for another? Under his steely
gaze, she felt a wave of fear, but she kept her eyes glued
to his and bit her lips against the tremor threatening to

expose her emotions. Rigid as a statue, she waited for his reply.

"I love you." His voice was brusque and cold, in total contrast to the words he spoke. She laughed hollowly at the contrast.

"Do you?" she mocked. "How odd. How very odd that you claim to love me, but you have yet to answer any of my questions. To whom do these lovely, *female* clothes belong? Why is it that Mrs. Gavin thinks nothing of a woman spending the night in your bed? Why did you send me from your room the moment that horrid Simon came to the door with his mysterious 'tidings'?" To her frustration, her voice quavered and broke on the last words, but she regained control after one gasping second. "And why did you refuse to bring me to Boston with you when you left Salem? Why, why, why? There are so many things I don't understand, so many things you refuse to discuss! I have a right to know!" she cried and angrily brushed tears from her cheeks. "If you truly love me, I have a right to know the answer to these questions and more!"

Justin shoved back his chair with a violence that sent it toppling. He advanced around the table and grasped Belinda's arm, yanking her from her seat. With one hand in her hair so that her head was bent backward, he clamped her in an iron embrace and stared down into her startled face. "Damn you, Belinda Cady! Damn you! If you still doubt me after last night—after this morning—then perhaps there really *is* no love between us!" His lips seized hers, but there was nothing gentle or loving about that kiss. It was filled with anger and brutality, and she whimpered beneath the ruthless onslaught of his mouth. Finally, he released her, her eyes narrow. There was a distinctly unpleasant edge to his voice. "I forgave you for the first promise you broke to me, firebrand. But last night you swore to something else, and already you've betrayed that trust. If you really think me the scoundrel your comments insinuate, I won't discourage you. In fact"—he smiled caustically—"I shall let you discover for yourself exactly what kind of rogue I really am." He pushed her back down into her chair, laughing roughly. "Have a pleasant day, my pet. Unless I am much mistaken, you will find it most enlightening."

With these cryptic words, he turned on his heel and strode from the dining parlor.

Belinda sat rigidly in her chair. She was too devastated even to weep. Agony seared her insides, spreading with fiery intensity throughout her body. Disbelief that Justin could treat her so cruelly and callously overrode even anger, and she remained motionless and sick for nearly half an hour, her reeling mind replaying over and over the terrible scene of wrath just enacted. A small voice inside her whispered, *You've lost him,* but another voice mocked her: *No, you foolish wretch, you never even had him.* Shock held her captive, until finally the tremors started, deep in her core and rippling outward until her entire body shook like a stone wall about to crumble. With the shaking came the rage, venomous, boiling, mindless rage. She snatched the china plate before her and hurled it toward the head of the table where Justin had sat, finding momentary release in the crash of splintering china. Mrs. Gavin came rushing into the room from the direction of the entry hall.

"Goodness, what in the name of—"

Belinda shoved past her, too enraged to apologize or explain. She hurried toward the staircase and up to her room, where she pounded her fist against the mantel. *I hate you, Justin Harding!* the little voice shrieked over and over until her temples throbbed and tears flooded down her face. *I wish Cousin Jonathan had arrested you and whipped you before the tail of a cart!* She gave a scream of

pure rage and whirled a moment later to see Mrs. Gavin
burst into the room, pale and upset.

"Miss, miss, please, what is this all about? Try to
calm yourself! You'll make yourself ill—"

"Oh, no, I won't! I wouldn't let that bastard have
the satisfaction of making me ill! I'd die first!" she
screamed, losing all sense of logic in her overwhelming
wrath. She once again charged past Mrs. Gavin, hurtling
down the stairs like a cannonball and out the front door.
She had no clear idea where she was headed, but merely
ran blindly, following the urge to escape. She ran straight
into a short, wiry man with thick reddish-brown hair,
whose arm shot out and gripped her as she fled headlong
across the courtyard.

"Let me go!" she cried, striking out at him in her
rage. "Get out of my way!"

"Wait just a minute, mistress!" the wiry man exclaimed. He stared at her in amazement and dropped his
voice. "Mistress Cady, where do you think you're going?"

"How do you know my name?" she demanded,
shaking him off. "And who are you?"

"Simon Foster." A hairy, gnarled hand swept off his
brown felt cap. "Pleased to meet you, ma'am. Justin asked
me to keep an eye on you. After the way you ran off
yesterday, he wasn't about to take any chances." He
squinted at her. "Now just where do you think you're
running? Don't you know, mistress, that it's dangerous
to go wandering around Boston—you being wanted by
the authorities and all?" He nodded toward a stern-look-
ing gentleman in a scarlet-coat and heavy buckled shoes
who was making his way down Oliver Street at the moment and who was staring intently at the couple in the
courtyard. "You don't want to be drawing attention to
yourself—especially with that red hair. Someone will
identify you for certain if you show yourself about the
town."

"I don't care!" she said crossly, but she lowered her voice, watching uneasily until the scarlet-coated man had disappeared from view. "I won't be a prisoner in this house. Especially if Justin Harding is to be my warden. I would sooner hang on Gallows Hill than allow that man to keep me as a pet!"

Simon shot her a twinkling glance. "Now, mistress, 'taint as bad as all that, I'm certain. Come along now to the stables, and we'll talk a bit. You can tell me what's troubling you, for I'm a good listener, and my own sister used to run to me whenever she was in poor spirits to spill out her troubles. I'll do my best to help, you can count on that, you know."

She followed him, not quite certain why. Something about his plain, simple talk and open face inspired trust. Now that her head was cooler, she realized the folly of showing herself openly on the street. As Simon had pointed out, her red hair was an unusual feature, one which would help to identify her as the escaped witch from Salem Village. She had to exercise some caution, or she would indeed find herself on Gallows Hill, and despite her defiant words, she *was* frightened of that possibility. So she allowed herself to be led toward the stable, a small, square frame structure set beyond the house, beside an ancient, weathered oak. Inside it was cool and dark. Several horses were inside their stalls, including, she noted, Justin's stallion. Simon followed her glance.

"The master took the carriage," he said rather hastily in response to her unasked question. "He had to meet someone at the harbor this morning."

"Oh, yes, the mysterious guest," Belinda scowled. Suddenly, she glanced at the wiry, rough, gravel-voiced man before her. Something he had said moments before had just penetrated her thoughts. *My own sister used to run to me whenever she was in poor spirits to spill out her troubles.* Simon's sister. Elizabeth Foster, the girl who had been hanged the very day Belinda arrived in Salem.

"I...I'm sorry about your sister," she said suddenly, turning to him with huge, haunted eyes. "I...I saw what they did to her....It was horrible, and I want you to know...you have my sympathies."

"Aye, Justin told me what you said about it. I thank you for your kind feelings." Simon's pleasant face tautened into one of fury. "Those damned bastards. Hanging Eliza for a witch! Why, never was there a sweeter, gentler girl! I tell you, mistress, if I had been there to know what was going on, I would have burned down the whole village to stop them from hurting her!"

"I know you would have." She spoke quietly. "It wasn't your fault, Simon. You couldn't have known what was going to happen."

"Madness, that's what it is!" he muttered, and his fists clenched until the knuckles whitened. "All the more reason, mistress, why you ought to be careful. They'd do the same to you if they caught you, and that would be a sad day for us all, especially for Justin."

"Justin!" she exclaimed scornfully, her hands on her hips. "He wouldn't care a shilling if they hanged me or burned me at the stake! If you had only heard what he said to me this morning!"

Simon chuckled. "Aye, he can be fierce all right, that's Justin for you. But he can be kind, too, when he's of a mind to be, and generous and fair-minded. You won't find a better man to have beside you in a pickle."

She watched as Simon sat down on a three-legged stool and began to repair the stitching on a worn-looking harness. She took a step nearer and followed suit, perching atop an identical stool, her violet skirts draped gracefully about her knees. "You seem to know a great deal about him," she ventured.

"Aye, mistress." He grinned crookedly. "I've known Justin Harding all my life. We were boys together in Old

England. I've got a year or two on him, but that never mattered. He was always big and strong enough, and smart enough, to get on with the older lads. Never met a fellow who could beat him in a match, that's for certain.

"Tell me about it. Please." Belinda felt strangely fascinated by the idea of Justin as a young boy. Despite her anger with him, and her fervent desire to revenge herself on him for his callous treatment, she couldn't help wanting to know more about him. After all, if he wouldn't tell her anything himself, she would have to look elsewhere for answers. Simon Foster seemed the ideal source. She waited, holding her breath to see if he would respond to her plea, and she smiled in relief when he began to talk freely and openly.

"Oh, he was a rough and tumble boy, for all his wealth and position. My father was the silversmith in the town, far beneath the Hardings, yet Justin and I became fast friends from the time we learned how to toddle. He never showed off his wealth, mistress, if you know what I mean. No, he was never that way at all. We fell into plenty of scrapes, the two of us, bad ones too, but we always managed to find a way out." He chuckled. "Yes, indeed, we had our share of lickings, but we got off light considering some of the pranks we pulled on our elders!"

Belinda's lips curved upward in a smile. For a moment, she envied the two boys who had frolicked so freely in the peaceful English countryside. Her own spirit had driven her to the same sorts of games and pranks they had no doubt engaged in, yet what was deemed boyish high spirits in them had been roundly condemned in her. While their behavior had probably been amusedly tolerated, if sometimes punished, her own escapades had brought real censure down upon her. Females were not allowed such indulgences. They were meant to sit and sew stitches, to recite prayers, to perform upon the pianoforte. And Belinda knew that while she had probably found it necessary to be even more cunning and clever than Justin and Simon to escape punishment for some of her tricks, no one would ever believe her or credit her for that. "Go on," she urged Simon, eager to know more about Justin's past.

"Well, as boys do, we grew up," he laughed and scratched his stubbly brown beard. "I learned the silversmithing trade from my father, and Justin learned how to be a young gentleman. Quite right and proper he grew, ready to assume his place in the family. He was all set to marry that chit and then—" He choked suddenly, coughed, and wiped the back of his hand against his mouth. His faded blue eyes shone suddenly brighter. "Never mind about that part," he said hastily. "I'd be obliged if you'd forget I said it. Justin would—"

"Never mind Justin," Belinda interrupted. "Tell me more about it. Justin was engaged to be married?" For some reason, jealousy sparked within her, and her eyes smoldered at the thought of this disturbing news, but Simon was adamant, refusing to continue.

"No, mistress, I won't talk of that. If you want to hear more of the story, you must hear what I choose to tell."

"But Simon—"

"No." He set his lips together firmly.

For a moment they glared at each other. Belinda felt anger rising within her. Then, abruptly, a smile tugged at her unwilling lips. "Oh, very well. Do go on. I won't badger you if you're going to be so bull-headed."

He nodded in satisfaction. "Aye, bull-headed. Justin tells me so all the time."

"He should certainly recognize the symptoms," she muttered, and Simon, catching her meaning, grinned.

"Well, Justin ran into certain...uh, family problems, mistress. He abandoned the rich future awaiting him in England, and instead used all of his inheritance from his grandfather to buy himself a ship. The *Gray Lady*, he called her, and he became the *Gray Knight*. Aye, mistress, those were glorious days. Wild and free we were, sailing the mighty seas. Justin hired our services out to merchant vessels seeking protection from pirates. We fought their battles for them, you might say. And many battles they were. Several times we came in danger of losing our ship, but just like in the old days when we were green boys in England, Justin always managed to get us out of our scrapes."

"So you went with him when he left England," Belinda said softly. "You were a part of his fighting ship. Why?" She leaned forward, fascinated. Her eyes glimmered in the duskiness of the stable.

"He was my friend." Simon shrugged. "He needed me. He needed someone who cared, much as he might not have liked to admit it. He had grown reckless, mistress, from being hurt. He fought like the Devil, and drank like him, too. Bent on self-destruction he was, for a long, long time. Aye, mistress, we saw some dark days. He was half-mad for a while, savage and cold and heartless as any buccaneer you ever imagined. But he came about. That's something you can always remember about Justin Harding. He always comes about in the end."

There was a brief silence. Belinda stared at the white toes of her slippers. Her hands were clasped in her lap. "There is so much I don't know or understand about him," she whispered, and her voice was filled with the agony of doubt. "Oh, Simon, what am I going to do?"

Suddenly, there was a commotion in the courtyard. Gravel crunched, and harnesses jingled. She heard Justin's voice shout an order.

Belinda jumped off her stool and started toward the door. Simon grabbed her arm. "Wait, mistress—"

"What is it?" She glanced at him in surprise. "Justin has returned with the carriage, I gather. And with his guest." She squared her shoulders. "Much as I don't want to see your abominable friend, I do wish to meet the mysterious visitor. So please release my arm. I'm going to—"

"No, don't." Simon's blue eyes blinked rapidly at her. "Don't go yet. I've more stories to tell you... fascinating stories..."

"Simon, what is this? Why don't you want me to leave?" she demanded in amazement.

He chewed on his lip, saying nothing.

"Well?"

"I... I just think you ought to wait and talk to Justin privately. Later. There's... things afoot which I know he'll be wanting to explain to you, mistress. If you'll just give him a chance."

"Really?" She lifted her chin. "I doubt that Justin Harding intends to explain anything to me. He has certainly had enough opportunities to do so, if that is what he wanted. No." She removed Simon's hand from her arm. "If you'll excuse me, I will return to the house and meet Simon's guest. Perhaps *he* will be an interesting, kind gentleman whose company and manners I'll enjoy. If anything, by comparison to Justin's, they will be admirable."

With these words she left Simon, who watched in chagrin as she opened the stable door and stepped out into sunlight. A servant was already leading the horse and carriage toward the stable, and Belinda stepped aside, noting that Justin and his guest had already gone into the house. She walked forward, shaking the stable dust from her skirts. They had become somewhat soiled, she observed in dismay, and there was a wisp of straw in her hair, which she plucked. Then she gathered her skirts in her hand and entered the house, heading immediately toward the parlor.

She saw Justin first as she sailed through the door.

He was standing beside an elegant wainscot chair, impeccably attired in plum-colored jacket, white holland shirt and cravat, and dove-gray breeches above gleaming black boots. He held a brandy glass in his hand. His eyes narrowed when he saw Belinda in the doorway. With an airy toss of her head, she ignored his gaze and bestowed it instead on the other person in the room, who sat just beyond Justin, near the small, cheerful fire. Belinda's eyes, sparkling so defiantly, lost some of their radiance as they perceived the mysterious guest. She was a woman. A most beautiful woman, with golden hair and breathtaking violet eyes, clad in soft, peach-colored silk taffeta.

Belinda stared in shocked silence for a moment. The woman met her gaze with slightly raised brows, taking in the flame-haired girl's rather disheveled appearance. Her nose wrinkled somewhat disdainfully, but she didn't speak. It was Belinda who spoke, her voice choked and hoarse.

"Who . . . who are you?" she demanded.

Justin smiled slightly and moved forward to take her arm. "Do come in, Belinda," he invited in his cool, nonchalant way. "We were just talking about you. I would like you to meet Mistress Gwendolyn Harding—my fiancée."

CHAPTER FOURTEEN

"YOUR...*fiancée?*"

Belinda's body chilled as if she had just been dunked into Massachusetts Bay. She stared at Justin in disbelief.

He nodded, his eyes like gray marble. "Allow me to present you. Gwendolyn, this is the child I told you about—Mistress Belinda Cady of Salem Village."

The golden-haired vision in the wainscot chair took her time summing up the girl before her. One gloved hand patted her impeccable coiffure. She spoke in a cool, silken voice subtly tinged with disdain. "How do you do, Mistress Cady?"

Belinda merely stared.

"Justin has been telling me of the bizarre circumstances which force you to seek shelter in this house. It is terribly kind of him to exert himself on your behalf. But then, Justin always did adopt the strays and misfits—you should have seen the mongrel dogs that forever followed at his heels when he was a boy."

Belinda's narrowed eyes glowed like emeralds as she met the hard stare of Gwendolyn Harding. She spoke in a low taut voice.

"Are you calling me a mongrel dog, Mistress Harding? How very uncivil of you."

"Of course not!" Gwendolyn laughed. "My dear, don't be a goose! I was referring to the fact that you are an outcast, a fugitive, akin in a way to the strays Justin always pitied." She sent a dazzling smile up at the man at her side, whose face was unreadable. "I am delighted to find that my dear Justin hasn't changed after all these years. The man I am going to marry is as kind and generous as I remembered."

Her words struck Belinda like dagger blows. Belinda, too, turned to stare at Justin Harding, but there was nothing dazzling about her expression. She looked as ill as a woman who has just been dealt a severe blow to the stomach, and Justin found it necessary to refrain himself from scooping her into his arms and laying her down upon the sofa to recuperate.

For a moment he wondered why he had chosen to play this cruel game with her. He could have explained the true situation in a far less painful way. Instead, he had allowed the truth to come out in the most brutal manner possible, leaving her to believe...what? Only what she had already accused him of. That she meant nothing to him, that his love for her was only pretense, that she was merely a temporary amusement before he turned his attention to someone else. He remembered the way she had promised to believe in his love only last night, and yet this morning she had questioned it again, hammering away with suspicions and doubts. However reasonable such doubts might be, they had infuriated him, and wounded him, too. Belinda was the first woman he had spoken words of love to in ten years, and though he had done everything he could to show her how much she meant to him, she still questioned him. Her doubt made him want to hurt her, to shock her, to prove her correct in her own suspicious eyes. And he had done so, cruelly. His damnable temper had led him to play this rogue's game with both Belinda and Gwendolyn. But then, he thought, his features tightening, why not? Why not amuse himself at their expense? Belinda had doubted him, mistrusted him. And Gwendolyn... His eyes narrowed as he shifted his gaze to her exquisite, patrician face. Yes, he had a score to settle with Gwendolyn, too. And despite what he had believed all these years, it was not one of love.

"Belinda, you look as if you need a glass of wine. Or would you prefer mead?" He spoke with easy nonchalance as he took the stricken girl's elbow and led her toward the sofa facing Gwendolyn's chair. "I can't imagine what has put you in such a state. Are you feeling faint?"

"Faint? Am I feeling faint?" Belinda shook off his arm, recovering herself in a burst of fury which superseded shock. "No, I'm fine, Justin. Perfectly fine. In fact," she spat, "I feel as if I've just awakened from a hideous dream. It is wonderful to know reality once again—to see the truth!" She turned to Gwendolyn with a brilliant smile. "May I congratulate you on your engagement? And offer all my best wishes? I'm certain you and Justin will find the happiness you each deserve!" She laughed, a shrill and hollow sound. "However, I do have one question. Did Justin indeed introduce you as Mistress Gwendolyn Harding?" Her stare was penetrating as she glanced from one to the other of them. "How can it be that this lady who is not yet your wife bears the same name? Perhaps it is stupid on my part, but I am mystified by how such a thing can come about."

Gwendolyn, to Belinda's surprise, colored faintly, and her gloved hands stiffened in her lap. It was Justin who spoke, with the same cool self-command he always possessed, yet she detected the underlying tension in his voice and in the drawing together of his brows. "That is something you need not be concerned with, Belinda. Indeed, it is quite impertinent of you to inquire. Let us suffice to say that Gwendolyn and I are related, and that is why we bear the same name. The details"—and here his icy gaze touched Gwendolyn briefly—"are no longer important."

"Indeed, no," she said in a voice that would have melted butter. "All that matters is that we shall soon be wed, and it is that thought alone that kept me from going mad all those wretched weeks at sea, dearest Justin!"

Belinda had had enough. She started toward the door, but as she reached it, it burst open and a tall, lanky young man crashed directly into her. He grabbed her shoulders to keep her from falling and gave a little exclamation of dismay.

"Oh, I do beg your pardon. I—"

"Let me by, damn you!" Belinda shoved past him. He stared after her a moment as she flew up the staircase and then turned to Justin and Gwendolyn with an eager smile. "Justin, who was that adorable creature? I demand an introduction."

His sister shot him a frowning look, which swiftly changed to one of amused tolerance when she saw Justin watching her. "Please, Timothy, do curb your tongue," she said lightly. "You have just met Mistress Belinda Cady, a poor orphaned girl being hunted for witchcraft. Justin has very kindly taken her under his protection, but in my opinion, she is wholly undeserving. Why, if you could have seen the rude manners she possesses, the impertinent, high-handed way she spoke to him—to both of us—you would have been appalled. It was shocking! And most unbecoming to a woman of any station."

Timothy laughed. "Oh yes, she even cursed at me! What a vixen. But she had the most arresting little face—and her eyes—"

"I think it is time for the noon meal," Justin interrupted. "Timothy, would you escort Gwendolyn to the dining parlor? I must attend to something. It will only take a moment, and I will join you both."

Gwendolyn rose gracefully and paused at his side. She touched his arm, and he could smell her perfume, the delicate lavender scent filling his nostrils. Her violet eyes shone softly as she gazed up at him with the ardent expression he remembered so very well.

"Don't be too long, my darling. I have waited eternities for us to be together. Now that I am finally here—with you—I cannot bear to be apart."

Justin kissed her gloved hands, his eyes glinting. "Gwendolyn, my pet, you are as charming as ever. You shall enrapture all the gentlemen of Boston at the reception in your honor tonight. Certainly your beauty will outshine that of all the local Puritan women invited to meet the future bride of the Gray Knight."

She inclined her head slightly at the compliment, but a slight cloud entered her violet eyes. "Oh, Justin, pray do not mention that...that odd nickname you have earned for yourself. I know you enjoyed those years of pretending to be a...a pirate, but now that is all behind you. My darling, I wish you would refrain from using it. After all, you know, it was not quite a respectable career and I know you have begun a whole new wonderful life in the colony of Virginia, where," she added with a glowing smile, "you are a gentleman of great esteem and influence. You have a grand estate there, do you not? A plantation? It all sounds quite magnificent and impressive."

"Yes, Willow Oaks is certainly magnificent," he returned, draining his brandy goblet. "I wouldn't dream of bringing my bride to any home less than magnificent. After all, Gwendolyn, you are accustomed to a certain

elegance in your life. My brother saw to that, I believe."
She stiffened suddenly, but he appeared not to notice.
He continued speaking pleasantly. "I have done everything in my power to equal and exceed the splendor to
which you are accustomed. I am certain that Willow Oaks
meets that requirement admirably."

"I will adore it," she whispered, moving closer to
him, but Timothy suddenly coughed, recalling them both
to his presence.

"Ah, Gwendolyn, shall we remove to the dining
parlor? I am famished for some decent food, after that
swine feed we existed upon at sea. I daresay you have
something better to offer us, Justin?"

"Most definitely. I will join you momentarily."

Justin waited until they had departed, then he stalked
off in search of Simon Foster. There was grim purpose
in his eyes, for he already knew the next move his little
firebrand would attempt, and he would take great pleasure in thwarting her.

Upstairs, Belinda paced her room. Her brain spun
with murderous thoughts, and the emotions roiling inside her made her feel physically ill. Her head throbbed,
and her hands were shaking. But she knew what she was
going to do. She couldn't remain in this house another
hour, no, even another minute. She would leave now
and seek refuge in a tavern house until she could find a
way to leave Boston safely. Perhaps a family passing
through would take her along. She could concoct some
story about her background, disguise herself in some way.
Even as these ideas swirled in her head she eased open
her bedchamber door and crept toward the staircase. She
stood there a moment, listening, and faintly caught the
sounds of voices from the dining parlor. Excellent, she
thought. They were stuffing their bellies. No one would
even notice her absence for some time, and surely, even

if he did, Justin would hardly mind her departure now that Gwendolyn was here.

She slipped down the stairs and darted toward the front door. She opened it slowly and edged outside. Then she froze, giving a small cry. Justin Harding stood before her, a diabolical smile upon his lean face. He gripped her arm and propelled her backward into the house.

"Running off again, Belinda?" he murmured. "How tiring of you. Surely you can think of a more resourceful way of dealing with your distress if you only but try."

"Let me go!" she hissed, trying frantically to break free.

He dragged her into the parlor and slammed the door behind them. When he turned to face her, she saw the grimness in his eyes. "I have just given orders to Simon Foster that the doors and windows of this house shall be guarded all day and night. I will not have you running off again, getting yourself into all kinds of trouble from which I have no interest in extricating you. Yes, I predicted you would try to leave—though I didn't expect you to move so quickly. Are you really that eager to escape me, firebrand?"

Belinda ignored this. She was breathing hard, still trying to free her wrist from his steely grip. "You . . . cannot keep me prisoner here!" she cried. "I will scream until every clergyman and constable in Boston beats down your door to investigate!"

"And where would that land you, my dear? Boston Prison?" His lips twisted into a smile. "Not that I'd mind, seeing you locked up in a dark, damp cell, but I very much doubt that *you* would enjoy it. No, upon reflection, I'm certain you'll feel that even this house is preferable to such a fate."

"Why? Why?" Belinda at last jerked her arm free and whirled upon him wrathfully. "Why won't you let me leave? You have your fiancée here now to warm your bed—you no longer need *me!* Or is she in truth as virtuous as that prim pose she adopts, insisting upon waiting until the marriage is official before allowing you to touch her?" Belinda laughed contemptuously. "Poor Justin. What *will* you do?"

Justin folded his arms across his muscular chest. He looked very tall, very strong as he stood before her in the intimate, elegant room. "I am keeping you here for your own protection, firebrand, whether you want to believe it or not. And as for Gwendolyn, I would rather not discuss her with you."

"Yes, that has been your attitude all along," she spat, her green eyes glittering like daggers. "Now the great mystery has been solved. I know these clothes you bestowed on me were intended for her—bride clothes, aren't they?" Her voice trembled on the words, and it took her a moment to regain her self-control. She bit her lip so hard it bled and grasped the back of a chair with rigid fingers. "You lied to me, Justin. You deceived me. You seduced me into your bed, swore you loved me, and all along you were—" She choked, swallowed hard, and continued doggedly. "You were engaged to be married to that . . . that detestable peacock! Do you deny it?"

She had never seen him so unreachable. His face might have been chiseled from granite. His eyes were pewter-colored, cold as lead. "No, I do not deny it. I have been engaged to Gwendolyn for many months. She sailed from England accompanied by her brother, Timothy, with the sole purpose of marriage to me."

Belinda's chest was tight. Her heart was bursting apart, exploding into a million jagged pieces that ripped her flesh like shards of ice. She nodded slowly, consumed by agony. "So it is true. You lied. You never loved me. You only used me, made a fool of me—"

"So you have accused."

"And you do not deny it!" Somehow, through tremendous willpower, she kept the hot, scalding tears from flowing down her cheeks. But her eyes were haunted and hollow when she raised her gaze to his face, and a shock wave rippled through him when he saw the emptiness there.

"Why won't you let me leave?" Her words were dull, almost dazed. "Haven't you hurt me enough? I will not stay under the same roof with you and that...woman. Besides, what reason can you possibly have for keeping me here?"

"I told you. It is for your own protection."

"My protection?" A bitter laugh rang out. She shook her head. "Why, Justin, what odd ways you have of showing your concern. Please, do think again. I'm certain you can concoct a more convincing reason if you try."

His face altered at her brittle words. For an instant, his gray eyes were alive with some emotion she couldn't decipher, but he quickly masked his feelings once again and spoke with icy calm. "Very well, Belinda. I am keeping you here for my own amusement. That is what you want to believe, isn't it? That I seek merely to torment you? Please, don't let me discourage your beliefs. In fact, believe whatever the hell you want. I don't give a damn."

"I know that." She raised her hand to slap him, fury getting the better of her fragile self-control but he seized her wrist, and his fingers clamped brutally around it. "Still the firebrand, eh? Always possessing enough spirit to fight back." She tried once again to break free of his hold, but this time he held her far tighter than he had before, so cruelly that she gasped, shutting her eyes. Her other hand fluttered upward and tried to tear his hand from her wrist, but he only grasped it in turn, staring ruthlessly down into her white face.

"You should have trusted me, firebrand. Your doubt was your undoing."

"Let me go." It was a whisper, none the less furious for its softness. Waves of pain enveloped her. She gritted her teeth against them and met his hard gaze with glittering eyes. "I hate you."

He smiled mockingly. "You will despise me even more when this conversation is finished. I have something to tell you, something you will not enjoy." He released her abruptly, watching as she rubbed her bruised wrists. "Tonight I am hosting a reception in Gwendolyn's honor. It has been planned for some time, dependent upon the date her ship arrived in port. The townspeople have been eager to meet the Gray Knight's intended bride and have been in a state of great excitement for the past week. They have held every evening available for the festivities. All the local dignitaries shall attend, so of course it is essential that you remain out of sight. You must keep to your room the entire evening and not make one sound, or I will not answer for the consequences."

"You . . . you expect me to cower upstairs like a frightened child while you toast your future bride?" she gasped. "Your arrogance amazes me!"

"I promise you, firebrand, if you are discovered, I will do nothing to aid you. I will watch them haul you off to Boston Prison and never lift a hand or speak a word in your defense. Is that clear?"

"Perfectly!" She tried to bolt past him, but he blocked her path, and she groaned in fury. "I understand! You've made yourself all too clear. Now, damn you, Justin, let me go!"

He stepped aside, silent as she fled to the doorway. On the threshold she halted and spun back toward him. He met her stare.

"I will never forgive you."

He barely caught the whispered words before she whirled once more and darted from the room. Her satin shoes made almost no sound as she ran up the carpeted stairway toward her bedchamber. Justin didn't move for several moments. He was staring at the doorway through which Belinda had fled. Suddenly, he raised his fist and brought it smashing down upon the gate-legged table beside him. The table splintered and collapsed beneath the force of that powerful blow. He gazed at it blindly. Then he strode forward toward the dining parlor to join his guests.

CHAPTER FIFTEEN

DUSK FELL like soft gray rain over Boston Town. From her window, Belinda watched the darkening sky, the hunched forms of men and women hurrying past Oliver Street, the gently swaying branches of the oak tree in the courtyard. Gloom had settled over the world and invaded her heart. She touched the cool pane of the leaded glass window with her fingertips, tracing an invisible pattern. The churning inside her had stopped. The grief and anger and humiliation were still there, simmering, but they bubbled quietly, with none of the violence that had brewed in her before.

She heard the door open behind her, but she did not turn. Mrs. Gavin entered bearing a tray. She cleared her throat to announce her presence, watching the girl at the window uncertainly. She did not know all the circumstances of what had passed between Belinda and Justin, but she knew that with Gwendolyn Harding's presence in the house, whatever problems might have existed before were now compounded. Poor child. The housekeeper shook her head as she saw her standing, slender and straight, by the window. Young and delicate as she was, she seemed no match for the master, in whatever scoundrel's game he was playing. This time the Gray Knight ought to be ashamed of himself!

"Miss, I've brought your supper." This announcement was greeted by indifferent silence. "Cook baked squash pie especially for you. It will taste every bit as good as that pumpkin tart they'll be having downstairs, I promise you that."

Slowly, Belinda turned from the window. Mrs. Gavin, watching her sympathetically, thought she looked more exquisitely lovely and more vulnerable than ever. Pale and slender as a rare flower she was in that small, softly lit room. The fire made her hair glow like burnished copper as it flowed over her shoulders. She had already bathed and was now wrapped in a soft peach-colored robe of shimmering satin, edged with ivory lace at the throat and wrists, which hugged the curve of her breasts and hips. Small bare feet peeked out from beneath the delicate garment. Mrs. Gavin's heart went out to her: the poor child looked so lost and alone. What had the master wrought through his wicked temper?

Belinda regarded Mrs. Gavin through eyes that had lost their sparkle. Her sculpted cheeks were pale as dawn. She shook her head slowly, as if it ached. "No, thank you, Mrs. Gavin. I don't want any supper."

"Oh, miss, you must eat," the housekeeper coaxed. She set the tray down upon the night table and stepped forward. "I have a message for you from the master. Perhaps that will brace you up a bit."

"What is the message?"

Mrs. Gavin beamed. "Master Harding wanted me to tell you that he has sent my husband, Ned, to Philadelphia in search of that Mr. March you're needing to find. So don't you worry your head any more about it. If anyone can locate that fellow, my Ned will manage it, and bring him back here quick as a lick."

At this news, Belinda did brighten. Even with all her own troubles, the specter of Lucy trapped in that dank Salem Village prison continued to haunt her. She clasped her hands together eagerly. "Oh! How good of Ned to go! When did he start out?"

"Noontime. Now, you see? Everything is going to be just fine." The thin, kindly woman smiled. "Why don't you try some of this supper I brought? The venison is Cook's specialty. And from the looks of you, you need your strength, my girl."

Belinda moved to the edge of the bed and sank down upon it. "I suppose you're right," she murmured. "After all, I'll need to think clearly later..."

"Later?" The housekeeper sent her a sharp look. "What do you mean, child?"

"Oh, nothing." Belinda bit her lip. She forced herself to smile despite the tension knotted inside her. "I...I'm afraid I'm not making much sense today. Please don't mind what I say."

From beneath her lashes she saw that Mrs. Gavin was still watching her suspiciously. Damn! Above all else, she didn't want anyone to suspect what she planned to do. She could well imagine what this kind little woman would say if she knew. She would scold and cluck and argue as vehemently as...as Sarah Cooke would have done. Belinda smiled to herself as Sarah's image loomed in her mind's eye as vividly as though she was really present. If Sarah were here, she would know immediately what Belinda intended to do this evening. She had known Belinda all her life and would have realized that never once had the headstrong girl ever refused a dare.

"Mrs. Gavin," Belinda said suddenly, watching as the housekeeper began moving about the cozy room, tindering candles. "Tell me, what do you know about this woman—this Gwendolyn Harding?"

Now it was the older woman's turn to look self-conscious. She flushed, busying herself with the candles. Her voice was a shade too casual when she replied. "Oh, miss, not very much. The master doesn't confide in me, you know."

"But you ánd your husband have known him for so many years. Surely he takes you into his confidence to some degree? You knew of the engagement for some time, didn't you?" Belinda persisted.

"Oh yes. Certainly." Mrs. Gavin turned and smiled woodenly. "I must be going now, miss. There are many things to attend before the guests arrive. I'll return later to fetch your tray."

"Mrs. Gavin, wait! Please!" Belinda sprang up and ran to her side. She closed the door, which the housekeeper had opened. "Please don't go yet. I need someone to answer my questions or I shall go mad! You've been my friend. I'm grateful to you for that." She grasped the old woman's hand and squeezed it. "I...I know I was rude to you earlier, and I'm sorry, but I hope you don't bear a grudge. I need a friend in this house, you know, I truly do!"

There was something so desperate and pleading in the girl's fragile face that Mrs. Gavin hesitated. Belinda plunged on.

"Justin won't tell me what I need to know. He's been horrid and abominable, and I don't know what to do! Please, just tell me what you know about him and...and that woman! I'm trying to think clearly, to understand everything that's going on about me, but I need information to do that, Mrs. Gavin! Can't you see that?"

The housekeeper studied her. Belinda's green-gold eyes sparkled with tears. All of her dismay and confusion was mirrored in them, and it was a painful thing to see. Poor mite. The housekeeper thought of that vain, frosty beauty down the hall who had been ordering the servants about so peremptorily all afternoon, always in that silken tone. Her teeth grated. That woman wed to the Gray Knight? Mistress of Willow Oaks? Never!

She nodded to Belinda and patted her arm. "There, child, don't fret yourself so. I'll tell you about the master and that harpy. You just see if I don't."

Belinda led her to the window seat and waited until the housekeeper had settled herself upon the blue and white embroidered cushion. Then she herself sat upon the bed, leaning forward eagerly. "What do you know of her?" she demanded. "Why does she bear the name of Harding when she and Justin have not been wed? For how long have they been engaged? When—"

"Hush, child, hush. I will answer all your questions. But it is a long and unhappy story. And you must promise me that you will never tell the master I told it to you! He would be deadly angry, you know—heaven only knows what he would do!"

"I won't say a word!" Belinda vowed.

Mrs. Gavin nodded and leaned back against the window. Her eyes grew clouded. "It all began ten years ago, in England. The master was a fine young gentleman with nary a care in the world. Until the day he met a beautiful young girl from a family as well born as his own. Her name was Gwendolyn Worth." She said the words with distaste. "She was a ravishing beauty, a woman courted by many, many men. He fell instantly in love with her."

"Go on," Belinda said through clenched teeth. Her stomach had begun twisting into hard little knots as Mrs. Gavin spoke, but she tried to ignore it. She had wanted to know this story, and now she was learning it. She listened with grim determination.

"Oh, the master loved her indeed. Quite besotted he was. I didn't know him then, but Simon once told

Ned and me how it was. The master even wrote sonnets about her, tributes to her beauty and grace and charm. He couldn't wait to wed her."

A log popped in the fire, startling Belinda. She twisted a finger through her silken hair, winding it and unwinding it slowly as she turned back to the housekeeper. "What happened?" she asked, remembering what Simon had said about an engagement. Mrs. Gavin shook her head.

"Two weeks before the wedding, she sent for him. She told him that she was not going to wed him after all." Here the housekeeper took a deep breath. "She told him...she told him that she was going to marry his brother."

"What?"

Mrs. Gavin nodded, her lips pursed together. "Yes, miss. You heard correctly. It seems that Mistress Worth had been thinking all about how Master James, Justin's elder brother, would be the one to inherit the family's title and the estate and the property and holdings, and so she chose *him*. It seems she had met him at the engagement banquet and had set her cap for him then and there. You can imagine how the young master felt, I'm sure."

"Yes. Oh yes." Belinda glanced down at her lap. She was thinking of the young Justin, love-struck and wounded, and her heart ached for him. Not for the Justin of today, so harsh and cruel, but for the young boy of the past who had been deceived and rejected so brutally. She bit her lip. "What did Justin do?"

"Oh, child, he was half-crazed with rage and pain and grief. He went out and drank himself stupid and then challenged some fellow to a duel. Nearly killed him, too. Simon tried to intervene, and the master knocked him cold, his best friend all the years of his life! Simon doesn't like to talk of it. Says the master was a wild man. Ran off and bought a ship and sailed off to fight pirates! For quite a while he drank and fought like the worst of blackguards, reckless as the devil himself! Almost as if he dared death to take him, if you can understand. But he calmed eventually. Like a storm that spins itself out. Only—"

She stopped, and Belinda leaned forward. "Only what, Mrs. Gavin?"

"Only he never quite got over it. Oh, he's always been a fine one when it comes to his crew and his friends, you know—generous and kind, and there's not one man who's worked for him who wouldn't lay down his life willingly for the master. But he's become hard, ruthless. It's as if the part of him that could write those sonnets had died. *That's* the lasting effect that whole awful business had on him. Especially as far as women are concerned."

"Oh?" Belinda clenched her hands together, her eyes glued to Mrs. Gavin's thin face. "What do you mean?"

The housekeeper shrugged. "Well, miss, it would be a lie if I was to say that the master hasn't been pursued by a great many women—some ladies and some not. They run the gamut from whores to widows to schoolgirls! But he never spends more than a few hours with any one of them. He . . . takes his pleasure, if you'll excuse me for saying it, and then he forgets all about them. He seduces them with that cold, deadly charm of his, and then . . . poof, it's as if they never existed. No one, from the day he left England and Gwendolyn Worth, has ever come near to touching his heart."

As she spoke, she looked across the room at the slender girl on the bed, the girl whose red-gold hair fell like a brilliant, shining halo about her lovely face. The girl looked saddened by this story, and Mrs. Gavin smiled to herself in satisfaction. Perhaps if Belinda could be stirred to sympathy, she would be more understanding of the master's ways, she would forgive him, encourage him to break off his engagement to that cold, haughty woman who had ill-used him so many years earlier. *This* girl truly cared. Despite the pain the master had caused her, she cared for him and, Mrs. Gavin thought sagely, she might be the only one who could save him.

Belinda broke into her thoughts. "What became of Gwendolyn after he left? She married the brother, I gather, since she now bears the Harding name."

"Yes, indeed. She married James, but bore him no children. I know little of their life together, but, miss, I doubt if it was happy. Who could be happy tied to a selfish, scheming harpy like her? Justin Harding was well rid of her ten years ago. Only then, Master James was killed in a hunting accident last year. And what do you think the master went and did? Waited until the mourning period had passed, and then he wrote to her, proposing marriage! He brought her here after all these years, after what she'd done!"

"He must have...loved her very much," Belinda said softly, her voice nearly choking on the words. "He still wanted her—despite everything."

Mrs. Gavin rose from the window seat, a grim expression on her small features. "Well, perhaps he did, or *thought* he did, but I don't think he does anymore." She put her hands on her hips. "He wants you, child. I'm certain of it!"

Gazing up at her in astonishment, Belinda gave a short, hollow laugh. "Oh no, Mrs. Gavin, you are quite mistaken! He has made it very clear that he does *not* want me!"

"Don't be so sure, child. Remember, I've seen him with you. I've seen the way he looks at you. I never saw such an expression in his eyes when he looked at any woman before, in all the years I've known him, ever since he and Ned and the rest of their crew settled in Virginia colony." Her eyes were bright and warm as they met Belinda's skeptical gaze. "Don't turn away from the master, I beg you, miss. He needs you, whether he realizes it yet or not."

"I can't believe that." Belinda spoke slowly, her eyes shadowed with pain. "I wish I could, but I can't. After the way he treated me today, after the things he said, I cannot believe that he ever cared for me. It is Gwendolyn he loves, and he always has loved her. What you've revealed to me proves that. I was only one final amusement before he claimed his bride. I can see that now." She made a sudden, impatient gesture with her hand, and her whole body stiffened, as if bracing itself up beneath a heavy burden. "Thank you, Mrs. Gavin. I'm grateful to you—more grateful than you can imagine. But I won't detain you any longer. The guests for the dinner will be arriving soon, and I know how busy you must be."

The housekeeper glanced pointedly at the tray still sitting on the night stand. "Your supper is fast growing cold, miss. You *will* eat it, won't you?"

"Yes, of course. Don't worry about me, Mrs. Gavin. I shall be perfectly fine."

Both women stared at each other a moment. Mrs. Gavin hesitated, then suddenly, jumped forward and hugged Belinda tightly. There were tears in her almond-shaped eyes. "Bless you, child. You're a sweet, good-hearted thing. Warm and real, with love in your heart. Not like *her!* I hope . . . I wish—"

She broke off, and Belinda squeezed her arm. Her own eyes were welling with tears, too. "Yes, I know what you wish! But it will never come to pass. Justin has loved Gwendolyn too many years. She is an obsession with him. No one can fight an obsession." She tore herself away, trembling, and after one breathless moment when she struggled for composure, she moved to the tray. With forced interest, she examined the covered dishes there. "You know," she remarked in a voice that was just a shade unsteady, "this looks quite appealing, after all. I...I believe I will eat my supper, Mrs. Gavin. So please do not bother about me anymore."

"Very well. It's true I've a bundle of tasks yet to attend. But I will return for your tray in a while, and I expect to find it quite empty, miss!"

Belinda forced a smile, watching as the housekeeper bustled out into the hall. When the door was shut behind her, she covered her face with her hands. Hot, burning tears slid down her cheeks. *Oh, Justin*, she whispered, *how could this all have happened? You have destroyed me, whether you know it or not.* She wept with all the pain of love that has been rejected, and her tears were for both herself and her lover. Poor Justin. How he must have suffered ten years ago. She knew how proud he was, and what a blow Gwendolyn's rejection must have been to him, and she also knew the agony of his loss, for she herself was experiencing it now. How much better she would have been never to have met him, never to have known his love, than to see all her foolish dreams snatched away by his obsession with another! As she sobbed, her pain churned through her, until her entire body ached with it. But gradually, the pain tormenting her changed instead to anger. Anger against both Justin and Gwendolyn. She had been cheated by both of them. She lifted her head, her hands clenching into fists. Her own love, every bit as strong as Justin's had been ten years ago, had been tossed aside, used and discarded, much as his had been. *She* was the one to suffer now. They would be together, after having made a fool of *her*. No! Her eyes

flamed with wrath. She slammed her fists into the softness of her bed, then quickly rose and darted toward the
wardrobe.

She had to dress. She had been made a fool of quite
enough, and she was sick to death of being Justin's pawn.
He had ordered her to stay in her room tonight, warning
her that he would not aid her if her presence and identity
were uncovered, but, stupid man, he had merely succeeded in raising her ire. Belinda Cady never turned her
back upon a challenge! Her defiant nature flared into
open rebellion when confronted with such dictatorial
commands, and she meant to make one final stand tonight, to show Justin that he could not rule her, that she
cared nothing for him or his advice. What she would do
tomorrow, she was not certain. If an opportunity presented itself this evening, she would make her escape; if
not, well, she would deal with that problem tomorrow.
She only knew that if she stayed in this room all evening
she would do nothing but brood about her broken heart,
thinking over and over about Justin and Gwendolyn and
of how cruelly she herself had been used and deceived.
And the pain would be intensified as each lonely minute
passed. She must take action, prove to Justin that she
dared not only face him, but defy him, and by so doing,
at least salvage a remnant of her pride.

She rifled through the wardrobe, smiling in triumphant satisfaction when her eyes fell upon one particular
gown. She lifted it out, running gentle fingers over the
gossamer material. It was a shimmering, dull gold satin,
with a gold lace ruff adorning the low-cut décolletage,
and a golden ribbon tied in flounces about the lower part
of the billowing skirt. Perfect! She laid it out upon the
bed and slipped free of her satin robe. Her mind was
filled with determination, anticipating the shock and fury
on Justin's face when he saw her gliding among his il-

lustrious guests. If deep in her heart was a pain sharper than any sword thrust, one which severed her straight to the core, she did not show it. She forced "the plan" to consume all her thoughts and emotions, ignoring the agony buried beneath. It was only later, when she eased open the door and stepped into the candlelit hall, that doubt assailed her. The sight of Justin and Gwendolyn together tonight would not be easy to bear. Her wounds would flare and bleed anew when she glimpsed that golden-haired, sly-eyed beauty on his arm, but she steeled herself. Pride made her lift her chin and straighten her shoulders beneath the luminous gold gown. Her green-gold eyes glittered like bewitching jewels. Belinda Cady run, frightened, from a confrontation? Huddle like a wounded sparrow in her room? Never! She swept regally down the carpeted hall toward the staircase, toward the voices and the lights. *Beware, Justin Harding*, the little voice in her head warned. *Beware the firebrand!*

CHAPTER SIXTEEN

THE SERVANTS of the house on Oliver Street had toiled all day to make the house "presentable" for the Boston dignitaries who would grace it that evening. Polishing, sweeping, and scouring, they had succeeded brilliantly. The silver candlesticks shone as brightly as the flames leaping above them, and the handsome, heavily carved oak furniture gleamed, as did the floors and moldings. Everything was bright and cheerful: the roaring fire in the parlor hearth, the crystal goblets waiting to be filled with wine, the plumped-up cushions of the sofa and chairs. Justin Harding strolled downstairs, casting an eye quickly about him. Satisfied with what he saw, he went forward into the parlor and poured himself a glass of brandy. In his white holland shirt, black satin coat, and black breeches, he looked coldly handsome, aloof, and somewhat dangerous. His intricately tied linen cravat, lace shirt cuffs, and gold buttons on his jacket bespoke a man of wealth and position, but something in the way he bore his powerful frame and the keen glint in his gray eyes warned one that he was still more pirate than gentleman.

Gwendolyn Harding, sailing toward the parlor in

time to see him toss off his brandy, paused on the threshold to regard her fiancé. A small smile curved her mouth. Justin Harding was even more intriguing now than he had been ten years ago. He had always been handsome and strong, but now there was about him an aura of danger and mystery which fascinated her. His rugged sexual charisma drew her potently to him. Watching him through violet cat eyes, she wondered now why she had ever rejected him for James. Oh yes, the obvious reasons of wealth and prestige which went uniformly to the eldest son had driven her to break off the engagement, despite her genuine attraction to Justin, but now, recalling the stuffy propriety of the tall, thin man she had been wedded to for ten years, regret stirred in her. She had been eighteen years old at the time, and it had not been an easy choice. It had been hard to reject the raven-haired, muscular Justin, who at twenty years old was already a reputed rake and who had made it clear he was head over heels in love with *her*. It was a difficult decision to give him up for the stiff, suave James, a difficult but pragmatic one. And it had proven enjoyable, having all that wealth and position right at her fingertips all those years. Quite enjoyable. Now everything was working out beautifully, far beyond her expectations. James was dead, and she was to have Justin after all. Her charms had apparently captured him on far deeper levels than she could have known, for he still wanted her, after all these years and after the way she humiliated him. Smug satisfaction crept over her, and with it, a sense of power. She had power over this man, this cool, formidable man whose very glance would make most women quiver like jelly tarts. He loved her, wanted her, and she alone could make him content.

For an unsettling moment, her serenity was punctured by the thought of that red-haired creature Justin had taken in. Belinda Cady. The girl was disconcertingly pretty, in a wild, rebellious way. Gwendolyn couldn't help wondering if all was really as innocent between them as Justin pretended. Yet she wasn't really worried. Whatever may have happened between them had happened before she, Gwendolyn, had arrived. Now Justin would have no desire to look at any other woman. *She* was the one he had desired all these years, *she* was the one who wielded power over his mind and heart. Belinda Cady may or may not have amused him briefly, but it was Gwendolyn Harding who possessed him. Smiling seductively, she glided forward into the parlor, knowing how beautiful she looked, knowing that Justin would not be able to resist her. He was hers. He always had been, and he always would be.

Justin glanced up as she came forward. The coldness in his gray eyes was unabated as he surveyed her in one swift, summing glance. Yes, she was beautiful. Her turquoise gown, of soft, rustling taffeta, set off her tall, willowy figure and generous breasts to perfection. Her golden hair, gleaming in the firelight, cascaded softly about her creamy shoulders, and her eyes, a fascinating violet color with lights that beckoned a man, sparkled alluringly. How well he remembered those eyes, filled with promises she had never fulfilled. Something tightened inside him. If Gwendolyn had been observant, she might have seen the hardness in his eyes, but instead she was watching his mouth as she leaned forward, put one gloved hand upon the back of his neck, and drew his lips down to hers.

Justin kissed her slowly, tasting her lips. When he lifted his head to regard her, his eyes were still cold. He spoke softly.

"Gwendolyn. You're ravishing. As ravishing as ever."

"I hope so." Her voice caressed him like velvet. "My

only desire is to please you, my darling Justin. It seems too good to be true, that we are to be united after all these years."

"Yes, doesn't it?" He smiled suddenly. "May I offer you a brandy or a glass of wine?"

"Wine, if you please." She frowned at the sound of footsteps running down the stairs. Timothy. Interrupting as usual. Well, soon she and Justin would be married, and they would have many, many private moments together. She smiled artificially as her brother surged into the parlor.

"Justin, are you sure I can't just stop by her room and introduce myself to that enchanting girl—Belinda, isn't that her name? It hardly seems fair that she isn't allowed to join in the celebration, you know!"

Justin handed him a brandy. He regarded the lanky young man with his usual air of nonchalance, yet there was subtle tension in his manner. "Belinda is confined to her bedchamber for her own protection, Timothy. Let her be. Or the consequences might be quite unpleasant—for everyone concerned."

Timothy stared at him. Was that a threat in Justin's voice? No, it couldn't be. He shrugged. "Certainly. I wouldn't go against your wishes, you know. It's just that I feel sorry for her."

"Don't waste your sympathy." Justin held the back of her chair as Gwendolyn seated herself prettily. "The little termagent is in no danger, provided she obeys me."

"It seems to me," Gwendolyn put in, still in that honeyed voice, "that Mistress Cady has brought a great deal of this trouble upon herself. Surely she has done something to make the authorities suspect her. Justin," she murmured, turning wide, innocent eyes upon her fiancé, "how do you know for certain that she isn't indeed a witch?"

"Gwendolyn!" Timothy exploded in exasperation, running a hand through his fair hair. "Don't be a ninny!"

Justin gazed down at her for a long moment before replying. "Do you truly believe in such creatures, Gwendolyn?" he inquired.

"Well, who is to say that the Devil does not have such servants? I hardly think the authorities would spend so much time prosecuting these people for witchcraft if they did not pose a real threat. Surely our leaders in the government and in the church know what is best, don't you think, Justin dear?"

"I prefer to decide for myself what is best and what is true and what is a threat to me. I have no need of protection from the likes of Belinda Cady," he returned, and there was an unsettling gleam in his eyes. They seemed to penetrate Gwendolyn right to her soul. "Do you have some objection to her presence in this house, my love? I can't help but notice that you don't seem to have taken to the poor girl."

Gwendolyn smiled and held out her hand to him. He took it in his large, strong one, watching her intently. "Oh, Justin, how can you say that? I hardly met the child! I merely hope *you* will not endanger yourself by protecting her. I would be mortified if she should be discovered and you should have to face punishment for harboring her! I daresay even *you*, my dear Justin, would not be above the censure of these Puritans. You might find yourself in prison, or locked in those dreadful stocks!"

"There is no danger of that," he assured her. "But your concern touches me deeply." His voice held an ironic tone which puzzled her, and she stared up at him, wondering what lay behind his nonchalant expression. She had no time to engage in further conversation or speculation, however, for at that moment there was a rapping upon the front door, signaling the arrival of the evening's first guests. Justin greeted them with his cool civility, and

Gwendolyn smiled dazzlingly upon one and all. Timothy, however, kept casting wistful glances toward the upstairs hall, a circumstance which made Justin murmur in his ear.

"Forget about her, my boy. She knows better than to make an appearance tonight. Besides, she is hardly the girl for you. Too stubborn and fiery by far; she'd have you running circles before you knew what she was about!"

To which young Master Worth blushed hotly, and he sent his host, whom he had previously thought a splendid fellow, a dark, scowling glance, which only made the Gray Knight laugh as he moved forward to pour wine for the Reverend Increase Mather, pastor of Boston's North Church. But despite his offhand manner, Justin Harding's thoughts centered much more than he cared to admit upon the small cozy bedchamber with the blue and white striped counterpane, where Belinda Cady no doubt fumed and chafed like a trapped wildcat. *Good*, he thought savagely. *It serves her well.* As his "fiancée" played her role of charming hostess to perfection, with the sweet, quiet gentility the Puritans admired in a woman, he strove to drive his thoughts away from that rebellious beauty abovestairs, though with very little success. Shortly before the company was about to assemble in the dining parlor, however, an unexpected guest claimed his exclusive attention. As he glanced idly toward the hallway, noting that nearly everyone invited had arrived, he caught sight of a face that made him start, nearly spilling the brandy in his goblet. He set it down on the mantel with a curse beneath his breath and turned toward the tall, gangly figure in the entry hall. Justin felt his muscles tensing, his hands automatically clenching into fists. Eyes narrowed, he moved swiftly forward, advancing with menacing purpose toward the gaunt, elegantly attired figure of Magistrate Jonathan Cady.

The two men's eyes locked, but before either could

speak, Jonathan's companion uttered in a hearty tone, "Master Harding? How do you do, sir? I am Reverend Cotton Mather. I believe my father has already arrived. I am most anxious to meet your future bride, dear sir, but first, may I beg a favor? My friend Magistrate Cady of the village of Salem arrived unexpectedly this morning on business of the court. He is returning to Salem on the morrow, but in the meantime, I took the liberty of inviting him to your reception. I believed you would have no objection. When he heard of my destination this evening, Magistrate Cady informed me that you are already acquainted." Cotton Mather, a young man of almost thirty years who possessed a large, bulbous nose, deep-set dark eyes, and a pair of bushy eyebrows, smiled into the rugged, arrogant face of his host. "He hinted of a slight altercation between the two of you, a misunderstanding, I am certain which can easily be resolved in the friendly atmosphere of a social gathering." He turned to Jonathan Cady, placing one scarlet-sleeved arm across the magistrate's narrow shoulders. "After all, two such esteemed personages as the king's good friend and ally and the magistrate of one of the colony's finest villages should have no reason to quarrel. Isn't that correct, my dear Jonathan?"

Jonathan's strange, icy eyes bored into Justin with a penetration that would have unsettled a more timid man. The Gray Knight merely met his stare with cool imperturbability, until Jonathan spoke harshly. "I beg a few moments of your time in private, Master Harding. There are a few matters which need urgently be discussed."

Justin surveyed the other man lazily. He noted that Cady, unlike the other guests at this social function, wore his rapier at his side. He was the only man in the room with a weapon. Justin's eyes flicked over the magistrate's green velvet coat with its rich gold braid, and falling lace ruff at his collar, his black velvet breeches and fine silken hose. This scarecrow of a man who represented justice in Salem stirred the embers of his wrath. Jonathan Cady had beaten Belinda, mistreated her, charged her with witchcraft. It was all Justin could do not to slam his fist into Cady's pasty face. But he restrained the impulse. This was neither the time nor the place to do battle. Instead, he nodded curtly to the man and jerked his head toward the small study beyond the parlor. "I shall be happy to oblige you in any manner possible, sir," he replied, though the cold contempt in his voice belied his civil words. He bestowed a slight bow upon Reverend Mather. "And you, sir, I bid you welcome. Is there some refreshment I may offer you before Magistrate Cady and I take our leave?"

"I should dearly love a glass of mead," the young reverend responded enthusiastically. "But don't let me detain you. I will see to it myself. However," he added, touching Justin's sleeve as the latter turned away, "I must insist that as soon as your business with Magistrate Cady is satisfactorily completed, you will perform an introduction to your fiancée. I shall be most honored to meet that estimable lady."

"Certainly." Justin bowed once more and headed toward the study, followed by the gangly, stiff-moving Jonathan Cady. They wove their way through the throng of guests toward the small study, then stepped inside, and Justin closed the door behind them. He lit candles in the dusky room, then moved to the writing desk. He sat upon the edge of it and folded his arms across his chest.

"Well, Magistrate? What may I do for you?"

"What might you do for me? You impudent scoundrel! I scarcely believe you have the affrontery to face me so boldly!" Jonathan exclaimed. He pointed a bony finger at Justin, who regarded him with raised brows. "Shame be upon you, Justin Harding! You eluded arrest in Salem by committing acts of violence against me, the good reverend, and our constable! I have only to announce that fact to your assembled guests, and you will find yourself sadly lacking in friends in Boston! In fact, you will no doubt find yourself in the stocks!"

Justin smiled mockingly. "Do tell them, Cady," he invited. "And I will share with them a few interesting pieces of information about you. Such as the fact that you beat your cousin and lusted after her. I'm certain the good people of Boston would be most interested in such activities."

Jonathan staggered backward under the force of this statement. His always pale face whitened sickeningly, and he clutched his stomach as though about to retch. "You—you—" His voice emerged as a hoarse rasp. An instant later, he answered his own question, leaning forward with a jerk. "You...you *saw* her! She told you! Where is she? What have you done with her?"

"You don't deny it, I see." Justin spoke with all his usual calm, yet he was exerting steely effort to keep from wringing Cady's scrawny little neck. He took a stride forward. "I ought to kill you here and now. A worm like you doesn't deserve to live. But I will spare you, Cady. For now. Provided you leave my house this instant and never set foot in it again. In fact, if I ever see your skeleton's face again, I will smash it beyond recognition! Is that clear?"

Jonathan's white face flooded with purple color. Rage shook him. "You...how dare you!...No one would believe...indeed, it is all lies! Lies! I don't know what that witch told you, but she has obviously spun a devil's tale! No one would believe..."

There was a quiet knock upon the study door, and Cady broke off his hysterical diatribe, spinning about. Justin strolled to the door and opened it. Gwendolyn stood upon the threshold. "Justin, I beg your pardon for interrupting, but Mrs. Gavin has informed me that supper is now ready. We ought not to keep our guests waiting much longer." She tilted her head, trying to see past him into the study. "Do you think your private business will delay you overlong?"

"No." Justin's mouth was grim. "As a matter of fact, it is now completed. Magistrate Cady and I have nothing more to say to each other. He will be unable to join us for supper this evening and must now take his leave." He opened the door wide and swung back toward Jonathan. "Thank you for coming, sir," he drawled. "I hope you have a pleasant journey back to Salem on the morrow. Good evening to you!"

Jonathan, still trembling, drew himself up to his full height. His hands opened and closed convulsively. He was unable to speak; the words froze in his throat. Finally, he stalked forward, straight past Justin and Gwendolyn. He made his way blindly through the glittering, crowded parlor, rudely elbowing aside all those who spoke to him. Suddenly, as he reached the entry hall, something did pierce the web of helpless rage which ensnared him. He froze, staring with bulging eyes at the spectacle before him. His mouth quivered, and then drooped. "You!" he rustled, in a voice like dead leaves. "It *is* you!" Then he blared forth a triumphant shriek.

Belinda slipped down the staircase from her bedchamber with pounding heart. She had her story all planned. She would introduce herself as Anne Beckwith, friend and companion to Gwendolyn Harding. She would say that she had accompanied her friend from England

out of devotion, wishing to witness her marriage cere-
mony, and that she planned a visit with relatives in Virginia colony. It was a daring ruse, but Belinda believed
she could carry it off. Especially with the full-powdered
wig she had "borrowed" from Gwendolyn's room, which
completely hid her own red-gold tresses. *That* had been
a stroke of genius. And once she had told her story publicly, before Justin or Gwendolyn or that young man she
had collided with earlier could unwittingly betray her,
she knew they would go along. They would not risk the
scandal it would bring upon themselves if she were discovered.

As she neared the foot of the staircase, the young
man with the fair hair wandered into the hall. He spotted
her and sprang immediately forward. Belinda's eyes sparkled defiantly as she saw the amazement on his face. His
eyes traveled swiftly over her slender, elegant figure,
noting the graceful swell of her breasts beneath the shimmering gold gown, the becoming glow upon her finely
sculpted cheeks, her brilliant eyes and proud smile. She
read, along with the amazement, another emotion: awe,
and felt the absurd rush of pleasure every woman knows
when a man greets her appearance with admiration. She
descended the final step and extended her hand.

"Good evening," she murmured, and then, in a lowered tone, "Quick, sir, tell me your name!"

"Timothy!" he replied at once, startled by her forth-
right manner as well as by her presence. "T-Timothy
Worth, Gwendolyn's brother. But you—Belinda, what
are you doing here?"

"Hush! Call me Anne—Anne Beckwith!" she whispered furiously. "I am your sister's friend and companion. Don't forget that!"

Suddenly, Timothy threw back his head and laughed.
He took her arm, and she could see that his blue eyes
were dancing with mischief. "You *are* a little minx, aren't

you? And a beautiful one, to be sure! Justin will be furious!"

"I certainly hope so," Belinda replied grimly, lifting her small, delicate chin. "If not, I shall be most disappointed—"

She broke off, gasping. Timothy, glancing down at her, saw that her flushed, lovely face had gone gray as dust and that she was rooted to the spot, her eyes wide as caverns. He looked in the direction they were staring and saw a very tall, gaunt man in a green velvet coat, who at that moment caught sight of them. The man, who had been hurrying toward the door, stopped dead in his tracks. He gaped. Then he spoke in a low, hoarse whisper.

"You! It *is* you!" Suddenly, he let out a shout.

"This woman is Belinda Cady—a witch escaped from Salem Village!" Jonathan Cady's voice reverberated through the house like cannon fire. Belinda shrank backward, the blood beating in her ears.

"Arrest her! Arrest her!" Jonathan's frantic shouting hushed the babbling company, drawing all eyes to the slender vision of gold at which he pointed. In the silence that followed one could almost hear the myriad candles flickering in their sconces. It was as if no one dared to breathe.

Jonathan jerked his rapier from his scabbard and thrust it toward Belinda's breast. "Beware—she is dangerous! A sorceress who knows how to elude righteous men. We must bind her, trap her, subdue the Devil within!" He broke off his shouting and advanced with slow, measured steps toward the girl who stood like a statue near the staircase. *"This time you shall not escape, witch! This time you shall die!"* His words thundered through her, and she felt terror strike the bone. Her cousin loomed before her like the very specter of death.

"No!" Belinda screamed in horror.

Timothy Worth stepped quickly in front of her, as if to protect her from Jonathan's advance, but the magistrate shoved him aside as the gasping, now muttering guests crowded angrily forward to surround the witch. "Don't interfere, sir!" Jonathan barked. "No doubt she has already cast her spell upon you, but it is a fie spell. Beware the witch's charms!" He held Belinda at swordpoint. The red glow in his eyes frightened her far more than the steel blade.

Dimly, she was aware of the pressing crowd, of angry mutterings, prayers, and curses, and from the corner of her eye she saw Gwendolyn Harding at the edge of the throng, a smug, satisfied smile upon her face. But Justin? Where was Justin?

Suddenly, Jonathan Cady chuckled. It was an ugly, triumphant sound, one which pained her ears. She could not tear her eyes from the gloating expression on his bony face.

"I've got you now, witch! There is no escape! You will meet your fate upon Gallows Hill! And there, like your evil companion, Lucy Brewer, you shall die!"

"No!" Belinda screamed again. Her knees felt as though they were buckling beneath her, yet she lunged forward, trying to flee. A dozen men charged toward her, and she felt herself roughly gripped and held. Surrounded, she fought against their restraining hands. Jonathan Cady watched her torment with an almost genial smile.

"Please!" Belinda sobbed, her borrowed wig tumbling loose in the fray, allowing her own flaming curls to cascade wildly about her face and shoulders. "Let me go! I've done nothing!"

"It will do you no good to lie, witch! Or to beg!" Jonathan boomed. "Justice will be served!" He nodded to the men who held her helpless. "Take her to Boston

Prison with the others. I'll bring her with me to Salem Village on the morrow." He watched with shining eyes as they bore the struggling girl toward the door. Then his gaze shifted to the throng of shocked onlookers, pausing as it discerned Justin Harding's towering, raven-haired figure among them. His eyes narrowed.

Belinda, too, had turned to the watching crowd, desperately searching for Justin's face. When she saw him, her heart wrenched painfully within her chest. He was now standing beside Gwendolyn, his expression dark and inscrutable. Their eyes met, and held. Belinda's gaze was filled with a silent, heartbreaking entreaty. Justin showed no emotion. For an instant, she thought something flickered in his cold gray gaze, yet he did not move or speak, and his iron features betrayed no softening. She caught her breath on a ragged sob as he continued to stare at her coldly. "Justin!" she cried, her voice breaking on the word. "P-please!"

Still, he was silent. There was no pity in his countenance. Her last view of his harsh features was cut off as she was dragged brutally from the house on Oliver Street. Tears streamed down her cheeks. Her body shook convulsively as terror and despair engulfed her.

Belinda felt as though she were enmeshed in a horrible nightmare, one from which there was no awakening. Warmth, safety, love, all seemed things from a distant past, gone forever. Heartbroken and abandoned, she was borne along in the cool, dark night, no longer resisting the men who imprisoned her. She had no strength left, no will. Of all the cruelties visited upon her, one alone had savagely destroyed her spirit. This was the final vision she had had of Justin Harding, so aloof and indifferent to her suffering. His hardened eyes and coldly chiseled features were engraved in her mind forever, killing every last ounce of hope and of faith in her heart.

* * *

Jonathan Cady waited until the door had slammed behind Belinda and her captors. Then he straightened his narrow, bony shoulders and, still holding his sword, advanced across the entry hall of the elegant, candlelit house. His thin lips twitched with a sneering, triumphant smile as he faced the host of the evening's reception.

"Well, Master Harding," Jonathan Cady intoned as all eyes in the room fastened intently upon the Gray Knight. "The good people of Boston are most eager to hear how this accused witch came to be found tonight in your house. Perhaps," he snapped, his pale, icy eyes ablaze with hate, "you will be kind enough to tell them!"

CHAPTER SEVENTEEN

IT WAS A HARSH, dreary gray day when Belinda returned to Salem Village. As she huddled in the crowded wagon, wedged between other prisoners bound like herself at wrists and ankles, with the icy rain slashing down upon her, she was reminded of the first time she had come to the village. That day, too, had been one of rain and darkness, with the gloomy trees and ancient hills closing in upon her. If only she had known what lay ahead, she thought wearily, maybe she could have somehow avoided the awful fate confronting her. If she had run away right from the beginning, that first dreadful night when Jonathan Cady had struck her with the switch and explained all too clearly the life ahead of her, perhaps she never would have found herself accused of witchcraft, trussed and guarded like a dangerous beast, hauled back to Salem in this wagon which bumped and jostled painfully along the rutted track. She laid her head upon her drawn-up knees, letting the tears flow freely down her mud-splashed cheeks. She didn't care anymore, she didn't care. Ever since her arrest the night before in Boston, she had been first in a state of shock, then filled with a fierce pride which had barricaded her against all other emotion. Now she simply didn't have the strength to keep up the pretense anymore. She wept softly, with anguished sobs which shook her slender form, heedless of the silent prisoners all about her, heedless of the tall, erect figure of Jonathan Cady who rode before the wagon, leading his captives to their deaths. Her tears blended into the rain which pounded upon her, soaking through the filthy gold gown of yesterday, chilling her flesh. Nothing mattered anymore. Nothing. She had lost everyone dear to her, so why shouldn't she also lose her life? Sarah was dead, and so, according to Cousin Jonathan's words last night, was Lucy. Belinda grieved for her quiet, gentle friend, unable to keep from imagining over and over the hideousness of her death on Gallows Hill. The image of the rope wound around Lucy's slender neck, of her thin face horribly twisted, kept repeating itself in pitiless detail, tormenting Belinda ceaselessly. Cousin Jonathan had refused to speak to her and so had not elaborated on what he had told her last night, but Belinda didn't really need to know more. She only knew that her plan to summon Henry March had not worked, that the court had moved all too swiftly on Lucy's case, and had condemned her to death before Belinda or anyone else could find a way to help her. She drew a ragged breath, rubbing her reddened eyes with her fists. *Lucy, forgive me, I failed you,* she cried in silent anguish, but her only answer was the roar of the wind in the trees.

She had lost Sarah, and she had lost Lucy. And then, finally, there was Justin. Justin, too, was gone. She would never see him again, never kiss those warm, strong lips or feel the strength of his arms around her. She told herself she was glad, she told herself that he didn't deserve her, that he had lied to her and deceived her and never even loved her at all, but it didn't help. She still loved him. For a time he had been gentle and caring, the one bright light in her dark, grim days. Even knowing that it had all been a game with him didn't change the way she had felt in his arms and didn't lessen the longing which made her quiver and ache. She still couldn't quite believe that he had really allowed àll this to happen. When Cousin Jonathan had accused her last night in the midst of the reception and dragged her off to spend the night in Boston Prison, she had felt certain, somewhere deep inside herself, that Justin would save her. But he had only watched with those cold, unfathomable eyes as she had been borne away. He had not spoken a word in her defense. In fact, he had not spoken at all. When she had last seen him at Gwendolyn's side, his darkly handsome face emotionless, her heart had cried out to him, but he was lost to her, a silent, far-off figure, one who no longer cared, if he ever had, what befell her. As the icy rain battered and soaked her, cold reality seeped in, along with the chill and the wet. Justin simply didn't care. He never had. And she was the queen of fools to have ever believed otherwise.

She thrust Justin Harding from her thoughts with savage determination. Lifting her head, she gazed about at the wind-whipped trees, the misty darkness, the pathetic figures of the women crouched about her, all of them Salem women accused of witchcraft who had been shipped to Boston Prison until the Salem courts could clear time to hear their cases. Now they were all being transported back to the Salem Village Prison, which was still overcrowded. And Belinda was now one of them, a witch, a servant of the Devil. She smiled grimly to herself, wishing for a moment that she really *were* a witch. She would strike down Jonathan Cady and the driver of this wretched wagon with a lightning bolt and free the captives. She would fly off through this murky forest until she reached the sea, and then she would soar home to England.

One of the women near her cried out suddenly, a

sound that pierced the leaden air, yet no one paid any heed. The driver, hunched on his wagon seat, never took his eyes off the muddy road ahead, and Jonathan Cady didn't even turn his head at the pathetic wail. None of the women responded either. Belinda leaned forward, her wrists chafing against the rough rope which bound them. "What is it?" she asked gently. "Can I . . . can I help you?"

The woman's head jerked upright. She regarded Belinda through glazed eyes. "H-help . . . me?" Her voice was a raw croak. She looked more like a skeleton than a woman as she sat shivering in a filthy gown of camlet whose color had possibly once been blue but was now a grimy gray soaking against wasted flesh. Her dark hair fell in wet, muddy strands upon her hollow cheeks and neck. "Y-you?" She gave a short, half-mad laugh, showing yellowed teeth. "You cannot . . . help me. You cannot even help yourself. You . . . are doomed . . . as I am. Doomed, doomed, doomed . . ."

Her teeth began to chatter then, cutting off her words, and Belinda spoke. "We'll be there soon. At least in the prison it will be dry, and warmer. Maybe they'll get us some dry clothing. . . ."

The woman's head drooped down upon her chest. She closed her eyes, sobbing silently. She appeared no longer aware of Belinda's presence, or anyone else's. She was lost in her private hell.

Belinda bit her lips to keep her own teeth from chattering. The woman was right. There was nothing she could do. Helplessness and despair clutched at her, clawing at the remnants of calm she still possessed. She felt her sanity slipping away; she fought the impulse to throw herself from the wagon, to roll, screaming, away from her captors. Useless, foolish, mad fantasies swirled in her head, and she sucked in her breath in an effort to regain her self-control. Any wild behavior now would only make her look more guilty. The case against her would be solidified. Suddenly, she laughed to herself, a grim, hollow laugh, as tears slid down her cheeks. It didn't make any difference how she behaved. Cousin Jonathan and everyone else in Salem Village believed she was a witch. Nothing she did or said would succeed in convincing them otherwise.

The two horses drawing the wagon strained and pulled to get their burden through the thick mud. The rain showed no sign of abating. Finally, just as the travelers reached the fork leading to the village, the wheels stuck and would not budge. The driver flicked his whip over the foaming beasts, but to no avail. Jonathan Cady turned and frowned.

"It's no use," the driver called, spitting disgustedly into the road. "The mud's too thick, and the wagon too heavy. The beasts are spent, Magistrate. They can't get through."

"Untie the women's feet, Zachariah, and they will walk behind the wagon. I will follow them, to make certain no one tries to flee."

Grunting his assent, the driver lumbered down from his perch and made his way to the rear of the wagon. One by one he cut the ropes binding the prisoners' ankles and lifted them to the ground. At first, Belinda almost collapsed. Her feet, still in their delicate white slippers of last night, sank into the oozing mud, and her legs were too numb to support her. She stumbled against the side of the wagon, using both hands, still tied together, to break her fall.

"Keep together now!" Cady ordered, casting an icy gaze upon his miserable prisoners. "I will have my eye on each of you, so do not think you can slip away. One after the other, in a single line, march!"

They reached the village in this manner, stumbling dejectedly along in their wet and filthy garments, covered with mud and drooping with exhaustion. Belinda expected to be herded into the prison along with the others, but to her surprise, her cousin separated her from them at the door and instructed her to proceed to the meetinghouse.

"These others have had their pretrial hearings already, before they were sent to Boston," Cady informed her, staring down from his horse as she stood in the drenching rain. "You, on the other hand, escaped before we could follow the procedure, cousin. So now that is the first thing that must be done. You must wait in the meetinghouse under guard while I summon the necessary officials and witnesses."

"Will you . . . will you have the decency to get me some dry clothing on your way?" Belinda's teeth were chattering so badly now that she could barely speak. Still, she held her trembling body erect, staring straight into Jonathan Cady's greenish eyes, despite the rain striking her upturned face.

Cady didn't answer her. He jerked his head toward the meetinghouse, and Belinda had no choice but to turn and walk toward that building.

Inside, at least, it was dry indeed. She sank down on one of the benches, her shoulders hunched. There were red, rough markings on her wrists from the tight rope binding them, and her once-beautiful gown, now filthy, clung in disarray to her chilled flesh. Her feet were steeped in mud well past her ankles. She dimly noted Constable Vining charge in, speak briefly with her cousin, and then come to sit on the bench opposite her. She felt his eyes upon her and, glancing up, realized that Cousin Jonathan had departed. She and the constable were alone. Suddenly, she became aware that he was examining her. She realized that her wet gown was clinging revealingly to her figure, exposing every curve of her womanly form. A hot blush rose in her cheeks, and she raised furious eyes to the constable's face.

"Sir, it is hardly decent to stare at me in my present state," she cried. "The least you can do is to find me some clean, dry clothing in which to cover myself!"

"I can't leave you unattended, witch!" the constable retorted. "You'll get some respectable garments for the trial, I am certain. Until then, do not be concerned. I am a righteous, churchgoing man and would not stoop to lusting after a witch!"

Belinda glared at him, but before she could respond, the meetinghouse door opened once again, and Goodwife Fletcher appeared, her arms laden with a large basket.

When she saw Belinda, relief washed over her wrinkled face. "There you are, mistress!" she exclaimed, hurrying forward. "I saw you marching down the road and came as soon as I could. You poor—" She broke off, casting a wary look at Constable Vining, who had risen upon her entry. She hugged her basket to her chest nervously. "Y-you surely cannot...object if I bring the poor child some food and dry clothing," she stammered. "She must be half dead from her journey."

"'Tis risky business, comforting a witch," the constable remarked slowly, his eyes narrowed upon the goodwife's plump, anxious countenance. "Some folk might wonder why you stand on such friendly terms with the Devil's servant."

"N-nothing has yet been proved." Goodwife Fletcher moistened her suddenly dry lips with her tongue. She pushed at a strand of gray hair which had fallen loose from her plain white cap and was straggling upon her brow. "It...it cannot be a sin to show human kindness to a suffering creature."

"Witches don't deserve human kindness." The constable frowned at them both, then suddenly shrugged his bearlike shoulders. "Oh, go on with you, then. But you'd best hurry, for the magistrate will return soon to begin the hearing."

Goodwife Fletcher sank down on the bench beside Belinda. She opened the basket and removed a heavy gray woolen cloak. She shook it out and draped it around Belinda's trembling shoulders, fastening the clasp for her. "There, now," she whispered. "That will warm you a bit. And here is some bread and cheese. Eat, child."

"Th-thank you." Belinda, grateful for the snug warmth of the woolen cloak, smiled into the gray-haired woman's eyes. "You are a true friend, Goodwife Fletcher, to bring me such comfort. I...I fear for you, though. I would never forgive myself if you were suspected because of your friendship with me."

"I...I am afraid, too. But I could not stay away, not when I saw how cold and weary you looked. I wish I had the courage, child, to tell them just what I think about all this witch-hunting madness. But alas, I am only a frightened old woman. Who would heed me? More likely, they would throw me in prison." She watched Belinda awkwardly bite off a mouthful of cheese, her wrists still tied together. "I must...warn you, child. Things do not look well for you. Frances Miles has screamed out against you often in the past days. She claims you torment her, pricking her with needles, beating her with sticks. And those girls who follow her about echo her words. The people are all stirred up against you."

Belinda nodded. "They will hang me," she said slowly. "I cannot foresee any other verdict in the trial."

"No!" Tears filled Goodwife Fletcher's eyes. "Have hope, my dear! Perhaps they will come to their senses. Be brave and strong as you aways are, and you may yet convince them of your innocence."

Belinda did not see how this could happen. Frances Miles and Jonathan Cady would both testify against her. What defense could she offer against their charges? Only the same defense offered by those before her, women such as Elizabeth Foster, Widow Smith, and Lucy, all innocent, and all condemned to death. She, too, would be convicted. Despair settled heavily upon her. Her shoulders drooped, and her entire body sagged beneath an invisible weight.

"I will pray for you," Goodwife Fletcher added, watching the girl's pale, weary face. She was about to say more, but suddenly there was a commotion at the door and she froze as Jonathan Cady, Reverend Wilkes, and Frances Miles entered the meetinghouse, along with a gust of bitter wind. "I...I must go," she whispered to Belinda, panic in her blue eyes. "I'm sorry, child...."

She edged away, nodding uneasily to the newcomers as she made her way past them to the door. Another blast of cold air surged in when she left. Belinda shivered inside her cloak, feeling more alone than ever. Even someone as kind-hearted and sensible as Goodwife Fletcher dared not raise her voice against the witch-hunts or speak in defense of an accused witch. Despite her loyalty to Belinda, she was too frightened to defy the community, and Belinda could not blame her. The villagers were too quick to point their fingers at anyone who disagreed with them. They would cry out against a pious and gentle neighbor as quickly as a stranger if that neighbor defended an accused witch. Goodwife Fletcher, for all her good intentions, could not help Belinda now. She had tried, bringing her food and a warm cloak, but there was no more she could do. Belinda was on her own. She watched as her cousin took his place at the front of the meetinghouse. A long pine table and bench had been set up at the right of the pulpit, and it was here that Jonathan

Cady presided. Frances Miles and the reverend sat beside Constable Vining. Belinda, alone in the opposite pew, waited with clenched hands for the hearing to begin.

"Let the defendant stand!" Jonathan ordered, and Belinda slowly rose. Draped in her flowing gray cloak, she stood straight and tall before the accusing eyes turned upon her. Her coppery-red hair was wet and muddied, and tumbled in disarray about her shoulders, yet despite her dirty, disheveled appearance and tense, pale face, she was a proud figure as she waited in the dusky meetinghouse, listening to the charges brought against her. She heard them all, the wild accusations of witchcraft, of torment, of service to the Devil. She did not flinch before them. When Frances Miles told of being pricked and beaten with sticks, of seeing Belinda's apparition accosting Peter Chadwick's cow, and killing her family's chickens, Belinda turned her head to give the hysterical girl a cold and contemptuous stare. Frances shrieked.

"She pricks me with her needles!" She wailed again and again. "The witch attacks me, aaaaah! Save me, oh, save me from the Devil's spears!"

Constable Vining spoke of Belinda's friendship with Witch Lucy Brewer, of how she had tried to comfort that witch upon her arrest. Reverend Wilkes spoke briefly about red hair being a sign of the Devil. And finally, Jonathan Cady charged her with trying to seduce him, with casting evil spells upon him which tempted a righteous man to sin.

"The Crown charges Mistress Belinda Cady with witchcraft and orders her to remain in Salem Prison until the time of her trial. It is the belief of the court that this particular suspect is one of the most dangerous ever to accost our village. She succeeded once in escaping, evidence in itself of her guilt. It is our recommendation that her trial be given precedence over that of less treacherous demons. The date and time will be set when the court's most pressing current cases have been settled." Jonathan Cady fixed his penetrating gaze upon Belinda's rigid countenance. "This hearing is adjourned and the defendant ordered to await trial in Salem Prison from this time forward!"

Constable Vining shuffled to her side and seized her arm. "Make haste!" he barked. "I want to get home to my supper!"

He dragged her toward the door. As she passed Frances Miles, that young woman sent her a gloating glance. Her pudgy cheeks were flushed in triumph. Belinda's own face colored with her pent-up rage, but she kept her silence, brushing past the girl without a word and bracing herself for the cold rain she would meet outside. Her cousin's harsh voice stopped her just before she reached the door. Constable Vining released her arm, and she turned slowly to face Jonathan Cady.

"So, my cousin, we see what has come of my charity to you." His lips curled in contempt as he regarded her cloaked, mud-spattered form. He nodded thoughtfully, almost to himself. "I thought I was taking in a poor, orphaned relation, one who would be grateful for the pity shown her, and instead, a witch entered my house. A wicked, scheming creature who sought to corrupt me, a sorceress who plays Devil's tricks upon my neighbors and lures good people toward evil." His tall, thin frame towered over her. He looked as gaunt and bleak as a winter tree. "Now you shall pay the price of the wicked ones, Witch Cady! The good people of Salem Village will prevail. If you thought that I would protect you because you are related to me, you were sadly in error. I am a righteous man. I seek justice and cleanliness of spirit.

You never should have tried to practice your witch's wiles in this colony. That, Witch Cady, was your gravest mistake!"

"I am innocent," Belinda replied in a quiet voice. Her chin tilted upward defiantly as she met her cousin's blazing eyes. Her own were cold as ice chips. "The only wickedness, Cousin Jonathan, is in your own heart. Your own imagination torments you, not any spell cast by me. Look into yourself, before you accuse others. Your own soul needs cleansing, not mine."

"Devil!" Jonathan shrieked, shaking his fists wrathfully. He took a step forward as if to strike her for her words, then suddenly recalled himself to his surroundings. He seemed to take control of his emotions with an effort and spoke curtly to Constable Vining. "Take her! Take her at once! I do not wish to see her face again until the trial! Then we shall see where the wickedness rests! We shall all see!"

The constable grasped Belinda's arm once more and hauled her out into the darkening village. The rain had dwindled to a drizzle, but the wind still whipped at shutters and trees and blew Belinda's gray hood from her head. She bent forward against the wind and moved toward the prison, borne along by the constable. Hopelessness engulfed her. The hearing had been a mockery, confirming her worst expectations. The trial would be no different. She had no prayer of acquittal.

When they reached the squat prison building, Constable Vining led her into the dim, dank interior. Past a row of tiny cells they went, until they reached a small chamber at the farthest corner of the building. There was one small barred window set high in the wall. A figure lay huddled upon the floor. Belinda shuddered at the rancid odor of the place. Gloom and despair clung to every corner of this wretched building. The constable's key scraped loudly in the lock, and he swung open the barred metal door to the cell. Belinda reluctantly stepped inside.

The door clanged shut behind her. With a sickened heart, she heard the key grating in the lock.

"Here, hold out your hands!" Constable Vining directed, and when she held her hands through the bars, he began to saw at the tightly knotted ropes which bound her. It didn't take long for his knife to slice them. "There." He scowled at her. "The missus will bring round your supper later. Don't you make any trouble now, or 'twill be the last meal you get for a full day." With these words, he lumbered back down the darkened corridor, not bothering to light any of the candles in various sconces along the way. Belinda, rubbing her numbed wrists, watched him disappear into the murky hallway. She heard the door to the prison slam behind him and drew a deep, ragged breath. Slowly, she turned to stare once more at her new quarters.

The prison cell made her loft at Jonathan Cady's house look like a palace. Even smaller, it was filthy, laden with dust, and boasted no furnishings at all, save for two soiled straw pallets laid upon the floor. The slight figure she had seen when she came in was huddled upon one of these. She lay there limp and unmoving. Her fair hair was tangled, and she wore a grimy brown homespun. Belinda could not see her face.

She took a step closer. It was odd that the girl hadn't glanced up when she came in, or spoken. Perhaps she was sleeping...or sick...or...A hideous thought flashed through Belinda's mind, making her flesh crawl. Or dead.

She knelt beside the still figure. "Pardon...pardon me. I...are you all right?" she asked in a low tone. There was no reply. "You...girl...are you..."

Truly alarmed, she put her hand on the girl's shoulder and turned her. For the first time, she had a glimpse of her cellmate's face. She gave a gasp and dropped down on both knees beside her. Her entire body trembled violently.

"Lucy!" she whispered, touching the damp, pale face with icy fingers. "Lucy, you're alive!"

CHAPTER EIGHTEEN

LUCY STIRRED and moaned as Belinda lifted her head, cradling it in the crook of her arm. "Lucy, Lucy, can you hear me? It is I, Belinda!" She stroked her friend's white cheek. "Oh, Lucy, what have they done to you?" she cried brokenly. "Please, wake up!"

Lucy moaned again. Her hand fluttered upward to her head. Then she appeared to sink again into unconsciousness.

Belinda stared at her. After the first shock of finding her friend alive, wild joy had swept over her. She had realized that she had misunderstood Cousin Jonathan's remark at the reception when he had told her she would die on Gallows Hill like her friend, Lucy Brewer. She had thought then that Lucy had already been hanged, but now it became clear that Cousin Jonathan had merely been warning her that the same fate awaited them both. Her relief would have been tremendous, if only Lucy didn't look so terrible. Fear returned, wiping away her joy as she studied the unconscious girl. She was obviously very ill—perhaps, Belinda realized in horror, dying. Her flesh felt feverish and clammy. She was pale and...so still. Belinda sobbed, clutching her friend's hand in desperation. "Lucy, please, wake up," she pleaded. "Lucy..."

The girl's eyelids fluttered. Her head shifted to one side. "Yes, Lucy, I'm here. Wake up," Belinda whispered.

Slowly, the thin eyelids opened, and Lucy's brown eyes gazed up into Belinda's face. She blinked, putting an unsteady hand to her brow. "B-Belinda? Is... it really *you?*" she murmured.

"Yes! Oh yes! Here, let me help you sit up. You look dreadful, Lucy. For a moment I thought you were... never mind. Try, if you can, to tell me what happened."

Lucy, with Belinda's aid, struggled to a sitting position on the crumpled pallet. She leaned weakly against her friend, burying her small, fair head in her hands. "I took sick... with the fever... yesterday, perhaps, or... or the day before. I'm not sure. They sent the physician and he... he bled me. He gave me a potion of... barley water and wine and whey. It was dreadful, Belinda... and then they... they left me here. I don't remember much else."

"You still have fever," Belinda told her, "but I don't believe it is overhigh. You are getting well, Lucy, I'm sure, but you're still weak. Have you had any food?"

"I don't remember. No, I... I don't think so. Not since I took sick...."

"How could they leave you here alone like this in such a state?" Belinda demanded, anger rushing through her. "You need care and attention!"

"They did separate me from the other prisoners. They said they didn't want everyone to be infected with the fever. I... I suppose they don't want to be denied the pleasure of hanging us. For that it is worth keeping us alive," she said bitterly. "I'm... surprised they put you here with me, Belinda. There is barely space here for one... and I am so sick...."

"The prison is full. I rode back from Boston with a

wagonload of accused women. I suppose there was simply no place else to put me." Belinda smiled at her. "Whatever their reasons, it is fortunate. I will take care of you and make you well. Goodwife Vining is to bring some food later, and I will insist upon some hot broth—"

"It's no use, Belinda." Lucy shook her head. There was desolation in her eyes, the same hopelessness Belinda had seen in that woman on the wagon. "We're going to die anyway. Today, tomorrow. My trial is very soon. I know what the outcome will be. Maybe...maybe it would be better if I died of the fever. I...I prayed for that, you know. Perhaps it was wrong, but it...it seemed preferable to...to the gallows." She shuddered, and Belinda hugged her close.

"Oh, Lucy, I had given up, too. But now that I've found you are still alive, I feel...hopeful again. Together we must think of something—a plan. I know we can survive somehow!"

Lucy's eyes were clouded with pain and weariness. "No, Belinda, no," she whispered. Silence fell between them.

Outside, the wet wind lashed the village street. It was a lonely, mournful sound. Belinda wondered where spring had gone. That lovely, warm day when she had strolled through the woods and met Justin Harding beside that pretty little pond seemed long ago. Now the changeable April weather was as bleak and glum as her future. She knew that fair weather would come again, but she wondered, sitting there in the darkened cell with Lucy ill beside her, if she would be alive to see it. Probably not. She swallowed, trying to ignore the lump in her throat.

"B-Belinda." Lucy spoke with an effort. "Tell me what...happened to you. Where did you go when you escaped? How...how did they find you?"

"Later." Belinda took one look at her friend's chalk-white face, and her earlier alarm returned. "I think you have done enough talking and listening for now. Here, lie down again, and I will cover you with my cloak. Good-wife Fletcher brought it for me; it is warm and clean and dry. Rest, Lucy," she urged, helping her friend to lower herself onto the pallet once more. "Soon you shall have some food and find yourself feeling stronger. I will watch out for you and take care of you. And later, when you are stronger, I will tell you my tale."

Lucy nodded, her strength ebbing quickly. She closed her eyes, moaning as Belinda draped the warm cloak over her. Belinda watched her until she had sunk once again into slumber, then she rose and walked to the window. She stared out at the wind-swept darkness. With all of her self-control and determination, she fought to keep her panic at bay.

The days crawled by. Two, then three days passed, an endless time when Belinda was pushed to the limits of sanity, feeling as though the prison walls were slowly closing in to crush her. Always restless and impetuous, it was torture for her to be confined in that tiny, dark cell. She tended Lucy, paced, and thought. It was the thinking that hurt her the most. Her impending fate terrified her, weighing upon her with crushing force. She contemplated day and night what it would be like to be led to the gallows, to mount the steps and feel the noose fitted about her neck. Each night she awoke screaming. The others in the prison screamed and wailed, too, sharing her nightmare. Only Lucy was calm. She grew better each day as the fever subsided, and some of her strength began to return. Yet, in the duskiness of the cell, her skin was pale, her eyes bleak. She had accepted the fate that haunted Belinda. To her it was cold reality, not the stuff of nightmares.

Belinda was haunted, too, by her memories of one tall, arrogant, impossibly handsome man. Justin Harding's image kept reappearing in her mind, vivid and relentless. When she awoke from her nightmare in the pitch blackness of the prison, she comforted herself by recalling his lean, rugged face, by remembering how strong his arms had been around her when they had lain together in his bed, how his lips had rustled her hair and caressed her breasts, and how he had spoken words of love. It was his gentleness she remembered now, not the harshness of his later treatment. Every grin, every kiss, was etched in her brain forever, and she hugged the memories to herself. Lying upon her pallet, she could almost feel the thickness of his raven-black hair between her fingers and smell the manly scent of him in the darkness. She wanted him so powerfully her body ached. Then she thought of him with Gwendolyn Harding. She wondered if he were lying with her at that moment, making masterful, passionate love to that icy, golden beauty, and all of her precious memories shattered. She sobbed, silently, brokenly, into the filthy straw of her bedding. Misery sat upon her like a great smothering beast, crushing her with its awesome weight, cutting off air, light, and movement. After the third night of imprisonment, tormented by her memories, she began to wonder if death would not indeed be preferable to this bleak confinement, to the waiting and the fear, and the thoughts of Justin. This was slow death. At least upon the gallows, the end would be quick.

The morning of Lucy's trial dawned clear and mild. Birds twittered as they swooped from tree to tree, and through the prison window, Belinda saw wildflowers bobbing gaily along the edge of the village. It seemed a day befitting a picnic or a fair. Instead, it was the day when Lucy would face her accusers and learn her fate.

Belinda clung to the metal bars of her cell, watching

helplessly as her friend was led off down the corridor by the burly constable. Lucy had gone bravely, wordlessly, only exchanging one resigned glance with Belinda before leaving the cell. It was Belinda who had to restrain herself from bursting into tears. The unfairness of it all welled up within her as she watched her fair-haired, quiet friend marshaled toward the meetinghouse. Lucy was so good, so gentle! If she, whose only crime had been to save a child's life should be convicted, how much hope could a flame-haired hellion harbor, one who had raised eyebrows from her very first day in the village because of her proud, defiant carriage and outspoken ways—not to mention her "Devil's hair"! Belinda knew that if anyone deserved acquittal, it was Lucy, for a less wicked person she had never met. But she knew with a horrid certainty deep in her heart what the verdict would be when Lucy returned to her cell after the trial. Guilty . . . guilty . . . guilty . . .

And so it was. Lucy actually smiled when she told Belinda the news. She laid a hand on her arm, saying in her quiet way that Belinda should not be upset. "I knew the way it would be," she stated. "Mistress Miles cried out against me, and even Will Gersholm spoke of a Devil's vision that nearly killed his child. I always knew, Belinda, that if my secret visions were discovered I would be accused of witchcraft. People are terrified of what they don't understand." She gave a rueful laugh. "I don't understand it either. But I know that my visions are not evil—they're not messages from the Devil. They just come to me—good or bad. In this case, they helped save a child's life. And yet—"

"And yet you are condemned to death, despite the good you accomplished!" Belinda's green-gold eyes sparkled in the duskiness of the cell. "Why are people so stupid?" she demanded. "Have they lost all their senses?"

"No. But they are frightened and superstitious. They must explain away the dangers and problems besetting them and . . . and . . ."

"Oh, do not make excuses for them!" Belinda cried. "I am sick to death of them all. Lucy, we must not dwell on what has happened, or why. We must think. There must be a way we can escape from this place."

"No, Belinda." Lucy faced her squarely, her soft brown eyes filled with resolution. "I will not deceive myself with false hopes. I will face my death with dignity."

"We can escape, I tell you!"

Tears glimmered in Lucy's eyes. Her small face was very pale. "You also told me that you would send word to Henry—that he would help me!" Lucy replied throbbingly. Her lips trembled. "And yet—"

"I did get word to him! He still might come!"

Lucy shook her head. "No! He no longer cares! If he had, I would have heard from him long before now. Belinda, it has been so many months since—" Her voice broke and she struggled for control of her emotions. Belinda's heart twisted inside her. She knew all too well how it felt to be abandoned by the man one loved.

"It's all right, Lucy. I understand." She squeezed Lucy's thin hands. "I feel the same way about Justin. I can't understand how this could have happened between us—our love was so powerful, so real—or so I believed for a time." She straightened her shoulders suddenly, forcing away the misery which threatened to suck her into a quagmire of despair. "But we must face the fact that we are alone now. We have to find a way to save ourselves. It may take some time, but if we think and plan—"

"Belinda." Lucy gritted her teeth. "There is no time. Your trial is tomorrow."

"T-Tomorrow?"

Lucy nodded. "They will come for you in the morning."

Belinda sank down upon her pallet. The color drained from her cheeks. Tomorrow. Tomorrow. She felt suddenly cold, her body chilled by ice which rushed through her blood. Tomorrow.

"I'm so sorry, Belinda." Lucy dropped down beside her, and there were tears on her cheeks. She plucked at her brown homespun dress miserably. "It is all my fault, I know! If it had not been for me, you would not have been accused and—"

"No!" Belinda clung to her. "It is no one's fault! Only theirs!" She pointed toward the high window, outside of which were villagers going on about their daily business. "*They* are the ones who are guilty, not you or me! Don't ever blame yourself, Lucy! I don't. I know that we have done nothing wrong, but...but that doesn't help the fear...the dread....Oh, Lucy, what are we going to do?"

But Lucy had no answers for her. They sat there together, two young women filled with terror, locked in the village prison without friend or ally. They spoke little, for there was not much to say. The same gruesome fate awaited them both, and they were helpless to avoid it. Shadows deepened all about them as nighttime fell, yet the greatest darkness lay in their hearts, for there dwelled the blackness of despair.

In the morning, along with her breakfast of gruel and rye biscuits, Belinda was brought a clean gown. It was the black woolen one from her cousin's house, the one she had worn to Thursday meeting when Justin was in town. She donned it after washing as best she could with the bucket of icy water brought to the cell, and smoothed her thick, red-gold hair with her fingers. She shook her head when Lucy urged her to partake of breakfast, for she didn't think she could eat. Her stomach was churning inside her, and her throat was dry. She paced the cell in a frenzy of apprehension, wishing the day and the trial were over. A clamminess coated her body, as the hour for the ordeal drew near. She felt her heart thumping wildly inside her chest. She knew the nightmare would begin soon.

Constable Vining came for her shortly before nine o'clock.

"Come, Mistress Cady! This is your judgment day," he announced, rattling the prison keys in his huge hands. "Magistrate Cady awaits you."

Belinda was rooted to the spot. She couldn't move. Her hands had turned to ice and her feet to marble, and she stood like a statue in the center of the tiny cell, staring into the constable's ruddy face. For a wild moment, she thought of bolting past him, of trying to flee down that dim, dusty corridor and out into the village, of once more darting into the thick web of forest just beyond the village square. But in the same moment, she knew it was useless. They would catch her, drag her back. She would only delay the inevitable. She blinked, seeing clearly now the cold satisfaction in Constable Vining's face. He was enjoying her fear, relishing his duty of escorting the prisoner to her trial. No doubt he would enjoy it even more if he were forced to drag her forcibly to the meetinghouse door. Her hands clenched into fists. She straightened her back and tilted her chin, eyes darkening to stormy green.

"I am ready," she said evenly, in a tone as cold and proud as she could command. She moved with slow dignity toward the cell door. When she reached it, she turned suddenly to gaze back at Lucy, who stood near the window, tears streaming down her cheeks. Their eyes met, and held. Lucy mustered a ghost of a smile. "Good luck," she whispered, but they both knew the words were meaningless. Belinda nodded and turned back to the door.

Outside, the sun sparkled like a great golden coin in a crystal blue sky. A warm breeze danced in from the sea, fluttering the little green buds adorning the trees and bringing with it all the delicious, invigorating fragrance of spring. Belinda lifted her head and breathed deeply of the fresh air. It seemed ironic to her that on the day of her trial, when her death sentence would be announced, spring should return to Salem Village, bathing the commons in a shimmering glow, beckoning one to taste the sweetness of life. She longed to smell the wildflowers in the thickets, to lift her arms toward the sun, to race barefoot against the breeze. Instead, she walked along beside this burly Puritan, to the somber meetinghouse where her fate would be sealed. As they reached the meetinghouse door, she took one final breath of the sea-scented air, then, tightening her lips, stepped into the dark building to meet her accusers. Spring's glory was left behind. Grim, harsh reality awaited.

For the next several hours the trial went exactly as Belinda had anticipated. Frances Miles shrieked that she was tormented by the red-haired witch, and the half-dozen girls who customarily followed her about sat perched in the front pew like a row of birds on a tree branch, screaming when Frances screamed, clutching their heads when she did so, pointing and shouting at Belinda in imitation of their leader. "She stabs us, she stabs us!" they chanted over and over, while Belinda sat silent and unmoving before them. Two men guarded her, standing over her at the bench, yet everyone in the meetinghouse regarded her with terror and awe. She was a witch, Frances declared, of immense power, the most dangerous one yet to accost the village. Together with Lucy Brewer, she served as the Devil's chief accomplice in torturing the righteous. As long as Witch Cady was alive, Frances cried, she and others of piety and grace would have no peace.

When Jonathan Cady testified that Belinda had sought to weave her spells of seduction upon him, the meetinghouse roared in horror. People began screaming out, shouting against Satan's whore. Through it all, Belinda sat with clasped hands, her face pale but calm. Inside, she trembled like a feather caught in a windstorm, but through rigid self-control, she managed to keep up her stoic facade, holding her head proudly despite the barrage of accusations raining down upon her. She braced herself against the hatred and suspicion directed at her, determined to hide her agitation from her enemies. Then Jonathan Cady, imperious in his scarlet robes, called for silence in the babbling courtroom.

"The Crown now calls forth another witness against this woman," he announced, eyeing the assembly with barely concealed excitement. "It is our duty to hear every fact of evidence relating to this case, and the information offered by this witness has only yesterday come to our attention. It is pertinent to this trial, tragically pertinent, and I ask for complete quiet so that the witness may speak for all to hear." He paused, while the villagers hushed, and then went on in his harsh, cold tone, "The Crown calls upon Yeoman Tom Phelps! Step forward, in the name of the king!"

Belinda gasped, turning upon her bench as a man rose in the rear of the meetinghouse. In all the commotion, she had not even noticed him before, yet he had been seated there all the while, waiting for his chance to speak. Tom Phelps, his sandy hair neatly brushed and his great, bulging shoulders encased in a buckskin coat, surged to his feet and swaggered forward. He approached the magistrate, but as he did so, he turned his head to glance at Belinda, and his eyes glared fiendishly into hers. Involuntarily, she shrank backward in the pew, all of her careful composure shattered. Memories of that dark, windy night at sea when he had attacked her flooded back, prickling her with horrible revulsion. She tasted once again the liquor on his lips, smelled his sweat and lust, and felt his brute's hands fondling her, and she swayed in her seat. "No!" she cried, nausea choking her. "No! Not... *you!*"

"Aye, 'tis me, Mistress Cady!" he shot back triumphantly. "I've come to tell the truth about you—about what you did to me and my family! I've come to see you hanged for your witchery!"

"To you and your—" Belinda jumped to her feet, her breast heaving. "I don't know what you're saying, but it is lies, all lies!" She wheeled on the villagers, spreading her hands. "This man is a scoundrel, a molester of women! He ought to be locked up in the prison for all the days of his life!"

"Silence!" Jonathan Cady thundered at her, his eyes aglow. The guards on either side of Belinda seized her arms as if to prevent her from attacking the witness. She struggled desperately to free herself. "The defendant will be silent, or the court will bind and gag her to ensure that she is!" Cady threatened. "This witness has come from Andover to give evidence at this trial. He shall speak freely, and if the witch tries to hinder him, she will be dealt with severely! Is that understood, Mistress Cady?"

"You cannot listen to him!" Belinda turned pleading eyes to the assembled villagers. "He is a drunkard and a brute—he attacked me on board our ship—"

"Silence!" Jonathan banged his fist upon the long table. "This is your last warning!"

Belinda glanced wildly about her. Every face in the meetinghouse was set against her. Hatred and fear were an almost physical force which made her slump against the guards who held her. It was no use. They would not listen. What did it matter anyway? Her conviction was a certainty, with or without the testimony of Tom Phelps.

She nodded, biting her lips to contain her frustration. Cady ordered her to be seated once again, and the guards released her. She sank down on the pew, weakness seeping through her, watching through dazed and bleary eyes as Tom Phelps gave his testimony. He spoke with a rough forcefulness which matched his countryman's clothes, but he held the entire meetinghouse spellbound with his tale of seduction and murder.

"'Twas on board the *Esmeralda* that I first saw Mistress Cady," Phelps began, standing in the front of the meetinghouse and facing the assembly. Belinda noted that his blond, stubby beard was gone; he was clean-shaven now, so that his broad, raw-boned face had a more respectable appearance, although he still carried with him the air of a country lout. She shuddered merely watching him, comparing him unconsciously with Justin Harding. Both men were equally tall and powerfully built, but Justin, besides being dark in contrast to Phelps's sandy hair and ruddy complexion, possessed an aura of elegance and cool intelligence to match his physical prowess, while Tom Phelps was merely a big bull of a man, whose swagger and bravado concealed nothing more than a lusty coarseness beneath. Watching him, she trembled inside. Her memories of that night at sea sickened her, and her fingers clenched her black woolen skirt as she listened to his lies.

"She came after me on the ship, trying to . . . to seduce me, Magistrate, strange as that might seem. I told her plain I was a married man, with a child on the way, but she . . . she just laughed and whispered to me . . . oh, she whispered things a decent man cannot even say! I saw what she was up to and told her to leave me be, but she put herself in my path whenever she might, shameless as a strumpet, casting out her lures." Phelps eyed his audience, sensing their disgust with the girl he was accusing, and a light flickered in his eyes. But he continued his portrayal of a humble, grief-stricken man, keeping his huge, muscled arms limply at his side as he spoke, his voice low and sincere.

"Then she stopped my poor wife, Lettie, one day, near the end of the voyage. I saw them talking on the ship's deck, but I wasn't near enough to hear what they said. But Lettie, she was crying, Magistrate, when this witch finished with her. She came running back to me, scared as a rabbit, and she told me what Mistress Cady had said."

Belinda, rigid in her seat, stared in shock at the man before her. She couldn't believe he was actually testifying to these outrageous lies, yet there he stood, going on and on with his wicked tale, mesmerizing everyone in the meetinghouse. Cousin Jonathan, his strange, icy-green eyes gleaming, leaned forward on his bench, his bony hands tightly clasped on the table before him. "Go on, Yeoman Phelps," Jonathan Cady rasped, nodding his head. "Tell us what this young woman said to your wife."

"She told Lettie she would put a spell on her and the unborn child! She said they stood in the way of what she wanted, that she would rid herself of them both! Oh, Magistrate Cady, she terrified my poor wife. I went to see Mistress Cady and warned her to leave us alone, and then, sir, I prayed for protection against her witch's ways!"

Phelps turned his sandy head to stare at Belinda, straight-backed in her pew, with her red-gold hair spilling loosely down her back, brilliant against the blackness of her woolen gown. "I hoped, I *thought*, we were rid of her when we docked in Salem Town!" he continued, anger throbbing in his voice. "Lettie and me settled in Andover and by accident soon met a woman named Hannah Emory. She had come from Salem Village to nurse her sister who was ill, and she told us that she was used to work for you, Magistrate Cady, but now your orphaned kinswoman, a wench by the name of Belinda Cady, had come to replace her."

Jonathan nodded. His pale face looked more ghostly than ever in the dimness of the meetinghouse. "Continue."

"Hannah Emory spoke ill of Mistress Cady. She feared her for her Devil's hair. I grew more and more worried, though I didn't say a word to Lettie." He shook his head, sadness creeping into his voice. "Then, Lettie's time came. She was in terrible pain, oh, 'twas awful to hear her, and she screamed over and over that the witch was killing her! I was afraid, but I prayed for her all the hours she struggled. But...she died birthing, Magistrate, and the child with her! I was left with a dead wife and son, robbed of my only family!" He swung angrily toward the pew where Belinda sat in horror and jabbed a finger at her. "She killed them!" he bellowed. "That red-haired witch cast her Satan's spell and killed my wife and child!"

"No!" Belinda surged to her feet. "It's a lie! I barely knew Lettie Phelps, but I...I liked her! I never argued with her or threatened her. You've got to believe me! None of this is true!"

"Hang the witch!" Frances Miles shrieked, clutching her head in apparent agony.

"Hang the witch, hang the witch!" the girls chanted in their high-pitched, wailing voices.

"Aye, hang the witch!" Tom Phelps shouted, his huge fists waving in the air. "Avenge my wife and son with her death!"

"No!" Belinda screamed, fighting off the solemn

guards who tried to subdue her. "I am innocent! Innocent! My only crime is the color of my hair—an accident of birth! I saved the life of Will Gersholm's child—I found him before he could drown in the pond! Don't you see that? I have never treated anyone ill in this village—or anywhere else! I defy you to prove differently!"

"You killed my family!" Phelps lashed at her.

"You torment me and these other poor girls night and day!" Frances cried.

"Hang the witch!"

Jonathan Cady banged upon the table, shouting for order. At last the uproar subsided. Belinda, each arm tightly gripped by a guard, was dragged before the magistrate's table. Jonathan regarded her, his thin, pasty face harsh and unyielding. "It is the duty of this court to inform you that you are found guilty of witchcraft in the Massachusetts Bay Colony established in the name of the Crown," he intoned. "I hereby sentence you to death upon Gallows Hill, where you shall hang by the neck until the last wicked breath is squeezed from your body." His lips twisted venomously. "The hanging, Witch Cady, will take place tomorrow. You and Witch Brewer shall die together. Both of you shall mount the gallows at dawn!"

Belinda was vaguely aware of commotion all around her: shouting, shoving, mutters, and prayers. She felt rough hands on her arms, seizing her, dragging her forward, and became aware that she was no longer in the meetinghouse, but outside in the sunlight, being propelled across the square, back toward the prison. She blinked against the blinding brightness, stumbling as her guards drew her forcibly along. Dazed, she tried automatically to free herself from their brutal grasps, but was without the strength or energy to accomplish this. She next found herself in the corridor and then back at her tiny cell. The door swung open and she was pushed inside. She went sprawling down upon her pallet, dimly hearing the cell door slam shut and the guards muttering as they retreated. Then she heard Lucy's voice, filled with horror. She gazed upward, still too stunned to focus clearly on her friend's agitated face.

"Belinda, Belinda, can you hear me?" Lucy's voice seemed to come from a long way off. "What did they do to you? What happened?"

Belinda moistened her lips with her tongue. She tried to speak, but only a hoarse croak emerged. Then she cleared her throat and shook her head at Lucy slowly, dazedly. "We're going to hang, Lucy," she whispered. "You and I. Tomorrow at dawn—on Gallows Hill." She began to tremble, as Lucy dropped down, weeping, beside her. "We're going to hang."

CHAPTER NINETEEN

JUSTIN HARDING WATCHED as dawn broke through the last fleeting shadows of the night. Faintly, it spread a warm, pinkish glow through the sky, growing stronger, surer, as darkness retreated and the moon went into hiding. The day promised sunshine. The air was calm. Justin buried his head in his hands.

Nearby, Simon Foster stirred on his pallet, glancing up at the man he had known all his life. "Justin?" Simon's voice was a gravelly whisper in the darkness of the cell which imprisoned them. "Are you . . . all right?"

Slowly, Justin lifted his head, staring at Simon through bleary eyes. "Yes." His voice was terse, but his filthy, drawn face betrayed his misery. Simon pulled himself upright, stretched, and then moved forward to clap a hand on his friend's broad shoulder.

"You didn't sleep again," he remarked quietly. "Are you thinking about . . . the Bastard?"

"No. Not this time." Justin's lips twisted at mention of the name. Six years ago, when he had commanded his ship against the pirates who preyed on merchant vessels, the Sea Bastard had been the one pirate captain who had succeeded in capturing the Gray Knight. Justin had spent a full week on board the Bastard's ship, imprisoned and tortured, before his crew had managed to rescue him. It was a week he would never forget. Last night, the first night of his imprisonment in Boston Prison, he had lain awake nearly till dawn, fighting off the memories that this black, cramped confinement stirred in him. Horrible, gruesome memories. He had slept finally, when the hour was near sunrise, but had awakened shortly after, his body soaked with sweat and panic shining in his eyes. The nightmare of the Sea Bastard had come to him again. He had not been plagued by it for some time now, but here, in this prison cell, it tormented him anew, and it had taken all of his self-control to drive it from his mind. Tonight, however, after a full day of questioning by Boston officials, it was not the Sea Bastard who had kept him awake. No, someone else. Someone who had smitten him with even greater power than that vicious pirate. A woman, whose power lay in her beauty, her gentleness, her grace. Belinda.

"What do you think they've done with her, Justin?" Simon had been watching his friend's eyes. He knew what Justin was thinking of as surely as though it had been spoken.

"She is probably in prison in Salem Village, just as we are here." Justin Harding's mouth was grim. He moved restlessly and came to his feet, a tall, formidable figure in the gloom of the cell. "No doubt there will be a trial. I just wonder how soon it will take place and how much time before they—"

"Before they hang her?" Simon, too, scrambled to his feet. "Justin, we can't let that happen to her! Bad enough they murdered Eliza!" he exclaimed savagely, "without being able to kill Mistress Cady, too! Damnation, I wish I'd been there when that cousin of hers showed up. I'd have..."

His voice trailed off and Justin wheeled to face him.

Their eyes met for a moment, and then Justin spoke, quietly. "You'd have done what, Simon? Fought the entire throng of men in that house? Rescued her?" He shook his head. "I wanted to, don't you know that? I wanted to break Jonathan Cady in two and kill every other man in that room! But fortunately, common sense prevailed. I realized that the only real chance to save Belinda would be to wait. To play the innocent and claim no knowledge that she was wanted for practicing witchcraft in Salem. If I had tried violence on the spot, and failed, the situation would be even worse than it is now. The way things stand at present"—his eyes narrowed, consideringly—"we will either convince them that we had no complicity in hiding a fugitive, and by doing so attain our release, or...we shall manage to escape."

"Escape?" Simon glanced bitterly at the solid walls of their cell, at the heavily barred door. "And how do you expect to do that, might I ask?"

Justin's eyes glinted dangerously. "I don't know," he muttered. "But believe me, Simon, I will find a way—even if it means bending these bars with my bare hands!"

Simon gave a rueful smile. "I don't doubt you, Justin. I've seen what you're capable of, and getting free of these Puritans will not be too difficult for you. But I hope we won't be too late. The poor girl's life is at stake, you know."

"I know." Justin turned away from the other man. He strode to the window, ignoring the three other prisoners still asleep in the cell, all of whom had been arrested for various crimes, such as drunkenness, thievery, and idleness, in the past two days. He stared out the window, watching the sun shed its golden light upon the awakening town. Despite his calm appearance, he chafed inwardly. Terror filled him, not for himself, for there were few things that held fear for the Gray Knight, but for

Belinda. He couldn't banish from his mind the heart-wrenching way she had gazed at him as they had dragged her out of the house that night. It had taken all the self-control he possessed not to try to rescue her by force then and there, but he had succeeded in taming his fierce emotions, in maintaining the posture of indifference which was crucial to his strategy. He had realized immediately the importance of convincing the officials that he knew nothing of Belinda's escape from Salem or the impending arrest which had spurred her to flee. His story had been that they had met by accident in Boston, renewing their brief acquaintance, but that she had told him nothing of the truth, only that she had left Salem Village to make a new beginning for herself and he had offered her employment as companion and maidservant to his future bride. She had come to the house on Oliver Street the day of Gwendolyn's arrival to meet her and had been hired immediately. That was why she had been in the house, on her way to join the reception. He had maintained all along that Belinda had lied to him from the start, that he had had no idea she was being sought by the authorities. After a full day of relentless questioning, his story was intact. Always cool under pressure, he had frustrated every attempt by the Boston officials to confuse or contradict him. Simon, arrested the same night as himself, had told the same story. And, he concluded, Gwendolyn had kept her end as well. Not that she had been arrested. Only he and his menservants had been taken for questioning immediately after Belinda had been seized, taken ironically to the same Boston Prison where Belinda spent the night, though in separate wings, so that she had not even known of their arrest. Gwendolyn had merely been interrogated at Oliver Street the following day, and, since he had not heard otherwise, she must have repeated the story precisely as he had hissed it in her ear while Belinda was being led away. So everything was in order thus far. Justin knew it was only a matter of time before he and his men were released, yet he gritted his teeth as the tension coiled and slithered inside him, like a snake about to lunge. Just thinking of Belinda in Jonathan Cady's power made him half-mad. If she was hurt in any way, any way at all... His powerful hand gripped the bar of the window, tightening around it until his knuckles went white. Then, suddenly, he gave a curse, his voice harsh in the new morning. *If she was hurt.* Of course she was hurt. But not, to his knowledge, by Cady or Salem's superstitious villagers. At least, not yet. No, Belinda had been hurt more deeply than any physical pain could wound her. She had been hurt by none other than himself.

Thinking now of the way he had deceived her made him groan. Why, why had he been such a bastard? Instead of telling her the truth about Gwendolyn and explaining that he no longer wished to marry the bitch, he had deliberately allowed Belinda to believe that *she* was the one who meant nothing to him. He had done it out of anger, when she had doubted him, to teach her a lesson, but it had been a cruel notion, a coward's way of dealing with a situation he wasn't quite sure how to handle. Fury raged within him, all of it directed at himself. Gwendolyn had become unimportant to him the evening he had first made love to Belinda, that inky, wind-swept night when they had lain before the fire in her cousin's house. He had known then that his heart belonged completely and forever to the glowing, enchanting rebel with the hair of flame. She had freed him from the obsession which had plagued him ten long years, made him realize that what he had felt for Gwendolyn all those years was not love, but a desire to possess what had been promised him and then denied. It was his pride which had made him long for Gwendolyn so bitterly, not his passion. Belinda, wild and beautiful and loving, had shown him that. She had stirred his passion in a way he had never known before, and more, she had stirred in him a tenderness long forgotten. She was a woman who would stand beside a man, strong and loyal, fighting every obstacle with as much strength as he. Her love was true, not a whim or stratagem. And yet what had he done to her love, to *her*? He had mocked them, torn them to pieces with his vicious game. Remembering the pain in her eyes when she had first seen Gwendolyn, thinking herself betrayed, made Justin suddenly slam his fist against the wall of his cell. He had to reach Belinda! He had to rescue her, get her to safety, and then he had to explain what he'd done and pray that she would forgive him. He didn't dare imagine what he would do if she did not. Life without her would be intolerable. He closed his eyes, praying with desperate fervency that she was safe from harm. If anything happened to her...

"Justin, you have a visitor," Simon muttered at his elbow.

He spun around to find Gwendolyn Harding outside the door to his cell, accompanied by Magistrate Edmund Lyon and a sour-faced constable. With a start he realized that it was no longer dawn, but well into morning, and that he had been brooding about Belinda for more than an hour. He composed himself swiftly and moved with long strides toward the cell door. "Good morning," he said to Gwendolyn in a voice that was cool and dry. "To what do I owe the honor of this visit?"

"Oh, Justin, are you all right?" She looked him over in horror. He had not been allowed to change from the dress clothes he had worn the night of the reception, and he made a filthy, unkempt picture as he stood in the dingy cell. His lips twisted into a smile.

"I am quite fit, Gwendolyn," he drawled with lazy mockery, "though not quite as presentable as you." He raked her voluptuous form, elegantly clad in cerulean blue silk, and his voice tautened. "You are looking quite lovely today, my darling. I am glad this abominable mess has not in any way infringed upon your splendor. I see you have taken quite as much time and effort with your toilette as always. But tell me, have you come to escort me from this place? Are you here, Magistrate, to at last release me and my men? We are fast growing weary of being detained in this way when we have committed no crime at all."

Magistrate Lyon, a florid, periwigged man of less than average inches, who only two nights earlier had been a guest at Justin Harding's reception, watched his prisoner with needle-sharp eyes. "No, I'm not here to release you, Master Harding. Not yet. I have more questions for you, as a matter of fact. I'm going to bring you to the Town Center. But Mistress Harding came to me and begged to see you. She said she wanted to be certain that you were well. I told her she could come here with me if she chose."

Justin nodded. "Might I have a few words alone with my fiancée, Magistrate?" he inquired.

The sharp-eyed little man frowned and crossed his arms across his chest. The silver buttons on his satin jacket seemed about to burst.

"I think not—" he began, but Gwendolyn interrupted, putting a gloved hand upon his arm.

"Oh, Magistrate Lyon, if you would but relent? I dearly wish a moment of privacy with my betrothed husband," she pleaded prettily. Her voice tinkled like little bells in the gloom of the prison. "This unseemly business has caused a delay in all of our plans, and there are several personal matters I must discuss with Justin." She smiled into the magistrate's eyes as though he were the kindest, most understanding man in the world. "I know that ordinarily such a request would be out of the question, but I thought that a man of your influence would be able to grant such a small request without too much trouble. Please, sir, I would be forever, and most gratefully, in your debt."

Magistrate Lyon cleared his throat. He glanced from Gwendolyn's radiant countenance to Justin's dark, arrogant one, and then gave a little shrug. "Very well. Constable Sawyer and I will wait down the hall for you to conclude your discussion. And then," he added with a warning glance at his tall, raven-haired prisoner, "I will personally escort you to the Town Center for further questioning! Today, Master Harding, it is my intention to learn from you the truth of this matter!"

With these words, he gestured to the sour-faced constable, and they both shuffled off down the hallway of the prison. Gwendolyn stared at Justin, her gloved hands gripping the metal bars dividing them.

"Justin!" she whispered. "How *could* you have gotten us into this horrible predicament?" Anger flushed her cold, beautiful face. "I have never been so humiliated in my life! To think that my fiancé is imprisoned like some wild beast and that *I* am being questioned by the authorities like some kind of common lawbreaker! It is dreadful!" Her violet eyes smoldered as her rage spilled out. "You never should have taken in that disgusting girl! You ought to have summoned the authorities as soon as you found her in Boston and learned that she was a fugitive! I don't know how you could have exposed me to such a scandal!" she declared.

Justin's eyes narrowed. "If you've finished your hysterical rantings, Gwendolyn, there are *important* matters I need discuss with you." Her mouth fell open at his ruthless tone, and she would have stepped backward, but the force of his words and his dangerously gleaming gray eyes held her immobile. "Did you tell the authorities what I instructed you to tell them? Exactly?" he demanded.

"Yes...yes! Of course! Do you think I *want* you to remain in jail?" she flashed. "I am doing everything in my power to attain your release, and so is Timothy!"

"Timothy?" Justin stepped closer. He knew that all of his own men, those working for him on Oliver Street and on his ship docked in the harbor, had been taken into custody, mainly because the town's officials feared they might try to rescue him if they remained free. Apparently, though, they had spared Timothy Worth, a fact which might prove useful. "Do you mean he wasn't arrested?"

"No. He's been trying frantically to persuade the authorities to free you. He keeps babbling some kind of utter nonsense about trying to rescue that...Mistress Cady!"

Justin nodded almost to himself. "So only my own men and I are prisoners."

"Only? It is bad enough!" she replied, regarding him bitterly. "I came to the colonies to wed a respectable man, a man of influence and power and—"

"Wealth?" he supplied for her, an ugly light in his eyes. "Like my brother, eh, Gwendolyn?" He gave a short laugh. "But you have found more than you bargained for. Well, my darling, if it is a staid and stuffy gentleman you wish to wed, you have chosen the wrong man."

"Justin..." Her eyes fixed themselves upon his harsh face, and she bit her lip. "I...I'm sorry. I have behaved like a...shrew. I know how upsetting all this must be to you, as it is to me! Pray don't think I wish to marry anyone but you! You are the one man I have always loved!" She bestowed on him a sweet, dazzling smile.

"How touching." Justin's lips curled. "Tell me, Gwendolyn, did Mrs. Gavin bring the food and clothing to Belinda yesterday morning, as I instructed? I warned you she must set forth early, before Cady took Belinda back to Salem."

Gwendolyn's lashes veiled her eyes. She hesitated only an instant before replying. "Oh yes, yes. I told Mrs. Gavin exactly what to do. She took Belinda all the provisions you ordered for her comfort. Only..." Her voice trailed away and she shrugged.

"Only what?"

"Well, Justin, if you must know, Mrs. Gavin dawdled on the way and was too late to reach the girl before she was carted off to her little village." Gwendolyn gazed at him innocently, spreading her hands. "It wasn't *my* fault, you know—I told her to set out quite early and to be quick about it, but you know how servants are."

Murderous rage surged through Justin as he realized that Belinda had not even received the warm clothing and food he had intended for her. That meant that she had made the entire journey to Salem clad in nothing but that damned satin gown she'd been wearing! And it had rained all through the day! His hand shot between the metal bars to grip Gwendolyn's wrist. He pulled her close against the bars separating them.

"I don't believe you."

"What do you mean?" Her eyes, meeting his, reflected a dawning fear. She tried to shake free, but failed. "I...I did exactly what you ordered....I..."

"You're lying! I'll wager you didn't even give Mrs. Gavin my instructions until it was too late. Did you? Did you, Gwendolyn?" He shook her until she cried out, then, with a curse, he released her, knowing that if he didn't, he would probably break her arm. Gasping, she jumped backward, staring at him as though seeing him for the first time.

His eyes were as cold and hard as steel. "Gwendolyn, I have one word of advice for you."

She waited soundlessly, shocked by the contempt upon his face.

"Get out of here—now. Go back to Oliver Street, pack your things, and get yourself on the first ship back to England!"

"What?" Gwendolyn's hands clasped her lace-adorned throat. She gasped in dismay. "But...Justin...we are to be wed....My darling, what are you saying?"

He laughed, a sound as cold and deadly as the thrust of a sword. "At this point I have no intention of marrying you, Gwendolyn. None whatsoever."

She paled. "Justin...you wrote to me, begging me to come here, to join you in the colonies and be your wife!"

"Quite true, my dear. My intentions were honorable when I sent for you from England. I thought you were the only woman I would ever love, the only one who could ever satisfy me. But I was wrong, Gwendolyn. I was a fool." He smiled down at the woman facing him across the bars, a cool, mocking smile. "I met Belinda. I fell in love with her. And you cannot begin to approach her, my darling. She is the only woman I will ever love. Or marry."

"Belinda!" Gwendolyn's wide, violet eyes narrowed on the word. "Do you mean to tell me that you prefer that...that child...to me? Justin, don't be a fool! You waited ten long years for the chance to marry me! Now we are together and—"

"Get out of here, Gwendolyn."

"No! I...I can't!" Panic rose in her breast and spilled out her violet eyes as she realized that he was speaking in earnest. "Justin, you can't do this to me! How can I return to England? What will I tell them? It...it would be too...humiliating!"

"I know exactly how you feel, Gwendolyn." His eyes met and held hers, and she caught her breath. Silence quivered between them. He broke it after a long, purposeful moment. "But I give you fair warning, Mistress Harding. I will be out of this place soon, and if I find you on my premises, I'll wring your lovely neck. And if Belinda Cady has suffered any illness because you neglected to send Mrs. Gavin with the provisions in time, I will follow you to England and...but no, you don't wish to know my intentions! You'd be far too frightened to sleep nights."

Gwendolyn swallowed. Her beautiful, cold face was white as parchment. "But Timothy might not agree to accompany me. He keeps talking about staying here...helping you and that...girl."

"I suggest you persuade him." Justin spoke curtly now. He had grown bored with the conversation, for he had other things on his mind. "It is fortunate he was not imprisoned with the rest of us, for now he can take you off my hands. That is service enough; tell him not to bother about me. I will get out of here and take care of Belinda myself."

Fury shone in Gwendolyn's violet eyes. She leaned forward. "Belinda! That little fool! She had not even the wits to hide herself in her room as you advised her. And what did she get for her stupidity? Exactly what she deserved! She's going to be hanged, Justin! There is nothing you can do to save her!" Gwendolyn's voice rose viciously, but Justin remained calm. "You'll never see your precious Belinda again, and you'll have lost me as well!" She gave a short, malicious laugh. "Justin Harding, you're going to find yourself alone!"

"There are worse things," he responded evenly, his gray eyes bright and hard.

She lunged forward suddenly, her nails poised to rake his face, but he merely took one step backward, regarding her coolly. "Remember, I want you gone by the end of this day. Consider yourself warned, my darling."

Watching him, Gwendolyn felt a knot of fear twisting inside her. Despite the fact that the heavily barred cell door divided them, Justin Harding looked very dangerous. He looked every inch a pirate, one who would stop at nothing to get what he wanted or to obtain his revenge. The expression in his eyes made her shiver. She took a step backward. Another. "I am going," she uttered in a strangled voice. "I...I never want to see you again!"

"The feeling, Mistress Harding, is entirely mutual."

She gave a little gasp then and whirled about. He watched her disappear down the murky corridor in a flash of blue satin. Beside him, Simon Foster coughed.

"I can't believe I was such a fool for so many years, Simon," Justin remarked, glancing ruefully at his oldest friend. "To think I would have actually wed that heartless bitch if not for Belinda."

"'Twould have been a sad day." Simon shuddered and shook his head. "I'm glad you finally have seen that she is not nearly worthy of you."

Justin paced the cell, ignoring the other three inmates who huddled against the wall, watching him and Simon warily. He felt amazingly free. Unfettered. A burden under which he had labored for ten years had finally been lifted from his shoulders, and the surge of release flowing through him was almost intoxicating. It was as if he had been reborn and was ready to begin life anew. Only one thing was lacking to make that life worthwhile. *And*, he thought, straightening his broad shoulders beneath the much-wrinkled and dusty black satin evening coat, *that will soon be remedied. I will reach Belinda and save her from the gallows, or I will die in the attempt.*

He turned slowly, watchfully, as the footsteps of the magistrate and constable approached down the prison corridor. The simplest and quickest way to get out of here was to convince them of his innocence in aiding an accused witch. He was prepared to spend the entire day doing just that. He was even prepared to be civil to that pompous, arrogant little Lyon if it would help free him any the sooner. Such a tame course was repugnant to one who had spent years battling openly with his enemies, but he accepted the fact that in this circumstance, open confrontation would not serve him to advantage. So, as the constable shoved open the cell door and barked for him to extend his hands for the manacles, he obeyed in silence, hiding his contempt. Both the magistrate and the constable had eyed his tall, powerful frame with unease on the previous day, insisting that his hands be manacled together behind his back, in obvious anxiety that he might try to overpower them. And well he might have, if they hadn't taken such precautions. Now he maintained a cool, impassive expression as they escorted him from the cell. He knew that later, when he returned, they would repeat the procedure with Simon, hoping that one or the other of them would tell a slightly different story, leaving themselves open to attack. But he wasn't worried. He knew how to handle himself, and he had complete confidence in Simon. If they both watched their steps, the authorities would find themselves with no choice but to release them.

Unfortunately, an unpleasant surprise awaited him when he at last faced his accusers in Magistrate Lyon's small, shuttered office in Boston's Town Center. Seated upon a chair, his hands manacled behind him, Justin regarded the sharp-eyed magistrate with nonchalance, until the latter picked up a roll of parchment from his desk and waved it in the air with a slight flourish.

"Master Harding, you have denied any knowledge that Mistress Belinda Cady was a fugitive being sought for the practice of witchcraft in this colony. You claim you met her in Salem Village while attending to some private business there. I find that most interesting." The magistrate's wigged curls bobbed as he leaned forward eagerly in his ornately carved chair, a chair that looked much too large for his diminutive form. "I have here a missive left yesterday morning by Magistrate Jonathan Cady for my perusal. He had left instructions with the tavernkeeper who was his host during his brief visit here, that this be delivered to me, but that worthy man nearly forgot to carry out his mission. Fortunately, he came upon the document by accident last evening and at once sent it to my door. I have read it with great interest. Great interest," he repeated, a shrewd smile playing about the corners of his lips.

Inwardly, Justin swore. He ought to have killed Jonathan Cady long ago. He felt fairly certain what the document contained, but since he had no other choice at the moment, he continued to play the game. "And what was it that claimed your interest, sir?" he drawled, his dark, arrogant face as unperturbed as though he had been the questioner and the other man a manacled prisoner. He didn't even bother to glance at the stoop-shouldered, scowling constable who stood over him armed with a rapier at his side and a stick in his hands, in case the prisoner became unruly. He kept his keen gray eyes riveted upon Lyon's florid, smirking face.

"Magistrate Cady informs me in this document that your business in Salem was directly related to the witchcraft trials in that village. He says you questioned Mistress Cady about the death by hanging of Witch Elizabeth Foster, admitting that your purpose in the village was to investigate her death. Do you deny this?"

"No."

"Magistrate Cady also maintains that he, Reverend Wilkes, and Constable Vining called upon you at the Four Bells Tavern to question you about your activities, and that you responded with violence, resisting their authority and escaping the premises, and then Salem—in the process doing them all bodily harm!" Lyon jumped up from his desk and minced toward his prisoner. His eyes shone with triumph as he gazed down upon Harding's rugged face. "Do you deny *this?*" he cried.

"No." Justin smiled coldly up at the flushed little man. "I admit that I defended myself when they attempted to arrest me. You see, Magistrate, I had no desire to spend any time in the Salem Village prison, nor to be whipped at the lashing post. You, I am certain, would have done the same."

"I would never have interfered in Salem Village business, or in the business of any other community!" Magistrate Lyon snapped, his victory diminished by Harding's damned nonchalance. "But more to the point, Master Harding, this information casts grave doubts upon your claims of innocence. It shows you have involved yourself in matters relating to the witch-hunts previously and that you have not scrupled to resist authority. Based on your past actions, I now seriously doubt your story that you knew nothing about the Cady girl's escape from that village! I believe you conspired with her, hiding the witch against all considerations for the community and the law! What do you say to that?"

"Prove it." Justin shifted his long legs impatiently. "You have no evidence that I did any such thing, Lyon. This is all a bluff. Why don't you simply release me and my men and let us be on our way?"

"Release you?" the Magistrate barked. "No! I will have you whipped at the post until you confess!"

Justin leaned back in his chair, to all appearances completely at ease. His eyes as they pierced directly into Magistrate Lyon's, were cool and gray as a storm-lashed sea. "You will have no confession from me, Lyon. Do what you will."

Staring into that arrogant, unreadable face, Magistrate Lyon felt the frustration mounting inside him. Questioning this man was like hurling pebbles at a fortress. He pressed his thin lips together. "Constable, take this man to the whipping post and administer fifty lashes! I will interrogate Simon Foster as he listens to his master's shrieks!"

But there were no shrieks from Justin Harding. He withstood the lashing in silence, his eyes shut against the spectators who crowded about to see the Gray Knight publicly chastised for his refusal to cooperate with the authorities. The constable raised his arm again and again, striking with all the force he could muster, but the tall, black-haired prisoner, stripped to the waist to reveal a broad, powerful chest, mighty arms, and a muscular back, made no sound as the whip sliced his flesh. In disappointment, the constable had to content himself with the knowledge that the prisoner's body flinched involuntarily every time the whip struck. Still, he would have been better satisfied if there had been even one cry of pain.

When the fifty lashes had been administered, the constable led his prisoner from the square. It was then that Justin saw two familiar faces in the throng of observers. One man was barrel-chested and stout, with dark, grizzled hair. He wore a fierce frown upon his rough face, and when Justin's eyes met his, Ambrose Cooke's gleamed. He nodded ever so slightly. Justin returned the glance with deliberate casualness, and walked on, though his heartbeat had quickened. Then, just as he reached the end of the square, he saw another face which almost made him start, but he controlled his reaction swiftly, letting his gaze wander without recognition past the man he had seen, and his companion. The man, tall and thin and gray, with bent shoulders, was as familiar to him as Simon Foster, but his companion was a stranger. Yet Justin guessed who he must be and smiled to himself. He was so relieved that his pain ebbed and his step lightened. *Three allies*, he thought to himself as the constable marshaled him back toward the prison. *Now we cannot fail.*

Later, when darkness had fallen over Boston Town, Simon Foster fumed helplessly over his friend, for he had nothing with which to tend his wounds. But Justin merely grinned at him, waving a hand as he sat wearily upon the floor. "Do not heed me, Simon. The pain is not so bad."

"After fifty lashes? Justin, don't try to tell your tales to me!"

Flexing his muscles, Justin winced. "Well, it is not pleasant, but...after the Sea Bastard, my friend, this is nothing. I have endured far worse."

Simon scowled. The other prisoners in their cell had been released after having spent the day in the stocks, and they were alone now. Through the barred window they could hear the mournful cry of gulls and smell the saltiness of the sea. "Ah, Justin," he groaned. "The sea air, the gulls, it all reminds me of those days on the *Gray Lady*. If I close my eyes, I can imagine we are out to sea this very minute, free...ah, free." He ran his gnarled hands through his reddish-brown hair in frustration. "Justin, how can you sit there so calmly? We're rotting here in this prison, and your Mistress Cady is facing her death in that damned Salem Village! What are we going to do?"

"We're going to wait, Simon. Rest, gather our strength, and wait."

"For what, blast it?"

"Freedom." Justin smiled at him, his gray eyes curiously alight and glowing in the dusky cell. "You, I, and the rest of our men have only to wait." As Simon stared at him in mounting amazement, Justin nodded. There was about him an air of contained excitement which Simon had seen many times before. It was the same expression he wore just before commencement of a sea battle. A dangerous, disturbing expression, boding disaster for all those opposing him, inspiring complete confidence in his own men. "Yes, Simon. I have a feeling that our escape is imminent. Unless I am mistaken there are plans being made at this very moment. Soon, my friend, very soon, we will be free."

CHAPTER TWENTY

IT WAS ALMOST MIDNIGHT. Black night draped Salem Village, silvered by a crescent moon. The air was still and heavy, fragrant with the perfume of cowslips and violets growing wild in the forest beyond the square. One could almost hear the whisper of the sea, five miles distant at Salem Town. Almost. The village slept, its citizens tucked into their small, snug beds, resting their bones before the morning's toil began. But two men did not sleep. Like tall, dark shadows in the night, they made their separate, secret ways to the prison at the corner of the square.

Belinda Cady lay upon her pallet, listening to the noises of the night. She could not sleep. She had been counting the hours till dawn ever since supper, and now there were precious few hours left. The sick, twisting fear inside her intensified as each minute passed. Her flesh was clammy and as cold as if death had already come. She was in the grip of terror, more frightened than she had ever been before. Death stalked her, a ghastly specter creeping ever closer, preying upon her mind and heart long before He struck the final blow. She lay still, silently fighting the hysteria which made her want to scream or weep, for she knew that neither would help her now. Nothing, in fact, would help her now.

"Oh, Justin..." It was a thought, a prayer, one which gave her no comfort, though, only a stab of pain. For a short time, the world had been so beautiful, so full of promise. When she was with Justin, anything and everything had seemed possible, and even the raindrops had glistened like crystal gems. Now everything was flat and gray and dreary. She knew it was mad to think such thoughts, but she couldn't help wishing she could see him one more time before she died. Even after everything that had happened between them, she just wanted to see him. To hold him and have him kiss her in that gentle yet excitingly masterful way that stirred all the flames of her passion and her love. Tears scorched the back of her eyelids and burned her cheeks. She began to weep with small, aching sobs. She surrendered to her grief, letting all the misery and pain she had tried to suppress escape, no longer able to dam the flood of pain. Her face was wet with tears, and she trembled violently upon her straw pallet, burying her head in her arms. *Justin, Justin... why didn't you love me? I loved you so! I love you still! Always, despite everything... Justin...*

Gradually, her sobs diminished. She lay spent and broken, like a twig rattled too long by the wind, finally sent tumbling to the sodden earth. As she lay there, visions danced in her head. Unbidden they came, lovely, joyous visions of love. She saw once again Justin Harding's darkly handsome face, his eyes, which would always flutter her heart, their gray gaze keen and piercing. She saw his mouth, so warm and strong and exciting. And she saw his magnificent, powerfully muscled body as he had leaned over her in his bed, naked and gleaming in the glow of the fire.... The visions continued, more vivid every moment. She saw herself and Justin making love before the kitchen hearth in Salem, and she saw their twined bodies together in her loft... in Justin's bedchamber on Oliver Street.... She saw him grinning at her, handing her a cup of coffee in the morning, kissing her in the woods. She could almost feel his lips upon hers once more as she remembered their first meeting near the pond, when he had kissed her beneath the maple tree, his hands tangled in her hair. How her heart had pounded when his mouth covered hers, when his arms enclosed her soft form and pressed her against his lean, powerful frame. That was the first time Justin had awakened her passion, the first time she had felt the searing heat of his desire. There had been so many more, so many beautiful moments of love...

Memories merged with dreams as gradually she drifted into a kind of slumber. She was so immersed in these poignant imaginings, floating in a misty state of half-sleep, that she did not at first hear the key scraped into the lock of the cell door... or the door creaking open. These sounds might have penetrated the outer edges of her consciousness, but it wasn't until she sensed someone looming over her that she came fully awake, her heart freezing in her breast as she felt another presence in the cell.

"What... who... *Cousin Jonathan!*"

She bolted upright, terror written across every feature of her small face. In the glimmer of moonlight which trickled in through the window, she saw her cousin's gaunt form towering above her, and it seemed to her that he swayed slightly in the gloom of the cell. She couldn't speak for a moment, staring in shock at his thin, pasty face and weirdly glowing eyes. Tonight more than ever he appeared a strange and grotesque figure, a bony skeleton of a man whose lips were twisted in a mocking smile.

"Good evening, my cousin," he whispered, and his voice echoed softly in the tiny chamber.

Goose bumps rose on her skin. Belinda took one

swift glance at Lucy, asleep on the pallet near the wall. She stumbled to her feet, her black woolen dress sticking to her clammy flesh, and brushed the thick mane of her hair from her eyes. "What are you doing here?" she demanded, a new and different kind of fear chilling her. "You have no right to be here now like this! Go!"

"I had to see you...one more time." Cady took a step nearer, and Belinda retreated. She moved backward until she reached the wall below the window and could go no more. Jonathan Cady moved within inches of her trembling form. "You're frightened of me, aren't you, Belinda?"

"Get out of here! Or I shall scream and wake the village!"

He shook his head, a faint, sneering smile upon his thin lips. "Idiot girl. Screams from the prison will not wake a soul in the village. Such sounds are common."

"What do you want?" Belinda hissed from between clenched teeth. "Are you mad to come here at such an hour?"

"Mad?" Cady shook his head. "No. I am sane once more! Sane and content, now that you are gone from my house, now that I know you shall die in a very few hours." He reached out a hand and touched her hair, almost absently stroking the thick, red-gold curls, ignoring the fact that Belinda had stiffened in revulsion. "I knew you were wicked, Cousin Belinda, from the moment I first set eyes upon you. You reminded me of...Alice. She was beautiful like you. Beautiful and wicked. I suspected from the first moment I beheld this Devil's hair that you were like her—a sorceress, a Devil's servant bent upon seduction of innocent men. And time proved me correct." His eyes, those small, strange, icily gleaming eyes of palest green, bored into her face. His fingers tightened on her hair until she winced. "And now you shall die. On the gallows, as befits a witch of Satan!"

Belinda raised her arm and shoved his hand away. Her cheeks were very white in the slender web of moonlight illuminating the little cell. "If you despise me so, Cousin Jonathan, why do you come here in the dead of night? Why do you touch me?" she demanded. Her own eyes shimmered with fury. "You are not as righteous as you claim to be, my pious and respected cousin, or you would not sneak into this cell for a private visit with a convicted witch!" From the corner of her eye, Belinda suddenly became aware of the open cell door behind him. A wild hope ignited in her breast.

Scarlet color suffused Cady's face and burned his long, bony neck. Wrath lit his eyes as he stared into her defiant countenance. "Insolent witch!" he rasped. He raised his arm to strike her, but Belinda dodged the blow, throwing herself sideways.

"Lucy!" she cried. "Wake up!"

Lucy started upright, her eyes wide with fright. When she saw Jonathan Cady in the cell, she screamed.

"Get up!" Belinda shouted, giving Jonathan a shove with all of her might. "He has left the door open! Run!"

Both girls leaped toward the door, but Jonathan recovered himself and lunged after them. He grasped Lucy's arm and jerked her backward, sending her flying to the floor. Belinda whirled to face him. She kicked his knee and at the same moment hurled a fist at his jaw, even as Lucy staggered to her feet and added her strength to the struggle. With a screech, Jonathan Cady toppled sideways. Belinda and Lucy dived once more for the door, but suddenly froze. Their screams died in their throats. The door was blocked. Another man faced them in the tiny cell.

"You!" Belinda gasped, her heart slamming in her chest. "Oh no!"

"Yea, Mistress Cady. 'Tis me!" Tom Phelps grinned at her, his brawny frame barring her escape. "Or should

I say, Witch Cady? For that's what you are, wench, you're a murdering witch!"

He laughed suddenly as Lucy clutched Belinda's arm in terror. Behind them, Jonathan Cady shoved his way forward.

"I demand...to know what is going on here!" he began, tugging agitatedly at his disheveled cravat. "Yeoman Phelps, what—"

"I came for the witch."

"What?"

"You heard what I said, Magistrate. I came for the witch, Belinda Cady. Just as you did. But I'm the one who is going to get her."

"How dare you!" Jonathan Cady drew himself upright. He glared at the grinning yeoman with all the dignity he could muster, and his thin form trembled with a combination of rage and apprehension. "Get out of this cell, you impudent scoundrel! You have no business here!"

"Neither do you, Magistrate!" Yeoman Phelps licked his lips. He flexed the muscles in his powerful arms as he eyed the two young women and the gaunt, shaking man before him. "We both came with the same purpose, Magistrate, but you're going to be bested! Witch Cady is mine!"

"No!" Belinda grabbed the cell door, trying to slam it shut so that Phelps would be locked on the outside and the other three within. But he grasped the door and with easy strength yanked it wide, nearly knocking her over. His other arm shot out and seized her waist, tugging her to him. Desperately, she tried to wrench away. Lucy, too, tried to pry Phelps's arm from her, and Jonathan Cady began to shriek.

"I demand that you release her! You have no right!"

Phelps swore as Belinda raked his face with her nails. He flung her to the floor, brushed Lucy away as though

she were a pesky insect, and reached out to grab Jonathan
Cady by the scruff of his neck. "That's enough noise from
you, Magistrate! This gentry bitch is going to pay for what
happened when we were at sea! I swore revenge on her,
and Tom Phelps keeps his vows!" His face was ugly with
hatred as he shook Jonathan off his feet. "And you—
you, Magistrate, with your fine clothes and fancy words—
you're in my way! I watched you sneak in here, and I
heard what you said to her! You want her! But you won't
have her! She's mine!"

Furiously, his fingers tightened around Cady's neck
as Jonathan fought to free himself. Belinda, watching in
horror from the floor, scrambled to her feet.

"No, no, don't!" she cried, and threw herself upon
Phelps' arm, trying frantically to loosen his deadly hold.
But Tom Phelps was like a crazed bear. His huge hands
twisted Jonathan's thin neck with mighty strength, and
his victim writhed helplessly. Sobbing, Lucy joined Belinda in her attack, but their desperate effort made no
impact as he slowly and savagely broke Jonathan Cady's
neck. Both girls screamed as Cady slumped suddenly in
his captor's arms. Phelps pushed him aside with a grunt.

"You . . . you're insane. . . ." Belinda whispered, staring with sickened eyes at her cousin's hideous corpse.
He looked . . . he looked as Elizabeth Foster had looked
swinging upon the gallows, her neck also broken. It was
a ghastly sight. "You . . . you killed him!"

Phelps sneered at her, scooping her into his arms.
"'Tis nothing compared to what I mean to do to you,
mistress! Come, Witch Cady, to the gallows we go!"

"No, leave her be!" Lucy threw her slight form upon
him, sobbing desperately, but Phelps just threw back his
head and laughed.

"I've little time, or I'd take you, too, little one." Suddenly, his huge fist shot forward, hitting Lucy square on

the jaw. The pale blond girl went down upon the floor of the cell with a heavy thud, her head striking the wall. She lay there unmoving as Belinda gasped in terror.

"Lucy!"

There was no answer, no movement from the fallen figure. Belinda tried to get to her friend, but Phelps held her helplessly in his grasp. "Let me go, you monster!" She kicked at him again, writhing and struggling with all the strength she possessed, but he only gripped her more cruelly. His gloating eyes shone with a wild light as he turned Belinda's white face up to his. Chuckling, he leaned downward to press his mouth to hers, but before he could do so, she spit venomously into his face.

"Why...you damned bitch..." He struck her hard across the cheek with the back of his hand, a blow which sent Belinda's head snapping back, her senses reeling. "You'll pay for this, Mistress Cady, this and all the rest. I promised you that you'd pay, and so you will!"

He wiped his face with the coarse sleeve of his shirt, then, just as Belinda began to struggle again, still dizzy from the blow, he hit her once more. Pain exploded in her head. Pinpricks of light flashed and extinguished, and flashed again. She cried out and sagged limply in his arms. Faintly, through a fog of agony, she heard him muttering to himself, chuckling with satisfaction. She felt herself lifted in strong arms, carried forward.

"No...no..." Again, she stirred, weakly trying to throw herself free, but no sooner did she do so than another blow struck her head. Life faded, returned. Dazed and sick, she felt herself drowning in a sea of pain. Vaguely, through half-closed eyes she saw frightened faces pressed against bars...prison bars...then night air assaulted her...darkness, darkness. *Lucy!* Leaves brushed her face. They were wet and clinging. Something was holding her, hurting her...darkness. Her head lolled sideways. Her arms dangled as though weighted. Her legs were numb. The world ebbed and flowed in her ears. She was drowning, drowning, drowning...in darkness.

Justin!

It was a silent wail from her very core, but there was no one to hear. The single word, a kind of prayer, rippled and flowed in the same vast, painful sea of darkness.

CHAPTER TWENTY-ONE

TOM PHELPS PLODDED through the forest path with his drooping burden clamped in his arms. The moonlight dusted the trees with silver and sent a pale shimmer of light upon the track. All about him was silence, except for the shallow breathing of the girl in his arms and the crackle of twigs beneath his heavy, booted feet. He smiled as he walked. Gallows Hill was nearly a quarter of a mile from the prison, but he didn't mind. The time for his revenge had come, and he was savoring every moment of it. Excitement charged through him, beating like a drum in his veins. He had Belinda Cady all to himself at last, completely at his mercy. He would make her pay for that night on the ship when she had stabbed him with her damned knife, when she had escaped and hidden from him. He would make her pay for having spat in his face tonight. Oh yes, the fiery little bitch would pay dear for that fighting spirit of hers. He knew how to tame her kind. And he had till dawn to do it. Plenty of time. Yea, plenty of time.

He reached the foot of the hill and shifted her weight in his arms. He was panting now, his broad face flushed with the exertion of carrying her such a distance, and now uphill. Yet his huge arms gripped her as tightly as ever. She would not escape him again.

Belinda's swimming senses rendered her only semi-conscious during most of that midnight journey through the shadowy woods. But as Phelps climbed Gallows Hill, her head began to clear, and the confused clamor in her brain subsided. Danger. She was in danger. Those were her first coherent thoughts. Then, suddenly, her memory came back with a jolt, sending heartbeats of alarm pulsing through her body. Cousin Jonathan was dead, Lucy hurt. And I, she thought, I am in the power of a murderer. She forced herself to remain motionless in Tom Phelps's arms, despite the panic ripping through her. Her eyes remained tightly closed. She had to think. *Think*. How could she get away?

Slowly, cautiously, she opened her eyes the merest fraction. All was dark trees and shrubs and jutting rock around her. She shut them again, dizzy, her head aching. Once more, desperately, she tried to think.

Her only chance, she realized, was in feigning helplessness. If Phelps knew she was conscious again, he would probably hit her or bind her or do something to keep her from fighting back. As long as he thought she was unconscious, his guard would be lowered. She must watch for her opportunity, all the while letting him think her senseless. If she stayed alert, he might unwittingly give her the chance to flee.

An owl hooted nearby. She heard Phelps grunt as he continued to carry her up the hill. Once, his foot tangled in the underbrush and he staggered forward with her, but he managed to regain his balance before they fell. Swearing, he clambered on.

At last they reached the crest of the hill. By this time, Belinda could feel the muscles in his arms bunching as he held her. She braced herself, expecting him to toss her onto the ground now that they had reached the top. Her prediction was correct. She felt herself thrown from him and landed in the damp grass a moment later. Pebbles scratched her cheek, but she made no sound, allowing herself to sprawl exactly as if she had been still unconscious. Then, slowly, little by little, her eyes opened.

He was standing about three feet away, with his back to her. He was staring at the gallows. One arm lifted to wipe the sweat from his brow with the half-sleeve of his shirt. She saw the thick, pale hair bristling on his arms in the moonlight which beamed brightly onto the hilltop. She felt as if she were back on the *Esmeralda*, reliving that awful night at sea. She would never forget the terrifying power in those arms as he had held her, fondled her, drooled on her. The sight and nearness of him made her queasy. A shudder shook her from head to toe. She didn't know if this was the moment to run or not, but she didn't know whether there would be another chance. He wasn't watching her or holding her, that's all she knew. She would have a precious five seconds' start.

Her muscles tensed, and she sprang up. Now! She darted away from him, down the side of the hill. Through the thunder of her heart she heard him cry out in fury.

"What the devil...? No, you damned bitch! Not again! You'll not escape me this time!" he roared.

He lurched after her, covering the steep downhill ground with surprising and frightening agility. Belinda ran as fast as she could, terror slamming through her. If she could make it to the woods, if she could lose him in the trees...

Suddenly, she heard him shout just behind her, and before she even realized what had happened, he tackled her in a flying leap, sending her crashing to the ground. He fell with her, in a tangle of arms and legs which swiftly resolved themselves to her disadvantage. In a few seconds' time she was pinned tightly to the ground with Tom Phelps's brawny frame atop her.

"Aye, Mistress Cady, I've got you now!" he crowed, panting and chortling at the same time. "You're much too comely to lose a second time, don't you know that? And I've got plans for you, fine plans! You just wait till we get back up to the top now, and you'll see."

He dragged her to her feet, one arm wound about her neck, with her body clamped to his, the other hand twisting her arm ruthlessly behind her back. "Come along, now, mistress, and we'll have some fun."

Belinda could scarcely breathe, so tightly did he hold her. She managed to gasp, "Let me go, you madman. I...I will fight you...till my last breath. I...will not submit!"

Phelps threw back his head and roared with laughter. "Aye, that's the spirit I remember! Many is the night I recalled the fire in your eyes when you faced me on the *Esmeralda*! I have thought of you over and over, my pretty gentry miss, wanting to get my hands on you again!" He continued to drag her back up the hill as he spoke. She resisted every step. "When Hannah Emory came to Andover and happened to mention your name, I started to plan. I wanted to come to Salem, and find you, and wait for you on some deserted village road. But Lettie, that whining, stupid girl, wouldn't let me leave her. I told her I had business in Salem Village, but she begged and pleaded because the hour for the birth was near, so, I waited." They reached the top of the hill once more, and again he flung her down upon the grass. This time he stood over her, his giant legs apart and his hands upon his hips as he stared down into her dirt-smudged face. Triumph lit his eyes, making them glow crazily in the night. Belinda pushed herself to a sitting position. Her breath came in short, ragged gasps as she listened to his excited chatter.

"Then that idiot girl died while birthing—and the babe with her!" He spat in disgust. "But at last I was free to come to Salem Village! I finished my planting, and set off, only to find when I reached the village yesterday that Mistress Cady was in prison, a suspected witch!" He rubbed his huge hands together with satisfaction. "So I decided to add some proof to the suspicions against you, mistress. Did you like that tale I told at the trial? It sealed the case, I thought! I had to keep from laughing when the magistrate sentenced you to hang! A fine revenge, it seemed to me, though not quite fine enough. I had more than hanging in mind for you, mistress. So I waited till night."

"I don't understand. How...how did you hope to get into the...prison?" Belinda croaked. All she could think to do was to keep him talking as long as possible. She didn't want to think about what would happen when he stopped.

Tom Phelps shrugged. His shoulders bulged beneath the coarse white material of his shirt, and his buckskin-clad thighs looked enormous. "I was going to break down the prison door and then take the keys to all the cells from the hook just inside. I've been in jail myself a few times, mistress, and I know how things are set up inside. But as it turned out, I didn't need to break the door or take those keys. I saw the fine magistrate go in and I just followed him. He was so set upon seeing you that he even forgot to lock the door behind him." The corners of his thick lips turned upward in a smirk. "Neighborly of him, it was, most neighborly. He made it easy as pie to get to you."

"You...you will be caught and punished for this." Belinda tried to keep from trembling, but her shoulders would not be still. "My cousin, Magistrate Cady, will be found when they come for me at dawn. They will come after you, for taking me, and for killing him. You...you should run away. Now." She moistened her lips. "If you go immediately, you might...get away. Leave me here, and go. I will run off, too, and they will never know who..."

Phelps chuckled. He reached forward and seized her arms, jerking her to her feet. She gave a cry of pain but didn't struggle as he grinned down at her. "You think you have it all figured, don't you, my lady? But I have a better plan. I know exactly what I'm going to do." He dragged her forward, forcing her to look at the gallows, where the thick rope was already knotted into a noose for her execution. "See that? That's where you'll be in a few short hours, mistress! Swinging like a monkey for all these Puritans! And all the while they're walking you up there, putting the rope about your pretty neck, you'll be thinking of how you were here with me tonight, in this very same spot, and what happened to you. You'll remember, just before you die, how I tamed you, you gentry bitch! And I'll be there to watch you. I'll see the whole thing!"

"No! I'll see *you* hang!" she cried. She twisted futilely in his grasp. "I'll tell them how you killed Cousin Jonathan and—"

Again, he laughed. His broad face was brimming with merriment. "And tell me, my fine lady, who's going to believe a witch? You and that friend of yours in that cell can babble all you want, but no one will believe you! I'll bring you back before dawn, and when they come for you, they'll find your cousin dead. They'll wonder how the good magistrate came to be in your cell at night, and they'll think: 'The witch lured him, and then killed him with her powers!' There's not much they don't think a witch can do, mistress! Breaking a righteous man's neck is easy magic for Satan's servant!" Phelps shook her, his fingers biting into her flesh. "And I'll be there, dressed in my Sunday best, looking as shocked as them all. So who will believe your accusations? I'm a respectable farmer, and you are a witch, my lady, so that will be that! You'll hang, and I'll rejoice." Suddenly, his voice changed. It lowered to a guttural growl as he ran his eyes over her slender, quivering form. He yanked her closer against him, squeezing her with thick arms. "Ah, but not yet, Belinda Cady. Not yet." One big hand fondled her breast as he nuzzled into her neck. His fingers plucked greedily at the black gown. "The hanging is still hours away, and we've the rest of the night for pleasure. And pleasure we'll have!"

"No!" Belinda's scream rang from the depths of her heart. Terror engulfed her, and her bones shrank from his very touch. She pushed against him with all of her might. But the yeoman only laughed, and forced her down upon the earth. As she twisted beneath him, he stared into her wild, shimmering eyes, his own ablaze with raw desire. His breath was foul as he panted into her face.

"Ah, Mistress Cady, what a beauty you are! I've waited long for this chance! I thought to have you on the *Esmeralda,* but you escaped me! But now you've no knife, my lady, to spoil it. You've no weapon at all!"

"No, she has not. But I have."

A deep, dangerous voice spoke from just above the struggling couple. Shocked, Phelps turned his head to see a very tall, raven-haired man who stood less than three paces away. Attired in an elegant white linen shirt with lace cuffs, fine olive breeches, and heavy boots of black leather, the towering, muscular newcomer presented a formidable appearance. He looked as strong, dark, and menacing as the Devil himself. But for Tom Phelps, the most alarming thing about him was the rapier he held extended, inches from the yeoman's thick neck. Phelps could not take his eyes from the long, glistening silver blade, which the stranger held so expertly.

"Who...who the Devil are you?" he stuttered, his hands falling from Belinda to hang limply at his sides.

"Justin!" The single word tore from Belinda's throat in a rush of relief so great it made her weak. She pushed at Phelps's heavy body, still sprawled across her, but it was Justin Harding who roughly gripped the yeoman's shoulder and hurled him from atop her. With his eyes still riveted to the sandy-haired yeoman, who had gone sprawling in the grass, Justin dropped to one knee, and helped Belinda to sit upright.

"Belinda! Are you all right? Did he hurt you?"

His voice shocked her. Despite his calm appearance, his voice betrayed all his fear. It was hoarse with terror as he questioned her. She clung to his hand, cradling it against her cheek, which suddenly, was wet with tears.

"I...I am all right. He was about to—"

"I know what he was about to do." Justin sent one quick glance at her pale face. "Don't worry, my darling. Don't fear anymore. This swine will never touch you again."

Before she could reply, he had surged to his feet. Phelps, who had begun to inch to his knees, froze as Justin advanced on him, sword extended.

"Who *are* you?" Phelps gasped, his ruddy complexion whitening. Moonlight spilled over the hilltop, bathing all three of them in a silvery glow.

"I am your executioner, you bastard." Justin's gray eyes glinted with steel. They were every bit as keen as the sword. "Now get up."

"I...I have no weapon. You are surely not going to

murder me, a defenseless man, are you, master?" Phelps hadn't moved. Justin jerked the sword impatiently.

"Get up, swine!"

Slowly, Phelps came to his feet. He rubbed his hands nervously upon his massive thighs. "I . . . I've no sword, master! You can't kill an unarmed man!"

"Can't I?" Justin's mouth curled. A muscle worked in his jaw. There was an aura of controlled rage about him more chilling than if he had been wild with it. He was in command, holding rein upon his emotions, though it was obvious that they guided him. He regarded the man opposite him in cold contempt. "But you can attack a defenseless woman, eh, my friend? Do you think that entitles you to a gentleman's death, or one due a wild beast one comes on in the forest? What do you think?"

"Please . . ." Phelps swallowed hard, his eyes on the glinting rapier. "I . . . I didn't mean nothing."

"Silence!" Justin's eyes narrowed dangerously. "I've already decided that it will please me more to tear you apart with my bare hands than with my sword." He tossed the rapier aside and faced Tom Phelps with an ugly smile. "So let us get on with it, you worthless scum!"

"No!" Belinda darted forward and grasped the sword. She lifted it, her eyes glittering. "Let me kill him!" she cried, and took a step toward the towering Phelps. "I will slice him to pieces!"

Justin laughed then, the first natural sound she had heard from him. With something of his old relaxed manner, he placed a hand upon her shoulder. Phelps stared from one to the other of them in horror.

"No, my bloodthirsty firebrand. Stand aside."

"I want to kill him!"

"Yes, my love, I know you do. So do I."

Her voice throbbed. "It is *my* score to settle!"

"Belinda." Justin's voice seemed to caress her suddenly on that moonlit hilltop with the gallows looming beyond them. "You speak from anger now, my darling. I don't blame you. But later, when your head and your heart are cooler, you might regret having killed an unarmed man, however deserved his death might be. Allow me to perform this service for you. I will kill him in a fair fight. And it will be my privilege to do so."

Before she could reply, Tom Phelps took matters into his own hands. He had had enough of listening to them debate his fate, and raw anger pierced through his fear of the sword. Head down, he charged toward Justin, bellowing like a bull.

Justin sidestepped, pushing Belinda aside. He faced the enraged Phelps with a mocking smile.

"You'll have to do better than that, you filthy cur. Come on, don't you know how to fight any better? Or are you only capable of doing injury to women, and scarecrow old men?"

"I'll smash you to bits!" The huge yeoman snarled. His hands were doubled into massive fists. He lumbered forward once again and swung his right arm at Justin's jaw. "You damned bastard—"

Justin ducked, countering Phelps's blow with a punch that crashed into the yeoman's belly. He bent over double and Justin slammed his fist into his opponent's chin. Phelps went down in a heap, blood dribbling from his mouth. His eyes shone with red wrath. He lurched to his feet.

Belinda watched with hammering heart as the two men circled each other. Her eyes flew back and forth between them. Justin Harding was every bit a match for Tom Phelps in height and build. They were both tall, immensely powerful men with broad shoulders and brawny thighs, with muscled arms and broad chests. But while Phelps moved with lumbering awkwardness, Justin was quick, almost graceful. The raven-haired Gray Knight dealt his blows with staggering strength and swiftness. Yet Phelps fought with the passion of a maddened beast. He threw his huge body into every punch, and when his fist connected, the effect was sickening. She gasped as Justin reeled backward under the force of a blow. Phelps drove forward and hit him again, and Justin sank to one knee.

"No!" Belinda screamed, as the yeoman crashed down upon his stunned opponent. Phelps straddled Justin on the grass. His hands closed on the black-haired man's throat.

"Justin!" Belinda darted forward with the rapier, ready to run the yeoman through, but before she could reach him, Justin's body gave a powerful heave. She never knew where that incredible burst of strength came from, but he succeeded in overthrowing Phelps with one giant effort and instantly gained the upper position. One fist slammed into the yeoman's face, mashing it to a bloody mess. Phelps twisted desperately, but could not throw the other man. Instead, Justin hit him again, then again, until Phelps sagged unresisting beneath him. Justin's fists were bloody.

"Enough! Justin, please, that's enough!" Pale and sick with fear, Belinda called to him as if from a distance. He looked up and saw her trembling form, her tear-stained face. "I can't bear it anymore. Leave him be!" she pleaded.

He took one last, disgusted look at the battered man beneath him. Then he rose heavily to his feet. "Belinda!"

An instant later she was in his arms. The sword had gone clattering, forgotten, as he enfolded her in a crushing embrace that threatened to break her bones, but felt as deliciously comforting as a wool blanket on a winter's eve. She buried her head in his shoulder, holding him as tightly as she could.

"Justin, I thought I'd never see you again. I thought—"

"I know what you must have thought, my darling." His hand cupped her chin, and forced her eyes up to his. "I have much to explain. But now is not the time. We must go, my love, at once. We—"

Belinda's scream froze the words in his throat. He spun around, his muscles tautening.

Tom Phelps had come hazily awake. Bloody and in terrible pain, he had lain momentarily still, then his hand had moved slowly, weakly, toward the small dagger he wore at his hip. He grasped it in fingers that shook, slid it free. His great body braced itself for its final effort. He would have his revenge upon this bitch and her protector. He would kill them both.

He staggered to his feet while they stood in each other's arms. A leering grin spread across his face. He raised the knife and advanced.

When Belinda screamed, he lunged forward, but Justin had turned just in time. One hand shot out, seizing Phelps's knife arm, holding it immobile. With a yell, the yeoman tried to hit his opponent with his other fist, but Justin slammed his powerful frame forward, knocking the yeoman off balance. Twisting his opponent's arm, Justin gained the knife. Phelps's eyes widened. His mouth fell open in a desperate scream, just as Justin Harding drove the dagger into his heart. Blood spurted everywhere. Harding stepped back, panting, as the big yeoman collapsed. A shudder seemed to run through his huge body, then he was still. Justin flipped him onto his back and knelt a moment.

"He's dead."

Belinda covered her face with her hands. She was sobbing.

"He deserved to die, Belinda." He was at her side, his voice rough. "You know that. You wanted him dead."

"Yes, yes. But...it's horrible. Please, let's get...away from here."

"Gladly." Justin glanced upward. The sky was lightening to lavender. Dawn was not far off. "We've got to get to the ship, Belinda. Come, my horse is tied in the woods below the hill. We must hurry before the village awakens."

"Lucy!" Belinda turned a determined face to him. "I won't leave without her. We have to go back to the prison!"

"Lucy is in good hands. She's on her way to the harbor now."

"But how?...Justin, I don't understand! How did you find me? What...?"

His brows drew together and he ran an impatient hand through his black hair. "This is not the time for questions, woman! We're both still in danger until we reach my ship. Now, are you coming or do I have to carry you?"

She recoiled as though he had struck her. Something died in her eyes.

For a few minutes she had forgotten. She had forgotten how this man had hurt her, deceived her. She had been ready to throw herself at him again. Now Gwendolyn's cold, beautiful image rose up to mock her, and she saw once more, with vivid clarity, Justin's heartless countenance the night of her arrest. The memory of his indifference that night, when she had been dragged away to Boston Prison while he watched in silence at his fiancée's side, surged over her, drowning all other emotions.

All the love and trust and gratitude which had overwhelmed her in that first rush of relief vanished, and wariness took their place. Pride reasserted itself as foolish love receded. "I am coming," she said quietly, her face very white. "Let us go!"

She was still shaking, her black wool gown blowing slightly in the breeze that had begun to rise with the morn. She looked very fragile and very alone, standing on the hilltop before the gallows where she was supposed to be hanged.

Justin grasped her shoulders and pulled her to him. He lowered his lips to hers, kissing her gently, caressing her mouth with his. "Forgive me, my love. I'm a scoundrel to speak to you so roughly after all you've been through, but—"

She jerked out of his embrace. She was trembling even more than before, and she felt her knees buckling beneath her. "Don't worry about me! I'm fine!" she retorted, through clenched teeth. "Didn't you say we must hurry to your precious ship? Well, then, let us hurry!"

He gave her a long look. She glared back at him, chin tilted, her shoulders back. Slowly, Justin nodded. "Later, then, my firebrand. We'll finish this later. Come."

Together, they descended Gallows Hill.

CHAPTER TWENTY-TWO

BELINDA WATCHED at the rail of the ship as the *Gray Lady* glided from Salem Harbor. In the town, the first pink and gold streaks of dawn brushed the lavender sky. Smoke from just-built morning fires puffed from the chimneys of the unpainted frame houses beyond the wharf, and shutters here and there were flung open. The townspeople were just beginning to stir with the new day. In Salem Village, she knew, a procession would shortly begin for the prison. A grim, bloodthirsty procession. She could well imagine their reaction at what they would find, and a tremor passed through her. Her fingers clutched the slippery rail as she turned her face away from the harbor and stared out to the open sea. She could scarcely believe she was really here, on this ship instead of locked in her cell, awaiting death, but it was true. Thanks to Justin, she was safe. Thanks to Justin, she had lived to see the dawn, and would live to see the morrow.

A soft, breathless voice interrupted her reverie. "Belinda! Oh, Belinda, is it possible? We are safe, both of us! It is a miracle!"

She turned as Lucy ran into her arms. Behind her friend stood a slim, fair-haired young man with blue, serious eyes and a tight-lipped mouth. As Belinda watched him, he smiled, and immediately the grim look was gone, replaced by warm friendliness as he held out his hand.

"Mistress Cady, it is good to meet you. My name is Henry March. I believe Lucy has told you that we are betrothed."

"Henry March!" Belinda gasped. She shook her head in amazement. "Oh, forgive me!" She grasped his hand. "I am delighted to make your acquaintance at last, but...I am wholly bewildered! How did you come to be here?"

Lucy laughed. The change in her was overwhelming. Although she had a bruise on one cheek, her usually pale face was otherwise transformed into one of sparkling happiness. A lovely pink color bloomed in her cheeks, and her brown eyes shone as she gazed upon the slim young man. She looked very young and full of joy. Her voice was light and eager, soft as the new morning. "Oh, didn't Master Harding explain anything to you at all while you rode to the ship? Henry has told me all about it."

"No. We...we didn't speak on the way to the harbor." Belinda bit her lip.

"Well, it is all quite simple, really, though *most* heroic." She sent an adoring smile at Henry, who grinned and put his arm across her thin shoulders. "And it is all because of you, Belinda! If you hadn't insisted that Master Harding send word to Henry in Philadelphia about my arrest, I don't know what would have become of us! You see, the manservant, Ned Gavin, found Henry in Philadelphia. The reason he hadn't sent word to me, Belinda, is that he was injured! He had been involved in an accident while working for his uncle, and then when he finally did recover enough to write..." Her brown eyes darkened. "Frances Miles stole the letters before they could reach me!"

"What?" Belinda stared at her, aghast. "How do you know this?"

Lucy spread her hands. "It is the only explanation.

Henry wrote three times since his recovery, but never heard a word in response. I never received a single message. I am certain that Mistress Miles kept the letters from me deliberately."

"It would be like her," Belinda muttered grimly. "I would like to get my hands on her just one time!"

Lucy smiled. "And so would I! But she doesn't matter anymore. We will never see her again, and I don't need my 'gift' to tell me that! She will undoubtedly live out the rest of her days in Salem Village, and neither you nor I will ever set foot there again!"

"What happened when Ned Gavin found Henry?" Belinda asked, still trying to piece together the story. "No doubt you were shocked, Master March, to discover Lucy had been arrested?"

"Yes, indeed." Henry's lips tightened again. "I was never more dismayed in my life."

"Henry and Ned traveled back to Boston as quick as they could, only to find that not only you but Justin Harding and all his men had been arrested! You may imagine their chagrin!"

"Justin . . . was arrested?" Belinda asked dazedly. "When?"

"The same night you were taken into custody. The authorities suspected that he had knowingly hidden you from them, which, of course, was true. They held him in the prison for days and whipped him at the lashing post to try to make him confess. Finally, Henry and Ned and a blacksmith named Ambrose Cooke helped him and his men to escape!"

Belinda listened in stunned silence to the tale. She had had no idea that Justin had been imprisoned. When she heard of the whipping, tears stung her eyes. And at the mention of Ambrose Cooke, she shook her head in amazement. Henry March continued the story, telling her how he and Justin and all of Justin's people had fled to the ship and made their escape from Boston, sailing directly to Salem Harbor. They had arrived at midnight, when no one was about, and a small party consisting of Justin, Simon Foster, Henry, and Ned had made their way to Salem Village Prison. They had found Lucy unconscious on the floor of the cell, with Jonathan Cady dead only two paces away, and Belinda vanished.

"Master Harding was near wild," Henry said. "He'd been cool as you please until then, commanding everything with great calm until we came to the prison and you were gone. Then he turned white as a ghost, and I thought he was going to tear the walls apart. He was frantic, Mistress Cady. I've never seen a man so desperate."

"Henry woke me then," Lucy went on, "and when I saw his face, I thought I was dreaming. But it was really him, and for a moment I couldn't even speak, but only weep with happiness. Then he stopped me and asked me about you, and everything came back to me, all the horrors we'd gone through. Belinda, I remembered that that awful man had said he was taking you to the gallows. I told Master Harding, and he bolted out after you. Then Henry brought me to the ship." She squeezed Belinda's hand. "I never doubted that Justin Harding would rescue you. There was such a ferocity about him, a determination. . . . Belinda, he is not a man I would ever care to cross!"

Henry March chuckled. "No, indeed. Nor I."

Lucy was watching Belinda's face. Suddenly, she turned to Henry and spoke quietly. He nodded, and with a slight bow, moved off toward the stern of the ship. He busied himself watching a sailor adjust the mainmast, while Lucy turned back to her friend.

"What is it, Belinda?" she asked gently. "What is wrong? You ought to be wild with happiness, as I am.

We are both safe, sailing far from Salem Village. And we are with the men we love!"

"Yes, I love Justin!" Belinda cried. "But...he doesn't love me. It is torture for me, Lucy, being here with him and knowing that he will never be mine! The sight of him pains me more than you can imagine! It is unbearable to be near him, to fight the urge to reach out and touch him, knowing all the while that his love belongs to another!"

"But...didn't he rescue you from that brute? Didn't he withstand flogging and prison for you, and sail all the way to Salem to save you from death? Belinda, he loves you! Don't you know that by now?"

"No." Belinda raised her eyes to gaze into Lucy's face. They were gold-flecked in the morning light, beautiful, deep green pools mirroring heartbreak. "It is not love he feels. I think perhaps Justin feels guilty about me. He feels he owes me something. But he doesn't love me. He loves Gwendolyn Harding. I...I have been dreading seeing him. No doubt she is in his cabin at this moment. I...don't know if I can face seeing them together again, Lucy!"

Suddenly, she froze. A tall, dark figure appeared on the quarterdeck, staring down at her. Lucy, seeing the expression on Belinda's face, glanced upward. Justin Harding stood above them, looking virile and impossibly handsome as the wind tousled his raven-black hair, and whipped at the full sleeves of his linen shirt. His booted feet were planted far apart, and he looked every inch a deadly pirate captain. He wore a grim, determined expression and radiated raw power in his stance and bearing. As Belinda watched, he turned and began to descend the companionway to the lower deck.

"I will leave you now," Lucy whispered quickly. Then, before Belinda could stop her, she flew off to join Henry at the stern.

Belinda gripped the railing, her heart pounding. The sea wind tore at her hair, sweeping it back from her small, fine-boned face. She stared blankly at the foaming waters, seeing nothing but a man's harsh image in her mind. Suddenly, a voice spoke beside her, and she whirled to face the image of her love in person.

"It is cold here, Belinda. Come below with me."

She stared at Justin. "Where?"

"To my cabin." He gripped her arm. "We can talk there."

"No!" She gasped and drew away. "I don't want to go there! I don't want to...disturb Gwendolyn."

"You won't." Again he grasped her arm and drew her inexorably along with him. "It is time for us to talk, firebrand. I won't allow any more delays."

It was useless to struggle. She allowed herself to be borne down a narrow companionway and to a cabin in the bowels of the ship. Justin opened the door and she stepped inside. She half-expected to see Gwendolyn Harding draped across Justin's bed, but the cabin was unoccupied. Despite the emotions churning wildly inside her, she couldn't help noticing the comfortable, masculine charm of the cabin. A huge four-poster was set against the far wall, with a thick brown and pumpkin-colored counterpane, and a brass headboard and foot-board. The other furnishings were of oak: a writing desk, two carved chairs, and a court cupboard, with plenty of brass wall sconces and candles, and a silver pitcher and basin set upon a small trestle table near the bed. She walked to the writing desk and stood there with her back to Justin, twisting her fingers in her black skirt. After the harrowing events of the long, sleepless night, she was weary almost beyond endurance. She tried to muster strength to withstand this confrontation, clutching at her ebbing stamina in desperation. Her heart was heavy in her chest.

"Belinda. Look at me."

His voice compelled her to turn slowly until they faced each other across the cabin. Belinda swallowed.

"What is there to talk about, Justin? There is nothing for us to say. I suppose I owe you my gratitude for rescuing me and bearing me to safety. I thank you for that. I will always remember it." She could not meet his eyes. Instead, she found herself staring at his mouth. How her own lips hungered for his. Quickly, she lowered her gaze to his chest, but the ignited desire inside her only intensified, flickering in a widening arc. "Where...where are we headed, by the by?" she asked nervously, reaching behind her to grasp the writing desk for support.

"Barbados. There will be an uproar and a search for a time," he replied calmly. "The island will be a pleasant place to hide until the fervor abates. Then we will take your friend Lucy and her husband-to-be to Philadelphia, if they so wish, and we will sail to Virginia colony. No one will dare disturb us there. Besides, I suspect the witchcraft madness will subside fairly soon. You see, I made some inquiries about it when I returned to Boston after first visiting Salem Village. I learned that Sir William Phips will be arriving in Boston next month to assume his duties as royal governor of the Massachusetts Bay Colony. Phips is a sensible man; he will inject some degree of reason into the situation. Unless I am mistaken, he will eventually succeed in bringing this madness under control and perhaps to a complete end." He began to walk across the room toward her. "For you, Belinda, it is already at an end. Salem Village is behind you. That is in the past now. Our future lies ahead."

"*Our* future?" Belinda gaped at him. Her eyes shone with bitterness. "We have no future, Justin! You are engaged to be wed! Or have you conveniently forgotten? If you expect me to play mistress to you, while you marry that golden-haired snake, think again!" Anger flowed through her, hot and vibrant. "Though it no doubt hasn't occurred to you, in all your damned, impudent arrogance, there is a limit to my gratitude. If you think that because you rescued me from Tom Phelps I will let you—oh, what are you doing? Let me go!"

He had reached her and suddenly, while she was talking, stretched out his strong hands to clasp her shoulders. He pulled her to him, enfolding her in a tight embrace. His hand cradled her cheek and turned her face upward to his.

"Let me go!" Belinda's voice throbbed as she tried to free herself, but he held her captive. Tears sparkled in her eyes.

"I love you, firebrand." Justin's voice was like silk against her skin. "I love only you."

She stared at him, her face very white and still. In contrast, her green eyes, flecked with gold, looked even larger and darker than usual. Watching her, Justin felt he could drown in those eyes. His heartbeat quickened to match hers as he held her tightly against his chest.

"But...Gwendolyn. You love Gwendolyn," Belinda whispered, searching his face.

"No." His grip tightened. "I wanted her. I wanted her the way a boy wants to win a prize at the fair. But it is you I love, and have from the first moment I met you in the woods. Something flowed between us then, Belinda, like two rivers with a common current. I felt from that first time I kissed you that we were joined somehow, but I resisted the bond. Until that night at your cousin's house, when we made love before the fire. Then I knew. I knew that you were the only woman in the world I wanted—that I would ever want! I have loved you ever since."

She was trembling, clinging to him, wanting to believe him, yet afraid that this fragile happiness would shatter at any moment. "Justin, I wish I could truly believe that this is true. I don't understand! In Boston you flaunted your love for Gwendolyn. You hurt me so! You made it quite plain that you cared not at all for me!"

He grimaced. "It was an act, my darling, a cruel, unforgivable act! I played a vile game with you, Belinda. With both you and Gwendolyn. Perhaps she deserved it. You did not." He caressed her hair, gently entwining his fingers in its satiny mass of red-gold curls. A strange, aching warmth spread through her at his touch. It was as if something inside her were beginning to melt. "I beg your forgiveness, firebrand. You angered me by doubting my love, and I, who had not been able to give love to anyone for so many years, reacted like a vicious, stupid fool! My senses failed me, but my heart never did. I knew all along that you were the one I loved!" His voice in her ear ran through her body like a lightning bolt, thrilling and hypnotizing her.

Belinda hardly dared to breathe. She felt her pulses racing. "And...Gwendolyn? Where is she? Have you told her of your feelings?"

He nodded. "She is gone. I sent her back to England, the damned sly bitch! Do you know that she prevented Mrs. Gavin from delivering provisions I had ordered you to receive in Boston Prison? I could have wrung her neck for that!"

"It doesn't matter. Oh, Justin, it doesn't matter!" Tears of happiness streamed down Belinda's cheeks. She stared up at him. "It is true, then? You do love me?" His obsession with Gwendolyn had seemed so strong, so permanent. The idea that it was broken stunned her.

Justin's lips were warm on her throat. "I do." His voice was husky. "More than any man ever loved a woman. But...can you ever forgive me, Belinda? I'm a damned scoundrel. What I did was cruel. I wouldn't blame you if you hated me."

"Hate you?" She slid her hands up his back and across his wide shoulders. "I love you! I will always love you!"

They were locked in an embrace so tight it seemed as if their bodies were one. Justin's mouth crushed down upon hers, bruising her tender lips with a fierce, devouring kiss, one which Belinda returned with an ardor more than equal to his own. She plunged her tongue into his mouth, giving herself up to the raging fire that consumed her. Justin's hands were warm and strong upon her body as he cupped her breasts and stroked her bottom, pressing her close against him. Her own fingers tore suddenly at his clothes, wanting him naked, wanting him inside her with a wild desperation that could not wait.

He chuckled, a deep, growling sound as he in turn ripped the black wool gown from her flesh. For a moment, Belinda froze, hesitating, and he instantly sensed her withdrawal.

"What is it?" he demanded, and she raised doubtful eyes to his face.

"I have been...in prison. I...I haven't bathed in days!" she whispered, fearing he would be repulsed.

He threw back his head and laughed. "Do you think I care about *that*, firebrand?" Grinning devilishly, he pushed her, naked, down upon the bed. "Don't move, my silly, foolish love. I have a solution to your problem."

She watched as he strode to the court cupboard and removed a towel. Then he went to the trestle table and poured water from the pitcher into the silver basin. He moistened the towel and lathered it with soap, then turned back to Belinda.

"Allow me, my darling." Slowly, he began to slide the soft, damp towel over her flesh.

She had been watching his lean, powerful frame with burning eyes. Now she gasped in pleasure as he leaned over her, stroking and rubbing with the soapy cloth, caressing every part of her. Her nipples tautened into rosy peaks when he glided the towel slowly, gently across her breasts, then down her belly and hips, and over and between her thighs. Her body trembled as he cleansed her, his eyes glinting like gray coals. She felt her flesh grow warm, then hot, until it seemed to burn beneath his fingers. By the time he had rinsed her skin with warm, clear water, and briskly dried her with a fresh towel, the tingling between her thighs had grown unbearable.

"Justin, come to me," she whispered, and reached up a slender arm to pull him down beside her. He tossed the cloth aside as her fingers stroked his hard, muscular body, eagerly caressing the entire pulsing length of his manhood. She arched in pleasure when his lips captured her nipples, teasing them with his tongue and leaving a trail of burning kisses across her creamy breasts. His mouth moved lower, tasting the sweetness hidden between her thighs until she gasped in ecstasy. Delight rippled through her, and every sensation seemed heightened. Her fingers moved in circles across his taut buttocks, traveling upward across his muscular back. When she touched the welts inflicted by the constable's whip, she paused in horror, stricken by the thought of his recent suffering, but he whispered in her ear, reassuring her, and she kissed him, every inch of him, with soft, gentle lips.

"Ah, Belinda. My lovely Belinda." Justin drew her mouth to his, exploring it with growing urgency. "You are mine."

"And you are mine," she breathed. "Always. Forever."

Desire imprisoned them in a single, searing flame. Passion burned from every pore as their bodies twisted and twined in tormented pleasure. She cried out in whimpering need as he poised above her.

"Now, my darling, now!" she cried, and pulled him close. Flesh to flesh, they held each other, rocking and writhing in wild motion as he thrust deep within her, as if pounding away at the last of the barriers between them.

Belinda's senses reeled and spun. Rapturous pleasure engulfed her. Her hips thrashed and she tossed her head from side to side. Justin's breath was warm and rapid on her neck.

"Justin, my darling, I love you so!" she gasped, her fingers digging into his muscled back, clutching him ever closer and tighter against her. Her lips clung to his as their bodies thrashed with even greater intensity. "Hold me, never let me go!" she begged as their passion exploded in splintering fury. "I love you!"

His hard body took hers with fierce mastery. "Belinda! I love *you!* My beautiful, wild firebrand!"

They shuddered and shook, their bodies glistening with sweat, until the crest of their passion subsided. For a while there was silence, but for their heavy, labored breathing, then, Justin rolled aside.

He put his arms around Belinda and kissed her hair. They lay quiet together, finally at peace.

Justin spoke after a time, his breath rustling her damp hair. "Ah, firebrand, what a life we shall have together. If, that is, you will consent."

"Consent?"

"To be my bride."

She sat up, a radiant smile upon her flushed, delicate face. "Yes, Master Harding. I consent."

"Good." He watched her lovingly. "Mrs. Gavin will be most pleased. She fretted about you the entire time we were sailing to Salem for your rescue. Oh yes, and Simon Foster will be glad also. He is quite fond of you, you know."

"Justin!" She narrowed her eyes. "Are Mrs. Gavin and Simon Foster the only ones who will be happy I accepted your proposal?" she demanded.

"Certainly not. I'm certain all the other servants will be delighted to have a mistress at last and—"

He laughed as she dived upon him, fists pounding his chest. He grasped her wrists and tumbled her down beside him, leaning over her with a grin. "Oh, did I forget to mention that I am most honored and delighted by your decision? How careless of me!" He kissed the tip of her nose and released her wrists to gently stroke her breasts. "I am truly the happiest man in the world, firebrand. You have my word that I will do everything in my power to make you the happiest of women."

"You already have, Justin." She sat up, her flaming hair spilling like silken ribbons over her bare shoulders, nearly to her waist. Her green-gold eyes glowed with love as she gazed at this dark, handsome man who had won her heart. "I never thought I would see you again. Locked in that prison cell, thinking you cared nothing for me, I nearly wished for death at the gallows. I...I almost can't believe this is true. It seems like a beautiful, fleeting dream from which I will awake."

"No." His gray eyes held hers. They were tender and warm. "It is not a dream. We are together, and we shall be together until the end of our days." Slowly, languorously, they kissed. Belinda's heart brimmed with joy. She leaned against Justin, shutting her eyes. A happy drowsiness came over her.

"I think it's time to sleep," he chuckled, lowering her gently onto the bed. "After we've rested, we shall have a proper bath—together—and then there is something I want to show you."

"What is it?" she murmured sleepily, snuggling into his shoulder.

"Later, Belinda." He kissed her cheek, "Sleep now."

Peacefully, she closed her eyes. Slumber overtook her almost immediately. The next thing she knew, she and Justin were strolling hand in hand, through a meadow of flowers. A breeze was ruffling her hair, lifting its heavy red-gold mass from her neck. The sky above burned bright blue. Justin's face looked tanned and rested in the sunlight. His gray eyes smiled down at her tenderly. Belinda was aware of the perfume of the flowers and of Justin's clean, invigorating scent. His arms went around her waist, while hers encircled his neck. She laughed, pressing closer against him. Then they sank together into the sea of flowers, their clasp of each other never loosening. She was kissing him then, the world a blur of flowers, perfume, and passion, as together they lay upon the soft, fragrant earth. Her arms enclosed him, holding him tight within her embrace, as her lips caressed his warm, strong mouth. She kissed him, passionately, lovingly, yearningly. She heard him chuckle.

"Again, my firebrand? Already?"

She opened her eyes to find Justin indeed enclosed in her arms, her lips pressed against his neck. He was gazing down at her in fond amusement as they lay upon his bed in the ship's cabin.

Her green-gold eyes blinked dazedly up at him, as the fog of sleep slowly ebbed. "I was dreaming." Her lips curved in a tender smile. "The most beautiful dream," she whispered.

"Tell me." Justin's hands began to stroke her body as he leaned over her.

"No, I'll show you," she murmured, and gently drew his face down to hers.

Hours later, when they had both rested and bathed, they mounted the companionway to the deck and he walked her all about his ship. Mrs. Gavin, observing them from the railing, where she stood with Ned, thought they made a matchless pair, Belinda with her brilliant hair and slender figure, adorned in a gown of soft lilac muslin, with a lace shawl about her shoulders, and the master as tall and powerful as ever in his black broadcloth coat and breeches, every bit the raven-haired, commanding buccaneer. She longed to felicitate them upon their obvious reconciliation, but at the same time, she didn't want to disturb them. They looked so rapturously happy. So she merely smiled, and squeezed Ned's arm, well remembering the days when she had been young and hopelessly in love.

Belinda gazed about her in admiration as they reached the quarterdeck. The afternoon was soft with sunshine. Brilliant gold light danced upon the dark-blue sea in sparkling patterns and warmed her face despite the salt-tanged sea breeze. The air was fresh and invigorating, and she almost imagined she could already smell the lush, tropical flowers of Barbados.

"The *Gray Lady* is magnificent," she told Justin. "Much finer than that awful *Esmeralda* I sailed upon when I came to Salem Town!"

"The *Gray Lady?*" Justin smiled down at her. "We are not sailing upon the *Gray Lady*, my love."

"No?" She wrinkled her nose in puzzlement. "But I thought this was your ship? I thought—"

"This is my ship. Once she was called the *Gray Lady*, but no more. This is what I wanted to show you. Perhaps you cannot see the prow very well, but I can point out where the letters are painted. My darling, we are sailing upon the newly named *Belinda.*"

She stared at him, her eyes widening. "You renamed your ship in honor of me?"

He nodded. "When I first left Salem Village, after

that night in your loft. I gave orders for the repainting as soon as I reached Boston." His voice changed as he gripped her shoulders. "That was before you even arrived there, firebrand. Before Gwendolyn arrived. I told you I had already decided that I loved you, and it is true. I named my ship for you, before any of that horrid charade even began." A glint entered his eyes. "Gwendolyn requested to see the ship the day I brought her home from the harbor, but I refused. I hadn't yet decided how I was going to cancel our betrothal, much less explain that I had named my ship for another woman." He chuckled. "How fortunate I am that I met you, Belinda Cady! To think I might have shackled myself to that cold-blooded bitch for the rest of my life! It makes me shudder merely to think of it!"

"Then don't think of it." She snaked her arms about his neck. "In fact, if you ever think of that woman again, I will—"

His lips clamped down upon hers, cutting off whatever gruesome threat she had been about to make. He kissed her long and hard, his hands tightly circling her waist. Belinda's soft lips clung to his, demanding more.

At last, they drew apart, both of them trembling. The light afternoon breeze cooled their warm, flushed faces.

"Careful, my firebrand. I could go on kissing you forever," Justin warned, his hands in her hair.

"Perhaps we should return to the cabin," she suggested softly. Justin laughed.

"I see I have a lusty wench upon my hands," he remarked. "My pet, you are insatiable. What am I to do with you?"

"Come with me to the cabin, Justin, and I will show you."

It was an invitation he had no wish to refuse. He

smiled down into her luminous eyes and nodded. "Very well, firebrand. Come along."

Hands clasped, they descended the companionway. Belinda knew that soon it would be sunset and the sea would be splashed with glorious color as the sun sank into the swirling water. But she would not be on the deck to watch. She didn't care. There would be other sunsets. Many sunsets. She would see the dawn and the dusk, the storm and the sun, the night and the day. And they would each belong to her. To her and Justin. Together.